"Veteran short story author and Shirley Jackson Award cofounder Cox (coeditor of *Crossroads: Tales of the Southern Literary Fantastic*) brings sly humor and a tone that's nostalgic, quintessentially American, and unfailingly uncanny to this haunting and excellent first collection of 25 reprints and two new stories . . . Cox is a master of subtle, understated chills that lurk just behind the familiar, and each story conveys a solid sense of history and place. Readers who enjoy literary speculative fiction (with shades of Flannery O'Connor and, of course, Shirley Jackson) will find much to love: there's not a disappointing tale in the bunch."

—*Publishers Weekly*, starred review

"Many writers center their stories around the arrival of the uncanny in their characters' lives, as Cox does here. But few writers are as interested in the aftermath, the withdrawal of this same unsettling and inexplicable notice. Brett Cox is a master of nuanced horror. Think of him as a kinder, gentler Edgar Allan Poe."

—Karen Joy Fowler, author of *The Jane Austen Book Club*

"As T.S. Eliot's enlightened twin brother once put it, 'We shall not cease from savoring the stories of F. Brett Cox—with their lapidary prose, beguilingly haunted characters, cosmic regionalism, wistful edginess, understated apocalypses, and laid back moral urgency—and the end of all our literary revels will be to arrive at a place of exceeding strangeness and never want to leave.'"   —James Morrow, author of *Towing Jehova*

"Brett Cox's glorious stories are a treasure map to a hidden America: *The End of All Our Exploring* will take you on a journey you won't soon forget, with a new discovery on every page."

—Elizabeth Hand, author of *Hard Light*

"Inside the wonderfully weird *The End of All Our Exploring* you just might find southern Gothics, and northern ones too, and UFO's, secret societies, alternate histories, a sea monster, and an amnesia helmet. But what you'll consistently find is great writing. Intelligent, sometimes angry, always honest, these are stories that not only make you feel something, but make you want to feel something. Brett Cox knows the difference is a delightful and dangerous one. Buy this book, now."

—Paul Tremblay, author of *A Head Full of Ghosts*

"Breathtakingly inventive, with prose tight as Marcia Brady's braces, *The End of All Our Exploring* is a joyful romp through the darkness on the other side of the mirror." —Sarah Langan, author of *The Keeper*

"Even in tales that feel borderline mainstream, F. Brett Cox slips in elements of the uncanny or the macabre that make the mind run hot and the blood flow cold. *The End of All Our Exploring* merits not just exploration, but focused scrutiny of its very vivid foray into American places, history, culture, childhoods, literature, music, psychic phenomena, and a host of other national obsessions. This brave collection unlocks them all. And rocks doing it."
—Michael Bishop, author of *Other Arms Reach Out to Me*

"The wonder of this long-overdue collection is how effortlessly Brett Cox jaunts between so many different literary modes. He understands the unique challenges not only of the fantastic genres of horror, science fiction and fantasy, but also of historical fiction and contemporary literary fiction. His deft touch with dialogue and narrative voice allow him to inhabit a cast of vivid characters, some as ordinary as your next-door neighbor, some well and truly estranged from reality. What I like best about these people is how decisive they so often are, even when they're dead wrong and bound for disaster. The stories in *The End of All Our Exploring* will make you laugh and shudder and shake your head at the absurd and marvelous things we humans do."
—James Patrick Kelly, author of *Wildlife*

"Replete with social comment, humor, and tragedy, the surreal and the haunted, F. Brett Cox's fiction is quietly devastating. These stories are intellectually clever, historically illuminating, and humanely affecting. Detailed, dry tales of the astonishing things that are considered "normal," they start in the ordinary life of fallible human beings and move to a place where the human heart is exposed through its encounter with strangeness. I am glad to see these stories at last gathered in one place, where we can arrive where we started and know the place for the first time." —John Kessel, author of *Pride and Prometheus*

"Brett Cox's stories range through American history, moving in and out of a succession of vividly and sympathetically rendered characters. In these narratives, women and men confront the mysteries and opacities of the self, family, and history. When their lives intersect the supernatural and supernormal, they do so less as otherwordly intrusion and more as irruption of forces at work in the underside of their experience. Deeply human and humane, attuned to the particularities of place and time, this is a book of marvels, and a marvelous book." —John Langan, author of *The Fisherman*

THE END OF ALL OUR EXPLORING

STORIES

THE END OF ALL OUR EXPLORING

STORIES

F. BRETT COX

FAIRWOOD PRESS
Bonney Lake, WA

THE END OF ALL OUR EXPLORING: STORIES
A Fairwood Press Book
August 2018
Copyright © 2018 F. Brett Cox

All Rights Reserved

No part of this book may be reproduced or transmitted in any form or by any means, electronic or mechanical, including photocopying, recording, or by any information storage and retrieval system, without permission in writing from the publisher.

Fairwood Press
21528 104th Street Court East
Bonney Lake, WA 98391
www.fairwoodpress.com

Cover © Getty Images 2018
Cover and Book Design by Patrick Swenson

ISBN: 978-1-933846-71-2
First Fairwood Press Edition: August 2018
Printed in the United States of America

To my brother Chip, who got me started

To my wife Jeanne, who keeps me going

And in memory of my parents, James and Frances Garrell Cox, who never tried to stop me

CONTENTS

11	Introduction by Andy Duncan
17	Legacy
31	The Amnesia Helmet
47	See That My Grave is Kept Clean
52	The Light of the Ideal
78	Flannery on Stage
82	The Serpent and the Hatchet Gang
99	Petition to Repatriate Geronimo's Skull
107	Consider the Services of the Departed
111	When John Moore Shot Carl Bell
118	Mary of the New Dispensation
132	What We Did On Our Vacation: My Whole World Lies Waiting
146	The Deep End
160	Nylon Seam
165	Up Above the Dead Line
173	It Came Out of the Sky
205	Suspension
212	The Last Testament of Major Ludlum
220	Road Dead
223	Madeline's Version
234	The Sexual Component of Alien Abduction
238	Maria Works at Ocean City Nails
255	Elimination of Restraint and Seclusion
258	What They Did to My Father
268	What We Did on Our Vacation: She Hears Music Up Above
277	They Got Louie
282	The End of All Our Exploring
288	Where We Would End a War
299	*Notes and Acknowledgements*

INTRODUCTION

by Andy Duncan

What a pleasure to hold in my hands a fiction collection by F. Brett Cox! Reading it, even scanning the contents, is for me like visiting a family album. Brett is a brother of mine, in the sense of the families we choose for ourselves.

Brett and I have been friends for almost a quarter-century, and would have met a decade earlier, when we both were students at the University of South Carolina in Columbia, had our aim been better. I was a journalism undergraduate, not an English graduate student like Brett, but I went to a number of author readings and other English-department events, and he and I were in the same room at the same time more than once, but just missed one another. Clearly the world was not ready.

In our timeline and, I trust, yours, Brett and I finally met at one of John Kessel's parties in Raleigh, North Carolina, circa 1994. I was one of John's master's students at North Carolina State, while Brett was a Ph.D. student at Duke. But our first extended conversation took place in January 1995 at a regional science fiction convention, Chattacon in Chattanooga, Tennessee. Most of the attendees were there for gaming, or for media fandom, but four or five of us dutifully trooped from one author reading to another, and bonded pretty well by weekend's end. (Another in that group was Christopher Rowe, whose own splendid collection, *Telling the Map*, came out in 2017.)

Brett and I quickly realized that though we grew up about 180 miles apart, me in rural South Carolina and him "up north" in rural North Carolina, we had basically the same upbringings, the same extended, fitfully genteel families (in the sense of blood kin and married-in kin) and the family secrets to go with them, the same pushmi-pullyu relationship to the American South, and certainly the same obsessive, all-encompassing reading habits; as a result, we both were determined not to turn out like Quentin Compson. (So far, so good!) In conversation, we frequently tell one another, "We are the same," a sentence we usually deploy as a transition device, where others might say, "I can top that one."

But Brett discovered science fiction fandom at a much younger age than I did. As a teenager, he briefly corresponded with Richard Shaver, a thought that has kept me awake nights. Brett's collection of first-edition UFO books inspires awe, and wherever he lives, he erects monumental towers of science fiction paperbacks and digest magazines that tease the visitor out of thought, like the *moai* of Rapa Nui. Sometimes (I can attest) these topple onto visitors as they sleep, and enrich their dreams.

Unsurprisingly, we have spent countless hours together at science fiction conventions, and we have shared many mild adventures on that circuit, for example our brief encounter in a hotel bar with a morose Scottish Highlander, dressed as for battle, who responded to our cheery greeting by snarling, "Don't touch me sword." Our panicked retreat can be imagined. At the International Conference on the Fantastic in the Arts, held each March in Florida —Y'all come!—Brett and I often wind up as co-stars onstage, I suppose because we've had so much opportunity through the years to perfect our timing, like the Sunshine Boys. We've played astronauts in zero-g; we've played fawning minions at the feet of Brian W. Aldiss (typecasting); we've played Frankenstein's creature and a rampaging villager (further typecasting).

But enjoyable as all that has been, I value more all the time we've spent together *not* wearing name tags: visiting the Thurber House in Columbus, Ohio; rescuing a snapping turtle in Georgia;

attending a production of *Julius Caesar* at London's Globe Theatre; having dinner with Fannie Flagg. (I'm unclear how that last one happened.) We've prowled through a number of cemeteries, for example the stonemasons' graveyard in Barre, Vermont. We both married well, better than we deserve; Sydney and I were present for Brett's wedding to Jeanne Beckwith, and we have spent a lot of time with that brilliant, lovely couple since, though never as much as we'd like. Sydney and Jeanne are good at getting Brett and me to talk about something *other* than, say, the 19th-century rat trap that Tom Waits demonstrated (sans rat) to David Letterman, which for Brett and me was a sort of apex of television.

A longtime member of the Cambridge Science Fiction Writers Workshop, and a tireless supporter of other writers' work, Brett has helped a lot of colleagues improve their manuscripts. I'm one of them. For example, during a conversation in the car, I believe en route to *Moonrise Kingdom* at the Savoy Theater in Montpelier, Brett suggested the crucial plot twist of my novelette "New Frontiers of the Mind." My favorite example of Brett's story-doctor skills came at ICFA one year, after John Kessel read aloud a chunk of his Mary Shelley-Jane Austen mash-up then in progress. John confessed, "I have no idea what to title this thing." In the audience, Brett calmly raised his hand and said, "Pride and Prometheus"—and that is, indeed, the title engraved on the base of John's second Nebula Award.

Looking over this remarkable assemblage of stories, however, I cannot recall being a damn bit of use to the drafting of any of them. I was sort of present at the dawn of "Road Dead," as I remember exulting long distance with Brett, right after he moved to rural Vermont, at his discovery that the town's only decent cell-phone reception was in a hilltop cemetery. But the funny, terrifying, fully inhabited and immersive story that resulted, which takes up barely three pages in this volume, was all Brett.

This whole book, in fact, is all Brett: his fascination with the sucking undertow of history, his determination to defy the sanitized,

Convention and Visitors Bureau view of community, his keen sense of the grotesque in daily routines and everyday people. Consider, for example, the story that accompanies the matter-of-fact title "Maria Works at Ocean City Nails," in which nothing fantastic happens, other than everything. One gets the sense that for Brett—should I use his last name, now that I'm in literary-critic mode? Nah—the whole United States is a Gothic construction, and the overhead vaults are beginning to crumble.

As I re-read these, I think of course of Shirley Jackson (whose memory Brett has done much to sustain, as a co-founder of the Shirley Jackson Awards) and of Flannery O'Connor (who shows up as a character in this volume, along with Herman Melville, Geronimo, Madeline Usher and multiple Bette Pages), but also of the late Irish writer Frank O'Connor, who kept throwing his cap over the wall of his childhood and jumping after it, no matter what he found on the other side.

You will meet some of my favorite fictional characters here, including the young air-raid warden in "Suspension," the angry villain who vents, Sam Hall-like, throughout "The Last Testament of Major Ludlam," and, well, just about everyone in "The Light of the Ideal" and "The Amnesia Helmet," both of which should have been awards contenders, both of which were published by zines that folded moments thereafter, in time-honored fashion.

For that matter, "Madeline's Version" was written for *Crossroads: Tales of the Southern Literary Fantastic*, an anthology co-edited by Brett and me, commissioned by a publisher that folded *before* the book came out. Tor came to the rescue, somehow persuaded by agent Shawna McCarthy, but it was a near thing. Short-fiction publishing can be precarious, like America. (Heads up! Another chunk of the vault just fell.) Still, we're very proud of *Crossroads*, which was animated from the start by Brett's determination to include genre authors and mainstream authors, the traditional and the experimental, science fiction and fantasy and horror and magic realism—all broadly defined, or not so much defined as half-remembered, like a joyous evening among friends. Brett does not believe that good fences make good neighbors; he loves genre fiction too much to isolate it.

The same eclecticism animates this volume. Sure, you will find zombies, UFOs, sea serpents and so forth, but they are seldom deployed in the way you expect. A Brett Cox character is likely to respond to an intrusion of the marvelous, the supernatural, the horrific by walking away and trying to forget about it, which of course is just the way we handle them in daily life.

In format, too, these stories would be all over the map, if there were a map. Some of them may be poems; a couple are definitely songs. At least one is a stage monologue, but several others are performance pieces: I've heard Brett perform them, though the convention program promised only a "reading."

I can't help wondering, with happy anticipation, what the fantastic Mr. Cox—no, sorry, *Dr.* Cox—no, sorry, *Colonel* Cox, Vermont State Militia (you'll have to ask him about that)—will come up with next. The title notwithstanding, I'm sure these are not the end of all his exploring.

In the meantime, enjoy these stories—and watch your step!

Andy Duncan
Andy Duncan
Frostburg, Maryland
May 2018

LEGACY

He brought her flowers every day. There was a patch halfway between his house and hers that belonged to no one he knew of, and there was always something there. Nice ones in the spring—daffodils and jonquils, magnolia blossoms from the lone tree near the edge of the road. But even in the cold months there were small blossoms to be had, and he always stopped and picked some of whatever was there. It was the least he could do. If things continued as they were, it was all he could do.

She met him at the door and took his gift for the thousandth time with the appearance of as much gratitude as she had the first time. He did not know after so long if appearance and reality were the same. He supposed it really didn't matter.

He carefully removed his hat as he crossed the threshold of her home. Rather than waiting for his hostess to take it, he hung it himself on the dark maple coat rack that stood by the door. She allowed him that familiarity. He followed her into the parlor and paused as she placed the flowers in a waiting vase on a table beneath a picture of her grandparents—not the ones who were the source of all the troubles, but her mother's parents. They stared rigidly from the wall, the man's forehead just to the edge of baldness beneath his white hair and above his crooked tie, the woman's mouth drooping at the corners, the left side of her head obscured by a diagonal white cloth. Two years after he first started calling on her, she had told him that the cloth was there to hide a tumor that her grandmother never had removed. God had placed that mark on her, her grandmother said, and no man was going to cut it away.

They're lovely, Franklin, she said. You shouldn't trouble yourself so.

It's my pleasure, Constance, he replied. Always.

They sat side by side on the divan and talked pleasantly, neutrally before going in to the supper she had prepared. Her students were undergoing their first encounter with a complete play of Shakespeare; one of the girls, her favorite of the term, had asked if Juliet wasn't going to get a beating from her father for being so disobedient. The demand for auto supplies was increasing so much Franklin had determined to double his orders for the month and set up a display in the store. There was talk of war in the papers, but President Wilson promised not to shed American blood over European complaints, and the state house in Montgomery seemed more concerned with how, or if, to pay for flood control along the Tombigbee river. Her hands rested comfortably in her lap and her skirt brushed the floor. Franklin had seen pictures in the catalogs that came into the store of newer fashions, skirts that hung only to the tops of the ladies' high-button shoes, but Constance had not changed yet. He sometimes dreamed of her ankles.

After a decent interval, they went into the dining room, where he sat at one corner of the dining table. The table was absurdly long. Her parents had been known for their dinner parties, but after their passing Constance had not kept up the tradition. She served the meal—green salad with fresh garden tomatoes, cream of spinach soup, pork chops with gravy, new potatoes and sweet corn, peach cobbler for dessert—and then sat across from him. She did not have a maid, although with what her parents had left her, she could easily have afforded one. She did not really need to earn a living teaching. But she preferred to do these things. They ate heartily. Constance was a wonderful cook.

You've outdone yourself, he said. A man couldn't ask for a better meal.

Thank you, she said. Here, have some more potatoes.

After dinner he helped her clear the table and stack the dishes in the kitchen sink. He always offered to wash them, and she always declined. She was so precise about some things, less so about others—in sharp contrast to his own mother, she had no objection to letting the dishes wait until bedtime, or even until the next day. It was one of many things he loved about her.

They returned to the parlor. He reclaimed his spot on the divan, and she sat at the piano and played for him. Some of the old songs—"Flow Gently, Sweet Afton," with the perfect air of melancholy that had brought tears to the eyes of the old men and women at the Burns Society fundraiser last winter. Some of the new songs—she had just acquired the music for the latest from Mr. Berlin, and she played it with total, uncalculated delight. He tapped time gently with his foot and felt himself smiling. When the sun finally set, he turned up the lamps and she sat back down beside him. It was March and the days were getting longer.

At this point it was all right to take her hand, to hold it and relax into the divan and look into her eyes, so deeply blue in the day, turned slightly green in the lamplight. She laid her head carefully on his shoulder and stroked the top of his hand with her own.

I could stay like this forever, she said.

You can.

No, we have to work tomorrow. And the day after, and the day after that.

You can stay with me forever. I can stay with you. I don't have to leave. If you'll just—

Franklin, she said. It was a self-contained statement, not a prelude to anything. In the early days of their courtship, five years gone, even a hint of the topic would cause her to stiffen and pull away. Now, after such a long time, she offered no resistance. And no acquiescence.

We could be married, he said. It was the first time he had uttered the word in months.

No. You know we can't.

Surely if nothing has happened by now—

Franklin. She sat up straight beside him, rose from the divan, walked over to the piano, and rested her hand near the picture on top. Her great-grandparents on her father's side. The source of all the troubles. An old man and woman, plainly dressed, surrounded by two younger couples and a young woman, Constance's grandmother Alice, centered in the frame, looking neutrally at something far beyond the photographer. She stared at the faded portrait in silence.

Franklin waited for her to speak, but knew there was nothing to say that had not already been said a thousand times before. Great-grandfather Henson. Peg Donovan. A dispute over slaves. The old woman's lawsuit. Her rage at the verdict. The disturbances that followed: *I am Peg Donovan's witch, and Ethan Henson shall know no peace.* The inexplicable torment of the grandmother: pins stuck in flesh, hair pulled out by the roots, obscene voices in the empty air. The family become a public spectacle for four years until the great-grandfather finally died and the grandmother's engagement to Franklin's grandfather was broken off. *I am Peg Donovan's witch, and they shall never marry.* Only then had the sticking and pulling and voices stopped. Years later a New York paper said the grandmother was a liar, a ventriloquist, a fraud like those Fox girls up north. She had sued the paper for libel, and won. Sometimes Franklin thought that, more than anything, was what kept Constance convinced.

And we shall throw away our own happiness, Franklin said, the bitterness he thought was past creeping back into his voice. The sins of the grandparents shall be visited upon the grandchildren?

Apparently so, she said, still staring at the picture. You know what our families have been through since then.

All families have misfortunes, he said. Everyone dies sooner or later. It's not preordained. It's not a curse.

We can't take that chance, Constance said, and then, more softly, I can't.

He wanted to say: It didn't want your grandfather to marry my grandmother, and what has that to do with us? It said it would come back, but it said it was an Indian, then a Spanish monk, then the ghost of another of Henson's dupes. Why should we believe it now? Peg Donovan was said to be in league with the devil, but Peg Donovan is dead. You will be thirty this year.

But all he said was, again, We could be married.

No.

It's the twentieth century. We are adults who can read and write. I can speak into that box hanging in the hallway and be heard a hundred miles away. In a few years, you'll probably even be able to vote. We have no room for witches and spells and curses.

There is still plenty of room for death and suffering, Constance said. Look at Europe. Read the newspaper.

And you are more afraid of a supposed curse than modern warfare? Our witch is more powerful than artillery shells and mustard gas?

Slaves, she said, as if he had said nothing.

Constance—

I wish we had left Africa alone, she said. I wish we had never heard of Africa.

He looked down at his empty hands. There was no use continuing. All right, Constance. All right. Come and sit back down with me.

She did, and they talked of other things. The lights shone through the scrolled globes of the lamps and cast familiar patterns on the wall. When they heard the grandfather clock in the living room strike nine, he stood automatically and she walked him to the door.

He kissed her in the open doorway before she turned on the porch light. She tasted of peach cobbler and her own skin. He looked at her until he was satisfied she was not angry or upset with him, and then he went home.

As he walked the half mile back to his own house, New Orleans came to him unbidden, as it sometimes did. Once, before his courtship of Constance had begun, when he was first taking the reins of his business, he went to New Orleans on a buying trip. He was a good man and had tried to be what his father had always called a True Gentleman. His father had warned him about the sins of the flesh, warned him how such activity was not only disreputable but debilitating, draining a man of much-needed vital energy. After Franklin had attained his majority, his father had even confided that he had marital relations with Franklin's mother no more than once a month for that very reason.

But New Orleans—its deep exotic layers, its sights and smells and very texture—was like nothing Franklin had ever experienced. One night at dinner in the French Quarter with some other young businessmen, he let himself get drunk, which hardly ever happened, and the others swore they could go over to Storyville and get whatever women they wanted, and it was perfectly legal. His mind told him it was wrong; his body and spirit followed the others over to Basin Street and a large house with a red lamp by the door.

He found himself in a cluttered but clean room with a woman whose auburn hair fell to her waist. She sat patiently in an overstuffed chair and crossed her black-stockinged legs so that her robe fell back from them. There were small signs on the wall with odd phrases: Oh! Dearie, I give U much pleasure; Dearie, U ask for Marguerite. An embroidered pillow balanced on the back of the chair announced, Daisies won't tell. From beneath the floor came the muffled clatter of a piano playing a song he had never heard before. He stood swaying in front of the woman as she opened her robe. She wore nothing underneath. He fell on top of her; she pushed him off, made him take off his pants, and guided him to the bed. She lay on her back and stroked her own nipples and said things he barely understood. He fell on top of her again. It was over too quickly and he wanted to stay, but he didn't have enough money. On his way out he noticed for the first time the pictures on the wall of men and women doing what he had just finished doing, and on the vanity by the overstuffed chair, a lone photograph of a little girl feeding ducks by a pond.

In the corridor he passed by one of the other young businessmen, who clapped him on the shoulder, gave him a wink, and walked on.

He burned with shame at such thoughts, especially after spending the evening with Constance. And he was not always so preoccupied after his visits. But he sometimes was. Of late, more often than not. He had to remind himself of what he truly loved in Constance, what the Storyville whore could not possibly have. The whore could not cook. The whore could not play the piano. The whore could not recite Shakespeare from memory. The sun did not rise and set in the whore's blue eyes.

By the time he reached his bedroom he was filled to bursting with his love for Constance and his memories of Basin Street. He took care of the matter, bathed, and went to sleep. He dreamed of marrying Constance and taking her to New Orleans for their honeymoon.

He did not see Constance for several nights after that. There was nothing unusual about it; as close as they were, it would have been an imposition to spend every evening with her. He did go by her house and leave her flowers every day. His father, who approved of both Constance and her family's money, had learned not to question him too closely. Instead, when the new and larger order of auto parts came in, he complimented Franklin on the resulting storefront display.

And then one day she called him at the store and asked him to come over that night. There was something wrong in her voice, but she refused to elaborate. He said of course he would.

She met him at the door but immediately turned and went into the parlor and sat down, ignoring the flowers in his hand. She had never done that before; he had no points of reference for such behavior. After a moment, he hung his hat and laid the flowers carefully on the table by the vase which still held yesterday's assortment.

She sat on the divan with her hands clenched tightly together. He stood mute, uncertain what to do.

Do you know Aaron Huckabee? she asked.

Jake Huckabee's brother? He has a farm over near Andalusia.

Yes.

He's two months behind on his account at the store.

She looked at him the way his mother used to if he ate his salad with the wrong fork. His daughter Ruthann is one of my tenth-graders.

Yes.

She was not at school today. Or rather she was there long enough to leave a sealed note on my desk. Constance rose, went to the table with the flowers, took a piece of paper out of a drawer, and sat back down on the divan.

Dear Miss Baldwin, she read. I am so sorry but I will not be in class ever again. My daddy has gone too far this time and I cannot stay any longer. I am sorry not to tell you face to face but I tried once or twice and I just couldn't. He has beat me more and more and done other things too. It hurts all the time and I can't look in a mirror I hate so what I see. Please don't be mad. I have learned a lot from you. My mother has people down in Mobile and I will go to them. Please don't tell my father. I love you Miss Baldwin you have been very good to me. Please don't tell. Love Ruthann.

She set the letter on the end table and held her head in her hands.

He sat by her and put his arm around her, removed it, put it back. Constance. I am so very sorry this happened.

She tried to tell me and couldn't? Or was I just not listening?

The Huckabees are a bad lot, Franklin said. Aaron's mother's family was the worst sort of trash, always fighting and cutting. My mother said when she was a child they could hear them clear across the creek. I'm not surprised this happened.

She had bruises sometimes, Constance said. I didn't think anything of it. She lived out on a farm. They all had hard labor to do.

This is not your fault.

Ruthann had a strange tone in her voice when she was asking about Romeo and Juliet. I realize that now. I should have realized that then.

This is not your fault. He tightened his arm around her and she leaned into him.

Other things, Franklin? What sort of man could do that?

His head suddenly filled with the room in Storyville and the photograph of the little girl on the vanity. He shuddered and held Constance even tighter. Don't think of it, he whispered. Don't think of such things. Her people in Mobile will see after her.

And who will I see after? She pulled away and walked quickly over to the piano. She stared at the photograph on top. And who will see after me?

I will.

I have been so careful. So very careful. I have preserved myself, preserved us. I wanted to make a difference with the children. She lowered her head. I wanted you to be proud of me.

Oh, Constance, I am. He rose and went to her. He wanted to embrace her fully but simply touched her cheek. I am so very proud. No man could ask for a better woman. You are everything I've ever wanted.

It doesn't matter, does it?

It doesn't matter that I love you?

It doesn't matter how careful we are. Terrible things happen for no reason. We can take all the precautions in the world. We can never leave our own back yard, and a tree will fall. We can confine ourselves to one room, and the lamps will turn over and burn us.

He had never heard her talk like this. It frightened him and made him hold her closer.

Constance—

We can't do anything to stop it, she said.

He turned her face to his and kissed her mouth. In the light from the window her blue eyes seemed nearly back. She kissed him back, wrapped her arms around him. He buried his face in her neck and almost fainted from the pressure and the scent and the warmth.

They returned to the divan and remained for a very long time. Then, without speaking, he rose and took her hand, and they walked side by side into her bedroom.

He had not known she kept a picture of him on her vanity. She took down her hair; it fell almost to her waist. At her request he helped her with the back of her dress, but when he tried to push it off her shoulders she gently stopped him and disrobed herself. The dress rustled noisily to the floor. He helped her again with her corset. To his astonishment, his hands were steady. She stepped away from him and removed her undergarments. She stood with her arms over her breasts; her face looked like her grandmother in the picture on the piano. He took her arms and pulled them gently toward him, kissed her hands, placed them on her breasts, and moved them in slow circles. She lay back on the bed and waited for him to undress. Her hands moved over her breasts, around and around. He came to her as gently as he had kissed her hands. She cried out in pain, once, and he thought his heart would stop, but she wrapped herself more tightly around him and it lasted a long time after that. He had never felt such things. He had never been to New Orleans.

And then when they were finished and lay side by side, Constance cried out in pain again, sat up and grabbed her shoulder. Franklin! It hurts!

My God, Constance, what is it—

It's sticking in me! It's on fire! She rose naked from her bed and clawed frantically at her side, then both her arms. A swath of her hair rose from the left side of her head, stood straight perpendicular to her body, and pulled itself loose. She screamed and fell to the floor, but before he could get to her a voice said: *Couldn't wait any longer, eh?*

No! Constance shouted. No!

I knew it was only a matter of time. I knew in the end you wouldn't disappoint me. The voice was harsh, distant, metallic, as if it were coming through a telephone from a distant place.

Leave her alone! Franklin shouted. This is not her fault!

Oh, come now. Do you really think I care if you fuck her? Your grandparents fucked like dogs. The words were horrible but flat, without inflection. *But they never married each other, and neither will you.*

We haven't done anything to you! Franklin was on the floor and held Constance as she sobbed. We haven't done anything—

Of course you have. You in particular, Franklin. You did that whore on Basin Street, didn't you? If you call that doing anything. You did better this time, boy. In Storyville you almost came in your pants before that whore got them off you.

Constance's sobs were uninterrupted; mercifully, she did not seem to take in what the voice was saying. Shut up! he shouted. Stop this!

I will stop when I'm ready to stop, prick. His picture rose from the vanity and smashed against the opposite wall. The corner of the frame scraped the top of his head as it flew by. Constance screamed again. No! Go away, please go away!

Oh, no. I'm just getting started. You're just getting started, too. But you have a lot to get used to, Franklin. The blood for starters. Didn't you smell it, that awful coppery stench when you came in here! Every month, boy, no amount of flowers or perfume can get rid of it—

Shut up!

Welcome to her body, Franklin. There was a rattling sound under the bed. The chamber pot slid out from beneath the dust ruffle, slid across the floor, leaped in the air, and shattered against the wall over the bed. The voiced laughed, an explosive, emotionless sound that frightened Franklin almost more than the rest of it. *My bowels moved for thee.*

God damn you, stop this!

Constance shits as much as you do.

Stop!

She does other things, too. She takes that picture of you and holds it in one hand and puts the other between her legs. You should hear what she whispers to herself—

Go away! Constance pulled away from him and rose unsteadily to her feet. She whirled in circles, seeking the voice. I don't care! Do what you want! I don't care anymore!

Of course you do.

I don't! I love him!

Of course you do.

I shall marry him!

No, you won't. The room shook as if in an earthquake. Franklin jumped up and grabbed Constance, tried to soothe her as the room rattled around them. He felt something on her back, cried out as he saw huge welts rise and run down to her buttocks. *Entertain yourselves, children, but expect my visits often.*

Merciful God, Franklin said. Our father which art in heaven—

Oh, please, the voice said. There was almost a hint of feeling. *What did He ever do for you? Your families? Ruthann Huckabee?*

—hallowed be Thy name, Thy Kingdom come—

You are bags of shit and piss and blood and you will die. With or without me.

And then the room was still.

When he finally stopped shaking, when Constance was finally still, he pulled on his pants, ran to the parlor, and drew all the drapes. He came back and picked up her clothes and took her with them to the parlor and left her to dress. He returned to her bedroom and put his clothes back on. He tried to pick up some of the shattered things but his hands started shaking again and he went back into the parlor.

Constance sat on the piano bench and did not acknowledge his presence. He sat on the divan and waited.

Finally she said, Take me out of here.

Of course. Come home with me. Or to my father's. There's room.

No, please walk me over to the hotel.

But Constance—

I do not want your father or anyone else to know of this.

What will you tell the clerk?

Something. Please take me there now.

He forced himself to stand. Then he walked her the half-mile to the town's only hotel. At her insistence he left her at the front entrance. As she walked through the doorway he felt his life fading away like the pattern on a much-trampled rug. Then he went home.

He returned to the hotel the next morning, but the clerk said she had left at first light. He endured two agonizing days and sleepless nights, and then he received a telegram from her saying she had gone to stay with her aunt in Tuscaloosa until the repairs on her house were complete. She was gone for over a month.

When she returned she looked well, if a bit thin. She asked him over the second night, and for many nights thereafter. They talked as they had always talked. Her cooking skills were undiminished. She played the piano for him, and he always brought her flowers.

A week after her return, he tried, tentatively, carefully, to talk with her about what had happened. He was afraid she would break down, be overwhelmed by the cold dead terror that had come and the desire that would not leave. But she simply put a finger to his lips and said, Hush, Franklin. It's all right. We are safe.

But Constance, I—

It will not come back, she said. Don't worry, Franklin. It will never come back.

Oh, my darling, my love, please—

Don't worry, Franklin. Dear Franklin. It will never ever come back.

As the weeks turned into months, he came by less frequently. The following year, Constance went back to Tuscaloosa and spent the entire summer with her aunt. When she returned in the fall she was engaged to a medical student. They married the following spring and he returned with her to set up his practice in her town. Franklin left her flowers the night before her wedding but did not attend. She and her husband lived in her house and were never disturbed.

Two years after Constance's wedding, Franklin married a second cousin who had admired him since they were children. By then he had opened more stores in nearby towns. Before his father died, he declared how proud he was of his only son.

Constance quit teaching soon after her marriage but occasionally gave music lessons. She had her husband and her home. Franklin had his family and his business. He found a whore in Mobile once, but he never went back.

THE AMNESIA HELMET

Buck Rogers came to the Rialto Theater in Clarksburg, Illinois, when Marlena was eleven years old and her brother Johnny was nine. Flash Gordon had been the highlight of summer before last and they couldn't wait for the new adventure. The fact that Flash and Buck were the same person made it even better. No worries about whether or not they would like Buck. The great movie star Mr. Buster Crabbe, who had played Flash, was playing Buck, so Johnny and Marlena were certain the new hero would not disappoint.

"You think he'll have the same uniform?" Johnny asked.

"Of course he won't," Marlena said. "Flash Gordon and Buck Rogers are two different people. They have different uniforms in the funny papers. They even have different colored hair on Sundays." Marlena loved the Flash Gordon and Buck Rogers comic strips, which her mother called "fanciful" and her father called "pernicious nonsense." Her father didn't like how wrapped up she was in those particular comic strips. But her mother had suggested, quietly and carefully as she always did, that these strips were "challenging" and might help Marlena's reading skills. Marlena did well with arithmetic and science but her teacher said she still struggled a bit with her reading. Shouldn't Marlena have every advantage? Her father grudgingly agreed.

Troublesome in a different way was Johnny's preference for the funny animal comics—the others, he insisted, had too many words.

But it was early yet and when he played with the other children Johnny showed what his mother called "recklessness" and his father called "proper vigor." He would be a man soon enough.

"If they have different uniforms," Johnny persisted, "then why is it the same man?"

"Because Mr. Buster Crabbe is the greatest actor of all time and nobody else—*nobody else*—could be Buck Rogers. Now come on," Marlena said, the matter settled to her satisfaction. "We want to get good seats."

On the way to the theater they met up with Pete Daniels, who was Johnny's age but acted more like Marlena's. Pete and his mother lived outside of Chicago but his father traveled for work and every summer Pete's mother would bring the two of them to Clarksville, where her own family lived. Pete and Marlena were veterans of the Rialto Theater and saw all their movies together. It had rained all morning and Johnny insisted on splashing every puddle.

The inside of the theater was packed, mostly with kids but with a few adults who were there for the main feature and were determined to get their money's worth. Saturdays at the theater before the show started were the loudest thing Marlena knew, louder than the playground, even. They made their way down the aisle to get as close to the screen as they could. Johnny was delighted with how his shoes squished with each step even though with all the noise nobody else could hear them.

They found three seats together in the middle of the fourth row and squeezed past a line of bouncing, brawling children to get to them. The noise subsided, but did not disappear altogether, during the newsreel (Johnny thought Hitler's moustache was funny, but Pete and Marlena just thought he was creepy), rose again during the cartoon (Popeye bought all the dogs in Olive Oyl's pet shop and set them free, but the dog catcher got them), and finally went away altogether when the serial started. Johnny grabbed his sister's hand and Marlena squeezed it. She was so excited she almost reached over and squeezed Pete's hand but caught herself just in time.

Afterward, Johnny said, "Where were the outer space people?"

"What outer space people?" Pete said.

"In Flash Gordon they were in outer space and there were people there. Ming the Merciless. This one doesn't have outer space people."

"It's only the first chapter," Pete said. "There's plenty of time for outer space people."

"I guess," Johnny said. "That airship was neat. Did you see when it crashed in the storm?"

"I was right there, stupid."

"Don't call me stupid, stupid! Anyway, it was neat. And how they woke up in the future? That was great! I can't wait for next week."

"Me, too," Pete said. "Too bad Mr. Delmore wasn't there to see that airship."

"Mr. Delmore?"

"Oh, you're too young to remember that," Pete said, always happy to ignore the fact that he and Johnny were the same age. "You remember Mr. Delmore's docking pole, don't you, Marlena?"

"What?"

"I said, you remember Mr. Delmore's docking pole, right?"

"Oh, yeah, sure." Mr. Delmore was what their mother called "eccentric" and their father called "crazy as a loon." Mr. Delmore had wanted to put up a tower for zeppelins to tie up to on their way from Chicago. He had seen a movie about a bunch of rich people in New York having a big party on one of the airships and had decided that was the future. The skies would be full of zeppelins, and with a docking tower Clarksburg would really be on the map and he would be rich. Everybody laughed behind his back but he actually got a couple of men from out of town to put up some money and had gotten an engineer from Urbana to draw up plans when that German ship crashed in New Jersey, and that was that. Marlena remembered the whole thing very well. She had thought it was a grand idea and was sad when it didn't happen. The piece of land where the tower was supposed to go was still empty and none of the adults had any idea what to put there.

"I said it's too bad Mr. Delmore wasn't there to see Buck and that airship," Pete said.

"You leave Mr. Delmore alone," Marlena said.

"I ain't bothering crazy old Delmore! Never mind him. What did you think of the show?"

Marlena paused before answering—not something she usually did. It made Pete and Johnny pay attention. "I liked it," she said. "I liked it a lot."

"There wasn't anybody from outer space," Johnny said.

"So what?" Marlena said. "Who needs them? I liked that it was here on the earth. It's like it could really happen."

"Could not," Pete said. "It's just a story."

"Maybe," Marlena said. She let Johnny and Pete keep talking as they walked home—it had quit raining and the afternoon sun had baked the puddles dry—and didn't tell them what had really gotten her attention: the girl, Wilma, who just appeared for a bit near the end of the first chapter but who was wearing trousers and didn't seem to be a princess. Marlena was even more eager for Chapter Two of Buck Rogers than she had been for Chapter Two of Flash Gordon.

They went back to the Rialto every Saturday. Johnny quit complaining when the villain Killer Kane showed up—"He's slick!"—and was overjoyed when Buck and Buddy and Wilma went to Saturn, even if he didn't understand why Saturn had Chinese people. Pete usually made a big show of getting up to go to the bathroom whenever there were any yucky hugging or kissing scenes, but this serial gave him no reason to leave, although in Episode Three when Buck and Buddy were sitting on Buck's bed while Buddy tried to talk Buck into letting him go with the team to Saturn, Marlena thought sure Pete was going to get up and go, he was squirming so much in his seat. Marlena certainly wasn't going anywhere, not with Buck there with his shirt off looking like Mr. Buster Crabbe had looked in the pictures from the Olympics.

But it was Wilma who truly kept Marlena in her seat. Wilma was awfully pretty, the way Marlena's mother had been pretty in the old pictures of her and Marlena's father when they were courting, but Wilma dressed like the men and seemed to be doing pretty much what they were doing. Buck was clearly in charge, of course—how could Mr. Buster Crabbe not be?—but Wilma could fly the space ship and threaten the Saturn men with a ray gun. And this wasn't some other planet in some other solar system. This was all coming from Earth, just in the future. Marlena had never seen anything like it. It made her want to do something.

It was two episodes later that Marlena decided what she wanted to do. She liked the way Wilma had a ray gun like the others, but she didn't have anything to work with since her father started locking his revolver away right after her mother had gotten sick and the doctor had said it would do her good to visit her family in Bloomington. But even better than the ray gun was the amnesia helmet, the device the evil Killer Kane used to control his minions. When you put the helmet on someone, he not only forgot everything, but he would do whatever you told him. Marlena could imagine all kinds of possibilities. Plus, she knew just what to use.

So she went back to the old carriage house behind their home where her father kept his tools and the family put things they didn't have anywhere else to put. A year earlier she had gone through what her mother called "a phase" and her father called "open defiance" when she had spent several winter afternoons after school using her father's tools to try to make an old radio do something other than be a radio. When her father found the scorch marks on the wall he whipped her, but she went back to work the next day and he had to whip her twice more to make her stop.

Marlena spent a couple of days observing her parents' schedules to make sure she knew exactly when her father would be leaving and returning, when her mother would be out shopping or calling on the neighbors or lying on the sofa listening to the radio and sipping what her mother called "her afternoon toddy" and her father called "dissolute behavior." She also kept watch on Johnny until she was pretty sure when he would be off playing with the other boys and not home sticking his nose in. Then she went back out to the old carriage house and went to work. She wanted to find a shirt and trousers to wear like Wilma but stealing from her father's closet was too much of a chance on top of everything else.

Four days later—it would have been three and a half if her father hadn't come home unexpectedly with one of his headaches, which seemed to make her mother as nervous as it made her—she finished the helmet and took it to show Johnny and Pete.

"What is it?" Johnny asked.

"It's an amnesia helmet. Like in Buck Rogers."

"Is not," Pete said.

"Is too."

"Where'd you get it?" Johnny asked.

"I made it myself."

"Did not," Pete said.

"Did too."

"Daddy's gonna whip you again," Johnny warned.

"I don't care."

"I'm gonna tell," Johnny said.

"Me, too," Pete said.

"Go ahead. But first you both have to put on the helmet."

"We can't both put on the helmet," Johnny observed.

"One at a time, stupid."

"I'm not stupid, stupid!"

"Put it on!"

"What's supposed to happen when he puts it on?" Pete asked.

"He'll forget who he is and he'll have to do whatever I tell him to do. Like in Buck Rogers."

"Nuh-uh!" Johnny said, jumping back like he'd just seen a snake.

"It's just pretend, dummy," Pete said.

"You're the dummy! I'm not putting that thing on!"

"It is not pretend! Now listen," Marlena said. "You both put this on, and whoever's the best amnesia man wins."

"Wins what?" Johnny asked, stepping back forward to take a look at the helmet. Any kind of a game was all right by him.

"If you win," Marlena said to Johnny, "I'll . . . I'll do your chores for a week."

"What if I win?" Pete asked.

Marlena considered. "If you win I'll let you kiss me."

"Huh? Yuck! Why would I want to kiss you?" Pete's face turned red and he jumped back as if he'd seen two snakes and a scary dog.

"All right then, dummy, if you win I won't let you kiss me."

Pete looked confused. "But why—"

"I'm in!" Johnny announced. "Gimme the helmet."

Marlena passed Johnny the helmet. He almost dropped it. "Careful!"

"It's heavy! Where'd you get this?"

"Remember when Daddy's company was delivering supplies to Lorena's Beauty Spot? A couple of the dryers were too small and Daddy never sent them back to the warehouse. Here, I'll do it," Marlena said. She set the helmet on Johnny's head.

Johnny's face went blank.

"Hello," Marlena called. "Anybody home?"

Johnny didn't say anything.

"OK, then. Walk over to that tree, turn around, and walk back."

Johnny walked over to the elm that shaded the roof over her parents' room, stiffly like the amnesia men in Buck Rogers. Then he turned around and walked stiffly back.

"So?" said Pete.

"He did what I told him to, didn't he?"

"He walked to a tree. Big deal. Make him do something else."

"Johnny," Marlena said, "take off your belt and go hit Pete with it."

Johnny unfastened his belt, slid it out of its loops, walked over to Pete, and slapped it over the top of Pete's head.

"Hey! Knock it off!" Pete grabbed at the belt but Johnny pulled away from him and walked back over to Marlena.

"Ha-ha, Marlena. Very funny."

"Still think it's not a big deal?"

"No! It's only a big deal if you make him forget something."

"Fine!" Marlena looked at her brother and said, "Johnny, I want you to forget that I told you that I made the helmet."

"I will forget that you told me that you made the helmet," Johnny said in a monotone.

"OK, then." Marlena lifted the helmet off Johnny's head.

"Do I win?" Johnny asked.

"Not yet. Your turn, Pete."

"Nuh-uh. How do I know he forgot like he was supposed to?"

"Johnny, where did I get this helmet?"

"I dunno," Johnny answered.

"Like fun he doesn't," Pete said.

"He's telling the truth!"

"How do I know?"

Marlena scrunched her eyes up like she did when she was working through an especially hard arithmetic problem. Then she opened them, went over to Pete, and whispered in his ear. "If Daddy doesn't whip me for working in the carriage house, you'll know that Johnny didn't tell him, and the only way Johnny wouldn't tell him is if he didn't know."

Pete thought about this. Then he stood on his toes—Marlena was two inches taller—and whispered in Marlena's ear, "How do I know if your daddy's really not whipped you?"

"What are you talking about?" Johnny demanded.

"Shut up, you," Marlena snapped, and then whispered back to Pete, "When has Johnny ever not told you when Daddy whipped me? So if he doesn't, you have to put on the helmet."

Pete stood up tall again, leaned in close to her ear, and whispered, "OK." Marlena didn't know why he had to whisper that last part, but at least the deal was done.

Marlena put the helmet back in the old carriage house, carefully hidden behind a camping tent nobody in her family had ever used.

The week went by. Johnny didn't say anything to their father and Marlena didn't get whipped. Saturday they went to see the latest chapter of Buck Rogers—a thrilling episode in which Buck himself fell under the evil influence of the amnesia helmet—and afterward Pete said, "OK, I'll put the helmet on. But—"

"What?" Marlena asked. He looked as nervous as he had the other day when she had offered to kiss him.

"I want to forget Uncle Baxter," Pete said.

"Huh?" Uncle Baxter was part of Pete's mother's family that they lived with here in Clarksville. He wasn't Pete's actual uncle, but his aunt Evelyn's brother-in-law who lived in the apartment over the family's garage, whom her mother referred to as "that odd young man" and her father referred to as "that bum." Marlena didn't really know Uncle Baxter all that well, although he had always been nice to her, and once when they were over at Pete's he had shown her and Johnny how to string two cans together to make them work like a telephone. "Why do you want to forget your Uncle Baxter?"

"I just do, that's all! Can you make me? Can you make me forget him?"

They were almost to Marlena's house. Johnny had run off with some boys his age who promised a game of pirates, even though the last time they kept making him walk the plank. "Of course I can make you forget your Uncle Baxter. You saw how it worked on Johnny, didn't you? But I still don't understand—"

"Then let's go. You don't have to understand."

Pete had never asked her for anything serious before. It made her feel good, like when she gave the right answer in class. But she had also never seen him look this way before, determined but nervous, even scared, and that made her worry that whatever she did would be wrong. "Are you sure?" she asked.

"Yes, damn it to hell, I'm sure! Come on!"

That did it. For all Pete's acting as if he were older than he was, she had never heard him use two cuss words in a row. Something was wrong, and she was going to use the amnesia helmet to make it right. "OK, then."

After Pete took the helmet off, Marlena asked him, "How's your uncle Baxter?"

"Who?"

"Never mind."

Marlena didn't see Pete for the next couple of days. Then Marlena's mother got a phone call from Pete's mother, who said Pete was acting as if he didn't know his Uncle Baxter. She had made him go cut a switch and bring it back for a whipping but that hadn't done any good. Pete insisted Uncle Baxter was a stranger and when they kept after him he ran up to his room and locked the door and climbed out the window. He had, his mother said, gotten halfway to Marlena's house when she had caught up with him and dragged him home. Now they were taking Pete to the doctor to see if there was something really wrong. Marlena was worried about Pete, but not nearly as much as she was overjoyed that her amnesia helmet had worked again. In the serial, once you took the helmet off, you were completely back to normal. She had not dared let Pete and Johnny know how much she wanted her helmet to do more, and how unsure she was that it would. Marlena's teacher had told them once that scientists had to do experiments more than once to make sure they worked, and if the experiments didn't work every time, something was wrong and they had to start over and try something different. The amnesia helmet had worked twice. That ought to be enough, she thought.

Late that night after Marlena and Johnny went to bed—they still shared a room, which annoyed Marlena no end, which her mother said was "not fit for almost a young lady," but which her father insisted would stay as it was as long as he "wasn't made of gold"—Marlena woke up and heard her mother crying. Then she heard her father say something that at first sounded like her mother sounded when she was trying to get Marlena to do something for her own good but then sounded like her father always sounded when he was complaining. Then they both started making the kind of sounds Marlena had heard before, as if they were both trying to lift something that was just barely too heavy for the two of them to lift, and by the time they finished moving the heavy object wherever it was supposed to go Marlena was almost asleep, thinking that scientists probably did their experiments more than twice.

The next afternoon, after her father had returned to work and Johnny was off on his pirate ship and before her mother could get situated with the radio and her toddy, Marlena asked her if she would play Beauty Parlor with her. Her mother had never been much for games and especially not for the last couple of years, but Marlena knew if she called it "Beauty Parlor" her mother would be so glad Marlena was showing an interest in something ladylike that she would agree to play.

Marlena ran to the garage, got the amnesia helmet, ran back a bit more slowly—Johnny was right, it was awfully heavy—and set it on the kitchen table. "I'll be the beautician and you be the customer," she said. She hurriedly gave her mother a pretend shampoo and then told her, "Now put the helm—the dryer on."

Her mother obliged, and Marlena waited for her face to go blank like Johnny's and Pete's had done. At first she was afraid the experiment had failed, and then she realized there wasn't that much difference between her mother's normal face and a helmet face. "Go stand by the sink," she said.

Her mother stood up and went over to the sink.

"Now come back and sit down."

Her mother returned to her chair and sat.

"Now," Marlena began, and stopped. Now what? What should she tell her? She tried to think of what she might want her mother to forget, and then she thought of Pete and how he was when he asked to forget his Uncle Baxter, and nothing she could think of seemed all that important. Then she tried to think of what her mother might want to forget, and after a minute or two she found herself wondering just how big a command she could give. She began to say, "Forget whatever makes you sad," but before she could get the first word out, she felt a hand on her shoulder. The hand whirled her around and she was looking up at her father, who looked not angry but utterly confused, the way Marlena felt when the teacher tried to make her read poetry.

She didn't know why he had come home so soon after lunch, but he had been standing there long enough to see her order her mother to stand and sit, and to see her mother obey. He asked her over and over again what they were doing, and at first all Marlena could say was, "Pretending," but when his voice got louder and he started saying "Pretending what? Pretending what?" over and over again, she did something she had never done before: raised her voice to her own father.

"It's an amnesia helmet! I made it! Like in Buck Rogers! Like the radio you wouldn't let me work on! It made Johnny forget, and Pete too! And it's going to make Mama forget everything that makes her sad!"

She knew she had gone too far but the only thing she could think of to try to make amends was to say, "It can make you forget, too. I can do that. Is there anything you want to forget?"

Her father stood there looking past her at her mother. He reached down and unbuckled his belt and started to pull it through the loops. Marlena flinched and then tensed, waiting for what was coming. But then her father stopped and refastened his belt. He walked over to her mother, lifted the amnesia helmet off her head, and put it in Marlena's hands. She almost dropped it but managed to hold on.

Then her father said, "I want you to take that thing outside and put it in the trash can."

Before she could stop herself Marlena did something else she had never done: she looked at her father and said, "No!"

"Marlena—"

"I won't!"

Her father hooked his right thumb into the waist of his trousers and patted his belt. "Are you defying me?"

The moment of determination she had felt vanished, and suddenly she knew how this would end, and knew that there was nothing she could do about it. "Please, Daddy..."

He walked over to the door and pulled it open. "Outside."

Marlena looked over at her mother, who was still sitting at the table. "Do what your father says, dear," she said, her voice sounding as if she still had the helmet on.

"Now," her father said.

Marlena held the helmet close against her chest and walked outside without looking at her father. She heard the screen door slam shut behind her, and her father's footsteps. He followed her and stood behind her as she placed the helmet gently in the trash can. Then she shouted as loud as she could, "Damn it to hell!" and ran back inside before her father could do anything else. Her mother was on the couch with the radio on and her toddy on the table beside her. Marlena ran up to her room and waited for her father to come upstairs and whip her for cussing but after a few minutes she heard the car pull out of the drive and all the energy drained right out of her. She wondered if she would ever get off the bed. She was amazed she was able to breathe.

When her father came home that night he acted as if nothing had happened. Johnny complained over dinner that the other pirates had made him walk the plank again. Her mother told them that Pete's mother had called just before dinner to say that the doctor could find nothing wrong with Pete and that her boy was acting fine. Just one of those silly games the children play. She also said that when she had gone to the garage apartment to ask Uncle Baxter yet again why he thought Pete had been acting like that she found a note saying he had been called out of town and didn't know exactly when he would be back.

Over the next week Marlena's father cleaned out their garage.

He removed all the things that had stacked up over the years and locked up all his tools in the same cabinet where he had locked up the revolver.

By then the Buck Rogers serial had reached its final installment. It was a grand finale, with Buck saving the day just as they all knew he would. Killer Kane was forced to wear the amnesia helmet, but everyone else was freed. On the way home from the theater Johnny wanted to be Buddy and do the final scene where Buddy makes a big deal about leaving Buck and Wilma alone but Marlena and Pete both told him to shut up. So Johnny went off to his pirate friends, and Pete said he had to go home and help his mother with something. Marlena didn't want to go home just yet so she started walking toward the edge of town until she found herself at the empty lot where Mr. Delmore was going to put his zeppelin tower. There was someone standing at the edge of the lot, and when she got closer she realized it was Mr. Delmore. He was just standing there looking at nothing in particular.

Marlena walked over to him. "Hi, Mr. Delmore."

He looked down at her, at first with no recognition at all, but then he said, "You're John Cantrell's daughter, aren't you?"

"Yes, sir."

"How are your parents." He didn't say it like a question and Marlena realized he didn't care how her parents were. So they had something in common. "Fine, thank you."

"That's good," he said. He was wearing a coat and tie even though it was Saturday, and he was thinner than he had been back when he had been planning the zeppelin tower.

He started to turn away from her, and Marlena said, "It was a grand idea, Mr. Delmore."

He stopped but did not look back at her. "What?"

"The zeppelin tower, Mr. Delmore. It was a grand idea. I'm sorry it didn't work out."

He turned around and looked down at her, and at first Marlena thought he looked like her father had in the kitchen, but before she could back away his face relaxed, and he almost smiled. "Me, too," he said. "But there's more than one grand idea." Then he went back to looking at the empty lot.

Marlena never made anything in the garage again. But when she finished high school her teacher made such a fuss about how a bright girl like Marlena needed to continue her education that her parents let the teacher find a way to get Marlena a scholarship to a big university in New England, a scholarship her mother called "a great honor" and her father called "charity." She graduated at the head of her class and went on to be one of the first women at that particular school to get a Ph.D. in Electrical Engineering. She was recruited by several government agencies but went to work for Bell Labs instead. She invented half a dozen remarkable things, three of which she received partial credit for and three of which her employers decided should not be released to the public. She retired early and became a teacher at her old university.

A year after the summer when they all watched Buck Rogers, Pete's father got a new job that didn't require him to travel so much, and Pete's mother took him back to Chicago for good. He and Marlena wrote faithfully for about two months, and then not so faithfully, and, eventually, not at all.

Johnny, to his father's pride and relief, grew up to be a successful businessman. He never lost his interest in games, however, and when, many years later, he was looking for an investment opportunity, he heard about a new board game where the players pretended to be dragons and wizards and knights. He put some money into the new game, and it paid off handsomely.

Johnny prided himself on seizing the moment and not dwelling on the past, so he never thought too much about his childhood with Marlena back in Clarksburg, Illinois. But every once in a while he thought about something that happened when they were kids that he never understood. It was a few years after the summer they watched the Buck Rogers serial. They went to a horror movie that was a sequel to another movie they had really liked about a woman who turned into a panther. The sequel was very different, much quieter—in fact, to Johnny, there didn't seem to be much going on at all. But Marlena was utterly engrossed until the part where the little girl tried to tell her father about an encounter with a witch, and her father thought she was lying and took her upstairs to punish her. When that happened, Marlena jumped up and ran out of the theater so abruptly that Johnny thought that something was really wrong—plus, the movie wasn't that interesting anyway—so he went after her. He found her a block down the street crying. Sobbing, crying so hard he was afraid she would choke. Eventually she calmed down, but he had never seen her cry that hard before, and he never saw her cry that hard again, not even when their parents died.

SEE THAT MY GRAVE IS KEPT CLEAN

I never understood what the fuss was about. It was just a job, and everyone needs a job. I needed a job. I had already decided that Billy was the one, but until we were married I was going to have to take care of myself. Not that Ma and Pa didn't take care of me, but you know what I mean. A girl always needs some money in her purse. You don't want to get caught unprepared.

And it's not like I had a lot of options. I could type but I wasn't very fast, and I was really good at filing but the offices weren't hiring for that right then. Waitressing was out of the question. I didn't want to serve anybody. I did think being a carhop at Renzo's Drive-In might be fun but then my cousin Theresa got a job there and it turned out the place was a front for something else they needed girls for and uncle Mike went over Theresa's first night and hauled her back home, so that was out.

But then I heard Marberry Funeral Home was looking for someone, and when I found out all they wanted was someone to sit with the bodies when nobody else was there, I went right over, and they hired me on the spot. In fact, they seemed grateful. I think I was the only one who applied.

Ma didn't like it, and Pa said I couldn't do it, but when I told him I'd kick in part of what I made to the household budget, he hesitated, and I could tell by the look on Ma's face that I'd won. Pa was doing OK at the plant but they were saying there might be another round of layoffs and that had Ma worried. If you ever saw the look on Pa's face when Ma acted worried or scared, and saw the look Ma had then, you'd know I'd won, too.

So I sat with the bodies. I never really understood why they needed someone to do that, but Mr. Marberry, who was the grandson of the man who had started the business in the first place, said that they had to guard against anyone disturbing the bodies. He said it was a matter of law. I didn't know how anyone could disturb a dead person, and I didn't know how I was supposed to stop anyone who did, but Mr. Marberry said they had hired girls before and never had any problems. He said again it was a matter of law, and even if there wasn't much chance of anything happening, they had to have someone there. My cousin Marcie used to say that Mr. Marberry was the ugliest man she'd ever seen and he gave her the creeps. He was ugly all right, but he had a steady voice and talked to me like I was just someone who was working for him and not like I was a kid. He was very matter-of-fact about everything, and I liked that. He even shook my hand when I accepted the job.

The late hours were kind of a struggle at first, but Ma said it was OK for me to sleep in since I was working late, and once I started doing that it was fine. I knew there were a lot more bodies down in the basement where they got them ready to be buried, but I just had to be there in the main area where they kept the bodies after they'd been prepared but before the funerals. I got to sit behind a desk in the main room, like I was running the place. From there I could see into the smaller rooms where they kept the individual caskets. The main room was fancy but very serious, with paintings that blended right into the walls. The smaller rooms were plain with maybe only some flowers on a table. Best of all, the whole place was air-conditioned, which wasn't common back then, but they needed to keep it all cool for obvious reasons.

And honestly, I didn't mind the bodies. The caskets were closed except when the families were viewing during regular hours, so from where I sat all you saw were these long polished boxes through the doors, and unless you went in and took a good look they could have been anything, really.

Of course, I did go into each room and check on things a couple times a night. That's what they were paying me for, after all. And for the first week or so that I was there, every once in a while I'd open up one of the caskets and take a look at the body inside. Maybe I shouldn't have, but nobody specifically told me not to, and I was supposed to be making sure the bodies weren't disturbed, right?

Sure enough there they all were in their caskets, but now they just looked like mannequins lying there with no expression. That was true even when every once in a while there was someone I had known, like Mrs. Nielsen, who had taught me and both my parents fourth grade, and Johnny Martin, who got killed in a wreck. Johnny was one of those kids who was mean to you until he decided to go after someone else, and I had never liked him. Of course that didn't mean I wanted him dead. The mortician had sure done a good job. You couldn't tell that anything had happened.

But I have to admit that after the first week I seldom looked inside the coffins. I poked my head in the rooms once or twice each night, just to make sure. Otherwise I just sat there behind the desk in this great swivel chair and read, mostly my library copy of *Gone with the Wind*. My cousin Kathleen claimed to have read the whole thing in a single day, starting first thing that morning and finishing after midnight. I don't doubt she did, but I can't read that fast, and even if I did I couldn't very well take a whole day to do nothing but lie around and read a book. My father's not rich.

So I sat there guarding the bodies against being disturbed. I read my book, and when I wasn't reading I was planning the life that Billy and I were going to have together once he realized that Alice wasn't the one for him. Even my parents talked about how sensible and down-to-earth Alice was, and how that was the sort of girl Billy needed. Maybe they were right about what Billy needed, but not about who. It was quiet and cool there in the main room and let's face it, I didn't have to do anything. Really, it was the best job I'd ever had.

And then one night right after I'd finished a chapter, I was resting my eyes and thinking how basically I really liked Scarlett although I didn't see why she had to be so dramatic about everything, I heard a noise.

I opened my eyes and looked around. Nothing. Then I heard the noise again. Second room to the left.

I got up and went into the room, taking my copy of *Gone with the Wind* in case I needed a weapon—it was certainly heavy enough. It was quiet, and then I heard the noise again. A scratching sound, coming from inside the coffin.

When I'd first heard the noise, I have to admit that I was a little scared, but now that I was in the room with the noise coming from the casket, I was just numb. I didn't know what to think or do. I wasn't even aware of moving, but I found myself beside the casket, leaning down with my ear practically on the wood. Scratch, scratch, scratch.

I put my book down on the floor and opened up the top half of the casket. There was an old man inside I didn't know. The scratching had stopped but now there was a different sound. It was coming from the man's head.

I looked down and realized his mouth was moving without opening. I guess they had to sew it shut, or glue it, or do something to keep it from falling open.

Then he sat up. The casket was still closed below his waist, but there was room for him to sit up and get his arms free. He reached up and pulled at his face with both hands, and there was a sound not much louder than pulling off a band-aid, and his mouth opened and he said, softly but perfectly clearly, "See that my grave is kept clean." And then he lay back down and didn't say anything else.

I stood there and waited. I don't know how much time passed, but he didn't sit back up, and he didn't say anything else. So I closed the casket, picked up my book, and went back to my desk.

I tried to read some more but I couldn't concentrate. I just sat there the rest of the evening and tried to decide what to do. To be honest, I didn't worry so much about the body sitting up or even talking. I'd never taken a drink of liquor in my life—still haven't—and I knew what had happened had happened. And there was that summer when we all read *Frankenstein* and *Dracula* and went to see that other Bela Lugosi movie about the zombies, so it wasn't like this was something I'd never heard of.

What I couldn't figure out was why he said what he said. Like I'm supposed to tend to his grave? Maybe he thought I had a different job here. Or maybe he didn't realize I was there at all. Maybe he was just hoping someone was.

I didn't read any more that evening. I just sat there and waited for another noise.

But there wasn't one, and when my time was up I got up and went home and didn't say a word to anyone.

It never happened again, which was just as well. If there had been more bodies sitting up and talking, I might have had to tell someone, and if I didn't, I might have had to quit my job, and neither one of those was something I wanted to do. Once Ma and Pa were used to me being there with the bodies, they would have been disappointed if I'd quit a perfectly good job. And if anyone was going to get Billy away from sensible Alice, it probably wouldn't be a girl dead people talked to.

So I didn't tell anyone, and like I said, it never happened again. When the summer was over I went back to school, and by the end of senior year, sure enough Billy saw the light about old Alice and started going steady with me. We got married, and here we are. Everything's fine.

I don't think much about what happened, but sometimes I have these dreams, and when I wake up it's hard to get back to sleep. When that happens I look over at Billy, and I'm so happy he's lying right there beside me. If Billy dies before I do, and he wants to sit up and pull his dead mouth open and start talking, he can just forget about it. He can just lie right back down.

THE LIGHT OF THE IDEAL

Stoddard was lucky to have a job at all. He understood that, and tried to be grateful. There were worse things a man could be forced to do; that he knew as a fact. At least this wasn't the foundry, which had bent his frame and broken his spirit beyond anything that might happen to him as an Inspector of Customs for the Port of New York. The poetry had been all that kept him going back then. It was really all that kept him going now. His wife Lizzie would scoff at such a statement, just as she had too often scoffed at his poetry, but it was true.

Thank God Hawthorne had understood, despite his enormous success—or perhaps because of it. It was Hawthorne's letter to his old college chum Pierce, conveniently President of the United States at the time, that had gotten Stoddard the job in the first place. It was not difficult to be grateful for that. Such generosity of spirit was hard to come by in this fallen world.

He scribbled his signature across the bottom of the paper which lay on his desk, put it on top of the others, initialed the copy below it, put that on top of the one he had signed. He looked over at the corner table where the package sat that he had brought back from his trip down to the Battery that afternoon. There were more papers left, but instead of signing them he pushed away from his desk and walked over to his office's only window.

Nassau Street lay below him, shadowed and unclean. Almost dark. The street lamps were being lit and the traffic was beginning to thicken; the carriage horses bumped their noses against the vehicles in front of them. As the distant figures scurried by three stories below him, they moved out of the shadows into the small pools of lamplight and back into the dark again. Stoddard wanted nothing so much at that moment as to go down onto the sidewalk and stand under one of the lamps and let the light surround him, illuminate him.

The lamp directly across the street from his office came on, and Stoddard saw a man and a woman standing under it. The man was well-dressed and held himself with dignity; the woman's skirts were soiled and her hat lay crooked on her head. The woman was talking and the man stood silently, listening. Her breath clouded the air between them; despite the cold, she had no gloves. Stoddard couldn't see their faces from here, but he knew the hard look he would find on the woman, the coarse features and cunning eyes. He knew also of the desperation the man so carefully hid: the desperation that sent otherwise good and noble men into the street for comfort. He turned away from the window in disgust, looked at his piled desk with even more disgust, and decided to go home. Perhaps Lizzie would have dinner waiting if she hadn't gotten lost in the composition of her new story.

While putting on his overcoat, he looked again at the package from the docks. It seemed insubstantial in the dim glow from the street that eased through the window, seemed to hover, mute and unreadable. He walked over to it, stopped before he reached it, turned around, and went out the door. He would deal with it tomorrow.

As he walked the seven blocks to his home, though, his thoughts returned to the box. His position in the Debenture Office of the Custom House did not call for him to go out into the city too often, a circumstance for which he was ever grateful. Nonetheless, from time to time he had to go see to business himself. His office was responsible for sending inspecting officers to all incoming vessels with cargoes from other countries; the ships' berths extended from the Battery to the foot of Twelfth Street on East River and to Gansevoort Street on North River, and so the staff was kept busy. Sometimes there simply were not enough men, and Stoddard would be forced to put on his hat and overcoat and go down to the shipping district and conduct an inspection himself, or clean up some subordinate's mistake. He was employed at an asylum for mediocrities; everyone who was fit for nothing elsewhere thought he deserved a job in the Custom-House, and so there were mistakes aplenty to go around.

That was what had happened this afternoon. Word had come that one of the inspecting officers had had a confrontation with the captain of the *Belle Amie*, a schooner just in from the Sandwich Islands. The outraged captain claimed the cargo was overestimated by the young clerk, who was in fear of bodily harm should the fees run greater than the captain thought just. Could Mr. Stoddard please come down to the dock and help facilitate the matter?

When he reached the shipping district he was struck, as always, by the spectacle. The waterfront of New York or any other great city was the opposite of beauty. Its grime and commotion reminded him of the foundry; all that was missing was the extreme heat. But there were elements of it that were undeniably picturesque. The bowsprits of the ships sometimes extended halfway across the street toward the warehouses, like medieval lancers ready to attack. Much of the cargo was prosaic, but much was of exotic appearance and even scent; a few of the poems in his volume *Book of the East* had arisen from these visits. And while the men of the foundry were gray haunts beneath their burdens, the inhabitants of the riverfront were a swirling patchwork of the world. He saw few of the ships' crew—no true sailor would remain near salt water once he was ashore—but the longshoremen surged continuously from the ships to the docks to the warehouses and back, clad in garments as outlandish as strolling players, their mouths full of strange pipes and strange words. Stoddard was never quite sure if it was the lure of the antipodes which appealed to him, or simply the fact that, although he was in a place he did not want to be, at least he was no longer a slightly-built youth carrying forty-pound ladles of molten iron in each hand.

He arrived at the *Belle Amie's* berth to find his clerk sitting on the edge of the dock, staring gloomily into the water. Behind the clerk stood a tremendous man in a coal-black greatcoat which hung down to the dock. The man stood impassively and puffed on a bamboo pipe half as long as his arm. The breeze from the water tossed his great flowing gray hair and beard. He looked a bit like Whitman, which, to Stoddard, was no recommendation.

The clerk, an underfed young man who had half the captain's size and a fifth of his hair, scrambled to his feet at Stoddard's approach. "Mr. Stoddard! I am very glad to see you, sir. I have done my level best to reason with this gentleman—"

"Be you this pissant's superior?" the gray-haired man asked. His voice was harsh and slurred, the voice of a man not used to talking below a shout.

"I am, sir," Stoddard replied. "Richard Henry Stoddard, Inspector of Customs for the Port of New York. Are you the captain of this vessel?"

"I am, Mr. Richard Henry Stoddard." He came up to Stoddard and the clerk but kept one hand in his pocket and the other on his pipe. He stank of sweat and brine. "Mardonius Cantrell, captain of the good ship *Belle Amie* and an honest man. An honest man, Mr. Richard Henry Stoddard," Cantrell said, his voice rising to its accustomed volume, "one who's never cheated another man on a game of chance or a load of cargo. There's 487 tons aboard this ship and not a pound more."

"If you please, Mr. Stoddard," the clerk said, "my estimates clearly indicate that 488 tons is a much more accurate figure. If you'll examine my report—"

"Quiet, you God-damned maggot!" Cantrell roared. "I'll have your balls for breakfast before you call me a liar!"

"Do you have proper documentation for your cargo, Captain

Cantrell?" Stoddard asked wearily. He should be in a sylvan glade, reclining comfortably beneath a tree. The Muses should be breathing poetry into him while Lizzie feeds him grapes.

"Paper. Paper and words." Cantrell reached into his coat and pulled out a wad of parchment. "I take the sorriest crew the company ever purchased, drag them around the Cape by their cocks, arrive in port three days ahead with only two men and no cargo lost, and what greets me? A company man with a bonus for my efforts? A fat whore with a jug of whiskey? No. Sniveling she-men with words on paper."

Stoddard examined the documentation, compared it with the clerk's estimate. "You're right, Mr. Van Ness," Stoddard said to the clerk. "There is most certainly a discrepancy here. Unfortunately, that is owing to your counting a dozen barrels of sugar twice." He pulled a metal stamp out of his pocket and pressed it to Cantrell's papers. "Please be on your way, Captain, and accept my apologies for the confusion."

"Apologies?" Cantrell spat on the dock. "All the whores will be taken in the time I've wasted here." He looked over at Van Ness. "If you had your manhood between your legs instead of a quill pen, maybe you could count higher than your fingers and you could count my cargo right."

"I'll—I'll not—" Van Ness began.

"You'll shit blood and be grateful! Out of my way." He pushed past the speechless clerk and went back aboard his ship.

Van Ness proceeded to beg Stoddard's pardon at some length, but Stoddard cut him off and sent him back to the office. Rather than following, he stood at the edge of the dock and stared down at the water. A thin oily film floated on the surface from where the ships had flushed their wastes. He felt profoundly depressed. It was not the captain's obscene tirade, or the clerk's incompetence. It was all of that and none of that. What could he hope for in such a place? What ideality was here?

He looked up from the polluted water and turned to walk

back to the office. A group of Negroes had gathered on the shoreline; they whooped and laughed as they looked out at the water at something Stoddard could not see. During the draft riots the good citizens of New York had hanged them from lampposts. What had they to smile about?

"Mr. Richard Henry Stoddard!"

Stoddard turned around. Cantrell had emerged from the ship and was walking toward him carrying a package. He came up to Stoddard and thrust it at him. "Here. Take this."

Stoddard looked at the package uncertainly. "Is this a bribe, sir?"

"A bribe? Christ, no!" Cantrell laughed, a harsh sound that betrayed no mirth. "If I'd wanted to bribe you, you damned fool, I'd've done it before you figured out that I was right and your ass-licking clerk was wrong. Go on, take it."

Stoddard hesitated, then reached out and took the package. It was unwieldy but light; it bore no outside marks.

"It's no bribe, man," Cantrell repeated. "I've seen your look in other men's eyes. I've been around the world too many times not to recognize it." He leaned in toward Stoddard, removed his pipe. His teeth were made of wood. "It's the look of a crewman who realizes too late what a mistake he's made signing on. The look of a man desperate not to be where he is."

Stoddard remained impassive, determined not to acknowledge the truth of what the captain said. "I am quite content with where I am, sir. But even if I weren't, what would this box have to do with that?"

"I don't rightly know, Mr. Richard Henry Stoddard. Maybe nothing. The man who passed it on to me didn't live long enough to tell me all its history. All I know is that it's for men like you, and I'm damned glad to be rid of it."

"What exactly is its history?" Stoddard asked, curious despite himself.

"For the love of God, man! I've wasted enough time here already. There won't be a whore left in New York by the time I get into town." He moved toward the street. "Throw it in the river for all I care. It's yours just the same."

That was how he had gotten the package. As he approached the entrance to his home, a grimy-faced boy stepped out of a doorway, emptied a slop bucket into the gutter, and retreated back into the shadows whistling a Yankee marching song. Stoddard breathed through his mouth as he turned his key in the doorlatch, trying to ignore the stench. He had outlived Shelley and Keats for this?

Stoddard found Lizzie sitting at the dining table, head resting in the crook of her arms on the tabletop, sound asleep.

"Lizzie," Stoddard said, gently shaking her shoulders. "Lizzie, dear. Wake up."

Lizzie started awake, looked up at her husband, and put her head back down on the table. "Lorry's asleep," she said. "He's been needing me all day. I had Millie put some supper on before she left."

"Good," said Stoddard, who was all too aware that their housekeeper was a much better cook than Lizzie. "Has the fever come back?"

"No," she said, and sat up. Stoddard sat down across the table from her. Lizzie had never been a great beauty, and the energy and wit that had always carried her through had been diminished in recent times. It had been almost five years since the death of their son Willy; Lorry's arrival two years later had helped considerably, but Stoddard knew full well his wife had never really recovered from the death of their second child. The first one had almost finished her off as it was. Night after night of the deformed creature lying silent in the cradle and Lizzie staring past it at something only she could see.... Better not to think of it. At least Willy had been born whole, and had lived long enough to warrant a name.

She asked him about his day, and as she laid the supper out he told her of the papers that had crossed his desk, and the many more that had arrived and stayed. She smiled and even managed a laugh at his tale of the inspecting officer who had complained about a procedural matter and whom he had referred to Jim Benedict, knowing that Benedict would dispatch the complainer with language coarser than anything Stoddard had ever heard on the docks. It was good to hear Lizzie laugh; there had been so little of that lately.

"You should have seen the look on the fellow's face," Stoddard said, smiling himself at the recollection. "It was as if he had just stepped off a curb and been splashed with mud by a garbage wagon."

"Did he tell you what Benedict said?" Lizzie asked.

"He did not, and I shouldn't repeat it if he had."

"Nonsense, Dick. Benedict is a classic study. I might be able to use it in my new story."

"Shush, Lizzie!" He pretended to be shocked, but he was used to her fancies. "As if any worthy magazine would print such a work."

"Shush yourself, Dick," she said pleasantly, biting into the last of her chicken. She chewed methodically and swallowed. "When Millie came back from the market today she said she had seen a boy with no legs who moved on a slab of wood with wheels under it. He propelled himself by pushing on the street with his hands, down to the ground like an ape." She poured herself another cup of tea. "There are worse things in the world than the words that come out of people's mouths."

"Indeed there are," he replied, holding his teacup halfway across the table while she poured. "All the more reason we should strive for the most beautiful words possible, arranged in an ideal fashion."

"Save your sermons for the choir," she said abruptly, rising and gathering the dishes. Her momentary good humor had vanished. "Boker is supposed to be up next week, isn't he? Talk to him of Beauty and Truth and Greece and Rome. Or go have lunch with Ned Stedman and pay homage to the Muse while he tries to sell you railroad shares."

Stoddard sipped his tea and said nothing. Millie should have known better that to come back to the house bearing stories of cripples; she knew Lizzie's dread of such things after the first child. He would fire her, except that she was such a good cook. He started to tell Lizzie the story of the package which sat in his office, but he decided not to. No reason to stir her up any further.

After dinner they sat in their chairs by the fire. Lizzie had sorted the mail earlier in the day, and Stoddard went through it while she scribbled at her story. A review copy of the first book of poetry by a young woman "whose excellent moral character is reflected in the purity and fragile beauty of her verse," according to the accompanying publisher's note. No doubt. A letter from Taylor complaining about bills and trumpeting his translation of *Faust*, which would be ready by summer—and which, Stoddard thought wearily, would no more pay the bills than any other poem, Goethe or no. More review copies, a handful of magazines, and several bills of his own.

Shining through the pile, however, was the letter of acceptance from *Harper's* for his latest sonnet. The enclosed check floated free of the envelope; Stoddard snatched it out of the air before it drifted toward the fire. He had published plenty of poetry by now, four books of it, but the thrill of achievement, however slight, still ran through him when he placed a poem. He looked at the check for fifteen dollars. A week's salary. If only he could write more and sell them; if only there were more *Harper's* to go around. If only wishes were horses, so beggars such as he could ride.

He passed one of the new books to Lizzie. "Look, my dear. It's the new Tennyson."

Lizzie took the volume and laid it aside without looking up from her writing. "Send it to Taylor. Show him what a real poet can do."

He started to respond, thought better of it, leaned his head back against the chair, and sighed. Tennyson had England. What had he and Taylor and the rest? New York was many things, but it was no place for poets. New York was a denser America, and America had no use for ideality. A nation of shopkeepers and engineers who wanted physical objects they could touch and, preferably, sell. That was why he had refused to support the war, a stance Boker and Taylor and young Stedman and the rest never understood. He had no use for the slaving South, concealing its brutality beneath a veneer of charm, but it was right about the North. It was not a culture worth defending; it was no culture at all.

Besides, Boker had his family money. Taylor had his travel books and lecture tours and still had to do the labor of three men to keep up that huge Pennsylvania house of his. And Stedman—Stedman worked on Wall Street during the day and wrote poetry at night, and actually seemed to prefer it that way. They all had money, but none of it had come from their poetry. And why should it, when the old boys whose coattails they kept grabbing for couldn't earn a living from their Muse, either? Holmes and Lowell had their professorships; Emerson and Longfellow had their wives' money; Whittier seemed content to exist on air and Quaker certitude.

Not that any of those old lecturers had the true gift, mind. When Stoddard had met Lowell for the first time, the elder poet had talked to him of poetry and those who wrote it. He had listened politely and then told Lowell—amazing, when he thought of it, to talk to such a figure in such a way—that poetry was more than a personal manifestation: it was the revelation of ideal truth and beauty. We must not pull the ideal down to us, but rise to the ideal. He believed that then, and he still believed.

But how to serve the Muse and Mammon, too? That young friend of Stedman's, Tom Aldrich, had said once that when he had sold his first poem and showed the check to the uncle with whom he and his widowed mother lived, the old banker had said, "Why don't you sell the damn fool one every week?" The first time Stoddard had seen ten dollars for a poem he had invested it in an accordion for a young girl with whom he had been infatuated. His poetic ability had improved since then, he hoped, but—judging from the bills which lay by his chair—he didn't think he could say the same of his ability to handle money.

A sleepy but insistent child's voice came from the back bedroom; Lizzie got up to check on Lorry. Stoddard went over to his desk and pulled out the manuscript of the sonnet *Harper's* had accepted. Old habits died hard; he always reread his work when he was notified that it would be published. He stared at the second quatrain:

Thou hast the laurel, Master of my soul!
Thy name, thou saidst, was writ in water—No,
For while clouds float on high, and billows roll,
Thy name shall worshipped be. Will mine be so?

Will it indeed? Will the name of Richard Henry Stoddard be remembered? He looked across the room at Lizzie, who had returned with a fretting Lorry in her arms, then returned to his poem. *I kiss thy words as I would kiss thy face,/And put thy book most reverently away.* Keats. The poor brilliant boy. Better for being released from the world, but so soon, so soon! He wished he could shake the hand that had soothed that fevered brow.

Eventually Lizzie got Lorry settled back down; Stoddard went into the nursery and dutifully kissed his son goodnight. He remembered from his own youth what it was like to be a child, and sick, not knowing what it was that had felled you, or why, or how to make it go away. With adulthood came the thin satisfaction of knowing what, and why; knowing how to make it go away was quite another matter.

Shortly after they went to bed Lizzie reached over and ran her hand up his nightshirt, tracing down his chest and the flaccid mound of his belly, touching him gently below. It surprised him, knowing how exhausted she must be after the day with Lorry, but he turned to her and complied. He almost failed her when his mind drifted to the man and the prostitute he had seen from his office window, but she spoke softly to him and he was able to lose himself again in her scent and the cushion of her skin. As they finished silently his mind was blissfully clean of the world. They parted, and he rolled to his side of the bed where he slept and dreamed of the disembodied head of Keats dissolving under a torrent of filthy water.

The next morning the package was still on the table in his office, unremarkable now in the daylight. He worked steadily at his desk through the morning, but his gaze kept wandering to the table in the corner of the room. Finally he put down his pen and walked over and picked up the package. It was not heavy and had been no trouble to bring back from the docks. It should be no trouble to bring home this evening, either.

Holding the package in his hands here in his office, he wondered again what he should do with it. Any unclaimed cargo was supposed to go directly to his supervisor, but Stoddard could not bring himself to surrender it. He had never gone against Custom-House procedure before, but the look in Cantrell's eyes, the tone of his voice, the unmistakable urgency of his message—there was no looking away.

Still holding the package, he walked over to his office window. The strong morning light poured into the room; as he moved toward it, his office receded into shadow. The details of the street below were sharp and clear. He could discern the colors of the cab drivers' waistcoats, the kinds of merchandise on display in the store windows, the texture of the mud in the street. From this distance, in this light, it all looked so lively and clean.

Stoddard knew better. In this bright world below him, men were kept from their dreams and children died for no reason at all.

He looked down at the mysterious object in his hands and found no immediate answers. He walked away from the window and set the package back on his desk. His hands, moving as if of their own volition, reached out and began to untie the frayed hemp wrapped around the box.

"Mr. Stoddard?"

Van Ness' troubled voice came from the other side of the door.

He had not heard the clerk knock. He hastily retied the rope and replaced the package beneath his desk.

Van Ness brought another problem—someone else's fault, of course—and as Stoddard left to repair the damage another clerk begged his intercession to correct another mistake, and the day promptly disappeared like so many others before it. He did not think of the box again until he was ready to go home. What a fool, to put credence in the obscene ravings of a ship's captain. He would turn the package over to Jim Benedict tomorrow.

Stoddard arrived home to find Millie running in and out of the kitchen under Lizzie's acidulous direction, setting the table for two extra people. Lizzie handed him the notes that had arrived from George Boker and Bayard Taylor. Boker would be up from Philadelphia today instead of next week; Taylor was in New York for a meeting with his publisher. Both would be at the Stoddards' for dinner that evening.

Their visit was not unwelcome; it had been months since Stoddard had seen his two oldest friends. But Lizzie, despite her outspoken contempt for persons overconcerned with social convention, was acutely conscious of the table she presented to dinner guests and resented the short notice she had received.

"But Lizzie," Stoddard protested, "why go to such a fuss? George and Bayard are family."

"And it's family who expect the most," Lizzie replied as she refolded the napkins Millie had already laid out. "George has spent a lifetime pampered by Philadelphia society twelve-course extravaganzas, and Bayard has sat at table from New York to Persia to Japan and back. I'll not have them returning to those wives of theirs with tales of their poor relations Dick and Lizzie."

Stoddard frowned. She was getting far more agitated than the situation called for. He started to remind her that, as many times as they had had to borrow money from both Boker and Taylor, neither one was likely to be swept away by fancy napkins and elegant china, but he thought better of it and held his tongue.

He wished Stedman were visiting tonight as well. Ned always had a soothing effect on Lizzie; not only was he genuinely fond of her, but he valued her writing, which was in fairness more than Stoddard could say of the others. By the end of the evening they would be sitting in the corner of the parlor, holding hands and reciting Mrs. Browning. But it was George and Bayard this evening, and Lizzie would have to make the best of it.

Their guests arrived within minutes of each other, and for all her apprehension Lizzie seemed glad to see them. Boker kissed her hand with the familiar upper-class charm, while the ebullient Taylor favored her with the same bear-hug he accorded Stoddard. Stoddard was relieved to see that Taylor had apparently gotten over the somewhat diffident review he had given his old friend's last collection of poems. He tried to be as supportive of his friends as he could, but Stoddard would compromise his literary standards for no one. That was one area where he and Lizzie were in full agreement, and they had both suffered the consequences of their honesty on more than one occasion.

Over dinner, as they all discussed the latest magazines and new novels, Stoddard regarded his friends. Boker was handsome as ever and still carried himself with the assurance and precision of one born to comfort—qualities that Stoddard had always envied, though he would admit it to no one but himself. But the gray in Boker's hair was more prominent than before, and the lines in his face just a little deeper. The years of battle defending his father's estate against the bank's lawsuit—and, more important to Boker, defending his father's good name from the taint of scandal—had clearly taken their toll. And the success of the hastily scribbled *Poems of the War* had in no way made up for the failure of his last few plays, or the oblivion into which his other, more ideal poetry had sunk. He hardly wrote at all any more, and his well-bred smile seemed a trifle strained.

Taylor, for his part, looked positively haggard. He had always driven himself harder than the rest, and for a while it had paid off. His travels writings and lectures had made him famous, almost theatrically so. Stoddard still remembered the New York lecture he had attended: as Taylor mounted the platform in the Bedouin raiment he had brought back from his latest Near East journey, the women in front of Stoddard had actually risen from their seats, straining to get a better glimpse of the exotic figure at the front of the room. "There he is," they whispered. "That's *him!*" Then the war had interrupted everything; the demand for lectures had dropped precipitously, and Taylor was now returned to journalism and translation to make ends meet. As always, the poetry brought next to nothing.

It had been so different at the beginning. They had had the shared vision of beauty to carry them through the prosaic days. Back in the '40s, he and Taylor would spend Saturday evenings together in Taylor's attic apartment, reading poetry to each other and pretending they were Keats and Shelley high atop Parnassus. Boker had joined them later, and for a while the three of them drew considerable notice—the *New York Knickerbocker* had even referred to them as a "Trinity." After he and Lizzie were married, they had offered their home as a *salon* for the brightest and most gifted poets and artists and actors and musicians New York offered. Stedman had joined their circle, and Aldrich; Taylor christened their gatherings "The Shrine of Genius," and they had believed him.

But children were born, and died; debts accrued; wives failed to get along; honest reviews went unappreciated; public taste failed to rise to the heights they had set for it. As they got up from the dinner table and retired to the parlor, Stoddard realized that his friends had simply grown old.

As the men lit their cigars, Lizzie retired to the nursery with Lorry to establish him for the evening. When she returned, Taylor was complaining about the state of the literary world. "Will we never see the end of glorified crudity in these United States?" he asked, waving his cigar and depositing a quantity of ash on the newly swept floor. "The public has become materialized. All they want is diversion and excitement. There's no appreciative class in this country. I'd thought after we whipped the Rebels things would settle down and we'd finally have an independent, cultivated audience—"

"Guardians of the temple," Stoddard said.

"Exactly! But no, all they want are new machines and cheap sentiment. It's no wonder an artist gets pulled down whenever he tries to rise."

"And what do you expect when no one appreciates or understands what we do?" Boker added. He rested his elbows on the arm of the easy chair he had sunk into after dinner and templed his fingers. "No one will believe the labor connected with all great literary achievement. It's enough to drive any but a man of genius stark mad, but the masses are still convinced that poets write as the birds sing. It's this false idea which robs us of half our honors."

"Absolutely!" Taylor said. "A man who means to write poetry must know how to *work*!"

"If poetry were forged upon an anvil," Boker said, "or cut out with an axe, my God! How men would marvel at the process!"

Stoddard looked over to Lizzie expecting a comment, but she had retired to the corner of the room and busied herself with sewing. Not at all like her. He grew worried. She had been lively enough at dinner. What was wrong with her?

He turned his attention back to his guests. "It's true," he said. "We've all given ourselves to the Muse, and she's extracted a dear cost. Who's worked harder than you, Bayard? You've done the labor of ten men with all your writing."

"And for what?" Taylor said. "I achieve a life-goal in translating *Faust*, and who will read it? Never mind my own poetry. I wrote a sonnet last week and it had been so long since I had written in lines I barely recognized the experience."

"You've written four novels, Bayard," Stoddard said. "That's four more than George or I. They were well-received. You still have a fine reputation."

Taylor snorted dismissively. "Reputation! I wouldn't swap the reputation earned by ten lines of good poetry for all the prose I shall ever write." He ground out his cigar in the ashtray on the mantelpiece.

"Perhaps we shall measure up to Keats, after all," Boker said. "Perhaps our epitaphs also shall be, 'Here lies one whose name was writ in water.'"

Stoddard rose from his chair and raised his wine glass. Enough was enough. "Come now, George, Bayard," he said. "Never mind such gloomy thoughts. We can take great pride in the work that we've done. Poetry is a flower which comes to perfection only in great minds. We can rest content. We have known that special joy which comes only to a selected few. We have served our Muse faithfully and well." He raised his glass. "To divinest Poesy!"

Boker stood, and he and Taylor raised their own neglected glasses. "To divinest Poesy!" they echoed.

They drank solemnly, taking comfort from the wine and the steady crackle of the fire. Stoddard looked over at Lizzie, who was still busy with her needles. "Come, Madame Defarge," he said with a cheerfulness that, despite the toast, he did not really feel. "Put your knitting aside and join us in our toast."

"I shall not, you frauds," Lizzie muttered.

"I beg your pardon, Lizzie?" Stoddard said, although he had heard her clearly enough.

"I shall not join in your delusions," Lizzie said, tossing her needlework onto the divan. She rose and walked over to them. The fire turned her eyes to two sharp points of light as she addressed them. "The whole lot of you have all been dreary failures as poets. Not a one of you has won even a third-class position in the field. Not a one of you can justly lay claim to popularity, and you know it. Even that weakling Longfellow, who is a third-rater himself compared to the mass of English poets, is a more exalted figure than any of you."

Boker and Taylor looked at her as if she had just slithered out from beneath the sofa. Stoddard's heart sank. Why could she never hold her tongue? "That is grossly unfair, Lizzie," he said.

"Is it? Never mind Keats. Can any of you match Tennyson, Arnold, Swinbourne, either of the Brownings? Since you lot began to write, all of them and more have arisen and secured the fame to which you aspired in vain." Her voice shook. "It isn't time or an audience you've lacked—it's poetic ability. The world is not unappreciative of real genius, as you flatter yourselves is the case. You are just not up to the required standard."

"The world appreciates genius, does it?" said Boker. "I trust that's why the novels of Elizabeth Barstow Stoddard have been such a rousing success."

"I am aware of my own limitations," Lizzie replied evenly, "and you should come of age and be aware of yours. You are all failures, and the sooner you stop writing the things that no public will read, the better for your peace of mind. Good evening, gentlemen," she concluded, and walked out.

The three men stood in silence. Boker took another sip of his wine. "What the deuce has got into her?"

"What is it that ever gets into her?" said Taylor, picking up a poker and thrusting halfheartedly at the collapsing fire.

Neither would react further to Lizzie's outburst, but Stoddard knew the effect her words had had. He tried to turn the conversation to other things, but it was no use. The evening was over.

After Boker and Taylor left, Stoddard went into the bedroom and found Lizzie stretched out on the bed, still fully dressed, staring at the ceiling. He went to the bed and stood over her. "And what in blue blazing *hell* was all that about?"

"The literary visit."

"What?"

"The literary visit," she repeated, not taking her eyes off the ceiling. "A finds B writing a poem. A insists on reading it. B reads and A says 'glorious.' Then A takes a manuscript from his pocket, which B insists shall be read. A reads and B says 'glorious.' A asks if B has seen his latest squib in the journal of the moment. B asks if A has seen his latest review of that book by C. They put their feet up, and then Tennyson, Browning, Longfellow, and their faults are discovered."

"I fail to see your point."

"You fail at all sorts of things, Dick."

He said nothing and turned to leave. There was no reasoning with her when she was like this, and he was determined she would not see how deeply he was wounded by her words. When he reached the doorway, he heard her say his name almost too softly to be heard.

He turned around. She still lay on the bed, but she held out her hand to him. The expression on her face, in different circumstances, might have passed for kindness. "Come here. Please."

Reluctantly, he walked over and sat by her on the bed. The folds of her dress obscured her body and ran into the bedspread, which was the same rich blue. Her head against the swell of the pillow seemed attached to nothing. There were circles under her eyes, and the lines on her face stood out against her powdered skin.

"Do you think I don't feel what you feel?" Lizzie said. "Do you think I don't want the same things, the same success? I hear what George and Bayard and the others say behind my back. They call me 'The Pythoness,' they hate me so."

"Now, Lizzie, no one hates you," Stoddard said quickly, alarmed by her sudden turn. He never knew which was worse, her sarcasm or her sincerity.

"As if I had not merely seduced them with knowledge but were the snake itself," she continued. "Is the truth so hard to bear? You know I'm right."

"It isn't a question of right or wrong. It's just that we've all worked so very hard for so very little."

"As have I!" she said, her voice rising. "I have endured fully as much as you. No one knows what an ambition I've had, or how my failure has broken me."

"I do, Lizzie. I know."

She squeezed his hand. Her voice grew softer. "You boys and your constant prattle about Beauty. Do you not think I desire it as well? The beauty I perceive is nothing against the beauty I long for."

He suddenly wanted to embrace her, dissolve with her and flee the world. Instead he squeezed her hand back and repeated, "I know."

"Poor Dick," she said, suddenly gentle. She placed his hand on her breast, pressed it down.

"This is where Beauty dwells," he said, feeling her heartbeat.

She slid his hand down low on her abdomen; his thumb brushed the top of her thigh. "This is where Beauty is supposed to be," she said.

"Lizzie—"

"What has Beauty's dwelling place yielded? A monster, a corpse, and a beautiful boy. If we enjoyed as much success with our work, we would have been dining with the Brownings tonight and basking in their praise."

Stoddard looked away from her and into the mirror above the washstand. The beard grows gray; the hair thins; the eyes droop and the lips move without words. George and Bayard weren't the only ones who had grown old. "Try to get some sleep, dear," he said finally, and went back into the parlor. He sat where Boker had and stared at Taylor's ashes on the floor. The room grew cold, but he did not bother to rekindle the fire.

By the time the clock said midnight he had made his decision. He put on his hat and coat and went out to his office. He did not bother to check and see if Lizzie were still asleep.

The blocks to the Customs house were much less busy than they had been during the day, but they were far from deserted. Stoddard was surprised at the amount of traffic, the number of other people going who knew where. As he walked, he felt an odd sense of comfort. The city was all too real during the day, and in the evening the falling light and rising shadows never failed to depress him as they made the streets an imperfect print, something on the verge of being. But here in the middle of the night the darkness smoothed over the manholes and concrete and left the city seemingly at peace. The solid pools of light from the street lamps were steady and reassuring. The sky overhead was clear; what stars were not obscured by the lamps glittered distant and pure.

A block from Nassau Street someone approached him from beneath one of the streetlights. A woman, poorly dressed. "It's a cold night, sir. Buy me a cup of something warm?"

Stoddard stared at her. Her pale gloveless hands seemed to float at the ends of her sleeves. It was the woman he had seen from his office window the previous day. For an absurd instant he wanted to talk to her, wanted to ask her questions. Where do you come from? How did you get here? Are the men dreadful? What beauty is in your life? "How—" he began, then turned and walked hurriedly away.

Once in his office he did not bother to take off his coat or light the lamp, but instead went straight to where he had left the box the Captain had given him. He placed the box on his desk, where it was fiercely lit by the moonlight through the window. His mind as empty as he could make it, he opened the box and stared inside.

Light poured from the box like a fog, surrounding him. His office went away, came back, went away again. The universal light cast no shadows. Stoddard stared into the box as if staring into the sun, but the light was soft and did not hurt his eyes.

He felt a wind, neither warm nor cool. The light moved around him like a palpable thing; he felt as if he could grab fistfuls of it if he wanted. The box dissolved, swirled and reformed in front of him. It was the figure of a woman, distinct from the light but made of it. She wore a long, full robe whose sleeves and hem disappeared into the light. A thick sea of golden hair hung loosely about her shoulders, surrounding a face of pure aching beauty. She held out her hand.

"Goddess," Stoddard whispered. Poesy Herself, come to take him away? It could not be. He could not possibly receive something he wanted so badly. Yet there she stood, beckoning him to join her.

Stoddard rose and moved toward her, deeper into the light. He took her hand. She smiled, and the light moved inside him. He could feel himself filling up, feel the emptiness disappear, the doubts and the pains and the fears drop away like pages from an old book he no longer had to read. He stared at her and let the light seize him, certain now that the shadows in the world were his own, not nature's. Nature herself was light. He could melt all nature in the furnace of his thoughts, and enrich the world forever. There was beauty to be celebrated, and truth to be taught. Now, at last, he could fix his eyes on heaven and sing as the stars do.

The Goddess pulled him toward her. Stoddard prepared himself to receive her, to melt into her, but rather than embrace him she leaned forward and kissed his eyes. As she withdrew her lips the light began to move again. Her hand dissolved and ran out through his fingers, and she melted back into the light. Stoddard leaned after her, but he felt no sense of loss. He knew what had happened, what he had seen and felt. Beauty Herself had accepted him, and he wept with the solace of her benediction.

As he wiped the tears from his face, his office returned. He had no idea how much time had passed. He closed the box, tucked it securely under his arm, and returned to his home. The traffic had abated; the woman beneath the street lamp was gone.

Lizzie had long since fallen asleep. He shook her awake. "Lizzie! Wake up!"

She muttered unintelligibly, stirred beneath the covers, then opened her eyes and was still. "Is Lorry all right?" she asked.

"Lorry's fine, dear. I have something to show you. Get up."

"What time is it?"

"It's late, dear, very late. But please get up. You must see this."

Eventually he coaxed her out of bed. As he led her into the parlor and sat her down, he told her an abbreviated version of how he had gotten the box. He did not tell her what was inside.

The box sat on the floor in front of the fireplace, between their chairs. They sat down. Stoddard leaned forward and stared at her now fully open eyes. She seemed startled by his intensity. "I have worked so hard, Lizzie, so very hard—as have you," he added hastily, before she could interrupt. "I have sought something outside myself, something healthier and larger, something that expressed the emotions of mankind and not my own petty feelings. But I never felt that I had attained it. I didn't know what it looked like, what it felt like. Sometimes I was frightened that it didn't exist at all. But now—"

He reached down between them and opened the box. "Here it is, Lizzie."

She looked into the box. The same light that had dazzled Stoddard back at his office poured out. At first it lit only her face, giving her a ghostly aspect in the otherwise darkened room; then the light grew and spread over her, covered her, conformed to the outlines of her body and clung tight. She stared into the box, eyes wide, mouth ajar. Stoddard sat transfixed.

Without warning, she jerked her head away. Her face was out of the light, which still covered the rest of her. She threw her arms in front of her and surged out of the chair, breaking free of the light like a bather breaking the water's surface. She ran out of the parlor and back to their bedroom. Stoddard was so stunned it took him several seconds to realize she was screaming.

He threw the lid back on the box and ran after her. "Lizzie! Lizzie, my God, what's wrong? What's happened?" She lay sobbing on their bed. He sat by her, reached for her, was pushed away.

"Where did you get that awful thing?" she gasped.

"Awful thing? I told you, the Captain gave it to me at the docks—"

"Evil!" she cried. "Ugly! Hateful! What does God mean by such agony?"

He did not believe what he heard. He pulled her up, seized her shoulders, stared at her. What little color her face had had was gone. "What did you see, Lizzie?" He shook her. *"What did you see?"*

"The child!"

"What child?"

"Ours! Our first child!" Her words came rapidly, as if she couldn't breathe until she finished talking. "It perched on my back, grasped my shoulders, it looked down at my scribbling on the paper, on the desk, I was chained to my desk and everyone filed by, laughing, they had so much *more* than we, and the words disappeared as soon as I wrote them, blood, blood flowing from between my legs onto the floor, the child climbed down and lapped it up—"

"Lizzie, God Almighty—"

"—it sat on my lap and cried, and the chains hurt my wrists, I could *feel* the chains on my wrists—" She stopped and gasped for breath. Her whole body shuddered. "Dick, my God, where did it come from, why did you bring it here?"

Stoddard hugged her to his breast, stroked her hair. "Lizzie, Lizzie—I saw Beauty herself! There was a wind, a wind of rhythm, a divine shape, fresh from heaven—a shape of loveliness and light, oh Lizzie—" The city had vanished, the soiled bricks and concrete, the money-grubbing men and the tainted women. "It was what we've sought. The pure light of the Ideal. Pure beauty. Pure light." He was sobbing now. "Lizzie, didn't you see it? You must have seen it!"

"No, nothing ... only blood and pain and ..."

"What? And what?"

"The people who walked by laughing—they all held my book in their hands. I was chained and bleeding and they walked past into another room, and a woman stood and began lecturing them."

"Your book?" For a moment, he felt wonder again, and then a twist of pain that burned him with shame.

"The child cried and cried."

"Your book endures?" *And mine does not?* But he stopped himself in time.

"I was not in that room, and neither were you."

"Beauty...."

"I saw what I saw," she said. "I saw what lies ahead, what lies inside me. Inside us."

"Beauty," Stoddard moaned again as he held his wife and cried for them both.

The morning found them both asleep. Lizzie roused herself to let Millie in; she came back to the bedroom with Lorry in her arms. She sat in the rocking chair by the bed and held him in her lap and sang softly to him. Lorry rested contentedly on her breast. Stoddard watched them from where he lay on the bed. He felt as if there were no floor below him, no ceiling above. Everything had been ripped away.

Millie served them a normal breakfast, which they ate in silence. On his way out the door Stoddard retrieved the box from where it still sat in front of the fireplace and carried it back to his office. He almost left it lying in the gutter, but as he approached his office building he began to feel the pavement beneath his feet and carried the box in to Jim Benedict, who received it without comment.

Later that afternoon a man of roughly Stoddard's age walked into his office and handed him a note of introduction from Benedict. The note read, curtly in Benedict's fashion, "He seems a good fellow, Dick, and says he knows you, though perhaps he doesn't, but anyhow be kind to him if this infernal weather will let you be so to anybody."

Stoddard rose, handed the note back to the man before him, and bowed slightly. "It's a pleasure to see you again, Mr. Melville. How many years has it been?"

"Too many, I'm sure," Herman Melville replied. He did not—could not?—look Stoddard directly in the eye, but stared in the direction of the window.

"I am most pleased to have a fellow man of letters on board. I don't know if I ever got the chance to tell you how much I admire your poetry."

Melville said nothing and stared out the window. Stoddard had no idea what he could be looking at. Another sacrifice at the altar, Stoddard thought. Another supplicant doomed to be forgotten.

At the end of the day Stoddard went home. The sky was overcast; the streetlamps made a ceiling of the clouds. Millie prepared an excellent dinner, after which he sat with Lizzie in the parlor and went through the day's mail. He could not tell to look at her what had happened last night, and he resolved then and there never to speak of it again. They had each seen what they had seen. They would go on from there. Lizzie put Lorry to bed and they retired for the night. Stoddard embraced his wife without making love to her, and then he turned away and slept without dreams.

FLANNERY ON STAGE

Her hair had thinned horribly during the illness, and she had been afraid it would fall out altogether. A petty vanity, she knew. When her mother had expressed her own worries she had laughed and reminded her that Jesus didn't care if she were bald or black or bowlegged. Deep inside herself, though, where no one was allowed but God, she wanted her hair.

And now to stand in front of this mob, head shaved like a penitent monk. She can taste the cold metal of the microphone; the stage lights heat her scalp. She feels naked. It thrills her.

She strums her guitar and begins to sing. Softly at first, as always, making them lean forward in their seats to hear. The explosions, the ecstasy, will come later. The metal taste stays in her mouth as the strings vibrate beneath her fingertips.

The first time she had spoken into a microphone had been back at Yaddo, when she gave her first reading; it had been a huge thing, like a metal sausage. (Actually it had reminded her of something quite different, an observation she shared with Elizabeth back at the apartment, but only after Lowell had gone out for cigarettes. They had laughed and laughed.) But this thing is no bigger than a half-dollar, and attached to the headset clamped tightly to her bare scalp, so she can move as she wishes. She can move, period: gone the aluminum crutches, gone the pain. Yes, this is better than Yaddo, much better.

I do not apologize, she whispers. The bass comes in now, signaling the move from confession to declaration. She looks out into the black expanse of the audience, their faces washed out by the lights pouring over her. A bright flicker here, there; exit signs off to the side, a lighter held prematurely aloft. As a child in Savannah she had gone down to the riverfront and seen pinpoints of light, running lights on boats speeding by, the city's illumination reflected in the water. There, too, the lights had not relieved the darkness so much as emphasized it; no more comfort than in Dublin, hiding on the rooftop from her mother's blows, the points of light below her as grimy and hopeless as the buildings from which they emerged.

Mother had problems, did her Mum. Once Dad left she beat them all every day, with whatever she could get her hands on. Starved them, locked them in closets. But she got away from all that, finally, and years later, when Mum died in the wreck, she thought she understood maybe a little bit. No divorce, no contraception, no abortion, no rights at all. Say what you want about their gift of gab; most of the Irish were as mute and desperate as the rest of the world. Especially the women. Her mother never said a word about any of it. Irish to the bone, but stolid and violent as those Jesus-shouters out from Milledgeville, filled with the same rage.

That was why she wrote things down, why all the stories, all the songs. Mama never understood why she didn't write things people liked, why she wasn't Margaret Mitchell. It always left her shaking and speechless, but she went ahead anyway. She would not be silent like all those other women.

Into the groove now; the bass and drums churning. She feels the bass drum through her spine. That reggae man, the producer from Jamaica she met in London when she was cutting the first album, had said that the drum was the heart and the bass was the mind. Walking, talking, I and I to you. Sacrilege, she would have thought before, all that Ethiopian hoodoo babble. But now, after the time in London, after the first album, she recognized the Rastas more fully than she had ever recognized the blacks of central Georgia. She regretted not looking more closely back then, not trying to understand (although one of them, that one that had the movie from the man who did the space films, had said that such honesty was one of her strengths). But it was now and there was plenty of time. She feels herself start to skank across the stage, chopping her guitar like wood. She begins to shout: *Go ahead and leave! You'll never get away.* The Rastas, they know. They know that faith is not some big electric blanket. Faith is not those prissy children back in Georgia; faith is not the old man in Rome. (She had learned; she would never rip that image up again—but she was who she was.) Faith is the cross.

The music swells and fills her up; she feels her lips pull back, her teeth bump against the microphone. Feral, some critic had called that look, when the song takes over. Predatory. Grotesque, like they said about the stories. But you had to be. You had to draw the pictures large and exaggerated, so that people would pay attention; you had to sing to make them listen. People are asleep, reading their books or listening to their music. You had to wake them up. And if they object, if they roll over and try to go back to sleep, you keep shaking them, you keep fighting. As she had in childhood, when she had practiced anti-angel aggression: she went in her room and whirled about in a circle, fists knotted, socking the angel the nuns assured her guarded each and every one of us. She didn't want to be guarded, chained, watched.

But now here on stage everyone is watching, and that is how it should be. The detour was valuable, the holy orders cleansing, but she belongs here. Now comes the ecstasy.

The music throbs, roars; she can feel the crowd at her feet. She is at their feet: the blind, reluctant prophet shouting the news so all can hear. She dominates the crowd as she submits to the mad, stinking, bleeding shadow of Jesus, carrying them with her, home. She doesn't need her hair. She is a slave; she is rapturously free. She does not know for certain how she came to this place, and the memories confuse her sometimes, drifting into her, merging, swelling, popping like a soap bubble. *You'll never, ever get away.* She is bathed in light. Her mother is buried, buried; her father is calling her home. To Georgia, to Dublin: the music stops, the audience roars, and she bows her naked head down. Pierced by the light, she dances.

THE SERPENT AND THE HATCHET GANG

The serpent in the sea was nothing compared to the serpent in the hearts of men. The serpent in the sea may or may not find you, Esther Lane said, may or may not be there at all. But the corruption in a man's heart, the malicious weakness that disguises itself as passion and autonomy, then drowns itself and all around it in liquor and violence and failure—that is inescapable. Its effects can be lessened, its power can be curbed, but it can never be banished entirely. Put the men in chains and pour their liquor out on the ground, she continued, and they will still find a way to do you harm. The serpent in their hearts will not be defeated. Better to take your chances with the monster offshore.

Julia Brooks listened attentively. The others, though steadfast in their commitment, were long used to Esther's grand pronouncements and greeted them placidly, nodding in agreement but clearly waiting for the old woman's rhetoric to run its course. But to Julia, the youngest among them, Esther's words flowed like the tide into Sandy Bay, and as they all sat—in three cases, stood—crammed liked netted mackerel into Rachel and Stephen Perkins' parlor, the temperate July night turned sweltering in such close quarters, she waited eagerly for Esther to continue.

Instead, there was the sound of an elderly throat clearing, and Julia turned with the rest of them to see Hannah Jumper look up from her knitting. "Don't say that, Esther. The whole point is to pour the liquor out. Ain't that why we're here?"

Esther looked momentarily annoyed, but quickly composed herself and said, "Of course, Hannah. I do get carried away sometimes. Of course we remain united in our purpose. Don't we, everyone?"

They all voiced their agreement. Tonight, only the leaders gathered for one last coordinated review of their plan. But come tomorrow, fully sixty of the women of Rockport, Massachusetts, would bring moral and economic sense back to the community. The halfhearted attempts of the town's agents to regulate liquor sales had been a miserable failure, and it was now up to the women who bore the worst of the burden, and the handful of men who understood what was at stake, to deal themselves with this public nuisance. No more men lying about in drunken indolence when the winter storms and summer doldrums kept the fishing boats docked; no more backbreaking grocery bills whose main item was rum. No more bruises to hide, Julia thought. No more knowing the back of your husband's hand better than his heart.

They had been meeting for weeks, in secret. And while Esther's eloquence kept them inspired, Hannah kept them going. She was not well-spoken, and seventy-five years old in the bargain. But it was she who had called the first meeting, she who had kept record as the conspirators discovered, and chalked with white X's that would not be seen by those not looking for them, every spot in Rockport where liquor would be found. It was Hannah who had invoked their Revolutionary ancestors, the twenty women who had banded together some eighty years back and raided Colonel Foster's supply store in Gloucester after their men marched off to Bunker Hill promising to bring back liberty but leaving their fishing boats idle and their families improvident and shivering. And it was Hannah who convinced them that hatchets were the only sufficient instrument for dispatching, if not the men who defied decency and the law, at least the wretched barrels of rum.

Mary Hale, at thirty-seven the next youngest after Julia, had objected. "Is there not too great a risk of injury? We don't want anyone to get hurt, do we?"

"Desperate cases need desperate remedies," replied Hannah, and continued with her knitting.

Now, on the eve of their action, the old woman sat calmly, the motion of her needles and yarn so smooth and continuous it scarcely seemed motion at all. Although she sat to the side, against the wall, the room seemed centered around her.

"But why all this talk of sea serpents?" asked Stephen Perkins, leaning forward from his perch on the edge of the room's only sofa. "Haven't we enough to do without digging up all that nonsense?"

"I agree," said Mary Knowlton. Her husband had enjoyed great success transporting stone south to Boston, prosperity that set her apart from the fishermen's wives and daughters who filled the room; some were surprised that she had joined enthusiastically in their conspiracy. But when Mrs. Knowlton was Mary Clarkson she had been a schoolteacher, and Julia, one of her students, still remembered the impromptu temperance lectures with which the young teacher would punctuate even a math lesson. "Do we want to be laughed at again? To the rest of the world we might as well have been Indians chasing spirits in the woods, and the nineteenth century might as well never have arrived. What we're doing is too important—"

"I was scarcely speaking publicly for the Boston papers," said Esther. "I merely invoked the serpent as a figure to dramatize my point. We're gathered here, after all, because of the depravity of men—"

"We're gathered here because of rum," Hannah said without looking up from her work. "Rum is real. So's our hatchets. Let's stick to them."

"Please, friends," said Mary Hale, "Hannah, Esther—we're all here for the same reason. Let us not divide ourselves from ourselves." She stood and brushed straight the skirt of her gray dress. There were some of the younger matrons in town who had left their Puritan ancestors firmly behind. Betsey Andrews, the current schoolteacher, periodically took the steamboat down to Boston to inspect the latest fashions, while Judy MacQuestion was rumored to own at least one hat imported from Paris. Mary was not among their number: the neatness of her clothing was matched only by its plainness. "Mrs. Knowlton is right. The task before us is too important. Esther, we all admire your eloquence, and are grateful for it. Who of us could have framed the issues so compellingly? How many will there be on the streets tomorrow because of your persuasion?" Esther smiled and nodded her head every so slightly.

"And if Esther's silver tongue has put people in the streets, it is Hannah's courage and strength that has put us all in this room. Please don't worry, Hannah. We know what needs to be done, and we shall do it."

Hannah did not reply. They all knew by now that, in a group at least, Hannah would speak only to prod forward or to object; her silence testified that the disagreement was settled. Mary sat and smoothed her skirts again.

"Well, then," said Mr. Perkins. "Are we concluded, then?"

They agreed that, barring unforeseen circumstances, this would be their last meeting; the plan was set and would be implemented tomorrow.

As they adjourned, James Babson, who had kept silent throughout, offered to escort Julia home. As an agent of the Granite Company, Mr. Babson had access to all manner of tools and an income not dependent on the vagaries of the ocean; both made him an invaluable ally. He was also corpulent and ill-kept, and the breath that whistled through two missing teeth was foul. Julia had had to accustom herself to such attentions in the two years since her husband's ship had returned to port with its flag at half staff, and she had no real reason to consider Mr. Babson's offer as anything other than honorable.

Still. "Many's the time, ma'am, when I saw your late husband, God rest him, with his hand so reverently on your arm as you walked home of an evening. I would be honored to assume that duty—even if only momentarily, this evening," he added hastily.

Julia instinctively leaned away from him, then steadied herself, sighed, and was about to agree when Hannah stepped in. "Walk home with me, child. I reckon I could use the company."

Hannah had no more need of company, Julia believed, than did Squam Lighthouse. But she quickly accepted the old woman's offer and left Mr. Babson standing in the middle of the parlor, Esther heading casually but directly toward him, already talking.

The night felt almost chilly after the warmth of the overcrowded parlor, and Julia pulled her shawl close about her shoulders. Inside, Hannah had filled the room; outside, her great height remained—Julia came barely to the old woman's shoulder—but, free of the press of walls and bodies, Hannah seemed reduced, distant. It was like walking with a scarecrow, Julia thought, although a most strong and determined one.

As they made their way down High Street, Julia, still full of the meeting and the righteousness of their cause, reiterated much of the evening's discussion. Hannah remained silent, her heavy shoes clopping on the cobblestones. When they reached the Inner Harbor, rather than turning right to continue to their respective homes, Hannah stopped, facing the water. Julia followed the old woman's gaze into the harbor. The fishing boats rested at their moorings, looking like charcoal drawings beneath the dim light of the half moon. They had not been out to sea for over a month. On one of the larger boats, at the outer edge of the harbor, several figures moved around the deck. Julia could not make them out individually, but she heard rough laughter, the shattering of glass, a bellowing voice: "She was mine, damn ya! Who said you could get under her skirts afore me?" More laughter, and the sawing of a fiddle. Although she knew it was impossible at such a distance, she could almost swear she smelled their liquor across the water.

Julia shuddered. "After tomorrow perhaps we'll have less of that."

Hannah stared out past the boats and the profanity. Julia looked up at her. For a moment, the old woman's face was obliterated by the darkness, and she looked like her bonnet and her dress and nothing else. "They should stay on the boats," Hannah said. "They should stay on the ocean. They can't harm the ocean."

"Maybe the serpent will get them," Julia said, and then instantly remembered Hannah's harsh dismissal of Esther at the meeting. "Oh, I know, Hannah, it's just nonsense, forgive me."

Hannah said nothing in response. Then she turned sharply away and said, "Long past time we were home, child."

They proceeded down Mt. Pleasant Street, past Hannah's house. Julia tried to get Hannah to stop and let her make the remaining short walk on her own, but the old woman refused. As they turned down Long Cove Lane, Hannah asked, somewhat to Julia's surprise, if the chamomile she had sent to Julia's Aunt Martha had helped with her digestive difficulties. The women of Rockport paid Hannah to mend their dresses, but far more valuable, and free in the bargain, was the harvest of Hannah's herb garden. Horseradish for a sore throat, catnip to sleep, pennyroyal for a chill, pipsissewa leaves for the heart.

Julia replied that her aunt was much better and expressed her admiration for Hannah's skills. "I wish I could cultivate herbs as well as you. I tried planting some rosemary last season and it just didn't take."

"Put rosemary close to the high-water mark. It gets its strength from the sea."

At Julia's doorstep, Hannah bade the young woman good night. "Rest well, child. You'll need all your wits about you tomorrow." Julia promised that she would and watched the old woman retrace her path down the street and disappear around the corner.

Later, with the lamps an hour dark and sleep nowhere close, Julia stood before her open bedroom window. The moon was gone, and the land and the ocean and the horizon were a dark unbroken carpet over the world. But she heard the ocean, and felt it in the breeze that chilled her through her nightclothes, and smelled it. If she opened her mouth, she knew she could taste it.

There was nothing to see, but much to remember. Two years ago next month.

She had heard the stories; everyone had. The summer of 1817, fourteen years before her own birth. Hundreds down in Gloucester, most more reliable than not, had seen it. From Ten Pound Island to Western Harbor they had shielded their children and grabbed their telescopes, or set out in their boats. The reports were almost all the same: fifty to one hundred feet long, thick as a barrel, dark on top, lighter on what of its belly could be seen when it raised itself from the water. A head the size of a horse's. Some claimed it was segmented; others noted its vertical undulations. It could turn on a dime and raced away when approached. Several had tried to kill it, of course, even as one newspaper suggested they should be grateful to it for driving herring into the harbor.

The Linnaean Society of New England had formed a committee—Harvard men, of course—to investigate, but, being too busy living inside their own heads to come and see for themselves, the committee members had sent a list of questions to the Justice of the Peace with a request for him to interview the witnesses and send them the results.

Things might have held steady at that point, or even faded away, but a couple of months later the Colbeys found a hump-backed snake, over a yard long, on the ground near Loblolly Cove. They killed and examined it, and they remembered one or two people claimed to have seen two serpents in the harbor. Could this be offspring? The Linnaeans got hold of it, dissected it, gave it a Latin name, and declared that, well, yes, it might be kin to the creature in the harbor. But then another Harvard man came along and proved that it was just a deformed black snake.

The next summer there were more sightings in the harbor, and things looked as if they were getting heated up again. But when the creature came up to Squam Bar, near the lighthouse, and a Boston captain chased it down in a whaleboat, only to discover that he had harpooned a horse mackerel, most of Cape Ann was ready to forget anything ever happened. The following year, dozens more saw the same thing just off the shore down at Nahant, but by then the Linaaeans had given up, the Boston captain had disappeared, and people were making fun of the gullible Yankees all the way down to Charleston.

They were all just stories Julia had grown up with, and she didn't regard them as anything more, or less. And then she saw it herself.

Her husband Joshua had been out with the boats, and she had not been sorry to see him go. The summer doldrums had lasted longer than usual, giving him more time to drink, and curse the fish because they weren't there, and her because she was. It could have been worse. Abigail Hancock's husband used her so badly that both the town constables had intervened, and Mr. Hancock, after he sobered up, left abruptly for a rumored family in the Maine woods. But the memories of the young man of promise and passion she had married, against the sullen wreck who stared emptily out at the waves as he swigged his rum, were almost as bad as the bruises she managed most of the time to hide.

Almost. A hundred fifty-seven dollars for nine months' work was no life for anyone; she understood, felt his entrapment. But he had no right to take it out on her. He had no right to do that.

She had been out on the rocks at Bearskin Neck in the early morning, looking out into Sandy Harbor. She had emptied the liquor as soon as he left and no longer cared how angry he would be when he returned. It was a clear morning and the sun was warm on her face, but the water still looked hard and gray.

She blinked, and felt as if she had just missed something. She looked intently out into the bay, and seconds later it rose up in front of her.

Immediately, she knew what it was. All the stories she had always heard, with all of their divergent details, now merged and came to life not fifty yards in front of her. It was black, and it undulated vertically through the water, and it did indeed seem about as big around as a barrel, and its head did in fact look about the size of a horse's. Its front end was several feet out of the water, and the sound of its churning and splashing was louder than the tide lapping against the rocks beneath her feet. The serpent splashed and glistened in the sun, and she reached out as if to touch it.

In an unbroken motion, it turned and plunged toward shore. Before she could even consider backing away, it was directly in front of her. It raised itself up from the water, its head level with her own. Its liquid gray eyes regarded her calmly. There was a hissing sound, but not that of a snake; rather of wind blowing through an enclosed space, or her husband's breath beside her when he slept without drinking.

Her heart felt as if it would hammer through her chest, but she was not frightened. At that moment she had no problems; there was nothing in her life but this wonder. She kept her arm outstretched, leaned forward.

And as quickly as it had come to her, it left. By the time she lowered her arm, it was gone. The water seemed scarcely disturbed. She turned away and went back through town to her home.

Two days later came the news that her husband was lost. She wept properly at his funeral and gave his clothes away.

She had never told anyone, ever, what she had seen, not even when it had been sighted a week later out from Loblolly Cove, and later that same month further south near Hull. It was not so much that she feared ridicule as that she wanted to keep the event for herself. She had given everything to her family and her husband while they lived, but that moment at Bearskin Cove, that splash of water and shining strange skin, was hers alone. Let the learned men have their theories, and let the foolish men try to hunt it like a whale. For her, the creature was not a disruption of the natural order; it was a reassurance, a guarantee of possibility.

And she so needed that guarantee. When her grandmother had died, she and Joshua had claimed the old woman's house. (Grandmother had loathed him, thought him beneath her only granddaughter; Joshua swore she had lasted as long as she did solely to keep him out of her home.) Modest as it was, it did for them, and certainly it had for Julia by herself. There was, of course, no pension for a dead fisherman, but there was still a bit left of the small inheritance she had from her parents, and it went farther without Joshua working his way through it a bottle at a time.

But it would not last forever. Sooner or later, Julia knew she would have to choose among gloomy options: join the relatives in Boston whom she barely knew but who had grand visions of her becoming a governess on Beacon Hill; strike off on her own and seek work in the inland factories; or cast her lot with the likes of Mr. Babson. These were not choices; these were sentences for the crime of being a widow.

Now, as she leaned out her open window into the dark, she breathed deeply of the ocean and thought about a new and wonderful possibility: a town without rum. A community of responsible and sober men who cared for their families. Surely in such a place, there would be true choices. She and Hannah and the rest would make it happen. Julia closed the window, buried herself under the bedclothes, and dreamed of swimming with the serpent, giving it sweet herbs from Hannah's garden.

By nine the next morning, Dock Square was more or less awake. The boats languished in the harbor waiting for July to pass and the winds to return, and the men who were about were already in the taverns. The shopkeepers had their doors open for business and what breeze might come off the harbor. But business almost always came from the women, and as Julia waited in front of Deacon Burns' shop, there were none anywhere in sight. Here were two men playing checkers in front of Johnson's Hall hotel; there was a cluster of neighboring merchants discussing the merits of Mr. Fillmore's audacious embrace of the Know-Nothings. An isolated scholar took his leisure near the checker players and perused the latest collection of Mr. Emerson's essays.

But where were the women? Julia smiled graciously at the merchants and restrained herself from wringing her hands. Where were they?

Then she saw a figure approaching from School Street, and two more down Broadway. Margaret Thurston, two of the Choate sisters. Then a group turned off High Street, Mary Knowlton among them, and more down Broadway, and when Julia looked up Mt. Pleasant she saw Hannah marching across the cobblestones, her hands hidden beneath the folds of her shawl.

As Julia moved to join the women, there was a commotion down past Jim Brown's shop. She turned and saw what looked like a small battalion moving in her direction, men as well as women. The women marched silently toward Dock Square, but Julia heard the cries of the men: "Watch out! They're coming for the rum! The women are going for the rum shops! Think they'll do it? Never in hell! Oh, yes they will, too! Ha! Let's go! Better hurry, boys!"

They're coming for the rum? How could these men know? She and the others had gone to such lengths to keep the plan secret. But as Julia saw more women treading resolutely toward the square, marching silently past the shouting men, she had a sudden sense of her own naiveté, and of the scope of what was about to happen. Of course others had found out. Not everyone. But enough. How could they not know what the problem was? How could they not see the ruinous effects of the rum in the idle men, in the drawn and haggard faces of the women? She moved quickly to join the others.

By now there must have been two hundred women on the square. Everyone from the meetings, of course, but plenty of others as well. The younger men stood to the harbor side and jeered. At least one woman, whom Julia did not recognize, complained loudly at being caught up in this lawless mob and swore to head straight for the constable's office. A few men were now gathered with the women: Stephen Perkins, Newell Burnham, James Babson—the latter of whom, to Julia's consternation, found her in the crowd, smiled, and tipped his hat. Joe Griffin, who worked for Perkins, waved an American flag.

Julia had expected Hannah to take command, but it was Esther Lane who separated from the crowd and planted herself to speak. Now the men as well as the women fell silent. The sun beat down on their heads as the gulls screamed over the harbor. Julia rearranged her shawl, and prepared for a lengthy discourse.

Esther started to speak, stopped, removed a hand from her shawl to wipe a tear from her eye. Julia marveled at the intensity of the old woman's face: for once, Esther Lane seemed to be yielding to what she felt, rather than to the sound of her own voice. "We know why we are here," she said, her voice quavering but loud enough for all to hear. "We are here to take back our town and our families and our lives." She paused, removed her other hand from beneath her shawl, and held aloft a hatchet. "Not one bottle left!"

In unison, every woman present produced a hatchet from beneath her shawl and raised it high. Every family in Rockport had one, or more—the common land was now mostly sold off to private hands, but most of the fishermen still cut their own wood as best they could from the ever-thinning landscape. To see them all at once, in the hands of these women, took Julia's breath away. As Joe Griffin waved his flag, Sally Norwood raised the banner she had promised to make: a cotton rectangle she held aloft bore a hatchet in black paint.

Julia held her own weapon over her head. She thought of Joshua and gripped the hatchet tighter. "Not one bottle left!"

With that, Hannah stepped forward beside Esther and shouted, "Let's get to work!"

The young men who had been so noisy before gaped as the women fell into formation, four abreast, and began their march down the street. Julia tensed when she saw the town's two constables, who had but recently arrived, but they looked on with the other men, and did no more to stop the women than they had done to enforce the liquor laws.

As they passed by Deacon Burns' shop, he stood in the doorway, his face twisted with rage. He looked like Joshua used to after a session with the rum, and Julia's step almost faltered. "Shame!" Burns shouted. "Where are your husbands? Are they men? Shame! There's nothing here for you! Go home!"

There was a sudden movement from the marching column, and Betsey Andrews darted toward Burns. Julia was shocked to see that the schoolteacher's latest fashion was a skirt that came just below her knee, exposing light yellow bloomers that ruffled down to her shoes. But the lack of a full skirt left her free to maneuver past Burns while holding a hatchet in each hand. She waved to the women, and as most of the column continued down the street, several broke ranks, shoved the deacon aside, and charged into his shop.

Julia followed them in, and they began rolling barrels out into the street, one after the other: rum, brandy, ale, beer. As Burns screamed and cursed in a manner not befitting a leader of the church, the women took their hatchets and went to work. The young men who had followed them from the Square were now cheering: "That's it, girls! Have at it! Damn, look at Burns! Better pour some on the Deacon, ladies—he needs cooling off, by God! Serves him right! Hurrah for the hatchet gang!"

Julia tried to weigh in with her own weapon, but there were too many women ahead of her. The aroma of the spilled liquor was overpowering, and she tried in vain to wipe off the rum that had splashed on her dress. She was mortified by the crude encouragement of the young men and unsettled by the gleam in the eyes of the women as they swung their hatchets down, again and again and again, on Deacon Burns' stock. Their hands were growing bloody, but they did not even seem to notice.

When she heard a voice from inside the shop announce, "That's the last one," Julia moved to rejoin the column. The gang now moved as with a mind of its own: several women would peel off to attack a shop or tavern, then rejoin the column as it wound through the streets. They took care of the Stage Coach Inn, the Laf-a-Lot cottage, Johnson Hall. When they got to Jim Brown's shop, they found him sitting atop a barrel, swearing, daring them to take his livelihood from him. They swept him onto his own front steps, smashed the barrel, and slopped over the foaming ale to get inside. Brown had hidden many bottles, and they found them all.

"Damn you!" Brown cried. "Whores! Devils! What are you trying to do? What do you want? Is this going to makes things better? Will this make the winds blow? Are your hatchets going to fill our ships? Give your men work? I'll be restocked in a month! We all will!"

They brushed past him and moved on to John Hooper's basement, reportedly the largest holdings in town. Julia stepped over a man she recognized as one of Stephen Perkins' crewmen as he lay beneath Brown's steps and tried to catch the dripping ale in his mouth. Mary Hale, her plain dress drenched with alcohol, evidently thought the man injured. She paused and tried to help him up, but he shoved her away.

And so it went for the rest of the morning. They ceased around noon, lining up to drink from the town pump, and then they resumed their work. They had marked many places with their subtle white X's, and they dispatched them all. As they moved through the town, the young men following them were joined by children, by dogs. The stench of liquor in the streets was suffocating, made worse by the boiling sun. The women's dresses were soaked through. With each stop, their eyes grew brighter, their hatchets cut deeper. Their laughter was punctuated by screams that might have been of anger or of joy. Some sang hymns that sounded here and now as rough as the sailors' chanteys.

Julia had never been so weary in her life. Her dress was ruined; her shoes squished from the spilled liquor. She had marched with the others from the square to Bearskin Neck and back, the fear she had felt at the beginning of the violence turning to exhilaration, and then back to fear as the violence continued, and then finally to numbness. The certainty of their cause, the care of their planning, her ache for a better life for them all—none of that had prepared her for the reality of smashed barrels and broken glass, the curses of the men, the jeers of the boys, the consuming ferocity that possessed the women. The unshielded, naked emotion on both sides. One of the merchants had actually wept as they smashed his bottles of brandy on the cobblestones. She had never before seen a man weep.

And still the women were on the hunt, and still the men did not try to stop them. Not really. She had heard one man shout to anyone who would listen that they should go down to the armory and come back and teach these women a lesson, but another man cuffed him on the head and called him a damned scoundrel. The women moved at will through the town. "Not a bottle left!"

Julia found herself staggering away from the hatchet gang down Long Cove Lane, her head spinning from the heat and the fumes, her hands bloody from her turns at the barrels. She had been unsure at first, and then she had thought about Joshua and the times she had tried and failed to fight back, and then her hatchet sank as deep as anyone's. Now she was in front of Hannah's house. Her head was so heavy. Her hands were trembling. It was so hot. Perhaps it would be cooler by the inner harbor. She walked around the house and through the back yard, past the herb garden, to the water's edge.

The sun was still relentless, but the wind had picked up, and the water was choppy. Julia shook her head as if to stir the air some more. She let her shawl drop from her shoulders. She did not know what had become of her hatchet. Behind her she could still hear the occasional sound of breaking glass, distant shouting. She stepped out onto the rocks. She wanted to be closer to the water.

Which churned, and bubbled, and produced the serpent. No sighting, no warning. The enormous head rose in front of her. The same gray eyes; the same hissing sound. And why not, on this mad day? Julia reached out to the serpent, as she had before. She leaned closer, and her soaked shoes on the slick rocks betrayed her.

The water was shockingly cold, and almost immediately her head struck one of the submerged rocks. Everything went away for an instant, and then she rose out of the water, and above it. The serpent's skin was like nothing she had ever felt before. She adhered to it without effort; she did not have to try to hold on.

As the serpent moved with her out into the harbor, she wondered dimly where she might be going, but a destination truthfully did not seem all that important. The stench of the liquor had been replaced with something equally strong, but it was the smell of the sea and not the weakness of men or the violence of women. To her still-spinning head, that was a great comfort. Esther's words came to her from what seemed like some other world: *The serpent in their hearts will not be defeated. Better to take your chances with the monster offshore.*

They raced through the harbor, plunging beneath the surface for seconds at the time, then rising, then plunging down again. It seemed the most natural thing in the world. Once the serpent paused on the surface and she could see the shore behind her. A figure appeared. A blotch on the horizon, but Julia dimly registered the outlines of a dress, a bonnet. Hannah? Was it over? Had they won? The serpent plunged again, but this time it stayed down. Julia held her breath and closed her eyes against the salt water.

When they surfaced, Julia opened her eyes. She was still facing the shore, but now it was different. The shore was yards and yards away, and yet she saw with perfect clarity as if looking through a telescope whose lens encompassed the whole world. Hannah stood motionless at the water's edge while behind her the houses, the shops, the cobblestones, all melted away, leaving no trace, leaving only a field of white, an appalling empty whiteness before which Hannah stood frozen like a carving before a piece of blank paper.

The serpent dove again. Julia closed her eyes and prepared to drown.

But when the serpent brought her to the surface she still breathed, and when she opened her eyes Hannah was still there on the shore, and the buildings had returned. Some of them. There was Hannah's house, and others. But now the telescope lens had become a stereopticon, and she could see past the houses on the shore to buildings she had never seen before, and bizarrely-shaped carriages that moved by themselves, without horses, and men and women dressed in bright colors, with some of the women dressed like men and some in nothing but what appeared to be undergarments. Before it all stood Hannah, still, and Julia heard a voice that was Hannah's, and was something else altogether. *Our victory will outlive us! It will outlive this century, and the next!*

The serpent was gone. Julia had never been particularly adept in the water, but she floated comfortably, without difficulty. She would not have noticed if fifty serpents had appeared. She did not know what she saw, but she knew that within this impossible scene was a cleanliness, a tolerance, a prosperity beyond anything she could ever have hoped, and at the same time a danger, an inexplicable poison that frightened her to the bone. There were options after all. It made no sense at all, and it made perfect sense.

Julia shut her eyes against the salt and the sun and the knowledge, good and bad, which overwhelmed her. She felt a hundred miles from shore and wondered if Joshua lay somewhere beneath her. She thought how pleasant it would be to remain floating there, like a leaf, like a hatchet, away from women and men.

When she opened her eyes again, the strange buildings and machines and people were gone, and so was Hannah, and her town as she knew it spilled down to the water's edge. She felt a gentle pressure on her back grow more insistent. She tried to keep floating, but soon her heels dragged the bottom, and she was returned to the shore.

Julia looked back to the water. The serpent was gone. So she turned and made her way over the rocks and across the yard and went back to the options that awaited, to the triumph and the wreckage of her town.

PETITION TO REPATRIATE GERONIMO'S SKULL

The initiate lies in his coffin and speaks his most intimate secrets. The first girl back in Ohio: in a grove of trees a hundred yards from the Labor Day parade, she left her summer gloves on as he slid her hand inside his unbuttoned trousers. The French girl, the kitchen help at the British prep school, with a single hair that curled out of her left nipple and a scent that left him breathless. He came within seconds and she laughed at him. Lucy, just last week. Not all the way, but far enough. He loves her and intends to marry her.

The members of the Order sit upon the overstuffed couches that encircle the coffin and voice their contempt. Is that the best you can do? My faggot uncle Cecil got more than that! There is a mirror on the ceiling, warped and cracked; in their hoods and robes, sprawled on the sofas, the reflections of the members look to the initiate like mushrooms sprouting in a pasture. Terrified that they will reject him, he quickly manufactures a story about a prostitute with a dozen wigs and a widow who proffered a riding crop and lay decorously across her late husband's desk.

Satisfied, the members of the Order permit him to rise from the coffin. They escort him down a darkened hall into a room lined with books and glass cases filled with bones, skulls, tattered scraps of cloth that might at one time have been clothing. There are three men in the room: a devil, a knight, and someone in the garments of the Pope. The members howl and chant and force the initiate to his knees. Finally the knight unsheathes his sword, touches the initiate on the left shoulder, and proclaims, "I dub thee knight of Ubarin within our sacred Order."

The initiate trembles with exhaustion, relief, and a consuming gratitude. He wants to own the world and present it to the sons he knows Lucy will give him. This first step accomplished, he has no doubt of his eventual triumph.

The warrior enters the circle and dances joyously about. He had fought well for his people and whoops his triumph. As the warrior dances, a dark spirit appears. The black figure coldly regards the dancing warrior. Evil is present.

Goyathlay, of the Bedonkohe Apache, joined the Council of Warriors when he was seventeen. Before being allowed to join the council, he went four times on the war path. Each time he humbled himself as a servant to the other warriors: not speaking unless spoken to, existing on poor rations, obeying all commands rightly and without hesitation. He learned the sacred names of all the things of war and proved himself in battle. After completing his four journeys, and there being no objection from any warrior, he was admitted.

To be a member of the Council of Warriors made Goyathlay very happy, for now all the privileges of manhood were his. He could fight for his people, and he could marry Alope, whom he loved. He presented her father No-po-so with a herd of ponies and took Alope away. The couple made their home near Goyathlay's mother, had three children, and lived a normal, proper life.

Twelve years after Goyathlay was admitted to the Council of Warriors, the tribe went into Mexico for trade and made camp outside a town the Apaches called Kas-ki-yeh. One summer day, on their way back from town, they learned that Mexicans had raided the camp, stealing everything of value, killing all the warriors and many women and children. Goyathlay returned to the camp to find that the Mexicans had killed his wife and his mother and all three of his children.

At the command of his chief, Mangus-Colorado, Goyathlay went to the Chokonen and Nedni Apaches to seek their aid in taking revenge on the Mexicans. The Chokonen chief, Cochise, and the Nedni chief, Whoa, agreed. The three tribes tracked the Mexicans who had destroyed the camp outside Kas-ki-yeh and killed them all. After the battle, Goyathlay was named war chief of all the Apaches. He took great pleasure in ordering the scalping of the enemy dead. He bathed in his vengeance.

From that day forward, Golyathlay was permanently at war with the Mexicans, who later named him Geronimo. He persuaded his fellow warriors to make many raids south from their native land in Arizona even when they were not particularly interested in killing any more Mexicans. He killed many whites within the territories claimed by the United States because it was necessary to defend his people, and he killed many Mexicans because he could.

The evil spirit fills the air with its dark power. The warrior falters in his dance. He tries to resist the spirit's black power but cannot. He falls, and the evil spirit dances in malevolent delight.

While training for war, the Initiate is given a task. He and a fellow Member will acquire a trophy to be displayed within the inviolate walls of the Order. A skull. A *memento mori*, not of their own inevitable death, but of the inevitable failure of the barbarians, the inferior teeming hordes who lie outside the Order, who labor and die, powerless and ignorant, as God intended.

Acting as if they are unquestionably entitled to everything they ask for (a strategy that has served them well thus far in life), the

Initiate and his fellow Member requisition a pick, a shovel, two crowbars, an electric lantern, and an automobile. They leave Fort Sill and drive to the grave where they will acquire their trophy. The night is stifling; the air swirls about in the open car but never really cools. The Oklahoma desert is flat and jagged and utterly removed from the green comforts of their homes back East. No Member would ever admit publicly to any degree of unease, but deep inside, in a space too intimate to reveal even lying in their coffins, they know they do not belong here.

The barbarian graveyard is unguarded. They find the grave they had been instructed to find. Digging away the earth is harder than they expected. The coffin gives them pause: so much flimsier than their own sites of initiation, but with a lid that will not yield. The fellow Member finally pries it open, removes the skull within, and places it carefully in the wooden box the Initiate holds in his battered hands. They replace the coffin and carefully recover it with the desert soil. They were told only to take the skull, and that is all they take.

The skull remains carefully packed in its box until they deliver it to the Order, except for one evening just before they returned east when they acquire a hotel room and two Mexican women and keep the skull in clear view on the bedside table all night.

The other Members are pleased, and the skull is given a place of honor in their collection. The Initiate goes to war and serves well enough. He has several children and becomes a very powerful and successful man. Although he never actually owns the world, he does, in time, present it to his sons.

As the evil spirit prances, a medicine man appears with a magic stick. His robes glisten and his headdress cascades gloriously around his shoulders. His magic stick is as tall as he is. The evil spirit stops his dance and knows he is now opposed by a powerful force.

Although a fierce warrior, Golyathlay was never a tribal chief. But in time he was the most famous of all the Apaches. It was said he had fearsome powers, that bullets did not harm him, that he could move through the desert without leaving a trail, that he could delay the sunrise to protect his tribe. When he was largely done killing Mexicans, he held out against the United States Army longer than any other warrior. At the end, it took over five thousand United States and three thousand Mexican soldiers to subdue Golyathlay and his band of fewer than twenty warriors.

The United States General promised a peaceful resettlement but broke his word. Golyathlay and some four hundred fifty of his tribe were forcibly removed to Fort Pickens and Fort Marion in Florida, where they spent two years sawing logs and performing other hard labor. In the summer the ground was covered with burning ants that killed a warrior and a child. They then spent an even longer time in Alabama, where more of the tribe died from disease. Two warriors killed their wives and themselves. Golyathlay decided that the lands this far east were clearly beyond the grasp of their god Usen, who had given the good land of Arizona to the Apache people.

Finally they were removed to Fort Sill, Oklahoma. There Golyathlay lived to be old, but he was never released from the supervision of the United States government, and he never saw his native land again.

Enraged, the evil spirit attacks the medicine man. He tries repeatedly to grab the magic stick, but the medicine man holds on. They struggle mightily. Neither combatant will yield.

The Initiate's son lies in his coffin and speaks his most intimate secrets. Surprisingly, he has the most to tell of any this year. The jovial clubability that, along with his father's legacy, makes the Initiate's son a natural candidate for the Order, masks a ruthless ambition. The Initiate schooled his children in competition above all and made sure they understood that history was written by winners.

Impressed, the Members lead the Initiate's son into the other room for the conclusion of the ceremony. As he is led down the hallway and the Members caper and howl around him, he passes the barbarian's skull. The room is as oppressively hot as was the night air in which his father pulled the skull from the Oklahoma desert, but he feels a chill as he regards the empty eye sockets. For a second the room shimmers, and the Initiate's son feels himself falling into the darkness where the barbarian's eyes had been, but he snaps himself back and finishes the march into the next room.

As the sword descends onto his shoulder, the Initiate's son tries and fails to dismiss the experience of the skull. It will linger in his mind the rest of his life, even when he fulfils the destiny his father had proclaimed for him and does, however briefly, rule the world.

As the battle continues, evil slowly gains control over good. The medicine man is bent almost to the ground, and the evil spirit is about to wrest away the magic stick.

Late in his life, while he was confined at Fort Sill, Golyathlay was invited to attend the World's Fair. With the permission of the President of the United States and under the supervision of the Indian Department, he stayed for six months in the city of St. Louis. He participated in a "Wild West Show" that purported to represent to the white audiences what life was like among the whites and the Indians but had little to do with how Golyathlay had himself lived. He attended other shows where men escaped from being tied up in cages and women emerged unscathed from containers into which swords had been thrust. He saw many other Indians and some small brown people the United States soldiers had brought in from some faraway islands. The white audiences were friendly and peaceful. He sold them pictures of himself and was permitted to keep some of the money.

The warrior lies motionless and can do nothing to affect the outcome of the battle.

The Initiate's grandson lies in his coffin and speaks his most intimate secrets, such as they are. A brief, halting catalog of furtive encounters: a finger in a debutante here, a masturbatory surveillance of a gardener's daughter there. Some of the Members stifle yawns. But his father and grandfather were of the Order, and there is a hint that his smug, ingratiating surface masks a will even more ruthless than his father's. He will do.

The Members lead the Initiate's grandson down the hall. They have forced him to wear his cheerleader's uniform and carry the megaphone he employs at all the home games. Giddy with the certainty of his confirmation and comfortable with the Members' diminished expectations, he raises the megaphone playfully to his right eye and surveys the corridor like Columbus surveying the New World.

As they pass the trophy case, the barbarian's skull appears in the circle of the megaphone. The Initiate's grandson blinks, there is a skip in the world like a poorly spliced film, and he is at the end of the hallway entering the room where his initiation will conclude. He is dimly aware that, in the previous stuttering moment, he fell completely into the darkness of those empty eye sockets and emerged with part of that darkness within him.

By the time he kneels, all thoughts of the skull are gone. The edge of the sword that touches his shoulder is chipped, the Pope's robe is ragged, and the devil's tail lies limply on the floor. The Initiate's grandson has no idea that one day he, too, will rule the world, no idea how the darkness now inside him will emerge.

On the verge of defeat, the Medicine Man calls out for aid. Three other medicine men enter the circle, each with his own magic stick. The evil spirit cannot combat four such sticks at once, and he leaves the circle, howling in hatred of the forces of good.

Near the end of his life, Golyathlay said: "I know that if my people were placed in that mountainous region lying around the head waters of the Gila River they would live in peace and act according to the will of the President. They would be prosperous and happy in tilling the soil and learning the civilization of the white men, whom they now respect. Could I but see this accomplished, I think I could forget all the wrongs that I have ever received, and die a contented and happy old man. But we can do nothing in this matter ourselves—we must wait until those in authority choose to act."

As the medicine men celebrate their victory, the warrior rises and resumes his dance. One by one, the medicine men depart. The warrior dances in triumph and gives his mightiest war whoop so that the evil spirit will hear and know what awaits him should he ever return.

CONSIDER THE SERVICES OF THE DEPARTED

"Men pay us to haunt houses." —Peter Barnes, *Red Noses*

At Rise: The Speaker, an adult of any age/gender, in formal attire on a bare stage, addresses the audience.

Consider the services of the departed. For too long we have hung in your imaginations like a molded apple in the back of the refrigerator, like a barely discerned whine in the inner ear, like a drip in the basement that, sooner or later, will rot your floor and bring you crashing beneath the ground. When you think of us at all, it is not fondly. Don't lie. You loved those whom you loved when they were here, and you love their memories still. But you do not love the departed. We frighten you and remind you of your unavoidable fate. But we can do more. Hear us out. Give us a chance.

The wise among you have noted the harshest aspect of departing is not the possibility of obliterated consciousness but the cessation of possibility altogether. The curtain comes down, and there is no encore. What you have done, you have done, and you will do no more. Hence your ambition, your monuments, your bucket lists. Your earliest evocations of us involved not hellfire and brimstone, not horns and pitchforks and charbroiled eternity, but shadows and dust: a dread congress of weary gossips encased in what they were and knowing they will not be anything else ever again. Stasis. Vacuum. None, you think, do there embrace.

But we are here to tell you it doesn't have to be that way. You have beneath your feet an untapped resource of unlimited potential. In the cemeteries you whistle past, certainly, but also in the layers of the world beneath your buildings, the particulate matter suspended in your streams, the dust in the air you can still breathe in and out. You have never hesitated to dig for treasure, solid or liquid. Why turn your back on wealth that you need not labor to acquire, riches that will present themselves to you?

Consider the possibilities. Think of all the things you really don't want to do. Think of your guilt, you who palm these unpleasant tasks off on the weak and the desperate. Think of your misery, you who are numbered among the weak and desperate. Now think of a world without guilt, without desperation. Would it not be better if we cut your flowers, polished your silver, pushed your infants in their strollers down the clean sunny streets? Would it not be preferable to make your way through a world in which the jobs to which you have access are by definition not bad, because the bad jobs, the ones that the desperate do for next to nothing, the departed now do, for nothing?

Wait a minute, you say. Hold on. Maybe there's an argument to be made for employing the services of the departed. If nothing else, it would certainly cut down on the paperwork. But do we really think that those of you still resident in the actual world could cope fully with having these invisible tasks performed by those who aren't supposed to be visible at all? After all, we're, um, well—

Dead? Is that the word you're looking for? We prefer "departed," as you know, but let's not stand on ceremony. What's your point?

Is it the creep factor? Are you worried by the prospect of some gothic carnival? Are you unnerved by the image of the skeletal janitor, appalled by the babe tipped back, blood gushing merrily through its plump new body, to receive the bottle from caring, competent hands of gristle and bone? Would you prefer not to hear the squeak outside your office window and look up to see the wraith from your most tormented dreams, urgently rubbing clean that one stubborn spot?

Well, we could point out that, based on pretty much any era of human history you care to reference, anybody can get used to anything. We could make that inarguable point and let it go. But consider this more carefully. Do you not honor us already? Do you not set aside observances, rituals, holidays? Have not some of you seen your own children having so much fun with the main holiday for the departed that you took it from the children and made it your own? Have not others of you refused to ever stop talking to us, witnessing us, factoring our reality into your lives?

Breathes there one among you who would not cheerfully crawl down a football field of ground glass if your special departed were waiting in the end zone? Surely our mowing your lawns or driving your taxicabs would not be such a stretch.

All right then, you say. Maybe this can happen. But what, you ask, is in it for us? Why do we offer our services? Why do we want this at all?

Were you not paying attention earlier? Shadows, dust, stasis, vacuum? Remember all that? We want this so we can have a tomorrow that will be different from today. We want something to do. We are bored. We are bored like you wouldn't believe.

So there's no hellfire and brimstone, you ask, perhaps a bit too eagerly? No punishment?

And then, upon further reflection, you have to ask: and no reward?

Punishment, reward: over eternity it's all the same. Difference is erased, as some of your more recent scholars might put it. Indeed, permit us to amend our previous statement: never mind a tomorrow different from today. We want a tomorrow.

And if we don't get it, you ask? If the spectacle of the departed is more than you can stand? If you decline, politely but firmly, our generous offer? What then?

Then we will have to think of something else. And next time, we will not ask.

But it doesn't have to come to that. Think over our offer. Take your time. Time is, after all, yours and not ours. We are not unreasonable.

And as you consider our offer, don't forget the thinning of your own bones, the desiccation of your own flesh, the finite number of beats in your own fragile hearts.

Give yourselves something to look forward to. Help us to help you. Consider the services of the departed.

WHEN JOHN MOORE
SHOT CARL BELL

When John Moore shot Carl Bell it was the Fourth of July, 1920. The shooting took place because Bell was "seeing" Moore's wife. In Kingston, South Carolina, in 1920 you didn't sleep with a woman or have an affair with her. You "saw" her, and that is how Mr. Allworth puts it when he tells the story in his living room on a rainy Wednesday turn-of-the-century afternoon. Mr. Allworth is ninety-five years old, looks seventy, maintains a part-time law practice, and puts on a tie to receive visitors. That was the proper thing to do when John Moore shot Carl Bell, and, for Mr. Allworth, it still is.

It was the Fourth of July, says Mr. Allworth in the year 2000, ten o'clock in the morning and already eighty-five degrees. Main Street was draped in red, white, and blue for the Independence Day parade scheduled to start at noon, and there was scarcely a house in Kingston that didn't have an American flag flying in the front yard or hanging from a window. When John Moore shot Carl Bell it had only been eight months since the end of the First World War, and Americans were still overflowing with pride at having saved Europe from itself. "We were all looking forward to the parade, because it was going to be the first one that all our veterans would be marching in, don't you see."

Mrs. Bryan nods her head in agreement. She is eighty-three years old, a near contemporary of Mr. Allworth and absolutely delighted that they are both in his living room on this turn of the century afternoon. She had completely forgotten about when John Moore shot Carl Bell because her parents had tried to shield her from the sordid event when it happened, and so her memories derive from what she was told in later years, which she has forgotten. Also in Allworth's living room are Mrs. Bryan's daughter, who is sixty-five, and the daughter's son, who is thirty-five. When John Moore shot Carl Bell, neither Mrs. Bryan's daughter nor her grandson had been born yet.

It was ten o'clock in the morning, then, and the middle-aged woman who was Mrs. Allworth's family's live-in servant was sweeping off the front porch. Allworth was twenty-one then and just getting started in his practice. He still lived with his parents, as did his married sister and her husband and their six-year-old son. It was a big house, there was room for everyone, families stayed together in those days, et cetera. The servant swept off the front porch and paid no attention to Allworth's nephew marching around the front yard, banging arrhythmically on a tin drum, leading his own imaginary parade. She paid no attention to the town's holiday preparations. It was not her time to celebrate yet, for when John Moore shot Carl Bell the African-American population of Kingston did not participate in the Fourth of July festivities. Instead, they waited until July 6th and went down to the lake three miles away and had the Colored Fourth. They laughed and danced and sang and ate and drank and swam and had the place to themselves. They could have stayed for the 7th and 8th as well, since no white person would swim in the lake for at least a week after the Colored Fourth.

When John Moore shot Carl Bell, the end of Reconstruction was little more than a decade further in the past than the end of the Second World War is in the year 2000. For Allworth's parents, the memory of Lincoln was every bit as fresh as the memory of Hitler was for Mrs. Bryan's daughter. And every bit as despised.

"Well, I had gone out onto the front porch to tell Bessie—that was our colored woman—that my mother wanted to see her in the kitchen, and my sister's boy Thaddeus—he couldn't have been more than six, and he was beating on this little old drum, because he was all excited about the parade, don't you see." Allworth remembers everything that happened when John Moore shot Carl Bell, although he cannot remember what he ate for breakfast this morning. "And at first I thought it was just Thaddeus hitting his drum extra hard, you know, kind of smacking it on the rim, but then he quit beating for a second and I heard the noise again. Then I realized it was a gunshot, and that it was coming from over somewhere around the Bell place, which was just down the street."

"Oh, my, yes. I remember that house so well," Mrs. Bryan says. She does not really remember it at all, but she sincerely believes that she does, and so the function of memory is served even without memory itself.

"I really didn't know what was going on at first, so I told Bessie to take Thaddeus inside. I remember that evening, after it was all over, Mother told me she had heard the shots and was sure that some of those Yankee anarchists had come to Kingston. . . ."

When John Moore shot Carl Bell it had only been two years since the Bolshevik uprising, and there were people in the United States who were more interested in continuing what had begun in Russia than with saving Europe from itself and making the world safe for capitalism. They had very grave doubts about the pride that was overflowing in Kingston and everywhere else, and every once in a while some of them expressed these doubts by blowing something up. Nothing had been blown up in Kingston, nor would anything be blown up, but when John Moore shot Carl Bell there was apprehension flowing just beneath the surface of the pride, and Allworth's parents felt it more strongly than most.

They were, in fact, seriously considering voting for Harding instead of Cox in November because they were afraid that Cox would not be firm enough to deal with the immanent threat. They would wind up voting for Cox, though, because Colonel Lereaux, a member of the South Carolina House of Representatives and their second cousin, assured them that Cox would keep the Reds out of the country and the Negroes in their place. In fact, Colonel Lereaux was none too sure of this himself, but he told the Allworths so because the Reds and the Negroes were nothing compared to having a Yankee Republican in the White House. And the Allworths believed him. Colonel Lereaux was a wise man and knew of such matters. He was from one of the oldest and most respected families in Kingston and had once broken a chair over the head of a black man who had called him by his first name.

". . . and then John Moore came up in the yard and told me he had shot Carl Bell and that I was to call the high sheriff to come and get him." The image of John Moore, whoever he was, coming over to the Allworths' and announcing his crime finally locks Mrs. Bryan's grandson, who had paid only passing attention at first, into the old lawyer's narrative. He had not wanted to come to this place on this rainy afternoon; he was there only because he had promised his mother that while he was home he would take her and her mother to visit some old friends. But as Allworth winds through his memories, the grandson finds himself more and more attentive. The fact that he is recently separated from his own wife may or may not have anything to do with it.

He can see it all now, very clearly before him as Allworth supplies the details. Virginia Moore had been "seeing" Carl Bell for several months, and in Kingston in 1920 (as in Kingston in the year 2000) (as in any small town, anywhere, anytime) it was impossible for such a thing to remain a secret for long. Sometimes it became public knowledge. Everybody, including the husband and the wife and the lover, knew what was going on, and that everyone knew that everyone knew. But neither the husband nor the wife nor the lover acknowledged the reality of the situation, especially not to each other. All three went about their normal lives as if nothing were going on. The sinned-against held their heads high, feeding off the clandestine admiration of the townspeople for rising above the inherent tackiness of the whole scene; the sinners pretended that all was well and that they were not aware of the whispers and the leers when they walked by.

But this was not for John Moore—"just as nice a man as you would ever want to meet, my family thought the world of him"—who was a prominent merchant and the son of a Baptist minister and would not bear the whispers and leers and bogus sympathy. No. None of that. That Carl Bell was essentially a stranger—unmarried, a man of "independent means" who did not mix with the townspeople and seldom stirred forth from the ancestral home Mrs. Bryan thinks she remembers—did not matter. Had Carl Bell been John Moore's brother, it would not have prevented Moore from doing what he did: upon discovering his wife's unfaithfulness, calmly picking up his gun (in Kingston in 1920, as in Kingston in the year 2000, owning a handgun was as simple and natural as owning a shovel or a watch), walking down to Carl Bell's place, and shooting him dead in his own yard. And then walking down to the Allworths', who were good friends and close by, and telling them to call the sheriff. What else was there to do?

". . . and so we went down to Carl Bell's and we went around to the back of the house and there was Carl Bell all right. He was lying down by the ditch that ran behind his house, and his left arm was hanging out over the ditch, his hand still quivering. He must have just died, because his hand was still moving, but he wasn't breathing, don't you see. John Moore had shot him twice in the head, and there was about as much blood poured out of him as out of an old cow. Some of it was draining into the ditch. . . ."

So the elder and younger Allworths, and the other men of the neighborhood who had heard the shots, dragged the body out of the yard and carried it down to the ice house down by the river because the coroner was out of town and wouldn't be back for two more days. They brought John Moore along with them but did not bother to restrain him. Where would he go?

When the men came out of the ice house they found Moore quietly regarding the oak tree covered with Spanish moss which stretched out and hung over the river, motionless and cool, in defiance of the century and the heat. He said, staring out at the muddy river, "I have done a terrible thing. I hope that God and you fine gentlemen can forgive me." In Kingston in 1920, that was a terrific thing to say at a time like that, and the Allworths and their neighbors were duly impressed.

"And they brought John Moore to trial all right, and he was acquitted..."

"What?" exclaims Mrs. Bryan's daughter. It is the first time she has said anything since Allworth began his story. "You mean they just let him off scot-free after he killed that man in cold blood? What in heaven's name for?"

"It was a matter of honor," explains Mrs. Bryan. She says this neither jokingly nor self-righteously, but matter-of-factly, as if she had said that it was a May afternoon in 2000 and it was raining outside. As if she had asked her grandson where his wife was, unaware that he couldn't answer her because he didn't know. Her daughter knew better than to say anything more.

Now Mr. Allworth goes on to other things and does not say what the grandson speculates about. He does not say that life returned to normal after the trial and that Mr. and Mrs. Moore returned to their respectable positions in the community, that the parade went on. He does not say what happened later—that John Moore walked the streets of Kingston with his head held high, that the other men nodded behind his back in grudging approval, jealously uncertain if they would have been able to do as Moore had done. He does not say that the women visited Mrs. Moore and chatted as they always had, their skirts above their ankles, their hair piled high and tight. He does not say that there was never any mention—and, eventually, no thought given—to the cause of it all. The adultery, the churning unsanctioned love between smooth, damp sheets. He does not say that, as long as Virginia Moore lived, nobody ever asked her how she felt about it.

He also does not say (and the grandson does not know until his mother tells him as he drives her home in the rain) that the murder was so spectacular it served as a point of historical reference. For years afterward, the residents of Kingston would locate events in time by saying, "That was before John Moore shot Carl Bell," or, "That was after John Moore shot Carl Bell."

And Mr. Allworth does not mention the most amazing fact of all—that when John Moore shot Carl Bell, it was only eighty years ago. The grandson tries to imagine Kingston in the year 2080, and cannot.

MARY OF THE NEW DISPENSATION

Mrs. Newton is nervous.
Her husband's assurances do not help. She does not need him to tell her how great a man the Reverend Mr. Spear is; she knows of the Reverend's good works in the past, and the promise of the future. Have they not all heard the spirits speak through the Reverend, received the plans for the New Dispensation and the machine that will bring it into being? Perfection! Joy! The fallen world will soon be set aright.

But now Mrs. Newton has been called to stand once again before the machine, the Physical Savior, the New Motive Power, and her belly continues to swell and press against her loosened corset, and she knows her husband had nothing to do with that. He and the Reverend and her dead sister Emily say she is Mary. She finds it difficult to think of her husband as Joseph. She cannot tell him how frightened she is as he helps her into the cab that will take them from Boston to the cottage at High Rock and the dawn of the new era. The rocking of the cab further disorients her. All things are possible. It is the year of Our Lord eighteen hundred and fifty-four. Invisible electric messages fly along metal wires, and slavery is not permitted anywhere within the Commonwealth of Massachusetts.

The machine waits on a dining-room table.
At this same table, Spear received his first messages from the

spirits. From a nest of metal plates, wires, and magnets rise two metal poles. Linking the poles, a revolving shaft of steel; resting on top of the shaft and perpendicular to it, a metal arm from either end of which hang two spheres containing magnets. Beneath the spheres alternating plates of zinc and copper seek correspondence with the electrical patterns of the brain. Other, smaller metal balls with magnets orbit the center of the device, hanging randomly from metallic protuberances. Bellows near the center breathe in and out. Extending through openings in the table, two segmented metal appendages run down to the floor.

Spear and his assistants have constructed the device according to the instructions of the Spirit Congress. Revealed to Spear at a séance in Rochester the year before, the Congress contains six major associations: Healthfulizers, Educationalizers, Agriculturalizers, Elementizers, Governmentizers, and Electrolizers. It is the Electrolizers, seven spirits who had been prominent engineers while resident on earth, all now supervised personally by the spirit of Benjamin Franklin, for whom Spear is the earthly representative. They speak to him, and he transmits their instructions. Spear himself is innocent of any scientific or mechanic expertise, a blessing that ensures the spirits' instructions will be transmitted without corruption or adumbration.

Thus the machine emerged, bit by bit, over nine months. None of its corporeal assemblers can hope to explain its workings, but they know its purpose. The Electrolizers, in Spear's mild but steadfast voice, had made that clear. The Associations, they said, are *charged to promote integral reform with a view to the ultimate establishment of a divine social state on earth.* To this end, the machine, bringing *new life and vitality into all things, animate and inanimate.* And now *Heaven's last, best gift to Man* awaits its final component.

The cab ascends the winding path to the summit of High Rock.

When the cab arrives at the stone cottage and Mrs. Newton steps down, her husband Alonzo wraps his arms beneath hers, encircling her torso above her swollen belly, and all but carries her up the additional steps to the wooden observation tower behind the cottage. They are greeted there by Mr. S. Crosby Hewitt, a chief assistant to Spear and, like Mr. Newton, editor of a journal in support of a better world. The mutual success of both Hewitt's *New Era* and Newton's *New England Spiritualist* is marked testimony, they all feel, to the profound appetite for improvement, in the greater Boston area at least.

One hundred seventy feet below them lies the city of Lynn, at once prosperous and shabby. A strange, unsettled place. She has heard the stories: accusations of witchcraft long before Salem; the fortuneteller Moll Pitcher, whose fame drew Mrs. Newton's own mother from Boston for a consultation and whose house had lain just below where they now stand. There is even a tale of a dispute among the Quakers that had led to a riot. Was the home of rioting Quakers, she wondered, an optimal site for the inauguration of the new era? But Spear had insisted. *This majestic eminence*, he declared, was *a high, sacred, consecrated place*. That the most famous spiritualist of the age, the seer of Poughkeepsie himself, Andrew Jackson Davis, had last year greeted the spirits from the observation tower undoubtedly provided further encouragement.

Mr. and Mrs. Newton and Mr. Hewitt enter the uppermost room of the tower. The machine sits on its table, surrounded by its assemblers, male and female. There is no other furniture in the room save a straight-back chair in which sits the Reverend, recently entered into his fiftieth year. Spear's collar is loosened against the growing heat of June, but his hair rests flawlessly in a careful halo around his head. His eyes are closed; his lips move rapidly, whispering. His daughter, Sophronia, holds a writing tablet on which his pen scratches frantically. As Mrs. Newton walks into the room, his voice rises to pulpit volume. —She is here! It is time! Let it begin!—.

John Murray Spear has devoted his life to others.
Since preaching his first sermon at the age of twenty-four, the Reverend Mr. Spear—baptized by his namesake John Murray, the founder of the Universalist Church—has given himself to the service of the poor, the downtrodden, the defenseless. Temperance, abolition, the rights of women and prisoners have filled his days and nights, his very soul. Many in his congregations recoiled from his activities. Ten years earlier, while he was speaking against slavery in Portland, Maine, a mob attacked him and nearly sent him to his maker; the months of recovery only deepened his faith, his determination to bring light to the darkened world. He redoubled his efforts to aid and comfort prisoners, railed against the merciless presumption of capital punishment, yielded not one inch in the sacred cause of abolition. When the captors of the slave woman Lucy Faggins made the mistake of visiting Massachusetts and Spear helped her obtain her freedom, the outcry from his parishioners cost him his New Bedford pulpit. Some who understood the energy of his passions and the nobility of his purpose offered him other appointments both civil and ecclesiastical, but he declined them all. Like Christ before him, he would labor misunderstood and alone.

And then his daughter, whose faith had never wavered even as her mother withdrew into a Stoic silence, showed him the way. Some years earlier they had both read the Reverend Mr. Davis's *The Principles of Nature, Her Divine Revelations, and a Voice to Mankind*: a vision of *Summer-Land*, a spirit world of joy and no punishment. Spear was intrigued; Sophronia was captivated. Davis had insisted that the spirits would soon provide a living demonstration of their existence; when the Fox sisters of Hydesville, New York, confirmed his prophecy, Sophronia sat herself and her father down at this same table on which the machine now rests. There the spirits spoke, not through enigmatic rapping noises, but through Spear's own hand as he transcribed their detailed instructions to focus his ministry on specific individuals. A woman in Georgetown, an elderly man in Weymouth; many others, all strangers to him. The afflicted were taken aback by Spear's unannounced arrivals but afterward confessed themselves mildly improved.

Following Davis, Spear published his own volume of spirit teachings, *Messages from the Superior State*, transcriptions of twelve communications from the spirit of the original John Murray. There followed public lectures during which Spear would sink into a trance and communicate the spirits' observations on topics about which he himself knew nothing. Most audiences were unconvinced that the lectures were anything other than Spear speaking in his own voice. Nonetheless, he continued his mission, speaking to any who would listen.

Then the visit to Rochester, the revelations of the Electrolizers, and the New Motive Power. He quickly secured the use of the cottage at High Rock from Jesse Hutchinson, fellow spiritualist and leader of the Hutchinson Family Singers, who had remained grateful to Spear since the Reverend had permitted the family to rehearse in his church. He gathered his followers, few but undaunted. Mrs. Spear retired to near relations in Gloucester, but Sophronia never left his side. The construction of the Physical Savior began.

Mrs. Newton also hears from the spirits.

She, too, had been inspired by Davis, and Spear, and her own dear husband. It was shortly after she read Davis's book that her departed sister Emily, gone from a fever these ten long years, began to speak to her. Whispers at first, a tremulous voice that seemed to emanate from a corner, from a heating grate, from nowhere:

(sarah)

(listen)

(there will be much for you to do)

Then the voice came into her own head and issued from her

own mouth. AS FIERY HOT AS WAS MY FINAL FEVER, SO COOL AND SOOTHING IS IT HERE. AS PIERCING AS WERE MY FINAL AGONIES, SO CALM IS THE PEACE THAT WAITS FOR YOU HERE. These words she spoke felt different from Emily's whispers, and Mrs. Newton was briefly uncertain. But Mr. Newton, who had just published his pamphlet, *Ministry of Angels Realized*, rejoiced at this reassurance, this confirmation of his deepest hopes, and regarded his wife with love and awe unmatched even on their wedding day. She chided herself for her lapse and continued to give voice to the voice in her head. Neither of their two young children seemed overly struck, although Mercy, the youngest, asked if Aunt Emily would be coming to her birthday party. And when they attended the Reverend Mr. Spear's delivery of a spirit message from Dr. Franklin, any doubts they may have had were cast aside. Mrs. Newton recognized in Spear her own state: an unimpeded transmission from the other side, yet with no loss of the transmitter's own consciousness.

By this time construction of the machine had already begun, and in the crisp air of September, 1853, Mr. Newton took her to the tower at High Rock. The initial sequence was under way, he told her. The spirits had instructed that the motor receive an initial charge of electricity, which action had led to *a slight pulsation and vibratory motion in the pendants around the periphery of the table*. Then several persons, male and female, had been presented to the machine, had laid hands upon it to transmit their own individual magnetism. They attended the machine, her husband explained, carefully ordered, from *ordinary or comparatively coarser organizations* to those of *finer and yet finer mould*, thus providing necessary links for the machine's progress.

At the cottage they found Mr. Hewitt, Sophronia, and several others clustered around the machine, on its table in the center of the room. Mr. Hewitt wrote rapidly on a closely-held pad of paper. Sophronia stood behind him, speaking softly to no one in particular. Mrs. Newton thought she heard, —Is there no other way? Does it have to be—, but she lost the rest.

To one side stood the Reverend Mr. Spear, although it took a moment for Mrs. Newton to ascertain that it was indeed him. The Reverend's body was wrapped in metal—wide bands, narrow strips, shiny and dull, with wires protruding in no apparent pattern. Some of the metallic bands were encrusted in what appeared to be jewels. Sheets of silver, gold, what could have been diamond caught the late sunlight that poured through the open windows that surrounded them and the open skylight in the rounded ceiling above.

Mrs. Newton must have betrayed her shock, for Mr. Newton carefully explained that the spirits had required an individual to submit to a potentially dangerous operation, to which the Reverend had consented only *from a rational confidence in the wisdom and good faith of the invisible directors.* The encasement was dramatic, perhaps, but necessary. Had not Spear himself written of God as *a Grand Central Electric Focus from which all electricity emanates? Was not electricity the grand instrumentality, the native element, by which all things move? Between the Grand Central Mind and all inferior minds there subsists a connection, a telegraphic communication, an Electric chain.*

Two men whom Mrs. Newton did not know picked up the Reverend in his metal casement and moved him to within inches of the machine. She could not see where the wires led or if the Reverend's metal was actually touching that of the machine. On the strip of gold where his eyes should have been rested two red jewels, but his lips were visible; she could see them move and recognized the trance state.

They stood together, metal-wrapped man and machine, for close to an hour. The room grew dark; someone lit candles. Sophronia was on her knees in prayer. At first Mrs. Newton thought the glow of the candles responsible, but she realized that a light was shining from a point near the center of the Reverend's casing. The light stretched, expanded, and enveloped the machine. Now others fell to their knees as Sophronia shouted, *Spiritus!*, and Mr.

Newton muttered, *umbilicus*. It seemed to Mrs. Newton that the light was on the verge of encompassing the table on which the machine rested and then making its way about the room and through the windows and upwards through the open ceiling into the empty night. Just as it appeared to come towards her, it disappeared. The Reverend collapsed within his cage; Sophronia frantically directed the two men who peeled the metal back and carried him away.

The next day, the spirits spoke through Mrs. Newton. With her husband and most of the staff of the *New England Spiritualist* present, the spirits explained the role she was to play. Her departed sister began to address her as Mary, and her belly began to swell.

Mrs. Newton lies on the floor.

Her husband dutifully places a pillow behind her head. It has been raining all day; the windows and the skylight are closed, she presumes to protect the machine. This June has proven unusually warm, and the room is close and hot. From her perspective the machine seems to rise to the very ceiling, in which there are, she notices, an inordinate number of cracks. She looks to her right and sees the Reverend scribbling and muttering. On each wrist is a thin golden bracelet that has remained since his encasement as if part of his skin. The others witnesses stand and look down on her like the spirits themselves.

She trusts the Reverend, her husband, their purpose and promise, but with each passing week since her previous visit to the tower she has grown more anxious and uncertain. Mr. Hewitt had said *the most refined elements of her spiritual being were to be imparted to, and absorbed by, the appropriate portions of the mechanism, its minerals having been made peculiarly receptive by previous chemical processes.* Fair enough.

But her swollen belly has brought memories of her two confinements and the unspeakable suffering that ended in joy but was suffering all the same. Do the spirits demand that of her? Did they instruct the Reverend to have her brought here wearing only a loose gown under her coat? Did they veto the presence of a midwife? Do they want these people here, men as well as women? She tries to bring her knees even closer together and smoothes the front of her gown.

Suddenly her abdominal muscles tighten and she is seized by pain. Her knees jerk up as if to confine the pain before it spills over the rest of her body, and she screams. Eyes clenched shut, she hears her husband and Mr. Hewitt ushering people quickly out of the room. The pain passes, and when she opens her eyes there is only Mr. Hewitt and Alonzo and Reverend Spear and Sophronia, whose eyes now glow like candle flames.

The pain seizes her again: a familiar pain, but no less awful for that. To this moment she has tried to convince herself that her outward condition was intended as a guide, a sympathetic sign of what might come. The spirits said she was to attend the machine, provide her *maternal feeling*. They said nothing of lying in agony on a hardwood floor. The Reverend is entranced, and Sophronia does not move from his side, but Mr. Newton squeezes Mrs. Newton's hand and waves Mr. Hewitt to stand behind them. She keeps her knees up, allows her legs to open, and howls.

(you are doing well mary)

Emily's voice whispers as it did when Mrs. Newton had first heard it, but it is there.

(take us to the new day beloved sister I love you so)

When Mrs. Newton brought her first two children to bed, she feared she would be defeated by the absence of the one person she needed most of all; she was surrounded by women, but none of them was Emily. Now she is grateful beyond expression for even her sister's voice. She clenches between her teeth the thick wooden handle of the spoon Sophronia has placed in her mouth and prays.

The contractions continue for two hours: much less than with either of her children, but within the too familiar agony of tension and release there is a hard, cold center that she has not felt before, and that frightens her more than the pain itself. Midway through she feels water pouring out of her; despite her sister's soothing whispers, she sobs in mortification. Shortly after she thinks she hears Mr. Hewitt cry, *It moves!*, but she is not sure.

When it finally ends, her husband helps her sit up. She shivers despite the heat, her skin clammy, her dress wringing wet. Sophronia chants in Latin; Mr. Hewitt is drafting aloud his editorial for the *New Era*. Her husband buries his face on her shoulder and weeps. She thinks she hears something from the machine; she thinks she sees it move. Her hand wanders to her collapsed belly, and she faints.

Mr. Hewitt announces their success.

The headline in the *New Era* reads, THE THING MOVES! Mr. Hewitt writes, *Unto your earth a child is born. Its name shall be called the ELECTRICAL MOTOR.* He declares the machine *the physical Saviour of the race.* He insists that it will *lead the way in the great speedily coming salvation.*

Visitors come, observe, leave. There seems to be some motion in some of the pendant attachments, but not in the two major orbs on top. The bellows occasionally appear to vibrate. An uncharitable letter in the *Spiritual Telegraph* testifies that the physical Saviour of the race cannot even turn a coffee mill.

The Reverend Mr. Spear reminds visitors that the machine is a newborn, still gathering strength, still finding its way.

Mrs. Newton takes a room in the cottage.

She spends several hours per day in the observation tower with the New Motive Power. The floor is stained where she lay. The fluids that poured from her traced a short path to the machine, terminating at the left-hand appendage beneath the table. Sophronia had ordered the floor scrubbed immediately, but the stain would not completely disappear.

Mrs. Newton sits by the machine. She knits shawls and covers, some small, some very large. She sings. On her children's first visit, she invites them to interact with the machine however they wish, but they are cowed by its presence and asked to be excused. Her husband, so ardent in the past to resume the full activities of marriage as soon as possible after her confinements ended, now keeps a respectful distance and busies himself with his newspaper.

Her breasts remain swollen. Periodically she shuts the door and loosens the top of her dress. The two orbs at the top are too far apart, but she lays her breasts on top of the steel arm that connects them. The cold metal always hurts at first, but it warms quickly. No milk issues, but she can feel something being taken out of her, a force that flows into the machine, nourishes it. Emily is most likely to whisper to her at these times and it is a great comfort to her, although once she grew most confused when she thought she heard two voices:

(it is the salvation of the race and the comfort I could not give you)

—God, why her?—

(it cannot love you but it will not die)

She turned and saw the door ajar and the dim figure of Sophronia quickly moving away.

None of this is what she expected, but the Reverend Mr. Spear assures her that all that has happened, that will happen, is at the instruction of the Electrolizers and therefore of certain benefit to all.

Reverend Davis himself pays a visit.

His return to High Rock, the site of *one of his most glorious visions*, draws back many of the people who had ceased their visits. Reverend Davis is deferential to Spear, who is twenty years his senior. After expending so much energy on the machine, Spear lacks his former presence that had drawn the curiosity of many and the devotion of a few, and surely lacks the swooping dark mane, the full beard, the resonant yet soothing voice of Davis. The younger man is particularly solicitous towards Mrs. Newton, who sits and receives his praise with a wan smile and the knowledge, intellectually understood if not deeply felt, that she is in the presence of a great man.

Davis' report in the *Spiritual Telegraph*, however, is a shock and a disappointment. Although Spear is *doing good with all his guileless heart*, he is *intellectually disqualified for the development of absolute science*—proof indeed that the machine was built at the direction of the spirits, but to what end? The motor is *artistically put together*, but its evident lack of any real application may suggest the influence, not of the unimpeachable Electrolizers, but of other, less responsible spirits. Thus the dangers of the *frightful and pernicious tendency to fanaticism among the true and faithful and teachable friends of spiritual intercourse*.

Sophronia throws the *Telegraph* to the floor and weeps. Mrs. Newton does not read the report. Mr. Hewitt reviews their expenditures. The New Motive Power has cost approximately two thousand dollars.

Mrs. Newton awakens one morning to find the machine is gone.

Her husband, who left their Boston home at dawn, comes to her room in the cottage and explains to her that, after consulting with the Electrolizers and Dr. Franklin, the Reverend Mr. Spear determined that the machine needed a change of venue. He has ordered it disassembled and removed. Even now, Mr. Newton says, it is on its way to its new home in Randolph, New York, where *it might have the advantages of that lofty electrical position*.

Before Mr. Newton can complete his report she quits him and races up the tower steps. Her head is spinning by the time she reaches the top. The room is empty; her chair and her knitting are also gone. She circles the room, runs from window to window as if the world below her or the sky above might tell her what she needs to know. She sits on the floor near where the table rested, knowing neither Randolph nor what might distinguish it from Lynn.

On the carriage ride back to their home in Boston, her husband declares his pride, his love, his utter adoration. He assures her that, although her work is done, it was both essential and successful. He repeats the spirits' declaration, as he witnessed through Spear's most recent trance, that the motor simply needs time. *It hungers for that nourishment on which it can feed and by which it can expand and grow. It will then go alone and pick out its own nourishment from the surrounding elements.* Mrs. Newton does not reply but runs her hand across the skin that hangs loosely from her jaw. She is thirty pounds lighter than when she entered the cottage and lay upon the floor.

When Mrs. Newton returns home she takes to her bed and does not rise for several weeks. Her children clamor for her attention, but she ignores them. The family physician can find no organic cause for her lying-in. Mr. Newton remembers her state after Emily's passing and is worried; there is still much to be done to understand the spirits and improve the world.

In time, however, Mrs. Newton emerges, rejoins her family. She has regained much of the weight she lost. She reacquaints herself with her children, and she and Mr. Newton resume the intimacies accorded husband and wife. For the next child, she will demand a physician in attendance, and ether.

Shortly after Mrs. Newton leaves her bed, the Reverend Mr. Spear reports to the world that an angry mob has destroyed the physical savior of mankind. However, there is no report of this in the newspapers of Randolph or surrounding areas. In time, the spirits explain to Spear the ongoing fraud of conventional marriage; he leaves both Mrs. Spear and Sophronia behind for a new community of freedom in Kiantone, New York.

The spirits continue to speak through Mrs. Newton and will do so for the rest of her days. Each time they do, she imagines her machine somewhere gathering strength, generating for a new world immune from suffering and loss. She weeps with joy at the final defeat of slavery but can only be stunned by the knowledge of the annihilated thousands, the mountains of the shattered dead, and wishes she would hear from more of them.

She remains honored to have been chosen, and she does not regret her actions. But after her final departure from High Rock, Emily never speaks to her again, and that she regrets so very, very much.

WHAT WE DID ON OUR VACATION: MY WHOLE WORLD LIES WAITING

Between Seattle and Bellevue, they drove past a door standing in a patch of woods.

"Did you see that?" asked Patrick.

"See what?" asked Carol, who was driving.

"There was a door in those woods back there. Just standing by itself."

"A door?"

"Yeah. The weirdest thing." Patrick turned around to look out the back window.

Carol sighed. "You want to go back?"

"Well . . ."

She pulled off the road and turned around. It was a gesture of resignation, not cooperation. Patrick looked carefully ahead and tried not to glance over at her. He had decided after the fight in the driveway back at her daughter Melissa's house that it would be best if for a while he paid as little attention to his wife as possible. He hadn't intended to say anything until they got to Bellevue, where they were having lunch with Susan Estridge, an attorney who had been one of Patrick's high school classmates. But the sight of the door got him talking despite himself.

As the car slowed down, their dog Monte sat up expectantly in the back seat. Patrick reached behind and lowered the back windows so Monte could poke his head through and sniff out where they were. They had been on the road for two weeks, driving from

Boston to Seattle, and whenever the car slowed down, Monte perked up and headed for the window. Monte the Hopeful, Carol called him.

Carol parked the car on the side of the road. It was a residential district on a weekday afternoon, and there wasn't much traffic. All the homes were set well back into their lots, many of which were left deliberately overgrown so you couldn't see the houses. The houses you could see spoke money. The door stood at the edge of one of the overgrown lots. There were two stone steps leading up to it, and it was framed by a thin tangle of vines and bushes and leaf-heavy limbs that hung down from the surrounding trees. The door stood by itself, unattached to anything.

"What the hell is that thing doing there?" Patrick said.

"That is really odd," Carol said.

Patrick reached behind his seat, rummaged around on the car floor, came up with their camera. "Just leave the motor running," he said. "I won't be a minute."

Carol turned off the car. "Monte probably needs a walk. Come on, Monte." Monte's tail hammered the back seat, all forty pounds of him twitching in delight, his hope rewarded. "Where's his leash?"

"Back there somewhere." Patrick was already out of the car.

Carol sighed again. They took long driving trips like this every few years, when they managed to save enough not to teach for at least part of the summer term. Usually to visit one of Carol's far-flung daughters or one of Patrick's equally far-flung friends, or sometimes both. At the end of each trip they joked about the need for some sort of stargate wormhole transporter thing that would pop them right home, or at least to the next motel.

It had been no joke back in Melissa's driveway when, just before turning the ignition key, Carol had a sudden vision of their leaving Seattle in two days for a long drive to Colorado, and her daughter Abby, before the even longer drive back east. Not that she didn't love her family, but. He thought he had replied to her concern in a supportive fashion, but evidently not. Her enumeration of his failings was prolonged, and his response was definitely not supportive.

Now Patrick leaned on the hood of their blue Chevy Malibu and took pictures of the door. It hung between two unpainted wooden posts, each of which was topped by a sphere that looked like the top of a chess pawn. There was no crosspiece on top. The door itself was vertically sectioned on its bottom third, with a horizontal strip across the middle, more sectioned vertical paneling above that, and another horizontal strip on top. The top strip and bottom paneling were etched with patterns that meant nothing to Patrick. The middle strip and top paneling were perforated with elaborate filigree, like a wrought-iron balcony. The door was a faint green that blended with the woods, but Patrick couldn't decide if that was the original color or if the elements had faded the wood. There was no doorknob.

"That is just the damndest thing," said Patrick. "Hey, don't let him do that." Monte had had his fill of sniffing and pissing in the leaves and bushes and was stretching his extendable leash toward the door.

"Do what?"

"Don't let him piss on the door."

"Why not?"

Monte sniffed the door frame deeply and with profound concentration.

"It's not our door."

"So? Is somebody going to run us off with a shotgun? We're in Seattle, not Little Rock." Patrick had had an administrative position and Carol had taught at a small college in Arkansas for three years, which had been at least two years too long. "OK, whatever. Come on, Monte." She tugged gently at the leash, and Monte trotted back to the car.

Patrick put the camera back in the car. "I wonder what on earth that thing is there for."

"I don't know. You don't suppose it could teleport us to Colorado, do you?"

He looked directly at her for the first time since the driveway. She was smiling. He let out a breath he didn't realize he had been holding. "Maybe so. We can come back and try it before we leave."

"Hey—no time like the present. Hold Monte." Carol passed the leash to Patrick and headed toward the door.

"Carol?"

"If I don't come back, go ahead to lunch. I'll meet you in Colorado."

Carol pushed the door. It hung loosely on rusted hinges and creaked when it opened. She stepped through and closed it behind her. Patrick could see her through the filigree, and then for a moment he thought he couldn't. Monte barked once.

The door opened, and Carol reappeared. "Damn. No magic transport."

"Sorry," Patrick said. "Guess you're stuck here for a while longer."

When they pulled away, Patrick asked, "Could you see the house from where you were on the other side of the door?"

"*Plonger au fond du grouffre*," Carol said.

"What?"

"*Au fond de l'Inconnu pour trouver du nouveau.*"

"What?"

"So you're certain you never dated this Susan?" She rolled up the back windows. Monte sighed, curled up, and lay down in the back seat.

Lunch with Susan went very well even though Patrick hadn't seen her for twenty years. She and Carol got along splendidly. Patrick had a vague memory of Susan having been president of their high school French Club, but he had taken Spanish, and Carol had barely gotten through German. He listened nervously to each sentence Carol uttered, but they all made sense.

Just north of Moab, Utah, they made a slight detour. Abby had told them Arches National Park was not to be missed, so they had dropped down to I-70 and were taking the southern route in.

Somewhere along the way Patrick had picked up a book called *UFO USA: A Traveler's Guide to UFO Sightings, Abduction Sites, Crop Circles, and Other Unexplained Phenomena*. ("A state-by state guide to weird shit and delusional behavior," Patrick had declared happily. "How did I ever do without it?") The book said that just off I-70 near Green River, Utah, was the Utah Launch Complex, which had been closed down in the seventies but had in recent years been the sight of much unexplained nighttime aerial activity. So when they passed by the Green River exit, Patrick, who was driving, turned off and headed south down a gravel road. Carol reached back and rolled the window down so Monte could check things out. There had been no more fights since Seattle.

Eastern Utah was brown and dry. The subdued rock formations in the distance promised scenery but didn't quite deliver. The air that blew through the open window felt like it came from a clothes dryer left on too long. To their left the interstate paralleled the gravel road. To their right were a few scattered buildings, prefab huts with corrugated tin siding. It looked as if there might be some larger buildings off toward the rock formations, but it would be a long walk off the road to find out.

"The book claims that this is where the military moved all its secret alien-related activity when Area 51 got too much publicity," Patrick said.

"Doesn't look too active to me," Carol said. "When was that book published?"

"1998, '99, I think."

"Uh-huh." A few years ago Patrick had found an online reference to some reported UFO sightings near the town in North Carolina where he had been born. The sightings had occurred in the mid 1970's, when he was in high school. Neither he nor anyone in his family had remembered hearing anything about it at the time. Patrick and his brother decided that they had been abducted and made a great show of plotting out a course of hypnotherapy to recover their lost memories. They had all had a laugh, but ever since then Patrick had been quietly accumulating UFO books. Carol had chosen not to worry about it.

"Oh, well," Patrick said. "Another of life's disappointments. It is kind of creepy, though."

"So it is. Ready to get back on the highway?"

"I guess so—no, wait." He pulled the car gently off the gravel road in front of one of the huts. "Got to record this for posterity." He lifted the camera out of the back seat and started to get out of the car. Monte's tail thumped expectantly.

"Patrick!"

"What?"

"You sure you want to get out here?"

"Why not? As you reminded me back in Seattle, we're not in Arkansas anymore. Afraid someone will shoot us?"

"Well, if this is still military property, then, actually, yes."

Patrick paused. The previous fall, while attending a conference in Washington, D.C., they had gotten lost behind the Capitol building well after dark. Patrick had stopped the car and gotten out to ask directions from a couple of security guards. He took three steps toward them when he realized he was a stranger approaching men with guns guarding the post-9/11 U.S. Capitol building behind a sandbagged barricade. He raised his hands, and the guards told him how to get back to the Beltway.

He got out of the car. "There's nobody around. I'm just going to take a picture. Be right back."

He walked closer to the hut, glancing frequently down at the ground to see exactly where he was placing his feet. At a rest stop in Montana there had been a sign urging travelers to stay on the marked pathways because of rattlesnakes. The hut was rectangular, about the size of a double-wide. The relentless sun brought out every stain and pockmark on the corrugated siding. There was a wide double door in the middle, as big as a garage door. It was padlocked. To the left was a utility pole leaning precariously away from the hut. To the right was a rusted-out fuel pump.

There was a rustle behind Patrick and he turned around quickly. "Mulder, it's me," Carol said. She had Monte on a leash.

"Watch where you step." Patrick turned back and snapped two shots of the hut, then walked around to the side of the building.

"Where are you going?" Carol called.

"Monte's not the only one who needs a walk."

Carol snorted. "God, guys will just pee anywhere, won't they?"

Patrick walked behind the hut and unzipped. When he was finished he looked at the side of the hut and saw there was a back door, a single door much smaller than the padlocked front entrance. It stood partially open. He walked over and looked inside, but he couldn't see anything. He looked carefully around, wondering with some degree of seriousness if the brutal sunlight would permit him to see a laser target point if one should appear suddenly on his chest. Then he pushed the door back and stepped inside.

Out of the sun the temperature immediately dropped, and then it seemed to drop some more. It was so dry outside he hadn't really been sweating, but the back of his shirt was damp from hours against the car seat. Now his entire back felt chilled, and he couldn't see anything in the dark. He blinked repeatedly and waited for his eyes to adjust.

When they did it didn't make much difference. The hut was empty. The floor was some sort of plastic and gave slightly under his feet. The whole place was covered in dirt and cobwebs and smelled like their basement back home. He started to walk further into the hut, and then the chill in his back spread all over his body as he realized that if he had been worried about snakes out there he also ought to be worried about them in here. He stood still and looked carefully at the floor around him. He saw nothing but heard something that wasn't a rattle, exactly, but it seemed to come from the floor on the other side, and it started getting louder, and he almost leaped through the back door.

When he got back to the front of the hut Carol and Monte

were both back in the car. He plopped down in the driver's seat and pulled back on to the interstate.

"See any aliens?"

"Nope."

"Sorry."

When they got off the interstate again to go to the Arches, Patrick looked in the rearview mirror and saw that his face was, not burned, but darkened as if by heavy makeup. "Guess I need a stronger sunscreen," he said.

"What?"

"Nothing."

By the time they reached the entrance to the Arches, Patrick was approximately the same deep gold as his wedding ring. By the time they reached the north end of the park, he was not. Carol had not appeared to notice any change.

They stared out at the Devil's Garden, at colors and shapes Patrick had never seen before, and he asked, "You can understand what I'm saying, right?"

"Most of the time," said Carol, and took another picture.

Southeast of Aspen, in a grove of aspens, Patrick had a meltdown. They had spent five days with Abby and her family in Eagle, Colorado, just outside of Vail. (Both Melissa and Abby were from Carol's first marriage. Mercifully, Patrick and his ex-wife had not had children.) It had been a good visit, although he was still unsettled by the odd moments outside of Bellevue and Moab. Truth to tell, he was unsettled by the fact that he was unsettled. Back home he had several shelves of books on unexplained phenomena. Now, confronted with undeniable phenomena and denied explanation, forced to deal with strangeness in strange places, he recoiled. He wanted nothing more to happen.

But on this trip as on all the others Patrick was still determined to see something he had not seen before at every stage of the journey. So instead of beginning the long drive home by heading east toward Denver, he suggested they detour and double-back to see more of the scenery and to check out Aspen, where they had never been. Carol was still on a contact high from the grandchildren and universally agreeable.

The result had been a prolonged and dizzying drive over mountain roads that were high and narrow even for the Rockies. Patrick, whose spirit adored the mountains but whose inner ear rebelled against heights, was terrified. Carol, whose love for travel had to be abetted by Dramamine before any long drive, and who was five days more exhausted than she had been in Seattle, forgot the grandchildren and was not happy. Even after they made it down to a lower altitude and slightly wider road, she reiterated her unhappiness. Not as profoundly as in Melissa's driveway, but profoundly enough. Monte lay in the back with his head between his paws.

Patrick pulled off the road and got out. He walked rapidly away from the car, more slowly down an embankment into the grove of aspens. He leaned against a lightning-blasted stump that was taller than he was and listened to the wind rushing through the tops of the trees.

Carol walked up to him. "Patrick, come on. Don't act like this. I'm just saying—"

"No, you're not." He looked past her at Monte's head poking out of the car window. "You're not just saying anything. You never *just say* anything. You declare, you assert, you belittle, you berate, you pontificate, occasionally you excoriate. You bitch and you moan. But you never, ever *just say* anything."

She stopped cold as if she had seen a snake. Patrick saw the hurt in her face and instantly regretted everything he had just said. He was exhausted and his head was still spinning from the drive down the mountain. But he kept talking. "I'm sick of this shit. Why do we do this? Why do we keep taking these trips? All we do is go out and come back. Why bother?"

"So what would you rather do? Stay home? What do you want?"

"I don't know." He sank down to the ground, squatting but still leaning against the stump. He looked up at the aspens. Their trunks were a mottled white. They looked diseased, but he knew they weren't. The branches didn't start until near the top. They were as tall as the Carolina pines of his youth but much thinner. The wind through the branches was unceasing and drowned out the cars from the road.

He looked back down. Carol stood over him with her arms folded across her chest, staring down at the ground. Not at him. He looked at her and suddenly, painfully, recognized her beauty. Middle age had been kind to her so far, kinder than to him. But her eyes looked tired.

She turned without speaking and walked back to the car. He thought of the worst fight they had ever had, ten years earlier on the way back from California. Carol had her own meltdown in New Mexico, and Patrick thought their relationship would end right there by the White Sands nuclear testing ground. But by the time they got to Roswell everything had been okay. "Carol—"

"Monte needs a walk," she said. He could barely hear her above the aspens in the wind.

What he did hear was the sound of a dog barking off to his right. He looked in the direction of the sound and saw a black tail disappearing into the bushes that grew beneath the trees. He looked back to the car and saw that it was empty. "You're going in the wrong direction," he called.

"What? Oh, goddammit, Monte! How did you get out?"

"He jumped out the window."

"He *never* jumps out the window." She ran to the car, reached in, and grabbed Monte's leash.

Patrick stood with some effort. The dizziness was better, but his legs were asleep. "Come on, let's get him."

They moved deeper into the woods. Monte stayed in sight but always just beyond their reach. Monte was the best-natured dog they had ever had, but also the most hard-headed. They had never managed to train him to stay put and were both almost morbidly afraid of his getting hit by a car. They never let him off the leash except in an enclosed run.

"Monte! Here, boy!"

"If we just stay put, he'll come back," Patrick said.

"Before he heads back to the road and darts in front of a car? Monte! God damn it dog, get over here!"

They made their way through the bushes, Carol calling Monte unceasingly, Patrick not taking his eye off the distant dark blot of their dog while cursing his decision to wear shorts. Then they abruptly found themselves in a clearing. On the other side of the clearing, less than a hundred feet from them, between two aspens that stood apart from the other trees, was an open door. The ground rose up sharply behind the trees, and the door leaned into the rise at enough of an angle to make it look like the entrance to a storm cellar. Monte was sniffing and pacing frantically in front of the open door.

"Jesus Christ," Patrick said.

"Monte! Don't you go in there!" Carol called.

They walked closer. The door was plain wood, white like the aspens but unmottled, with no knob. It lay open to the left of a perfectly even rectangular hole into the rise of ground.

"He was probably chasing a rabbit, and it ran in there," Carol said.

"If it had been a rabbit, he would have dashed right in after it. Do they even have rabbits at this altitude?"

"Come on, Monte," Carol coaxed, walking toward him. "Good dog."

"Hold on," Patrick said. He sat down on the ground. "You said sometimes he'll come back if you do this. Here, Monte!"

Monte took a few steps toward Patrick, then turned and ran through the open doorway.

"Great," Carol said. She started toward the door.

"Wait a minute. Let's just stay here. He'll come back out."

"Well, let's at least get closer."

Patrick got up, and they moved directly in front of the doorway. They waited. The wind continued to rush through the trees. Abbey had said that the root systems of the aspens were intertwined, and that a grove of aspens was essentially a single organism. Each tree seemed to carry the wind down to its roots. To stand in a grove of aspens was to stand in the middle of a living, breathing thing.

They waited, but Monte did not reappear.

Carol sighed and moved into the doorway. She still had Monte's leash in her hand.

"Wait! Let me go first."

"I'll go. I'm dressed for it." Unlike Patrick, Carol had dressed for the altitude in jeans, boots, and a light leather jacket.

"I'll go with you."

"Doesn't look like there's room for both of us." They couldn't tell how far in the entrance went, but it didn't look as if it widened out beyond the width of the door itself.

"I'll be right behind you."

"No, you just stay here." Carol paused. "Or is that too much of a declaration, or an assertion? God knows I wouldn't want to pontificate."

"Carol, look, I'm sorry, I'm just tired, we're both tired—"

"Bitch, bitch. Moan, moan," Carol chanted as she stepped through the doorway and promptly disappeared.

Patrick waited a few seconds, then called, "Carol? You okay?"

"So far. Here, Monte! Here, pooch."

"Can you see?"

"Yeah, there's still light from the entrance. It doesn't seem to go too far back. And there's some kind of light from the walls—that's weird. Dog, where are you?"

"What do you mean, light from the walls?"

Silence. "Carol?" No reply. "Carol, you OK?"

The wind continued to blow.

Patrick ran his hands through what was left of his hair and stepped through the doorway.

Carol was right; initially the entrance was no wider than the door. The sides of the hallway pressed in on him. Patrick knew that, technically, it was probably a cave, but caves didn't have doors, did they?

Then things widened out, and he found himself in a space about the same size as the hut in Utah. The walls were, indeed, glowing. He looked down at his feet and felt a plastic floor spring slightly beneath him.

He looked around. The walls didn't look like rocks or dirt. They seemed as smooth as the floor.

Carol wasn't there. Neither was Monte. He couldn't hear the wind in here, but he did hear something that sounded not quite like a rattle, and was getting louder.

The next thing he knew he was back in the clearing. He assumed he had walked out under his own power. He sank to his knees and then lay flat with his cheek pressed to the leaves and the dirt. The wind rushed above him and the trees swayed around him and beneath him the roots pulsed and pushed upward to answer the wind.

When he finally got up, it was getting dark. He made his way back to his car and stood by it, trembling. Other cars rushed by on their way to Aspen.

Then he got in the car and drove back to Seattle.

He stopped only for fuel and bathrooms and once to sleep fitfully at a rest area in southern Idaho. Each time he woke, he thought of the night in Arkansas he had gotten the call offering him the faculty position in Boston, and Carol coming home from an evening class, and the look on her face when he told her they were leaving for something better, a look that said, *I will love you anyplace and always*, and at the same time, *I no longer have to love you despite the circumstances*. Never had he felt more of a success.

The door was still there among the trees and the homes that spoke money. He pushed it open and walked through, bracing himself for a plastic floor and a not-quite rattling noise.

But what was behind the door was the same as what was in front of the door, except for a dim view of a large house back behind the trees, and Carol holding Monte safely on his leash.

He walked over and took her by the hand and led her and their dog back through the door to where they had been before.

"I don't understand any of this," Carol said.

"*Les vrais voyageurs sont ceux-la seuls qui partent pour partir,*" Patrick said.

"What?"

"I don't either. Let's go home."

In the electronics section of the Wal-Mart Supercenter in Salem, Massachusetts, they opened the pictures from their trip. Every last one was blank. A few had soft white spots radiating from the center, like a stain, or a peephole, or a newborn sun.

THE DEEP END

Breathless, Charlie floated toward the light.
He rose in silence with nothing to either side. No motion but his own. He lay as still as he could, rigid, legs together, arms stiff by his sides. A comfortable coolness surrounded him. He felt it on every inch of his body except the space around his eyes that let him focus on the light.

As he got closer, he could hear muffled sounds from above. Now there were dark shapes moving at the edge of his vision, but he ignored them. His goal was the light.

Closer . . . closer . . .

Suddenly one of the dark shapes moved directly above him. Instinctively, Charlie loosened his body and tried to float past it, but he was too late. He floated directly into it. A soft bump, a violent thrashing about, a sharp blow to Charlie's chest, and the coolness and the quiet went away.

"Ow! Watch it, doofus!"

Charlie whirled on the surface of the pool, clutching his chest where the boy he had collided with had kicked him. The boy looked older, but Charlie's diving mask had fogged up and he couldn't tell for sure. He was certainly bigger. "Watch where you're going! Jeez!" The other boy slapped both his hands on the water, giving Charlie what should have been a choking splash, but his mask protected his eyes and nose, and he had been splashed often enough to know when to close his mouth. Charlie fell back below the surface, flipped over, and swam away as fast as he could, scissor-kicking like his dad had taught him, left arm still wrapped around his chest.

Charlie followed the downward slope of the pool bottom toward the deep end. At the deepest point, directly below the diving board, there was a drain cover set into the concrete bottom. Just like the pool he swam in back home in Virginia, where it was trouble if anyone saw you getting too close. *You want to get stuck if the pump comes on?* (And rumors of much worse: *I heard some guy sat in the drain when it was on and it sucked his guts out of his ass!* Charlie didn't believe that for a minute. Who would be that stupid?) But also like back home, the pump in this Kansas hotel pool was loud, and you could tell immediately if it was on. Right now it was quiet, so the pump was off.

Except the drain cover was pushed to one side, and in the space between the edge of the cover and the side of the opening, the water was swirling. Not the whirlpool of the pump in operation, but churning like the water was boiling. Like there was something thrashing around in the drain.

Charlie wanted to edge closer for a better look, but the collision had knocked out whatever breath he had stored up. He was out of air. Two kicks brought him to the surface, where he gasped, inhaled, and dove back toward the deep end.

The cover was still off, but the churning had stopped. He floated to one side of the drain and peered into the opening but could see nothing except, a couple of feet down, the beginnings of the pump hardware. Maybe it wasn't as loud as he thought.

This time, as he made his way back to the top, Charlie made sure there was nobody above him. His chest wasn't so sore now. He broke the surface and immediately began sweeping the water with both arms while pumping his legs beneath the water in the bike-riding movement his dad promised would keep him both vertical and above the surface. *Your body wants to float. Unless something's weighing you down, you don't have to sink.* Unless you want to, Charlie had thought, even back then, when he was little and first learning how to swim.

Charlie lay back in the half-tread, half-float that was his favorite way to stay on the surface. He bit down on the snorkel attached to his mask, exhaled into it sharply to clear it of water, and then took several breaths through it, not because he needed to, but because he wanted to. The mask and snorkel weren't just prize possessions—they were the true signal of summer. When he pulled them out of the box that spent most of the year on the top shelf of his bedroom closet, that meant summer was here and it was time to go to the pool.

His big sister Katie made fun of him, as usual. *So you need to see the sharks coming in the pool? Or is there treasure buried in the deep end? I know—you're just waiting for a girl to lose her top underwater so you can get a good look!*

Charlie ignored her like he always did. The mask and snorkel made him feel—connected. When he floated face down, all he could hear was the sound of his own breath funneled in and out of the snorkel. Then the dive: bending the top half of his body down, throwing his legs up as straight as he could, and letting their weight push him beneath the surface. He could see clearly, even if it was just bare concrete walls, and the closest thing to treasure was an occasional hair clip or pair of sunglasses. Every once in a while, when people crashed through the water after jumping off the diving board, as they hurled toward the bottom, they did almost lose their swimsuits, female and male, kids and adults. Charlie couldn't help noticing the sudden curves of skin so much paler than the rest of their bodies—not that he would ever admit that to Katie. The mask and snorkel didn't just connect him to this underwater world—they made it his world.

Which was why when Mom had talked about packing as efficiently as possible for the trip to Kansas, he campaigned to take his mask and snorkel for the hotel pool he and Katie had been promised. The fact that he knew he couldn't take his swim fins—both heel straps had torn off—gave him some leverage, and he looked on in triumph as his mother wrapped the mask in his swimming trunks and laid them in his suitcase. He laid the snorkel by them himself.

Now, after a few more satisfying breaths, he spat out the mouthpiece, took off the mask, and clutched its strap tightly while he looked around. This pool was never as crowded as the one back home, but today there were a lot of people, both in and out of the water. He looked for his mother and saw her reclining in the glaring white lounge chair that was twice as big as any of the folding chairs they normally took poolside. She was reading a magazine and sipping through a straw from some big drink in a plastic cup. He turned a full circle in the water, looking quickly past the kiddie pool. (Ick! Might as well go swimming in a toilet.) He had never been happier than when, three years ago, when he was six, his rapid progress as a swimmer had convinced his parents to let him go in the regular pool. He saw some older girls talking with some older boys and noted that one of the girls was Katie, taking full advantage of Dad being in meetings all day. The lifeguard was sitting in a wooden chair built into the top of a narrow platform that rose above the diving board. The lifeguards back home were sometimes not much older than Katie, but this one looked almost as old as Charlie's dad. By the diving board there were three boys talking. He thought one of them might be the boy he had bumped into when he floated up from the bottom of the pool, and he quickly looked past them.

There were a lot of things Charlie just didn't get about this trip, beginning with why they were supposed to think it was a vacation to travel from their home in Virginia to Kansas City just to hang out at a hotel while his father attended yet another one of the conferences he had been sent to with his new government job—*a soldier in President Johnson's War on Poverty,* his mom had said, *and this time we're going with him to the front.* Or why he had to share a room with Katie instead of having his own room (and if it was too expensive like his mom said, then why not just all of them stay in one room and save even more money? *Grow up, little boy,* Katie had snorted—her answer to pretty much everything.) The trip out had been exhausting, although the parks in the mountains were fun, and Katie and he had found it equally funny that Dad had made such a deal about their having breakfast in Paris when they stopped in Paris, Kentucky. And there was the pool. Not as big as the one back home, which was a lot nicer than either the scuzzy old club house or the tiny golf course that went along with it. But he had a pool to swim in here, and that was enough for Charlie.

People swam differently out here, though. They spent all their time on the surface. Few of the other kids back in Virginia were underwater as much as Charlie, but most of them spent at least some time beneath the surface, diving, floating from the bottom to the surface, seeing how long they could stay under, how close they could come to swimming from one side to the other while holding their breath. Some of them had their own masks, although Charlie was by far the youngest who did. Sometimes a couple of the older boys who didn't care about lifeguards or parents or rumors about losing your guts would grab the drain cover and use it to help them stay submerged.

But here in Kansas everyone was either splashing around in the shallow end or just swimming back and forth from one end of the pool to the other, stroking and kicking like they were in the Olympics. Charlie wondered if it had anything to do with being in the middle of the country instead of near the coast where he lived, but truth was he just couldn't figure it out.

That was why he'd bumped into that guy. He wasn't used to everyone being there on the surface. It wasn't his fault.

Charlie put his mask back on, left the snorkel hanging, inhaled and exhaled three times, held the last enormous breath, and dove beneath the surface. Yesterday he had gotten halfway the width of the pool underwater with no problem, so today he ought to be able to make it. He knew he was supposed to empty his lungs rather than filling them if he wanted to stay submerged, but the extra time he could stay under made up for the extra effort.

He could tell there were people passing above him and kept pushing forward, determined there would be no more collisions. Between strokes, he looked down. The drain cover was now completely off, sitting on the bottom to one side of the opening. He tried to turn and push back down toward the deep end, but his momentum had carried him farther than he realized. When he bumped against the wall, scraping his right shoulder, he forgot about the drain cover and popped to the surface.

His mother was still sipping her drink and reading her magazine. That was another thing weird about the trip—how she kept to herself. At the pool back home, she was always with a bunch of the other moms, working on their tans, talking almost nonstop, ignoring him and Katie except when, at least once each visit, she made him get out of the water and lie out on a big towel by her folding chair. *I know you're half fish, but that doesn't mean you have to look like the belly of one. Now stay put and get some sun.* So he'd lie there, dying to get back in the water, and listen to her and the other moms talking:

—*Just look at old Jerry Stallings, strutting around like he's cock of the walk with that new wife of his.* —*I know, it's just a sin, with Marla barely in the ground.* —*He sure didn't make things easy for her, did he?* —*And those trunks! What is that, French?* —*Not like he has anything the rest of them don't....* —*That boy of yours loves the water, doesn't he?...* —*What about that boy Katie's been dating?* —*Oh, Don doesn't have much use for him.* —*Honey, Donald McGuire isn't going to have any use for any boy coming around after his daughter and you know it....* —*Sons are not one bit easier, believe you me. I swear I'd rather he went to a whorehouse every Saturday night than spend one more minute with that Creel girl....* —*The doctor said it wasn't anything to worry about, but I'm just not sure. At least I can count on him for the Valium....* —*All right, Charlie, you can go back in.*

But here, she just lay out with her magazine and kept sipping on her drink.

He threw his arms over the rounded stones that outlined the

sides of the pool and took off his mask. Despite all the water splashing over them, they felt hot. "Hey, Mom!"

She looked up, smiled, and said something he couldn't hear over the splashing and yelling. Someone's radio played "Summer in the City." Katie loved that song. On that, they agreed.

"What?"

He half-heard, half read on her lips, "You'd better go see your friend," and she pointed to an unknown spot behind him.

He turned around, keeping an arm on the hot stones. Gail, the girl he had met at the pool the first day they were here, sat on the edge of the other side, kicking her legs in the water and waving at him. He realized she was calling his name: "Chaaar-lie!"

He looked up at his mother, wanting to say something grown up like, "Gotta run," but she had already turned back to her magazine. So he braced his feet against the side of the pool just under the water, pushed off, and dove down at the same time. He looked down to his right and saw that the drain cover was still off. The water in the opening looked like it was churning again, but from this far away he couldn't be sure. He wanted to swim down and check it out. But he also wanted to swim to the other side completely underwater and surface right in front of Gail. Unfortunately, he didn't have enough air to do either.

When he came up he was more than halfway across. Gail was a blur through his mask, but he could tell she was still kicking her legs in the water. He went back under, and before he could decide which direction to take, he found himself on the other side, still underwater directly below her. As much as he wanted to reach out and grab her by the ankles and pull her in the water, he still remembered their conversation on their first day at the hotel and contented himself with popping up at the wall right by her.

She looked down at him accusingly. "Hey! Didn't you hear me?"

"Sorry. It's pretty loud around here." It was. As the day got hotter and more people poured into the pool, the noise level rose accordingly. There was a radio on this side, too, playing "Easier Said than Done," which was an old one—he only ever heard it back home on the Sunday night oldies show. And here it was the middle of the week. They even did radio different around here.

"I guess," she said. Her kicking slowed but didn't stop.

He still had his mask on. The first time he had it on in front of her, Gail said that with his nose covered he sounded like he had a cold. He thought it made his voice sound deeper. Not that he would tell her that. "So are you ready to try it?"

"Try what?"

"You know." Now he did reach out as if to grab her ankle.

"No!" She pulled her foot away and then brought it back through the water, splashing him. "I told you I'm not ready."

"I thought you said you liked to swim."

"I do! But I'm not ready to put my head under."

"Sissy."

"I'm a girl. I can't be a sissy."

"Can too."

"Can't can't can't can *not!*" She splashed him again. "Besides, Mama just fixed my hair." He thought Gail's hair was probably really long, but he didn't know for sure because she always kept it wrapped around her head, held in place by a huge hair clip. "And there's nothing to see, either. It's not like it's the ocean, with fish and stuff."

He had had this same conversation with her each day since their families arrived, and it always stopped right there. Charlie's home in Virginia was less than an hour from the coast. In the summer they went to the beach at least once a month, and while Katie couldn't wait to get there, Charlie was less enthusiastic. It was kind of exciting being in water that was always moving, but in the shallows, which was as far out as his parents would let him go, the water and the sand were constantly churning into each other. Even on a sunny day the water was gray, and if there was anything interesting beneath the surface it didn't matter because you couldn't see two feet in front of you. The pool was better.

"Besides, you told me it took you a long time before you could duck your head."

"When I was *six*. Gah." He looked past her to the people sunning on the patio beyond the pool. Katie was still there, still talking to the same group of boys. She looked in his direction, smiled and waved. Smiled? Waved? Something else that never happened back home.

"So you're just going to sit there and not come in?"

"Maybe in a little bit." She kicked her legs in the water again but this time without splashing him.

"Ok," he said, and pushed off toward the deep end. He paused to let the teenager on the diving board do her cannonball into the water. When she surfaced, shrieking happily, he bent at the waist and dove. As the water covered him he felt a sting where he had scraped his shoulder on the side wall of the pool. Halfway down he looked back up and saw the blurred image of Gail on the other side of the water. He thought she was smiling at him, but he wasn't sure. He also saw a small dark blob suspended near him. His shoulder must be bleeding. He'd need to get a band-aid when he got out of the pool.

The water still swirled from where the girl had cannonballed in. It looked like she had almost hit bottom before she shot back up. Charlie moved through the turbulence and went deeper. He wanted to see what was up with the drain cover. He wanted not to be talking with Gail and trying to think what to say next. He wanted, he realized for the first time since they had arrived, to go home where things were as he knew them to be.

But right now he just wanted to look at the drain cover. As he pushed himself toward the bottom, the pressure started against his ears. There was no nose clip on his mask, but he pushed its lower lip hard against his nose and blew until his ears popped. He kept moving down until he reached the bottom.

The cover still lay by the drain opening. It was coated in something that looked slimy. The water around the opening was still, and there was no sound. It was safe to approach.

Charlie pulled himself along the bottom with his hands. The chlorine was making his shoulder sting even more. His breath was Ok, but the air in his lungs kept pushing him up. He peered into the drain.

The water in the opening started to churn—and an arm reached for him.

It had a hand and fingers, but it wasn't a regular human arm. It was something else. The wrist was too thick for the rest of it, and it was all covered in the same slimy stuff that covered the drain cover. The hand touched the front of his mask.

Thirteen feet underwater, Charlie screamed. All the air went out of his lungs and bubbled in front of him, so that he couldn't see the drain or the arm that reached out of it. He backpedaled on the bottom like he was on land and felt the concrete scrape his feet. Then he pushed and shot himself back to the surface, kicking and thrusting as hard as he could.

When he broke the surface he choked and sputtered and gasped for breath, but before he could refill his lungs an arm pushed his head back under the water. He screamed again, thinking the arm had come out of the drain after him.

But when the arm quit pushing and he came back up, gasping, he saw that it was attached to the boy he had collided with earlier. There were two other boys with him.

"Hey, squirt," the boy said. He motioned to one of the others, who reached out, ripped Charlie's mask off, and tossed it away. Charlie heard a small splash where it fell, through the noise of all the people in the pool who weren't paying any attention to what was happening to him.

The other two boys were the same size as the first one. They were all older than Charlie, maybe in junior high.

"You know what this is, little boy? This is traffic court," the first boy said. "We need to teach you the rules of the road. You can't just be running into people."

Charlie sputtered and tried to tell the boy what he had seen, but the boy splashed water in his face, which started him choking again.

"Shut up, punk! I'm doing the talking here."

"Don't be looking for the lifeguard," one of the other boys said. "He's on break."

"Taking a leak," the third boy said.

"Getting laid," the second said, and they all laughed.

Charlie hadn't even thought to look for a lifeguard. He never paid attention to the lifeguard. He didn't need a lifeguard. He was a good swimmer. He looked around frantically for his mother, for Katie, but he couldn't see them anywhere.

"What'll we do with him?" the first boy asked.

"Take him and toss him in the ladies' room!"

"Take his trunks off!"

"Take his trunks off and then toss him in the ladies' room!"

They all laughed again. Charlie splashed and circled and looked for a way out, but they circled with him.

"Let's drown him for a while first and then we'll figure out what to do." The first boy moved toward him, followed by the other two. Three sets of arms moved in and pushed him back under the water.

The arms, and then their whole bodies, pressed down and kept Charlie under the water. He had been able to take a breath before they pushed him under, but not much of one. He swirled and punched and kicked and tried to get away. One of his kicks connected with something that felt like a swimsuit that had something soft and bulging beneath it. Suddenly there was an opening as one of the boys pushed away. He yelled so loud when he broke the surface Charlie could hear him under the water.

Charlie twisted, turned, and plunged through the opening. This was his chance.

But instead of getting to the surface where there was air and his mom and Katie, and his dad somewhere, he felt his body bend at the waist and push itself back toward the bottom. Toward the drain.

He knew he was out of air, but somehow he was able to keep moving. He had to keep moving. Something was pulling him down. His head knew he should be drowning, knew he should resist, but his arms and legs kept pushing him down to the bottom—and his lungs amazingly did not complain. He swam out of the churning water where the boys had corralled him into the clean transparency of the bottom of the pool. It was like looking through a telescope. It was like that song where the singer said he could see for miles.

When he reached the drain, the arm was still there. Now it was attached to a shoulder, and through the telescope view Charlie thought he saw a head emerging. It had eyes and teeth. It looked like the monster they had watched in that movie about Florida, then it looked like pictures he had seen of sharks, then it didn't look like anything he had ever seen at all. The eyes didn't change. They stared at Charlie and made him want to go closer. If he could just go a couple more feet things wouldn't be strange anymore. Things would be just as they were supposed to be, and he'd never have to get out of the water again.

The creature in the drain reached out, and Charlie felt as if he could breathe normally if he wanted to. He extended his own hand.

Then he felt another hand grab his left ankle, and yet another grab his right. He tried to kick them away. He didn't understand anything that was happening, but he knew where he wanted to go.

The hands on his ankles held firm. As they pulled him away, he could see the eyes and the teeth and the head squeezing back into the drain through the water that was churning and bubbling again. Then the shoulder and the arm followed, and finally the hand that, before it disappeared entirely, grabbed the drain cover and pulled it back in place with a clunk Charlie could hear as clearly as he had ever heard anything. And now the water was still. He felt his feet hit the air, and then the rest of his body, and finally his gasping, crying mouth and chlorine-burned eyes.

They laid him by the side of the pool. The sun filled his burning eyes, but he squinted and saw it was Katie. And Gail. Gail's hair was wet and hanging in tangles down beyond her shoulders. It really was long. Katie was yelling at him, and Gail may have been crying, but Charlie wasn't sure. His mother appeared, pushed the girls aside, and knelt down to see after her son.

Later Katie told him that Gail had seen the boys circling Charlie and had yelled for help. Katie heard and jumped in after him, and Gail followed her. When Charlie asked her what it was like to finally stick her head under the water, Gail said, "It was awful! It burned my eyes. I couldn't see hardly anything." Then she punched him in the shoulder, right where he had scraped it, and told him how scared she had been, using a word that Charlie had only heard other boys use.

His mother insisted that they go home. Dad wasn't too happy about missing the last day of his meetings—*He's all right, isn't he? Just keep him out of that goddamned pool*—but Mom just stood there and stared at him, and Katie, who, like Charlie, usually got as far away as she could from their parents' arguments, stood right there by her. So Dad tracked down the lifeguard who hadn't been there and yelled at him, and Mom found the parents of the boys who had gone after Charlie and yelled at them. The lifeguard just said something about boys being boys and didn't seem too concerned. Two of the boys' parents said they were sorry and would punish their boys. The third boy, the one Charlie had run into, only had his father with him, and his father just said the same thing the lifeguard had said. Katie said they ought to sue the hotel but Mom gave her the same kind of stare she had given Dad and Katie didn't say anything else.

Just before they left the hotel, Charlie's mom asked him if he had packed his mask and snorkel, and it wasn't until then that Charlie realized he had never gone back and gotten it from wherever the boys had thrown it. Katie went to look for it but couldn't find it.

Charlie didn't say anything immediately about what he'd seen coming out of the drain. He thought about it for the whole long drive back, and when they got home he decided he wouldn't say anything. He almost wrote to Gail about it after she started sending him postcards, but he didn't do that, either.

How could he explain to anyone that when he had moved toward the creature in the drain, he had felt safe, and when he had looked into its eyes, he had seen himself?

He couldn't tell anyone that. Ever.

When they got home Dad bought him a new mask and snorkel, and new fins that were full-foot and didn't have a strap that would break. Charlie put them in the closet, but it took him until almost Labor Day before he could stick his head under the water again.

Even when he did, he didn't dare open his eyes.

NYLON SEAM

I don't want nothing from no machine
With no ragged edges and crystal clean

Dave is into Eddie for two thousand dollars and has no idea how he is going to pay it back. He tried Harold, but Harold was tapped out. He tried Max, but Max's terms were even worse than Eddie's. He even tried Tight Albert Morrison. Tight Albert told him to fuck off.

Plastic, processed, boring, bland
Wouldn't make noise with a marching band

Worst of all, Dave knows that Martine will leave if he doesn't have any money. She says she won't, but he knows she will. It is for her he accumulated the debt in the first place. She says he didn't have to, but he knows he did.

I want a story with a twisted theme

Dave's only remaining option is to go see John Schwartz and offer his services. Dave does not want to do this. Word is Uncle John always has a job that will pay you more than you're worth, but what he expects from you later on may not be worth the price.

Trace down the length of your nylon seam
The breeze from the window fan does nothing to cool the room but ripples Martine's skirt as she adjusts her hose. She is talking to someone on the phone. She says it's her sister, but he knows it isn't. Dave sits on the edge of the bed, smoking, paralyzed by his insurmountable debt and the vision of her cherry-red toenails.

Neckline low and hemline high
A splendid evocation of the back of your thigh
There is a long-standing rumor that no one has ever seen Uncle John when he was not sitting behind his desk. His enormous gut starts at his breastbone and flops onto the desktop. He smokes a cigarette in a long black holder and reads a newspaper that lies flat on his desk. Dave's eyes rest on an upside-down headline. He deciphers, SENATOR BOXER GRILLS ATTORNEY GENERAL. "I'm Dave Johnson. I hear you have a job needs doing. Local. Quick."

Your half-open mouth as red as juice
A torn fishnet turns the seafood loose
Uncle John hangs up the phone, satisfied. "OK, kid." He hands Dave a package wrapped in brown paper and tied with twine. It is just big enough to hold a DVD player or perhaps an assortment of garden seeds. "Ocean Forest Hotel, Room 334. Give the package to Mr. Lawrence and nobody else."

A genuine pulp Technicolor dream
Brush my finger down your nylon seam
As Dave walks past Uncle John's secretary in the outer office she stands behind her desk with one leg in her chair. Her skirt drapes her naked thigh as she rolls her knee-high stockings down.

Ankle-strap, spike-heel, painted toes
Two thousand miles of open road
    He stops off to tell Martine they will soon have the money they need, but she isn't there. Perhaps she is at her sister's.

I don't know, but I've been told
A seam-legged woman don't never run cold
    The Ocean Forest Hotel is indeed by the ocean, but the nearest forest is ten miles inland. The front doors are bigger than Dave's apartment. He walks into the lobby and wonders where Martine really is. A newspaper lies on the phone table by the elevator. The headline reads, SENATOR CHURCH GRILLS CIA CHIEF.

Seize my breath and clutch my heart
A living work of cover art
    The elevator takes its time getting to the third floor. The elevator operator reads a paperback novel with a woman in the cover whose gauzy dress is flipped up nearly to her waist as she rolls her fishnet stockings down. Dave has read the novel. He remembers a passage in which the narrator discusses a mob boss whose wife was so wanton that when he was away he would not permit her to keep any clothes in their penthouse suite. When he was not there she was trapped, naked, in the penthouse, unable to walk out the door.

Down and dirty and a little mean
Split wide open your nylon seam
    Dave walks down the hallway to room 334 and knocks on the door. The woman who opens the door is naked and holding a pair of white stockings attached to a garter belt. She looks a bit like Martine, but not quite. She bends down and picks up the newspaper that lies in front of the door. After glancing at the front page,

she holds out a hand to Dave. It takes him a moment, but he finally says, "I was told to give this only to Mr. Lawrence."

The twenty-first century is blurred and faint
Give me cigarettes and lead-based paint
She steps aside. Dave sees a man sitting on a sofa, smoking, wearing a trenchcoat, but his legs are bare and he wears house slippers. "Stay out there. Slide it across the floor." Through a doorway behind him another woman who looks nothing like Martine sits on the edge of a bed and rolls her sheer black stockings down.

Sex in sinful and can ruin a man
Blot your lips 'neath that slow-turning fan
As Dave walks back toward the elevator, all the other doors open at once. Out of each doorway steps a naked woman. They all bend down and pick up the newspapers that lie in front of all the doors. Some of the naked women pause to read the headline: SENATOR KEFAUVER GRILLS SMUT PEDDLERS. And below the fold: STAG FILM STARLET TO TESTIFY. Then they all step casually back into their rooms and close their doors.

An engine room compressing steam
On the way down to the lobby, the elevator operator is reading a different novel.

A saucer thick with the sweetest cream
"Thanks." Uncle John hangs up the phone and hands Dave an envelope containing two thousand dollars. "I'll be in touch."

The hottest woman I've ever seen

When he gets back to the apartment Martine is still not there. Dave waits for two hours and she is still not there. Her sister lives in Illinois.

Don't straighten out your nylon seam

Dave goes to Eddie and pays him off. He stops at a convenience store and buys a newspaper and a paperback novel. Then he goes back to the Ocean Forest Hotel.

UP ABOVE THE DEAD LINE

It had happened for the last time. That was all there was to it. Ned Grainger had told his brother Joshua time and time again not to let his hogs feed on Ned's land and not to let his sons take water from Ned's well, but Joshua hadn't listened. He had never listened when they were boys, and he wasn't listening now. He kept on letting his hogs roam over onto Ned's land and mix with Ned's hogs and eat Ned's feed and drink from Ned's trough. And those worthless sons of his let it go on while they came over like hogs themselves and drank from Ned's well. So it had happened for the last time. That was all there was to it.

Ned told his own boys, Caleb and Little Ned, not to let it happen again. They were standing in front of their house when he told them. It was getting on toward noon and the summer sun beat down heavy on their heads as he spoke. The half-rotted boards of their two-room cabin sucked in the heat and shined dully in the hard light.

Ned was a huge man. He always wore coveralls, with no shirt when it was hot like it was now. His nose was flattened against his face from the fight with Joshua that had caused all the trouble to start with. The sheer bulk of him seemed to block out the sun as he told his boys that he was sick and tired of their uncle's hogs and boys on his land, and he meant for it to stop. He told them that he hadn't worked like a dog all his days to give food to Joshua's sickly hogs and water to his no-'count boys. He told them that if they saw any of their uncle's hogs on his property to chase them back across, and if they could catch one and kill it for themselves, fine. And if they saw either of their worthless cousins, chase them back across, too. Beat them with a stick if they had to. Do whatever they wanted, just get them off his land.

Caleb nodded, understanding. He was the oldest, the one Ned had the most hope for. Ned had never been able to do much more than scrawl his own name and puzzle out store signs, but Caleb had learned to read and write like he was born to it. He was twenty and had been the first one in Ned's family to finish the sixth grade. He had wanted to go live in Kingston and continue his schooling, but Ned needed him on the farm, and Caleb understood that, too. He was a good boy and had never been a problem to his father. True, there had been that business with the Purvey girl a few years back, but she had had the good sense to jump in the river before things had gotten out of hand, and nothing had ever come of it. The Purveys were trash, anyway. Nothing but trouble.

Little Ned nodded and seemed to understand, which was all Ned could hope for. He had come into the world two years after Caleb and taken his mother out of it in the process. Betsy had lain on a straw mat in the corner of the house and labored for fourteen hours before she died. And Little Ned slid out of her with the cord wrapped around his neck. The midwife had told Ned that that was liable to make the boy slow later on, but Ned hadn't believed her and had spent the first several years of Little Ned's life trying to beat some sense into him. Finally he saw it was no use, and from then on he took Little Ned for what the boy was. Caleb was good with him and managed to keep him in line even though Caleb had his mother's short, slight build while Little Ned had inherited all of his father's size and then some.

When their father finished with them, Caleb and Little Ned walked down to the watering trough to make sure their cousins weren't there. Little Ned followed his older brother quietly, watching the sunlight play off the smaller boy's blond hair. The four acres of tobacco that kept them alive shimmered in the June heat as they walked by, green at the top and slowly beginning to yellow near the bottom of the stalk. It was going to be a good crop this year, and after they endured the backbreaking weeks of hand-cropping the tobacco a few leaves at a time, they could look forward to a comfortable winter. Their dog, which they had never bothered to name, caught up with them as they walked and trotted alongside. Caleb threw sticks for it to fetch, and each time it brought a stick back Little Ned got down on all fours and circled the dog, growling, pretending to try to steal the stick. His normally blank face came alive as he played, his tongue lolling out of the side of his mouth, eyes flashing, untrimmed brown hair flopping in his face. Caleb laughed and shoved at his brother with his bare feet. The sun was directly overhead now and pounded down through the trees, making the brothers sweat.

The dog wandered away again as they approached the trough, where they heard human laughter mixed with the grunting and rooting of the hogs. They arrived to the sight of half a dozen of Joshua's hogs drinking at their trough while one of Joshua's boys threw rocks at their hogs in the pen. The hogs would stand frozen in the pen until the boys' cousin Matt would fling a rock inside. Then they would explode into motion as if they were all one animal, stampeding thunderously inside the pen while Matt stood outside and laughed and his father's hogs drank from Ned's trough.

When Matt looked up and saw Caleb and Little Ned coming toward him, he threw his last rock at them and ran. Joshua's hogs scattered and disappeared. Ned's hogs kept on stampeding in the pen, frightened now by the sudden burst of movement outside. Caleb and Little Ned ran after Matt, whooping and hollering. They weren't fifty feet from the trough when Matt, who was fat and clumsy and seldom moved faster than a shuffle, tripped on a rock and fell. Caleb was on him at once, punching him and rolling him around in the dirt, cursing and telling him that they were going to teach him to stay off their land.

Little Ned got to them a minute later, holding a thick piece of wood in his hand. He had remembered what his father had said to do and had broken a dead limb off a tree near the well. He ran up to his brother and cousin and swung the stick blindly, laughing.

When Caleb felt the first sting of wood on his shoulder, he rolled away from Matt, jumped to his feet, and whirled around. Little Ned was kicking Matt, kicking him hard, and hitting him again and again with the stick. Matt was howling and rolling around in the dirt like a hog. The dust the fight had kicked up hung like smoke around the two of them, and Caleb couldn't even see his brother's face. The stick came down and down and Matt rolled and howled, and then suddenly the howling stopped and he was perfectly still.

Caleb ran up to them, pushed Little Ned away, and knelt over Matt. There was blood and dirt smeared darkly all over him, and one side of his head was caved in like a rotten cantaloupe. His mouth hung open and his eyes were rolled back. Little Ned was still laughing.

Caleb slapped his brother across the face until he stopped laughing and then dragged him back to the house, where he told their father that Little Ned had killed his cousin Matt. Ned looked without expression at his youngest son, who regarded him solemnly, aware that something important was happening. Caleb was yelling, tears running down his face, demanding to know what his father was going to do. He told his father that he, Ned, was the one who told Little Ned to beat them with a stick, that he should have known Little Ned would take him at his word, that it was all his fault and what was he going to do about it? What was he going to do?

Ned looked at his sons and didn't say anything for a while. The afternoon sun hit him full in the face, brutally outlining the eighty years' worth of lines and crevices that had managed to appear in half that time. He told Caleb to shut up and show him where the body was.

So the boys showed him Matt stretched out in the dirt, and Ned told them to pick up the body and carry it back to the house and put it on the wagon. They did, and Ned hitched up the mule and the three of them rode out to Joshua's place, where they laid the body out in front of the house. Joshua's wife, a pale, thin woman who looked as if she had seen entirely too much, cried and hugged her dead son and would not let go. Joshua said nothing. The boys hung back in the edge of the yard, not knowing what to do.

Joshua sent his youngest son to fetch the sheriff, who came and heard everybody's story and arrested Ned and Caleb and Little Ned for the murder of Matthias Grainger. He hauled them into town and put them in jail to await trial. Ned tried to talk the sheriff into letting Caleb out once a day to tend the mule and the other livestock, but the sheriff refused. Instead, he ordered one of Joshua's sons to see after the place.

They were tried quickly, within the month. The courtroom was crowded. It had been two years since the last time a white man was accused of killing another white man, and the people of Kingston, South Carolina, were hungry for entertainment. The three Graingers told their stories, all of which were true. The prosecutor had some trouble with Little Ned, who was not used to talking to anyone besides Ned and Caleb, but he finally got the youngest Grainger to admit that, yes, he had hit his cousin with a stick and kicked him until he had stopped moving, and he had done it because his daddy had told him to. Then he sat down and spent half the rest of the trial staring at the portrait of President Cleveland that hung over the jury box and the other half staring at the black people sitting in the balcony. He had never seen a painting before, and he hadn't seen that many black people. The Graingers' farm was up above the Dead Line, beyond which black people were not permitted to live or work, as they were not permitted to sit on the ground level in the courtroom.

The jury did not take long to reach a verdict. The foreman, a prim little man in pince-nez glasses and a string tie who normally would have nothing to do with the likes of the Graingers, stood and read the verdict. Ned and Caleb were found innocent of all charges. Little Ned was found guilty of murder and sentenced to hang two weeks hence.

When the sentence was passed, Ned stood and asked permission to address the judge. He told the judge that he was grateful for the mercy shown toward him and his oldest son, and he accepted the judgment passed on his youngest. But he reminded the judge that he was a farmer, a poor farmer with a crop that had to be brought in. If he didn't have both his sons to help him with the tobacco, he would be ruined; he couldn't afford to hire an extra hand. So he asked the judge to postpone the hanging until after the tobacco was harvested. After that, the law could have Little Ned. The judge got a strange look on his face, but he agreed to Ned's request. Caleb stared at his father as if he had never seen him before.

So the three of them went home and brought in the tobacco crop. Ned and Caleb and Little Ned bent to either side of and behind the drag their mule pulled through the field, picking the leaves off the stalk by hand. Caleb stood to the left side of the drag and never once looked at his father and brother, staring instead at the damp, bristly hindquarters of the mule. Little Ned paused frequently and rubbed the tobacco leaves between his fingers as if he had discovered a new toy.

It took six weeks to harvest the entire field, six passes to crop the leaves as they matured from the bottom of the stalk to the top. And between the croppings the tobacco had to be hauled to the barn, strung on the poles and hung in tiers inside the barn, and cured by heat pouring through tin flues from a wood furnace outside the barn. Then the cured leaf was stacked inside the home since the Graingers didn't have a pack house. The three of them were usually forced into the kitchen, but during this harvesting Caleb decided that he and Little Ned would sleep outside. Caleb lay beside his brother in the dark and pointed out the stars to him, one by one.

During the final stages of the curing process Caleb and his father had to take turns maintaining a twenty-four hour watch on the barn. Once the leaf color had become fixed, the heat inside the barn had to remain constant to avoid spoiling the leaf or burning down the barn. They watched the thermometer through a small plate-glass window.

While they were curing the final barn of tobacco, the Rabon boys, who had helped Ned and his sons bring in their tobacco ever since the falling out with Joshua, celebrated the end of the harvest by getting drunk. Jugs of moonshine lay scattered in front of the barn as one of the Rabons twanged on a mouth harp and the others danced and hollered and clapped their hands. Little Ned didn't drink any of the moonshine—he knew his daddy wouldn't like that—but he joined in the dancing, linking arms with the Rabons and clomping around in skewed circles, throwing his head up and howling at the moon as if they were all going to live forever. Caleb sat at the far side of the barn, paying no mind to the rest of them, silently watching the thermometer hold steady at 180 degrees as the heat radiated out of the barn wall and through him and into the already sweltering August heat. His father slept fitfully beside him, tossing and turning, occasionally muttering things that no one could understand. The mercury in the thermometer burned into Caleb's eyes and he tried desperately not to think of anything at all.

When the last barn of tobacco had been cured and graded and the whole crop had been hauled to market, Ned went out to the woodshed and built a coffin. He told Caleb to help him put it on the wagon, but Caleb wouldn't do it. So he told Little Ned to help him, and little Ned did. They put the coffin in the back of the wagon, Ned hitched up the mule, and they both got in the wagon and rode into town. Caleb stayed home.

On the way into Kingston, Ned told his youngest son that he was mighty sorry for all of this, but that he had done a wrong thing by killing Matt and that the law punished people who did wrong things. The law was bigger than they were, he said, and they had to obey it. Little Ned nodded and seemed to understand.

It was raining by the time they got to the muster field on the outskirts of town where the local militia drilled and the hangings took place. Umbrellas dotted the large crowd that waited for the execution. Entire families were there. Some had brought picnic lunches.

Ned led his son through the crowd and up to the gallows, where he handed him over to the sheriff. Then he went and stood in the front edge of the crowd. Joshua was there with his wife. She was sobbing as hard as she had when they had brought Matt home, but her husband had a content, satisfied look on his face.

Little Ned didn't say anything when they put the hood over his head or when they put the rope around his neck or when the preacher read from the Bible. Just before the end, though, when the crowd was completely silent and all anyone could hear was the rain, he cried out from underneath the hood, "Pa?" Ned clenched his jaw and stared straight at his son as the trap door swung open beneath his feet.

When it was over, Ned took Little Ned's body and put it in the coffin in the back of the wagon and took it home in the rain and buried it beside his wife.

Caleb wasn't there. Ned never saw him again.

IT CAME OUT OF THE SKY

We were preparing for the argumentative essay assignment in my English 101 class, and I was trying, with predictably mixed results, to teach my students something about logic. "Another fallacy is the 'appeal to ignorance,'" I said, dutifully writing the term on the board. "An appeal to ignorance assumes that an argument is true because it hasn't been shown to be false, or that it's not false just because it hasn't been shown to be true."

Blank faces. It was a week before spring break, and none of them wanted to be there. Neither did I, for that matter. "If I were to say, 'Since no one has proven that depression does not cause cancer, we can assume that it does,' that would be an appeal to ignorance. You can't say an argument is valid just because there's no evidence on the other side."

I counted at least eight of the twenty students unapologetically staring out the window to our left, perhaps noticing the first leaves of spring. Or perhaps not.

"Try this one," I said. Turning back to the board, I wrote, *UFO's must exist because no reputable studies have proven conclusively that they do not*, and then read it aloud. "See how this works? The fact that nobody has proven that UFO's *don't* exist is not proof that they do."

In any class, there's always one student who will cheerfully ask questions, whether they have anything to do with the topic under discussion or not. This semester, in this class, it was a woman named

Myra Jansen, one of those aggressively pragmatic older students who's gone back to school after raising her kids and is convinced she knows more about what's what than her teacher. Maybe she's right. "Do you believe in UFO's?" she asked.

I paused, intending to tell her that my beliefs on the topic weren't relevant to our discussion, but instead I answered her question. "If by 'UFO' you mean an unidentified flying object—something you see and can't explain—then sure, there are obviously unexplained phenomena that people have witnessed. If you mean flying saucers from outer space, then no, I don't think so."

"Have you ever seen a UFO?" she persisted.

All thirty faces were now turned toward me. "No," I lied, and moved quickly on to *post hoc ergo propter hoc*, making sure that this time I used an innocuous example from the textbook.

The last time I had thought seriously about UFOs it was also almost spring break, but it was 1975 and I was a junior in high school. Remember when we're talking about, here. The Cold War was at a lull; the first wave of UFO reports and "flying saucer" cultural imagery had peaked before I was born; nobody had ever heard of Roswell, New Mexico, and if they had, it was only because it was John Denver's birthplace. Post-*Star Trek*, pre-*Star Wars*, marginal activity was still on the margins, nowhere more so than in Pine Heights, the small town in southeastern North Carolina where I grew up. Neither I nor anybody I knew was thinking about unidentified lights in the sky.

That's why it was such a shock when the first reports came in, not on the evening news or the daily newspaper, but over the dining-room table. It was Wednesday night, and my older brother Stephen, who taught at the community college one town over, was home for dinner. Somewhere between the fried chicken and the potato salad, he started talking about some odd things he had been hearing from the highway patrolmen, dutifully pursuing their

Associates' Degrees in Criminal Justice, who populated his Public Speaking class. "And he came up at the end of the period and actually apologized for falling asleep in class. He said he'd been out all night chasing blue lights in the sky."

"More likely he was out all night at the House of Blue Lights," said my father. Dad was a product of the Big Band era, but he had continued to follow pop music through the fifties right up to that week, which made my life a bit easier. He sometimes told me to turn it down, but he never bugged me about what I was listening to in the first place.

"Now, Fred," my mother said automatically, and then, "What sort of lights? Was he chasing someone?"

"Or some thing," Stephen said.

"Really? What do you think it was?" My mother had a healthy interest in the paranormal that led to occasional mutterings among the parishioners of the First Baptist Church. It was an interest my father emphatically did not share. One of my more vivid childhood memories is of watching my mother and my Uncle Vic sitting in the middle of our living room huddled over a Ouija board while Dad and Aunt Cathy cringed on the sofa. I don't remember what the message was, or even if they got one.

"He doesn't know, but they were in the sky, and they were moving awfully fast. Curt said he and his partner were out on late-night patrol, and they kept seeing all these lights all over the place. They said it was some kind of V-shaped object, with blue lights on the sides and a red light in the middle, and it was hovering beneath cloud level, close to the ground, and it didn't make any noise."

"Didn't make any noise?" I asked, looking up from the uneaten potato salad on my plate. Mom looked over and said, "Don't pick at your food, Leroy." I put down my fork a bit more forcefully than was perhaps necessary and gave her a look I hoped was just the right combination of pain and exasperation. I hated my full name and had spent a great deal of time and effort since junior high to get people to call me Lee. If they called me anything at all, that is.

"He said the thing took off like a shot, *woosh*," Stephen continued, putting his own fork down gracefully and making a sweeping motion over the table with his right hand. He kept his left, as usual, carefully positioned on his lap. Stephen had left Vietnam a lucky man; the grenade had only taken off two fingers and the tip of a third.

"They're probably testing something up at Ft. Bragg," my father said, helping himself to another piece of chicken.

"Probably," said Stephen, reaching for more potato salad.

As the conversation turned to other things, I munched on a roll and thought. For the first time in a good long while, I had something worth thinking about.

At age sixteen, I was maybe not as much of a deep geek as some of the computer wizards and game addicts who pass through my classes these days, but deep enough. Your basic alienated misfit: a fair number of acquaintances but almost no friends, more time spent with books than other people, and let's not even talk about dating. Hardly a unique situation. I know that now, and I basically knew that then. But knowing didn't help. All those starving kids of whom my mother tirelessly reminded me never increased my enthusiasm for the food I was expected to eat.

So I was never able to join in the nostalgia for the decade of my adolescence. I don't write it off altogether. There was cool stuff in the seventies, but my students never ask me about that. They don't want to know about Robert Altman or Richard Pryor or Patti Smith; they're all about *The Brady Bunch* and chunka-chunka cop show theme music. A few more adventurous souls, who maybe saw *Boogie Nights*, will occasionally press for an account of the libertine swirl they know I was lost in. Drugs without persecution, sex without condoms, woo-hoo! When I shrug and say, "I wasn't doing any of that, and neither was anyone I knew," they always seem vaguely distressed.

But that April night, in the reports from Stephen's highway patrolmen, was the possibility of something different. Maybe not a night at CBGB's or Studio 54, but something interesting, something beyond dinner and study hall and all the boredom that was in all the houses I had walked by all my life. I thought about the possibility that evening while we watched *Cannon*, and later, just before Stephen left, when I asked him to be more precise about where the sightings had occurred, and later still that night as I lay in bed and half-listened to a radio talk show out of Ft. Wayne, Indiana. The woman who hosted the show—something of a rarity, back then, to have a female radio personality—was chatting merrily with some guy from Bloomington about his new CB radio. Just before I fell asleep I stopped thinking about Stephen's story and wondered what it would be like to find a girl who would talk to you like that.

The next morning, though, my thoughts were back to the blue lights, and by lunch period I realized that I suddenly had, not just something worth thinking about, but something worth doing. Something worth doing with someone else. So I ran it by Marshall.

Marshall Kourkoulis had moved down to North Carolina from Rhode Island two years earlier. Although his visibly Mediterranean heritage and Yankee accent had marked him as exotic goods—"He doesn't look like anybody I've ever known," my mother said—Marshall had managed to acquire a degree of acceptance fairly quickly by throwing himself, with sincere enthusiasm, into the turbid waters of Southern culture. His speech slowed; his grammar eroded; his hair fell to his shoulders. (Back then, if you were a teenage boy and didn't look like a roadie for Deep Purple, your trustworthiness was under suspicion—not to mention your manhood.) Freed from the decadent foppery of the urban Northeast, he became an enthusiastic hunter, wearing his camouflage jacket to school, often still bloodstained from the weekend's killing. And the day after he received his driver's license, he arrived at school driving a pickup truck with a CB radio beneath the dash and a gun rack, complete with gun, hanging from the rear window.

Marshall had, in fact, embraced all the elements of contemporary Southern life that I had turned around and walked away from.

Nonetheless, we became friends. Despite his embrace of the exterior trappings of good-old-boyhood, that degree of acceptance he earned never really evolved into a full and unreserved welcome. His speech may have slowed and his accent moderated, but he was still verbally aggressive and doggedly literal in a way that sometimes didn't play well with his new Southern peers, who were laid-back to the point of indolence and schooled since birth in polite misdirection. And he didn't have anything to offset these failings: perfectly intelligent, he was indifferent to the classroom; a genuine outdoorsman, he was hopeless at team sports.

So Marshall, like me, was accepted, but never really welcomed. United in our disdain for our more successfully mainstreamed peers, in our insistence that we didn't want what we couldn't have, we became friends. Certainly he was the only person to whom I would propose, over lunch, a trip into the swamps off Highway 74 to look for UFOs.

"Stephen said that they had ten sightings Monday night and twice that many over Tuesday night and Wednesday," I said. We were sitting in his pickup gobbling our sandwiches, drinking Coke, and listening to an 8-track of Led Zeppelin's *Physical Graffiti*.

"And who's seeing them?" Marshall demanded. "Some half-blind old lady thinks the booger man's come for her?"

"No, man, it was the cops, the patrolmen," I said, and repeated Stephen's account of the mysterious blue lights. "They said the thing took off like a shot, *whoosh*, didn't make a sound," I quoted, imitating Stephen's gesture from last night and feeling irrationally guilty—not for the first time—that both my hands were intact.

"And you think we're gonna see this *whoosh* out over the swamp?"

"I looked at a map. That area off of that stretch of 74 is right on the same path as the other sightings."

Marshall considered this while John Bonham's drum kit rattled the inside of the truck. "Well, hell, might as well. Ain't nothing else to goddamn do around here."

I realized I'd been holding my breath, and exhaled. I wanted Marshall with me, but even more, I wanted his truck to get me there. "It'll be cool," I assured him. "You'll see."

"Whatever. You not gonna eat that other sandwich?"

Marshall picked me up promptly at eight the next evening, Friday night. My father set a preposterously early time for me to be home but, mercifully, didn't try to strike up a conversation with Marshall as the latter stood in the entrance hall swinging his key chain and staring in frank amazement at an ancient photo hanging on the wall of my great-grandfather Harold and his fourth wife Liza, neither of whom probably looked like anyone Marshall had ever seen. My mother urged us, in equal tones, to have a good time and to drive carefully.

As we drove off, I looked back at the house. The door was closed, but as we picked up speed it opened again and my mother stood in the doorway, as if she had something more to say. She had always been, and still was, concerned and attentive towards her boys, but after Stephen came home more or less in one piece, she acquired an air of resignation. No less love or affection, but thereafter, it was as if she had finally been convinced, on some fundamental level, that there were some things in this fallen world that were simply out of her hands. Her silhouette blurred, floated insubstantially for a moment, and disappeared.

Marshall's eight-track had jammed, so he had the radio tuned to an FM station out of Fayetteville, the only one in the area with what was then called an "album-oriented rock" format. They were playing side one of the Allman Brothers' *Brothers and Sisters*. "Wasted Words" cranked up and out, clear over the wind from the open windows.

"Dickie Betts can play the ass off that guitar," he said.

"Ain't been the same since Duane died, though," I said.

"That's the truth."

"I like this whole album, though."

"Damn straight."

I leaned back against the vinyl seat, stuck my hand out the window, and let the wind push me. It didn't take long for us to get past the city limits—Pine Heights was, as I said, a small town--and we headed west on Highway 74. The rush of air chilled my hand, but I kept it out as if I were trying to touch everything we passed. I closed my eyes, and behind the Allman Brothers and the roar of the truck I could hear the rush of the landscape we drove through: the wisk of mailboxes, less frequent as we got further out in the countryside; the muted roar of the iron bridge that marked the county line, and the sudden sense of empty space that marked the water below. I opened my eyes. The town lights were gone, and the stars were out. "Ramblin' Man" came on, and the song made perfect, irrefutable sense. I felt outside and connected all at once, not thinking about UFOs, not immediately aware of what year it was, not realizing that I was simply happy. I clenched my fist and held on.

"Where the hell am I supposed to turn?"

"About a mile further up, on Mill Branch Road."

As we turned onto the dirt road, Marshall said, "Wonder if Ray'll make it."

"Ray?"

"Yeah, I told him we were coming out here. He said he might come on out, too."

"Ray Hedgeford?"

"Yes, hell, Ray Hedgeford. How many goddamn Rays do you know?"

Only one, and I had had no thought in this world of his being a part of tonight. Ray was only a year or two older than me, but he seemed as remote as any adult. I had known him only as a distant presence on the far end of the schoolyard, talking as easily with the girls as he did with the boys. Not singular or dramatic enough for James Dean territory, Ray was still a bit of an enigma: whispers about drugs, without any proof; rumors of violence, but no arrests.

He sealed his uncertain reputation by dropping out of school without explanation. "I didn't know you even knew Ray."

"I bought this damn truck from that guy he works for, Henry. I see him sometimes when I stop for gas."

"Well, OK, cool," I said, more enthusiastically than I felt. The euphoria I had felt earlier had diminished. Marshall was a known quantity in my search for something unknown, but Ray made two unknowns, and that made me nervous.

"There's a clearing back over here," Marshall said. "That close enough to your flight path?"

"Sure," I said. Ray probably wouldn't show up at all. And if he did, well, what harm could it do? I decided not to worry about it. It was Friday night, I was out of that wretched goddamned town, and there was, maybe, perhaps, something interesting ahead.

Marshall pulled off into a clearing and we got out. He carried a battery-powered lantern in one hand and a shotgun in the other. I had a flashlight and an AM/FM radio only slightly smaller than the shotgun. I balanced the radio on my knee and tuned it to the station we'd been listening to in the truck. Marshall set the lantern down on the ground, turned it on, sat down in front of it, and laid the gun across his lap.

"You're not gonna build a fire?" I asked.

"Too warm."

I sat down beside him and placed the radio by the lantern. They were playing something by Golden Earring that wasn't "Radar Love."

"Now what?" Marshall asked.

"I guess we wait."

In the distance, I could barely hear the sounds of cars out on the main road. There was the slightest of breezes, just enough to move the tops of the trees. There was no moon, but the stars were everywhere. The trees were thick with moss and blotted out the bottom of the sky; in the starlight, they were a chalky swirl, like a poorly-erased blackboard. I leaned back on my elbows, raised my knee to block the glare of the lantern, and looked up past the trees at the sky. All the constellations were there, I was sure, but I couldn't identify any of them. When I was in grade school and discovered the Sherlock Holmes stories, I had for a while fancied the notion of being a great detective and ultra-rational thinker. Now I remembered how, when Dr. Watson expressed astonishment that Holmes didn't know anything about astronomy, Holmes dismissed the matter, claiming that whether or not the Earth revolved around the sun or vice versa had no bearing on his life and work. Marshall, thank God, was no Dr. Watson, but it occurred to me that maybe I was a bit more Sherlock Holmes than I should be.

Marshall had pulled a couple of sandwiches out of his jacket and was peeling the plastic wrap off one. "Want some?" he asked, gesturing with the unwrapped one.

"No, thanks."

He bit cheerfully into his sandwich, chewed, and swallowed. I could smell the bologna from where I was sitting. "I can't believe we're out here in the woods without any damn beer," he said. "Why couldn't you get your brother to buy some for us?"

"I told you he wouldn't do that. He's the responsible one in the family. I remember one time—"

"Whatever. I could just use a damn beer is all. I should have told Ray to get some."

"Think he's gonna show up?" I asked.

"I don't know. He's probably off somewhere getting laid. He's got more sense than to be out in the middle of a swamp waiting for a goddamn space ship full of little green men."

"Nobody said anything about any damn little green men. But there's something going on, that's for sure."

"'Cause your big brother said so."

"'Cause those cops said so."

"Oh, excuse the hell out of me. Those cops wouldn't lie, would they, Lee-roy?"

I sat up. "Don't call me that."

"It's your name, isn't it, Lee-roy?"

I got up, gave Marshall the finger, and walked over to the truck. Marshall laughed. "You got a license to fly that bird, boy?"

"Just got one today," I replied, wondering what I had been thinking to come out here in the first place.

"Let's see it."

I flipped him off with my other hand. He laughed again. "Well, hell, might as well. Maybe I'll get to shoot me a spaceman." He picked up his shotgun and aimed it at the sky.

"I still don't know why you brought that damn thing along," I said. I liked to think that it was just another level on which I was refusing to go along with the herd, but the truth was that guns made me nervous, especially ones, like Marshall's, that got a lot of use.

"Can't go out in the woods without my gun, Lee-roy."

"I *told* you not to—"

"Wait." Marshall looked over his shoulder. "I hear something." He stood up and aimed the gun just past the rear bumper of the truck. "Who's there?"

"Put that fool thing down, Marshall. Jesus."

"I said, who's there?"

To my considerable surprise, there was actually a figure approaching. I was sure it was one of the same highway patrolmen who'd made the original sightings, come to pack us off back to our parents.

But—what do you know—it was Ray Hedgeford.

"You heard the man, Marshall," Ray said, walking right up to Marshall and his gun. "Put that fool thing down."

"Hey, Ray," I said. "You came. Cool." I hoped so.

Marshall put down the gun. "Did you bring some beer?"

"Is a bear Catholic? Does the Pope shit in the woods? I got a case in the car."

"Where you parked?" Marshall asked.

"Back up off the road. I'll go get it in a minute."

Marshall walked over to the truck, opened the passenger-side door, and laid his gun on the seat. The promise of beer evidently made him less defense-minded. "I knew Ray'd bring us some beer."

"Hell, yes," Ray said. "Looking for space critters is thirsty work."

"Now, don't you start, too," I said. "It's like I told Marshall—"

"Hell, Lee, I'm serious as a heart attack," Ray said. Like Marshall, he was wearing a loose-fitting camouflage jacket over his tee-shirt and jeans. He took it off and threw it in the back of Marshall's truck. I had contented myself with the nylon windbreaker my mother had bought for me at Sears last month. At that point in my life, I was not one for fashion statements. "I heard some of those inbred sons of bitches going on about those goddamned blue lights on my CB radio. There's something out there, all right. And I want to see what it is."

I was surprised at the surge of gratitude I felt. "Told you," I said to Marshall, who ignored me.

"So it wasn't just cops, huh?" Marshall said.

"No, sir," Ray said. "I recognized Harley Turner's voice—can't miss how those folks from Crusoe talk." Crusoe Island was not far from Pine Heights and isolated even by southeastern North Carolina standards. Legend had it that the town was originally settled by French Huguenots on the lam; once they settled in, they never left, and their descendants' dialect was still distinct from that of surrounding communities. Many years later, when I was in grad school, I got a female linguistics student I was trying to get to know better to join me on a visit home on the pretext that she might find a dissertation topic waiting for her at Crusoe. But that's another story. "He sounded near about to piss his pants going on about those lights, and how they moved so goddamned fast and didn't make any noise."

"So they all saw the same damn thing," Marshall said, his voice less skeptical than before.

"Just about," I said. "Two of the cops in Stephen's class followed it clear down 701 into South Carolina, almost to South of the Border." You couldn't go five miles on a main road anywhere in that part of the state without seeing signs for South of the Border, a motel/restaurant/gift shop complex on I-95 at the North Carolina-South Carolina state line. The motel and the signs are, as far as I know, still there.

"That figures," Ray said. "I'd expect space aliens to be headed to that damn tourist trap. Gonna buy some souvenirs to take back to outer space with 'em."

"I'm gonna work there next summer," Marshall said.

"Outer space?" I asked.

Marshall glared at me. "No, idiot, South of the Border."

"What you gonna do?"

"I don't know. Mop the damn floor. Empty the damn trash."

"Get some damn pussy," Ray said. We all laughed. Believe it or not, at that point in my life I actually considered myself something of a burgeoning feminist. After all, feminism went against most of what I had been taught, which was good, and I liked the thought that, if I ever did get a date, I wouldn't have to pay for everything. I must confess, though, that genuine rejection of the patriarchy was somewhat later in arriving.

"Better take some rubbers with you, man," Ray continued. "Those women are nasty come through there."

"Like you know," Marshall said.

"Goddamn if I don't. My sister worked there one summer—"

"Oh, *right*," Marshall said, "*those* nasty women—"

"Fuck you, Marshall—"

"—nasty, crabby things, burn your dick off—"

"I said *fuck* you, Marshall. I said she worked there and she said those people just didn't give a good goddamn. They were just passing through, it's summer and everything, who cares? They were running back and forth from one room to another, just fucking like rabbits."

"For real?" I asked. This was more interesting than flying saucers.

"All day and all of the night," Ray assured me.

Marshall asked, "Anybody fuck your sister?"

I took a step back, ready to jump behind the truck if necessary, but Ray just said, slowly and deliberately, "Fuck you, Marshall. Just take your damn rubbers, is all."

There was a pause while Marshall pondered Ray's advice. The Fayetteville DJ, perhaps as an apology for confusing his listeners earlier, was now playing "Radar Love." Marshall asked no one in particular, "How big do you think it is?"

"Well," said Ray, "it's usually about six inches full hard, but by the time your mother got through with it last night—"

Marshall causally flipped Ray off and re-addressed his question to me. "How big do you think that flying saucer is?"

I considered. "Stephen said the cops said it was bigger than an airplane or a helicopter."

"What kind of airplane? One of them Piper cub jobs or a damn jet airliner?"

"They said it couldn't be a jet because it was too low," I said, "and it couldn't be a small plane because it was hovering, and it couldn't be a helicopter because it wasn't making any noise. I told you, they don't know what the hell it was."

"Uh-huh," said Ray, who had started walking toward the woods. "'Scuse me, gentlemen, I got to go commune with nature before I get the beer."

"Better watch out for snakes," I said.

"Too early for 'em," Ray said. He unzipped his pants as he walked. "Ain't but one snake out around here."

As Ray disappeared into the woods, Marshall walked over and turned off the radio. "Hey, what'd you do that for?" I asked.

He sat back down on the ground, pulled his hair back out of his eyes with both hands. Once Marshall had decided to let his hair grow, he had pursued the task as determinedly as he did everything else; dark curls radiated in all directions, occasionally subdued by a camouflage hunting cap. He didn't have the cap tonight, and his hair faded into the darkness. "Just wanted to listen to the woods."

"Listen to the woods? What the hell you talking about?"

"I'm talking about listening to the woods. Sit down," he said, gesturing to the ground in front of him.

I sat. "That's why you come out here," he continued, "to watch and listen. When it's night and you can't watch, you listen."

"Listen to what?"

"To the woods, dammit. This ain't home, it ain't school. It's the woods. Just listen."

I listened. There was no traffic right then out on the main road. We were too far from the river for any water noises. Evidently the crickets were asleep, and the owls weren't up yet. "I don't hear shit," I said.

"Keep listening."

I listened again. The ground I was sitting on was cold and damp. "You're right. I do hear something."

"Told you."

"I think I hear Ray jerking off."

A full second pause, maybe two, and Marshall made a noise somewhere between a snort and a laugh. "Crazy son of a bitch. You need to get out in the world more, is what you need."

"I get out in the world," I said.

"No, you don't. You're either at home or at school."

"That's not the world?"

"Not hardly. Don't you ever want to breathe some air that isn't run through an air conditioner? Don't you want to get close to the earth?"

"Well, damn, Marshall," I said, "I didn't know you were a hippie. Gonna start your own commune?"

"No, hell, that's not what I'm talking about." He got up suddenly. By the time my body had registered that he'd stood up, it didn't feel like moving. "I'm just saying I'd go crazy as hell if I couldn't get out here away from all that shit back there."

"What shit?"

"All that shit," he said, walking over to the truck and climbing into the back bed. He stood and leaned against the side panel and stared down at me. "All the school shit, parents shit, people telling you what to do shit. Y'know, sometimes I'm sitting there in class and it's like I can't breathe or something. Like I got to get out." He was talking faster than usual, more like when he first moved down here. I had never seen him this animated about something that didn't involve shedding blood. "And I come out here in the woods, and all that other shit goes away."

"I know what you mean," I said, and I meant it.

He stood up, moved to the other side of the flat bed, and sat on the side panel. "But you don't ever get away from it."

"Sure I do," I said. "I read, I listen to the radio."

"You're still in a damn box while you're doing it."

"My head isn't. You know what'd make me crazy?"

"What?"

My legs were almost asleep. I stretched them out, lay down flat on the ground, put my arms behind my head. Marshall looked a hundred feet tall.

"What'd make me crazy," I said, "is if I couldn't read or listen to music, listen to the radio, hell, watch TV even—stuff that tells me that this isn't all there is, that there are other places besides here."

"What's wrong with here?"

"I don't mean here here, right now this very minute. This is OK. This is different." When was the last time I had lain on the ground under the open sky? "I mean what you said before—school shit and parents shit and people telling you what to do shit."

"I thought you liked school," Marshall said.

"I can't fucking stand school."

"But you're smart. You make A's all the time."

"Doesn't matter. I still can't stand school. It's boring. Those people are all boring. I don't want to be there."

"You'd rather be home?"

"I don't want to be there, either."

"Then where the hell do you want to be?"

"I don't know. Just not here, is all." I started to say more, but stopped. What I was saying was in my head all the time, but I had never actually *said* it to anyone, and it felt—weird. Marshall had climbed down while we were talking and was leaning against the side of the truck. God knew what he thought of all this, but at least he wasn't laughing at me. "You know," I said, "I stay awake at night listening to all those radio stations up north, in New York and Chicago and Cleveland, and I feel—I don't know, not safe exactly, but—I feel like there's other places, other people out there. People who aren't these people, places that aren't this place."

"Is that why you're out here? Waiting for that flying saucer to take you someplace else?"

"Maybe. No. Hell. I don't know what that thing flying around is, and if it came to get me I'd probably run."

Marshall reached inside the cab of the truck and took out his gun. "I'd give it my shotgun, right up the ass."

I laughed. "Bet you would."

"Hey, spaceman! Get a load of this!" He aimed the gun straight overhead. "Blam!"

"Marshall Kourkoulis, Greatest of All Hunters."

"Goddamn right."

"Defender of Earth, protector of virgins, if he can find any."

"Fucking A, Lee-roy," he said, laying the gun back in the cab.

I jerked into a sitting position, took a deep breath, studied my knees. "Don't call me that."

"Don't call you what, Lee-roy?" His voice had returned to its acquired Southern cadence.

"Goddamn it, Marshall, cut that shit out."

"Aw, what's the matter, Lee-roy, you don't like—"

"I said cut that shit out! I ask you to do one goddamn simple thing, not to do *one thing*, and you keep *doing* it, son of a bitch—"

"Lee-roy! Lee-roy!" he chanted.

"Fuck you, Marshall!" I yelled, and launched myself off the ground and at him.

I don't remember the next minute or so too clearly, but I do recall being dimly aware that something was happening that had not happened since I was in fourth grade and, as it turned out, has not happened again since that night: I was in a fight. I don't know what it was—Marshall's abrupt turn from confession to taunting, my tension at the lack of results of our trip so far, the stars in their courses—but, as if someone had suddenly thrown a switch, I was in a blind, gibbering rage, and I wanted nothing more than to stuff my Christian name down Marshall's throat and make him choke on it.

Nothing of the sort happened, of course. I was a bit taller than Marshall, and had the element of surprise; when I slammed against him, he lost his balance and slid down the side of the truck to the ground, and for a few seconds I was on top of him. But he had fifty pounds on me and had obviously been in such a situation more recently than fourth grade; he quickly threw me off and jumped up. Like an idiot, I bounced up and rushed him again. To his credit, he didn't do nearly the damage he could have done, mostly just shoving me away each time I charged at him. But I was not to be deterred, and soon my hands hurt from where I had actually landed a few blows, and my head and torso ached from where Marshall had done the same.

"Don't call me that—"

"You want a fight, pussy—"

"Fucker—"

"Give you a fight, goddamn it—"

Suddenly there was a third person between us. "Girls, girls, please," Ray was saying, pushing us apart. "This is so unladylike—watch it, asshole—come on, knock it the hell off, Jesus Christ, all *right*, already!"

I was sprawled against the side of the truck panting for breath; Marshall staggered over near the radio and flopped down on the ground.

"My name," I gasped, "is Lee, goddamnit."

"What?" said Ray.

"Call him Lee-roy and he goes apeshit crazy," said Marshall. He bent forward and began to swat straw and leaves out of his hair.

Ray looked at me. "Lee, what is your goddamn problem?"

"I'm not gonna take that again like I did with those assholes," I said.

"What assholes?" Marshall demanded. "What the hell you talking about?"

"Are you still pussyed out about those fools used to pick on you?" said Ray.

"They didn't 'pick' on me, goddamnit! They mugged me!"

"What the hell you *talking* about?" Marshall said.

"Oh, shit," I moaned. My head was beginning to clear. My hands were throbbing, and my right temple was on fire. "It was before you moved here, back in sixth grade. These guys waited for me at recess. Billy Johnson and Matt Caine."

"They used to turn him upside down and shake the money out of his pockets," Ray volunteered.

"Glad you remember, asshole," I said. "You used to stand there and laugh." It was true; Ray was one of many who stood by and were amused by my being robbed and humiliated. I had forgotten.

Ray shrugged. "It was funny."

"Yeah, fucking hilarious, see how you like it."

"They didn't do it to me. They did it to you."

Marshall stood up and started to brush off his jacket and jeans. "What's all that got to do with anything?"

I paused, tried to slow down my breathing. Even now, thinking about it made me feel sick. "Every time they did, they'd chant 'LEE-roy, LEE-roy, pussy boy, LEE-roy!' Loud as a goddamn thunderstorm."

"So you try to kill Marshall because some rednecks beat you up," Ray said. "Makes sense to me."

"I just got sick of it, is all."

I crossed my arms over my chest; suddenly, I felt cold. Marshall walked away from us. Arms still crossed, I walked over, bent down, and turned the radio back on. "Lily, Rosemary, and the Jack of Hearts" by Bob Dylan blared out; I adjusted the volume as Marshall walked back over. "What happened to them?" he asked.

I didn't really want to talk about it any more, and was surprised that he did. "Oh, they got tired of me after a while and went on to someone else. Billy finally graduated. I think he's still playing football at State. Matt dropped out. I heard he got arrested."

"For being ass-ugly and sucking Marshall's dick," Ray said.

"What?" I said.

Ray walked over to us and clapped his arm ceremoniously around Marshall's shoulder. "Didn't you know, Lee? Marshall is a notorious homosexual. I'm surprised your parents let you out here in the woods with him."

"Fuck you," said Marshall, shrugging off Ray's arm and walking over to the truck. It had been six years since Stonewall, but we hadn't heard about it.

"Why, I was walking along the other day," Ray continued, "minding my own goddamn business, and this fool comes up to me and drops his pants and says, 'Suck my dick.' I said, 'Fuck you, fool, you're crazy.' And he looks at me and says, 'Isn't your name Marshall Kourkoulis?'"

I snorted and couldn't tell if what poured out of my nose was snot or blood.

"You'd choke on it, boy," Marshall said.

"Better mend your ways, Marshall," Ray said solemnly. "Connie ain't gonna go out with no queer."

"Connie?" Marshall asked.

"Connie Gore," said Ray, "that girl you want to fuck in fourth period study hall."

"I don't want to fuck Connie Gore," Marshall said.

"Yes, you do."

"No, I don't."

"Yes hell you do to."

"Nah. Her ass is messed up."

Silence. "Her ass is messed up?"

"Yeah," Marshall said. "It kinda pouches out on the sides, kind of hangs low."

"Her ass is messed up," Ray repeated.

"You deaf, asshole? That's what I said."

"If Connie Gore jumped stark naked in the bed with you, you'd toss her out."

"Now, shit—" Marshall began.

"You'd say, 'I don't like your ass.'" This time I laughed out loud.

Marshall seemed trying to restrain himself, whether from getting his gun and shooting Ray or laughing with me, I wasn't sure. "I'm just saying—"

"Marshall, you are so goddamn dumb," Ray said. "Why are you so goddamn dumb?"

"Well, if you think she's so damn hot, you fuck her."

"Not me, boy."

"Why not?"

"Are you blind? Her ass is messed up."

Our laughter drowned out Bob Dylan and the distant traffic and any chance of another fight. Ray walked over to a cooler sitting on the ground, and for the first time I realized he had indeed brought the beer. He opened the cooler, took out two cans, gave them to Marshall and me, and then took one for himself. "Drink up, boys."

Marshall popped the top on his beer and took a long, audible gulp. "Yeah buddy. That's more like it."

Ray followed suit; I opened mine, put it to my mouth, and hoped they didn't notice how cautiously I sipped. Truth was, the number of times I had drunk beer could be counted on the fingers of one thumbless hand—not nearly enough to develop a taste for the stuff. Later on, in college, I made up for lost time. But that's another story.

Ray said, "Are we going to stay out here all night or what?"

"Most of the sightings have been after midnight," I said.

"Don't matter to me," said Marshall. "Won't be the first night I've spent in the woods."

I took another, larger sip of beer. It went down better than before—better than ever before, in fact. Maybe the fight had toughened up my taste buds. I looked up at the sky. "Look at those stars. Sure won't have any trouble seeing that thing if it does show up."

"Hope it won't be the last, either," said Marshall. He gulped some more of his beer and started walking toward the woods. "I got to shit. I forgot to earlier."

"You forgot to shit?" I said. "How do you forget to shit?"

"I just did, that's all. Got things on my mind."

"Got Connie's ass on your mind," Ray said.

Marshall belched—long, loud, propulsive—and disappeared into the woods.

Ray stood by the lantern drinking his beer. I suddenly had an overwhelming sense of Ray, not as a friend, but as a friend of acquaintances, an acquaintance of friends, someone I had never really had a conversation with. I felt cold again and snapped my jacket shut. Ray, I suspect, would have been content to stand silently drinking until Marshall got back, but a comfortable silence was something I could only share—sometimes—with family and friends. Everyone else, I wanted to keep talking.

"You work today?" I asked.

"Hell, yeah. People's cars keep breaking down, they keep bringing them to Henry's, and I keep fixing them while Henry parks his ass in his office." He tossed back the rest of the beer, crumpled the can, dropped it on the ground, and walked over to the cooler. "He says he's keeping up the books, but every time I go in there he's reading the damn sports section." He got out two more beers, one of which I declined.

"You glad you're not in school any more?"

"I don't know," Ray said. He popped the beer open, slopped the foam off, sat down on the cooler. "Sometimes I kind of miss it. Sometimes I think there's got to be more to things than patching tires."

"Yeah."

"But I sure as hell never got anything in school that told me what it was."

"I hear you," I said. And then, "I wish I had the nerve to drop out." I couldn't believe I'd said that. I flinched, irrationally certain that my mother or father would be there instantly to rebuke me.

But Ray saved them the trouble. "Shut up talking like that."

"Huh?"

"Just shut the hell up talking like that. You need to finish school."

"You didn't."

"That's me. That's not you. You're good at that stuff. You need to do what you're good at."

"Like you're good at fixing cars."

Ray took a tremendous swig of beer, belched, looked past me and the lantern and the public education system. "I ain't shit at fixing cars."

"What do you mean? My dad said Henry told him just last week how glad he was to have you working for him."

"Henry couldn't find his own ass with both hands and a spotlight. He's glad to have me working for him so he don't have to get his hands greasy."

"He wouldn't keep you on if you didn't know what you were doing."

"Shit." Ray got up and walked over to the truck. "Fucking redneck and his goddamn cats. He keeps that trailer of his air conditioned down to about zero, and the place still smells like a litterbox."

"You hang out at his place?"

This time he didn't even bother to finish the beer before he crumpled the can. Drops of beer dripped off his hand and onto the ground. "Bite your tongue, boy. I just went by there a couple of times to drop off stuff he forgot from the office. Fool can't remember his own name sometimes." He pitched the can into the back of the truck and leaned against the side.

"Maybe he's getting senile. He's pretty old. Must be over fifty."

"I don't know what his problem is, and I don't care."

"My granddad thinks he's queer."

"Who, Henry? That pervert has a stack of *Hustler* magazines taller than he is."

"I guess it's because he isn't married."

"That don't make you queer."

"'Course not," I said quickly. If a UFO was going to show up, now would be an excellent time.

"Better not, 'cause I sure as hell ain't getting married."

"Why not?"

"'Cause. I saw what happened with my old man and old lady, and that's not gonna happen to me."

"Lots of people get divorced," I said. I was vaguely aware than Ray's parents had split up a while back.

"Lots of people don't come after your mother with a shotgun. Lots of people don't take a pair of shears to their wedding dress and then burn the rags."

"Christ, man." That, I had not been aware of.

"No sir. I'll get what I can, but I ain't settling on any of it."

I reached over and turned the radio back on. They were playing Aerosmith's "Sweet Emotion." Ray reached down into the back of the truck, retrieved his camouflage jacket, and shrugged it back on.

"I heard someone say once that all this 'till death do us part' shit got started when people didn't live much out of their twenties," I said.

Ray turned around and looked at me. "There you go. Told you to stay in school. You know all that shit."

"It was just something I heard," I said, feeling the same unease I always felt when someone said I was smart. Being smart was fine, but it wasn't enough.

"I tell you, man, you can look for your flying saucers all you want. Ain't nothing up there any weirder than what's down here."

I looked at Ray. The lantern light just barely touched him. His clothes seemed to suck in what little light there was, leaving his face to glow dully in the dark. For an absurd instant I thought of the Frankenstein monster model I had had in junior high, with the phosphorescent head and hands. Ray was no stitched-together monster, though. Nor was he the shrewdly obscene comrade-in-homophobia who had diffused the confrontation between Marshall and me. At that moment, slumped against the side of Marshall's truck, he just seemed young and tired—two words that ought never to go together.

I tried to think of something to say but was spared the effort by Marshall returning from the woods, fastening his belt. "Welcome back, son," Ray said. "Everything come out all right?"

"Yeah, 'cept I had to stop by your car and wipe my ass on that roll of twenties you had under the front seat."

"Damn. And I was going to buy your sister with that."

"I don't have a sister, asshole," Marshall said.

"You don't? Your father lied to me."

"Hey, I love this song," I said, and turned the volume up on the radio. The Rolling Stones' "Can't You Hear Me Knocking" blared out—gloriously overmodulated guitar, drums like boxes of contraband falling off the back of a speeding truck. I realized that I'd almost finished my beer and downed what was left in one swallow. Ray nodded along with the music; Marshall bounced over to the cooler and grabbed another beer, white boy in search of the beat. Soon we added our own voices to the Stones' shockingly pure harmonies.

There was a burst of static on the radio, and suddenly the music was gone, replaced by a male voice:

"Yes ma'am, we thank you . . ."

Another burst of static: *". . . modulating . . ."*

"What the hell?" Ray said.

The voice continued, periodically obscured by the static: *"we do not have . . . 104 and our equipment . . . we are clear . . ."*

"What happened to the song?" Marshall said, setting his beer on top of the cooler.

"*Robot, we are clear . . . we may be in violation of rules.*"

"Robot?" I leaned closer to the radio. At first I thought the voice sounded local, sounded southern, but the longer it spoke, the less certain I was what it sounded like.

"*You may be violating the rules and regulations of the National Loudmouth . . . by modulating with this one Robot. We may be violating . . .*"

"Aw, shit," Ray said. "Some dumb cracker's gotten his CB signal messed up. The radio's picking it up."

"No, wait, listen," I said. As I reached over to turn the radio up even louder, my hand looked different. It was blue, and so was the radio.

I looked around. Marshall and Ray and I, and the radio and the lantern and the cooler and the truck, were all bathed in a deep blue light, a light that seemed to make everything brighter and darker at once. There was no sound beyond the radio. I looked up at the sky, but I couldn't tell where the light was coming from.

The radio continued to belch static, and the voice droned on. "*. . . do not modulate with this one, Robot . . . we are circling around and checking out different . . . and they do not like for any voice to modulate with this one Robot.*"

The blood rushed out of my head and headed somewhere down around my shoelaces. My arms were numb. I don't know what frightened me more: the prospect of a close encounter with the source of the light, or the prospect of fainting in front of Marshall and Ray. Ray was keeping a game face, but he was also spinning like a gyroscope, desperately trying to determine where the light was coming from.

Marshall, on the other hand, seemed to have no doubts as to what the situation called for. Shouting "Goddamn!" a half-octave higher than his normal voice, he ran to his truck, pulled his shotgun off the front seat, grabbed a box of shells from the floor, and began loading. "You ain't taking me, motherfucker!"

"Marshall!" Ray yelled. "Goddamnit! We don't know what it is!"

The blue light held steady and was joined by a red light, above it, yet distinctly red, not filtered through the blue. Both the red and the blue grew brighter.

"*We are not a black man, we are not a white man, we are not a red man, we are not a yellow man, we are not anything. We are just a one Robot . . .*"

"Modulate this, asshole!" Marshall aimed his gun at the sky and pulled the trigger. Nothing happened. "Shit! It's jammed!"

Suddenly a bright white light snapped on behind the red and blue, bleaching them out without displacing them entirely. I had not moved since I had first noticed the blue light. I was reasonably sure that I could move if I wanted, but it seemed beside the point. I heard the voice on the radio, and I barely registered Marshall struggling with his uncooperative weapon, and Ray running over and yelling at him, but it was all like background action in a movie I was only halfway watching. I was encased in a bright, thick world.

"*. . . we are circling for the pleasure of our commanding vehicle. Anybody that does not like the sound RRRRRRR of this one Robot . . .*"

"That's got it!"

"Marshall, you dumb sonofabitch—"

"My god, my god, my god . . ."

There was a deafening burst of static, and "Can't You Hear Me Knocking" came back on, and then there was more static, and then the voice, and then the music again.

"Look!" Marshall pointed toward the woods. "There's one!" He pointed and aimed.

Ray looked where Marshall was aiming. "No, wait, that's not— Jesus Christ, is that—don't shoot!" He reached in and knocked the gun upward just as Marshall pulled the trigger. This time the gun fired—both barrels, a stereo pop like both rear tires blowing out at once.

A figure came out of the woods. It looked as if it were floating above the ground, moving erratically, first one way, then the next. It dropped to the ground, got up, kept moving. My mind told me to run. Instead, I made my first move since the lights came on—but toward, not away from, the figure from the woods.

"Here I am!" the figure shouted. "You want me? Here I am!"

The figure became a worn-out looking man somewhere in his fifties, wearing coveralls with no shirt and a narrow-brimmed fedora like my grandfather used to wear. "Beam me up, you bastards!" he bellowed. He was waving a bottle whose contents slopped out on the ground. "Beam me the hell up! I'm ready to go!"

"Henry!" Ray yelled. "You crazy sack of shit! What're you doing?"

"We are not . . . anybody . . . that we did from out there . . . we are not a computer, but we are a Robot; we are computerized . . ."

Henry dropped to his knees, took a swig from the bottle, and threw it aside. "Here I am! Come and get me! Beam me up!"

For days afterward—weeks, hell, months—I tried to put together in my mind what happened next, exactly what it was that I saw. I remember that the light grew even brighter, and I remember Marshall and Ray and Henry yelling, and what sounded like one of them crying. I remember that the radio fell dead silent at one point. I remember wondering what had happened to Henry's shirt.

But all I can honestly claim clear memory of was that one moment Henry was screaming "Beam me up!" and the next I was sitting on the ground, and the lights were fading, and Henry wasn't there anymore.

"We do . . . take the Earthling's words and twist it around and turn it against . . . We are more than you know . . ."

"Jesus fucking Christ," Ray said.

". . . more than you know." And the lights were gone. The long instrumental conclusion of "Can't You Hear Me Knocking" was still playing, guitar and saxophone floating out into the restored night.

I looked over at Marshall and Ray. Marshall still held his shotgun, but loosely, its barrels pointed harmlessly downward. Ray had joined me on the ground. Nobody said anything for a long time.

Then Ray said, "Will someone please tell me what the hell just happened?"

"They abducted Henry," I said. My voice sounded odd to me, like somebody selling something over the phone.

"What?"

"They took him. They came down and announced themselves on the radio and took him."

"That was some drunk trash on his CB," Ray said.

"What about Henry?"

"Like I said, drunk trash."

Marshall walked over to the truck and carefully laid his shotgun in the rear-window gun rack. Then he walked over to the cooler, took out a beer, popped the top, and started chugging.

"What about those lights?" I asked.

"I don't know," Ray said, "hell, a jet, they're testing something from Ft. Bragg—"

"Bullshit, Ray." I stood up. "Bull *shit*. And you know it."

"I don't know any such goddamned thing."

"I know what I saw," I said.

"And what did you see?" Ray asked.

"Something I've never seen before."

Marshall got two more beers out of the cooler, walked over to me, and handed me one. "Shut up, Lee-roy."

"Someplace else," I took the can of beer and calmly opened it.

"I said shut the hell up, Lee-roy."

"Someplace else." I took a huge swallow of beer. It went down with no trouble at all.

I looked at Marshall. "Got any of those sandwiches left?"

Marshall shook his head. He walked over and handed the other beer to Ray. Ray stood up and took the beer but didn't open it. "There's got to be an explanation for this," Ray said.

"No, there doesn't," Marshall said.

We stood there in the dark. The news came on the radio, but we weren't listening.

"I wonder where Henry's going?" I said.

"I wonder what we're going to tell people about this?" Ray said.

I looked over at Marshall, waiting for his question. Suddenly I wanted nothing more than for him to bring us back down to normal. I wanted him to speculate about Henry and those cats, or the attributes of Connie Gore.

But he just sat there, sipping his beer and saying nothing. I stared at him, and then at Ray, and then up at the sky, which was still there, just like before.

As it turned out, Marshall dropped me off before my father's appointed curfew— it just felt as if I had been out all night. My parents were watching the late news. Once we got past "Did you have a good time?" and "Did you see anything?" and I told them what they wanted to hear, I left them bathed in the soft, comfortable glow of the television and went upstairs to bed.

There were a few more reported sightings over the remainder of the weekend, but then there were no more, and within a very few weeks, the whole thing was forgotten. Neither Marshall nor Ray nor I ever discussed our experience in the woods, with the authorities or with each other. In fact, I never really spoke to Ray again. The good folk of Pine Heights didn't bother themselves about Henry's disappearance any more than the good folk of Sleepy Hollow had bothered themselves about Ichabod Crane's abrupt departure. I think a couple of people thought that Ray may have pulled a Brom Bones, or even something more sinister, but there was no evidence one way or the other. And, like Irving's bachelor schoolmaster, Henry had no family and owed no debts, so he wasn't missed. Ray took over the garage, and I saw him every once in a while, but we never sat and talked. One weekend when I was home from college, I learned that Ray, too, had up and left. Nobody knew where.

Marshall and I remained friends and finished high school together, but after graduation, we went our separate ways. After a year's rustication in the local community college, Marshall entered State and received a degree in Forestry and Wildlife Management. Last I heard he was working out in Wyoming, where, I understand, if you pay your fees and say your prayers at night, every once in a while they let you kill something. I heard he got married, too.

As for me, well, my appetite improved. I went to college and got a life, and I've been living it ever since. The high desert of New Mexico is a long way from the pine forests and swamps of North Carolina, but I've managed to adapt. It's a hard, dry place at first—shortly after I arrived, I emailed a friend back east that the aliens must have landed here because it reminded them of home. But after almost ten years, it no longer seems so strange. (Being able to buy hard liquor off the shelf at the grocery store, though—that still feels odd. Just too many years among the Baptists, I guess.)

The small college where I teach freshman composition and American literature is less than an hour from Roswell, but I still have never been over to visit the UFO museums. I've asked myself why, more than once, and this is the only answer I can come up with: Keith Richards once said he so loved the guitar solo on one of Elvis Presley's early records that he had never learned how to play it. There are rational explanations for what happened out there in the woods, and irrational explanations, and hyper- and extra- and post-rational explanations—and I finally decided that it doesn't matter. *Something* happened, and it touched me. If I pursued the matter to its logical conclusion, it might not be there any more, and I don't want that. Logic is logic, said Oliver Wendell Holmes—but the wonderful one-hoss shay had already collapsed.

I did tell my brother Stephen about what happened, many years later. He didn't offer an opinion, but he put his good hand on my shoulder and told me that he had seen some odd things during the war, and that one day he would tell me about them.

He hasn't to this day, but that's all right. I can still get in a car and drive a very short ways out from the small town where I live, and all the artificial lights go away. I can look up at the stars, clear and hard and beautiful, and know that there are mysterious things in and out of the world than I just don't understand.

And I can drive home content, knowing that Ray was right: ain't nothing up there any weirder than what's down here.

SUSPENSION

Daddy always told me I was too honest for my own good. "And that's especially dangerous for a girl, Caroline," he said the last time we talked, before he went off to the war. "People will lie to you, and they'll expect you to lie right back to them. Now, honesty is an admirable trait, daughter"—he always calls me "daughter" when he's being serious—"but you need to temper it some. Learn to tell little white lies. And learn how other people will do the same. If you don't, you'll get hurt very badly. And you'll never get a husband."

Well, that thought didn't make me particularly nervous, and I told him so. He smiled and said, "Just you wait, girl," and kissed me on the forehead, and Mama on the lips, and went off to England. That was a year and a half ago, when I was seventeen. Since then he has flown twenty-seven missions over Germany, but we haven't heard from him since April. It's now June. Mama says she isn't worried, but I know she is. I don't suppose I've followed Daddy's advice very well on the whole, but I can usually tell when mama's lying.

Here on the home front they all want us to feel as if we're doing our part to win the war, so everyone has a special task to perform. Mine is to watch for planes. Once a week I come up here to the steeple of the First Baptist Church, which is the tallest building in town, and I watch for the approach of enemy planes. Kingston is right near the coast, of course, and the air base at Palmetto Beach makes us a particularly tempting target. Or so I'm told. Personally, I don't think

Germany would send its airplanes all the way across the Atlantic. But the little roost Mr. Barlow has built up here—Mr. Barlow who is sixty-three and too old for the draft but who is still, according to Daddy, the best carpenter in three counties—is quite comfortable, so I don't really mind. It gives me time to think, even if it's only for a few hours a week. Things like that can be very important.

Kingston is a small town, only four thousand people, and viewed from on high it seems even smaller. I know I'm supposed to be looking up in the sky for planes, but, as I said, I don't feel any pressing danger about that, so I spend about as much time looking down as up. It's a whole new perspective. My old math teacher Mrs. Spivey told me, when Mama and I ran into her the other day at Jones' five and dime, that it was appropriate for me to be an airplane spotter since my head has always been in the clouds anyway. All three of us laughed. Had she said such a thing while I was in her class, I would have been mortified, but now that I'm an adult I can laugh at myself. Being able to laugh at yourself is a sign of maturity, I'm told.

Despite Mrs. Spivey's assertion, it was odd at first, being way up here and able to look down on everybody, watch them scurry around like mice, watch the cars slide down Main Street like electric trains. It took some getting used to. My best friend Virginia was afraid I would brood about Ben, up here all alone, but I haven't so far. Not really.

To be honest, I'm not at all sure that Ben is worth brooding about. Oh, I admit I had strong feelings for him. It would be foolish—and dishonest—to deny that. He was a sweet boy, and he was certainly handsome enough in his Army Air Corps uniform the same soft brown as his eyes, and that slightly crooked grin that brought him down to earth and kept him from looking too dressed up and official, the way some of them did. Well, there are still plenty of them here, and as Virginia so cleverly puts it, if your boy is one in a million, that means there's a hundred more just like him in the United States alone. Everybody didn't go away.

As it gets into the afternoon, the sun angles in from behind and the area in front of me grows brighter ever so slowly, like an oil lamp being turned up. By five o'clock, when I climb back into town, the shadows of the trees are starting to lengthen and the town lies hard and shimmering below me. On a clear day the sky overhead is like a blank piece of paper. Sometimes when I stand up to stretch, as far as I can stretch in such cramped quarters, I thrust my arm out in the sky and I write, *Dear Germany, where are your airplanes? Having a wonderful time—wish you were here.*

I don't really wish them here, of course. Nor do I expect them. Ben told me once, in one of the first conversations we had while swishing across the dance floor at the American Legion hut down at the beach, that the Carolina shore was the best spot on the East Coast for landing troops, which is why I think the invasion would be more likely to come by sea rather than by air. They should have me and the other girls standing sentinel on the beach instead of watching the skies.

After the first hour or so up here I confess I tend to get a little bored. It would be different if I could read, or if I had a radio. The only other thing up here besides me is an old hand-crank telephone for me to use if the planes arrive. Soon the novelty of my location wears off, and I find myself drifting—I suppose Mrs. Spivey was right. Oh, I try to keep watching, but it's difficult, and I usually settle on my favorite view.

South of the church is Kingston Lake, about a quarter of a mile away. Bordering it and running all the way back to the church is the cemetery where my grandparents are buried and my parents have their plots already reserved and where, I suspect, I will eventually join them all. Mama says she finds it reassuring to know exactly where she will be laid to rest, but, to be honest, I think it's rather morbid. Daddy has never commented one way or the other.

For true morbidity, though, all you have to do is go to the statue that stands at the center of the cemetery. Many years ago, before the first war, a brother and a sister, ages five and six, drowned in that lake. Their parents, the Stevenses, commissioned a stonecutter to mark their grave with a statue of two cherubim embracing each other, their stone wings stretched out behind them, their eyes looking upward toward heaven. Now that, I submit, is morbid.

Still in all, it's peaceful to look down and let my eyes wander over the cemetery and out to the lake. Some cemeteries look far too much like one of the golf courses down at Palmetto Beach, but this one manages to be well kept without looking overly manicured. From up here the grass blends effortlessly into the lake and the headstones are soft gray marks; the sporadic noises of birds and squirrels only emphasize the silence. It is peaceful down there, as only cemeteries and still water can be. The thought of a war somewhere in the sky seems utterly impossible.

The last time I saw Ben before he left, we walked around the lake. I had thought we had said our goodbyes the night before when he took me out to dinner, and then to dance to the orchestra that was playing at the Ocean Forest Hotel, and then to walk on the beach under the full moon shining through the clouds. It was early April and not quite spring yet; the wind pounded through my skirt, freezing my legs and churning the water clear out to the horizon. I let Ben put his arms around me and hold me close as if we were dancing. I told him yes, I loved him too, but no, I would not go with him behind the dunes and lie down in the sand with him. He took his arms from around me and said he understood, and the pain in his voice cut me worse than the wind. I had not wanted that to be the end of everything, but I had thought that it was until he showed up the next night also. He had driven up from the beach to see me one last time. We walked around the lake, passing the cemetery. The clouds from the previous night were gone. The moon and the stars shone down together, and although I knew it wasn't possible, I thought I could see the statue of the Stevens children out there in the middle of the dark. Ben took both my hands and we led each other away to a place I knew we wouldn't be disturbed, and I lay down in the grass and did what he wanted. What I wanted.

The war has caused hardships for us all. The rationing isn't so bad, since we never really went anywhere anyway. The scrap-metal drives just get rid of a lot of junk nobody needs. But I do confess some of the town's patriots, such as Mrs. Spivey for instance, get a little tiresome heading up their committees for this or that. As if people like my father weren't doing the real work of the war, anyway. Virginia once said that all we needed to do to win the war was to ship Mrs. Spivey over to Europe and get her alone in a room with Hitler, and she'd talk him to death and everybody could come home.

Mama in particular seems to benefit from the time she spends in her victory garden. I can just make out that small greenish-brown patch off to the side of the house, beneath my bedroom window. Most people from up North, like a lot of people I've met from the air base, seem to think that if you're not from a big city you automatically live on a farm. Like that oaf from Massachusetts or wherever it was who seemed genuinely shocked when I told him that I had never milked a cow or cropped tobacco. They don't understand how small towns work, and they surely don't understand the difference between being raised in the country and raised in town. My father was born on a farm and came to town the first adult chance he got and seldom leaves except when he has to go fight a war. My mother's people have lived within the incorporated limits of Kingston for several generations now; she doesn't know any more about tilling the land than my Boston Brahmin dance partner. So I think it does her good to work in her garden, growing her tomatoes and bell peppers and whatnot, doing her part for the war effort.

A few days ago we were on our knees in the garden digging new openings for seeds when she suddenly stopped and held up a handful of dirt. "It's real," she said. "I never thought this kind of stoop labor would agree with me, but it does. This is something permanent. It's something that lasts."

I picked up a clump of dirt in my own hands. It ran out of my fingers and was mostly gone. It agrees with you, Mama, because you can stop whenever you want. You don't have to go on if you don't feel like it.

I had hoped to hear from Ben after he left. I had wanted to mark the weeks with his letters even as I formerly marked the months with my periods, every twenty-eighth day like a memorandum from nature. I have had nothing to mark the weeks or the months since Ben left. And I am beginning to grow tired of marking the days.

The fact that Daddy is over in Europe has made it easier not to say anything. There may not be anything to say; it's only been two months; I understand these things can happen for any number of reasons. Keeping a secret from Mama is hard enough, so much so that I have perhaps been overly thorough, making it a point to buy my napkins at the usual time each month and leaving a visibly depleted box in the medicine cabinet. Business as usual. But the thought of being dishonest with Daddy is an impossibility. If he were here and so much as looked at me crooked, I would undoubtedly burst into tears and tell him everything. Mama has her garden and her bridge club and is, on the whole, easier to deceive.

I must admit that Daddy has always been honest with me in return. Once, many years ago before I entered high school, I asked him if he was ever sorry that he had had me instead of a son. Something had happened at school that day, I don't remember what, and I was in search of reassurance. He didn't answer exactly the way I might have preferred. "That's a tall one, Caroline," he said, leaning back in his chair and resting his head on the antimacassar Mama refused to move even though nobody used them anymore. "I did want a son somewhere along the line—every man does, I suppose. It was something of a disappointment when the doctor said that your mother shouldn't have any more children." He reached over and stroked my hair. "But I wouldn't trade you for a whole platoon of boys, daughter. You're the best a man could want." Two years later, when we had biology in high school and I learned that I had only been a chromosome away from giving my father what he wanted, I kept repeating to myself what he'd said as he stroked my hair, over and over.

Just before he got on the train, Ben kissed me and told me he loved me. I believed him.

Five o'clock. We are safe for another day.

As I descend from the steeple, I begin to feel dizzy, as I do when I haven't eaten for a long time. It can't be that, since I stopped by Neal's Drug Store on the way over and had a sandwich and a coke. My appetite has been irregular lately; I find myself eating at odd times.

I stop by the only window in the stairwell and look out on the churchyard. The shadows are getting longer, moving across the cemetery. The lake shines beyond the markers. I can just make out the statue of the Stevens children out in the middle. From here, halfway down with my head spinning, it blurs and looks almost as if it were floating above the ground.

I have heard of young women like myself who try to deceive their families as I have but who could only go so far before they ran away and did something permanent. Bury it in the backyard; sink it like a stone in water. I have never been able to imagine what went through the Stevens' minds as they commissioned the stonecutters. I thought I understood Ben. My mother is on her knees in the dirt, my father is not here, and the statue rises, rises and floats out over the lake, amid the birds that circle and dive like airplanes. Suspended in the air.

THE LAST TESTAMENT OF MAJOR LUDLUM

June 20th 1906

By the grace of God, amen. It has been advised by my lawyer Mr. Dole & others that I, Major Ludlum, put in writing a last will & testament so that my worldly possessions may be disbursed after I am gone. I am however profoundly certain that as everything else has been taken out of my hands since the Rev. Mr. Rabon's passing with no regard for my wishes nor the truth, that this most sorry practice will in fact continue after my death & that Sarah Williamson & the good citizens of Kingston will carve up my possessions as they see fit, & so to hell with them. As I have no wife or children nor relations who have meaning it is of no consequent to myself what becomes of my property. So in the stead of a will I shall make this document the final & true statement of the events leading up to my wrongful arrest & condemnation. Posterity & the vigilance of Almighty God in whom my faith is sorely tried but ultimately unshaken will witness to the righteousness of my claim & blast the rest.

It is two days now from when it is said that I am finally to be hanged, as my lawyer Mr. Doyle informed me that his meeting with the governor was of no good & is why I have been removed back to Kingston jail to await the payment of the debt it is claimed I owe. I owe no debt for I did not shoot the Rev. Mr. Rabon & so owe not one thing any more than I owed the Rev. payment on his rot-

THE LAST TESTAMENT OF MAJOR LUDLUM

ten lumber, which is why I suppose I am here in the 1st place, that along with the business of Sarah which was nobody's fault but my own as well as the sorry judgment of the community.

They have said that there was malice between myself & the Rev. Mr. Rabon as if this was proof enough that I did the crime. That this malice existed is a fact I have admitted freely both before my trial & during as well as after, & that this foresaid malice existed for good reason. I had contracted with the Rev. in November of the year of our Lord 1904 to purchase a quantity of timber for the shoring up of my barn which was in a state of lamentable disrepair & sundry other improvements on my property. Which timber I signed for in good faith only to find when I received said timber that it was in fact rotted & in generally poor condition with holes & soft places in it so as to make it worthless for my or any other purposes. I refused to pay & rightly so but the Rev. insisted on payment claiming I signed for the property & so owed him payment.

It was said during the proceedings of my trial that I was a rough man who lived outside the laws of man & God & that it was no wonder that I would not hesitate to take a human life. Perhaps I have failed to be a good Christian for which failing my Lord & Savior will judge me these two days hence but I have never taken human life, not the Rev.'s nor anybody's unless the two negroes I shot for crossing the Dead Line count as the prosecution seemed to think they did ignoring the fact that I was merely keeping the standards of the community which has been ordained by tradition in that no negro shall come north of the Dead Line to live or to work. The prosecution & the good citizens of Kingston seemed to have ignored that fact besides which one of the negroes fell in a ditch & crawled out & away & was not seen no more & so may or may not have died.

But even as I have not taken human life so I have always paid all debts which are truly mine & I so informed the Rev. when he tried to charge me for the rotted lumber. I told him that his lumber was no good as any damn fool could see & so I needn't to pay for it or any other damaged goods. I told him so reasonable & calm which I know I did as I had not anything to drink that day excepting water at my own well. The Rev. informed me in a loud voice so that all his workers both white & colored turned to look at us (for we were standing in his lumber yard at the time) that he weren't to be talked back to by a poorbucker like myself & that I had signed for the lumber & so owed him the money & that the few holes that was in the lumber was of no account & would in any case probably be an improvement on whatever I had in the first place. Not wanting to be stared at by the negroes or the trash he had in his employ I said in also as loud a voice as possible that I did not understand why the Presbyterians of Kingston could not afford to have a full-time preacher as rather a preacher & lumberman & that for the spiritual good of the community I hoped that he was better at the first than at the last for his lumber was rotten & I would not pay for it, & so turned & walked away.

It is of no import to detail here what followed in later days & weeks, for my time draws nigh & while my jailer has sworn to provide me with as much paper as necessary to my avowed purpose I do not trust the white trash who imprison me to be faithful to the truth any more than the high & mighty citizens who condemned me. Suffice it to say that after a powerful weight of discourse between the Rev. & myself that the following month the same Sheriff Hamacker who will I am told escort me to the gallows found that I was in the right & that as the timber was "demonstrably faulty" as he showed when he broke a four-inch thick board with both hands & little effort I owed the Rev. no money. I thanked him soundly & went about my business.

From that day on the wrath of the Rev. Mr. Rabon was directed at me. His sermons, I am told, begun to weigh heavy in their attacks upon the unrighteous & the unchurched & the flouters of God's law with most specific reference to some of those who existed outside the limits of the town of Kingston like they also lived outside the limits of the City of God. A man told me that the Rev. even cited my name as an example of the ignorant damned once but I have not in truth ever been able to confirm this.

Now I am used to the scorn of those who were born in town & fancy theirselves of higher station than the rest of us who do their work oftentimes & are no better than colored in their eyes. I say I am most used to it & it does not bother me one bit. I am not ignorant no matter what they say as I know for my schoolteacher Miss Sessions once told me that I had a powerful fluency with my language & should control & develop it which I never done until now as until now I had no need or desire of writing more than my name when necessary. I am neither ignorant in the ways of the world of men & know for a fact that the Rev. Mr. Rabon was mightily angry at me for having been made a fool of by a poorbucker & nothing he said or did would surprise me.

It did not even surprise me when he began to publicly stain Sarah Williamson & myself. I was aware when I took up with Sarah that the community at large would more than likely as not scorn us for we were not lawfully man & wife & thus sinners. Yet as the community at large has never seemed at all anxious to acknowledge me as other than rough & ill-bred & away from the center of their world it has not seemed necessary for me to do other than see after my own affairs & farm what I can & provide for myself & be left alone, occasionally to do the citizens a service by taking out their negroes when they stray across the Line which I would do anyway as they have no business up here. So if I choose to provide myself with a woman who pleases me I do not see where it is any business of the community of Kingston or the Rev. Mr. Rabon. Admittedly also it was known to me that Sarah was still in the eyes of the law married to Mr. Williamson but it was also known to all folks around & to Almighty God as well that he was a drunk who was unable to provide for her or satisfy her in a husbandly way & cared not what she did. It is said in the Holy Bible that King David partook freely of his handmaidens & if a king can do that with many women I do not see why a simple man as myself should not have an abandoned white woman of some comeliness & no use to anyone else.

& Sarah & I took up & I must witness here as God is watching & the gallows loom that I took care of her, good & proper. I saw to her needs & provided for her & never beat her except that she was ever showing me disrespect or refused to come to me when I wanted her as the Holy Scripture ordains woman to obey man. This never did her no harm & besides if she did not come to me & I beat her she more likely came to me the quicker & with enthusiasm. & as Sarah did washing & odd chores for the high & mighty citizens of Kingston she was able to tell me tales of them that amused me, not the least of which was that the Rev. Mr. Rabon's wife would meet Sarah regular to give her washing & have marks & sundry bruises on her face & elsewhere & claimed she had fell or some such when it was plain to anyone with eyes that she had been beat. Sarah would lay in my arms & tell me these things which pleased me near as much as the smell & touch of her herself.

Yet the Rev. maintained his persecution, & as I said this did not surprise me none too greatly. But it would be less than the truth which above all as God knows I want hard to convey if I did not say that it did surprise me when the Rev. appeared on my doorstep having driven in his mule & wagon all the way up from Kingston for the purpose of reading me scripture & to threaten swearing out a warrant against Sarah & myself on grounds of adultery. This was on July 18th 1905 & as the Rev. read the scripture the sweat poured from his brow from the heat & perhaps also as I have thought since from his nerves as he was right farther from town than he usually strayed & if he had been colored I could have shot him.

At this point I must as I am before God & posterity affirm that I was indeed drunk when the Rev. appeared, having just bought a jug of good corn & been sharing it with Sarah, who was also right drunken inside. When he told me the Savior's words that whosoever looketh at a woman with lust in his heart has committed adultery with that woman I laughed & asked the Rev. if he remembered what it looked like. He then became abusive & began to threaten me with the warrant, & I did shout back at him, & then Sarah came stumbling out the door to see what the shouting was about. She was as I have said prior drunk & only partially clothed, & I have after much powerful thought the thin satisfaction of knowing that the Rev. defied his Savior as he stared at my woman. But at the time in my drunkenness it enraged me & I struck him & shoved him off my porch, & then turned & hit Sarah & shoved her inside with my foot. & then I did turn to the Rev. Mr. Rabon & say that if he bothered me more I would kill him.

I have thought of those words often in the time that has passed since then & regretted them heartily, & if there was some way to unsay them I would. Yet I cannot lie now & say that I did not say them for I did. Yet I am not neither lying when I swear before Almighty God that I never did act on those words.

For it was not until the following evening when Sheriff Hamacker & his men came to arrest me & Sarah that I learned of the Rev.'s death. It was not until their questioning begun that I learned of the circumstance. That the Rev. was plowing in his field that morning & that he was shot in the back while plowing, that he fell on his plow & remained so for the afternoon so that a young high & mighty driving by in her horse & buggy thought he had fallen asleep at work, that when the Sheriff & his men finally arrived the sun had worked so on the body to where it was so hot they thought the Rev. still lived.

It is of no consequent to detail the events which followed our arrest as they are well known to all. Despite my protests of innocence & lack of direct evidence, Sarah & myself were in fact brought to trial & were both convicted. The prosecutor made much of us before the good citizens of Kingston & cited the business of the warrant for adultery besides which was all in all enough to convince twelve good men & true. My lawyer Mr. Dole, who moved here from other parts & has confided in me as we have grown closer throughout the weeks & months that he feels as much of an outsider as any poorbucker, fought good & proper for me but failed before the justice of Kingston. That is one thing I wish to note about the trial.

The other being that as Sarah sat on the stand & was questioned by the prosecutor as to did I in fact threaten to kill the Rev. Mr. Rabon she said "Yes he did" which I would expect no more as it is the truth & I had already admitted as much. But when she was asked if I was capable of carrying out such a vicious deed she stared into the stifling air of the court & said "Yes he is" & no more. Nothing in my defense.

My lawyer Mr. Doyle informs me that this is why Sarah was convicted but with mercy & not sentenced to hang. I say she also is no better than the rest.

Of the appeals which followed & which my lawyer Mr. Doyle so heroically pursued I will not relate neither as it has been a full day since the beginning of this my testament & I prefer to spend my last hours on this earth in contemplation of my fate & my God who awaits me rather than scratching on this paper. Suffice it to say it has none of it been to no use & I will die tomorrow. Only two things remain.

One is that my lawyer Mr. Doyle has been of great service to me, even to having me removed elsewhere for a time so that the Rev.'s kinfolk might not get me, & it is not his fault that I have come to this end. When he last visited me yesterday as I was writing this he embraced me & left with tears in his eyes. I have scorned such from men in the past but am moved by it now.

The second thing being that before my lawyer Mr. Dole came in yesterday I was visited by the Rev. Mr. Rabon's widow. She was & is an ugly woman & no better than the rest but I was curious that she should visit me now & more so that she should stand outside my cell & say nothing, just stare at me. The prosecutor said she did not appear at my trial in that she was too overcome with grief & three witnesses said where she was that morning which was elsewhere than the Rev.'s field. As she turned to leave I noticed that her bruises were almost healed.

THE LAST TESTAMENT OF MAJOR LUDLUM

I am most grievously sorry for what sins I have committed but do not apologize for those of which I am not guilty & say now what I will witness on the gallows tomorrow: you are hanging an innocent man.

Sarah tears at me. I never left a mark on her.

I trust the Rev. Mr. Rabon is satisfied now & is looking up from hell & laughing. God damn him, & the rest, each & all.

ROAD DEAD

There was no cell service in our town. The nearest tower was in the next county. The closest place we could get a signal was the cemetery north of town. Danny needed to make a call and the rest of us didn't have anything better to do. Jake drove and Danny called shotgun. Rob and I were in the back. Before the turn to the cemetery there was a turn onto a dead end road and at the turn there was a sign that said Private Road Dead End. It had been there ever since I could remember. But there were smudges over the Private and the End like someone had tried to erase them and if you just looked quick it looked like the sign said Road Dead. Well hell Jake said and turned onto the road. What the fuck I got to make my call Danny said. Sorry man got to check this out Jake said. Goddammit I got to make this call make it quick Danny said. Good luck with that Rob said. I didn't say anything. I couldn't remember the last time I'd been on this road. Jake kept driving. It hadn't rained in forever and the car kicked up a lot of dust. The sky was overcast though and you couldn't see the sun. There were plenty of clouds. It just wouldn't rain. We got to the end of the road and there was a log cabin. That prefab shit Rob said. No this one looks old I said. And it did. The wood was so worn it was almost shiny and there were patches on it where it looked like someone had tried to chop the house down. Jake pulled over on the far side of the road from the house and cut the motor. He rolled his window down and we could hear music coming from the house. Classical music like the teacher played in humanities unit. It sounded familiar and before I knew it I said Bach. Danny turned around and looked at me. Lah de dah Professor he said. Rob snorted like it was funny. Then Danny said to Jake now what? Don't know Jake said. Make up your fucking mind I still got to make my call Danny said. Jake looked at Danny and said well fuck all right then. Jake got out of the car and started walking towards the house. Dumb shit always got to be chasing something Danny said. Then he started checking his phone. God damn this sorry remote ass place he said. Rob snorted again. Fucking Bach he said. Jake walked up at an angle to the front door and moved toward the side of the house. He put his elbows out to the side and got up on tiptoe and made a big deal out of creeping up to the house like he was one of the Three Stooges. When he got up to the side of the house he made another big deal of peering into what I guess was a window and then he kind of shook and went forward like he had tripped and then he wasn't there anymore. You couldn't tell if he had tripped and fallen in through the window or if he'd been pulled inside. Fuck Rob said. Danny was still fooling with his phone. What happened he said. Goddammit I said and got out of the car and walked across the road over to where Jake had been. There was a window all right but it was closed. I looked inside. They didn't have any lights on and it was hard to see much but there were a bunch of people. More than you would have thought would have been inside such a small place. Some were men and some were women and they all wore regular clothes. I didn't see Jake. One of the men was lying on some sort of table. He was strapped down to the table and it didn't look like he had any clothes on. He was shaking. Not like he was cold but like he was riding down a rough road. A couple of times he seemed about ready to jump off the table but the straps held him down. Some of the people were holding things but I couldn't tell what they were. You could hear the music like the window was open. There was another window on the other side of the room that looked like it was covered in plastic until you realized the whole wall was covered in plastic and the plastic had dark stains all over it. I looked again at the man on the table and for a second I thought I knew him but then the one standing closest to him looked up. It was a woman. I don't know if she saw me or not but she stared like she was looking at something. I backed away from the window and into someone standing right behind me. I yelled and spun around. It was Danny. He and Rob had gotten out of the car and followed me over to the window. Fuck fuck fuck I said and ran for the car. Danny beat me there and got in and started it up. Rob and I piled in and we took off. We hauled down the road and turned and headed back up the main road towards the cemetery. What about Jake Rob said. I don't know I said. Danny didn't say a word but when we got up to the cemetery he pulled in and started driving up the path. The fuck you doing Rob said. Danny kept on as fast as he had been going on the main road. A loose rock flew up off the dirt and cracked the windshield. When we got to the very back past all the tombstones he stopped the car. The fuck you doing Rob said. Rob's right what about Jake we've got to go back I said. You looked through that fucking window fuck Jake it's his own goddamn fault Danny said. Then what are we doing here why don't we go I said. Danny looked at his phone and then looked and us. I've got a signal he said and got out of the car. It was Jake's fucking idea he said and walked away. Rob and I stayed in the car. I turned around and looked back at the main road. The tombstones ran down to the road in neat rows. One near the car had fallen over. Danny was standing by it talking into his phone low like he was trying to keep a secret but I could hear him. Hello? he said. Hello? I looked at Rob. Now what I said but now he was looking back at the main road so I turned back around. A car was pulling into the cemetery with another right behind it. About halfway up the path the first car stopped and then the second. The first car turned its lights on bright and the driver got out and then the rest of them. And Jake. Jake got out of the second car and started moving towards Danny but Danny didn't notice. He was still talking into his phone but now he was shouting. Hello? he kept saying. Hello? Hello?

MADELINE'S VERSION

She had been sick a long time, and when the physician finally declared recovery impossible, no one was surprised. Not even her brother, prostrate by her bedside, his lamentations shrill and echoing upward to be lost in the arched ceiling. His flesh and blood and very self. What would he do, what, what? The dim lamp by her bedside lit without illuminating; the torches on the wall flickered and cast random shadows. She could see the physician standing in the corner of the room, muttering to the nurse. "No, good God, they can't come in here. Tell them I'll be out presently." Her hearing was unusually acute. The nurse went out; her brother pressed her pale hand to his paler face. She tried to smile at him but failed, contented herself with what she hoped was a loving glance into his gleaming mad eyes. She was cold despite the covers. Everything seemed so far away.

She said nothing. For even longer than she had been sick, she had said nothing. There was no longer any need to speak.

II

They had been taught, when they still had tutors, that while brother-and sister twins were not uncommon, it was impossible that they be identical; the laws of biological science would not have it so. Nonetheless, there they were, she and her brother. The broad brow; the large, liquid eyes; the delicate nose. The thin lips; the finely-molded chin, wanting prominence. The soft, web-like hair; the death-pale skin. She fancied that all of these features were more pronounced in her brother than in her, that perhaps her chin was a touch stronger, her hair a bit thicker, her skin a shade less pale. But everyone who had ever seen them together—fewer and fewer as they grew older—remarked the same: they were identical. Not mirror images, as a mirror is a reflection and reversal; not a duplication, with one the original and the other a copy. Identical.

A servant, attached to the household since before Madeline's birth, had grown talkative in her dotage. Before her death, she had told Madeline that their parents had dressed them alike during their infancy and well into their childhood, sometimes in dresses, sometimes in breeches and coats. Madeline did not remember this. She barely remembered their parents at all: dim figures treading slowly, arm in arm, through the great house, or around the grounds, surrounded by the dull, gray mist that perpetually enveloped their home, that seemed to ooze from the trees and rise from the ground itself. Their faces had been the image of their children's. One day the physician had appeared and told her and her brother that their parents had died. She never saw the bodies, was not told of a funeral. Since then it had been only her brother, and her, and the vast, crumbling house.

III

She awoke, unaware of how long she had been asleep. The nurse, seeing her awake, came to her bedside, helped her with the chamber pot, and proceeded to bathe her. She could tell that the cloth was soft and the water warm, but she could barely register either sensation. She heard voices down the hall, in the upstairs drawing room: her brother's, and that of an unknown man. She looked at the nurse inquiringly. "His Lordship has a visitor, m'lady," she said, turning Madeline to reach the small of her back. "An old school friend, I'm told. His Lordship seems pleased for the company, though it's hard to tell, he's still so dreadful nervous. He worries about you so, m'lady. I hope his friend can revive his spirits."

She tried to take this in. Someone else in the house? She remembered the one period of her life when she and her brother had not been together, when he had been away at school. His visits home had included references to his schoolmates, and one in particular with whom he had established a relationship of some sympathy. She remembered her discomfort at this, and how he had had to hold her close and kiss her eyes and assure her that he would not leave. And he did not. Adam? Andrew? She could barely tolerate the presence of the servants, but something within in her needed to know. What was the man's name? With some effort, she pushed herself upright and pointed toward her wardrobe.

The nurse helped her as far as the drawing-room door; Madeline pushed her away, leaned on the doorsill, and listened.

"It is the curse of this family," her brother was saying. "The stem of our race, time-honored as it is, has put forth, at no period, any enduring branch. The entire family lies in the direct line of descent, and has always, with trifling variation, so lain. Small wonder that I am stricken so. There is nothing to alleviate our condition, which is passed on undiluted from generation to generation."

"But Rod, dear fellow," the stranger said, his accent marking his Southern origins. "Is there truly nothing to be done? Perhaps a sojourn from this—this too-familiar environment. Let me take you—"

"No!" he cried, his voice strangled with agitation. "No, Allan, I cannot leave this place! The most insipid food is alone endurable; my eyes are tortured by even a faint light—how, then, might I survive out in the ungovernable world? You are right; the physique of these gray walls and turrets has surely poisoned the morale of my existence. Yet, I cannot—I dare not—leave."

"But would it not also be beneficial to Madeline? A change of scenery, at least, if not in fact different treatment from a different doctor—"

"Madeline! She is gone!" His voice broke. "It is more than I can take. We have been together always; she is of me, and I of her. Her decease will leave me—me, the hopeless and the frail—the last of the ancient race of—"

Their conversation ceased upon her entrance. The room, as always, oppressed her. Dark draperies obscured the walls; armorial trophies rattled as she strode upon the black floor. The scattering of books and musical instruments left an impression not of activity, but of disuse. She was too weak to traverse the great length of the room, but passed through it at an angle, away from her brother and his visitor. They were obscured in the dim light; curious as she was, she could not bring herself to look directly at them. But out of the corner of her eye she apprehended the stranger: well-dressed, of an age with her brother, and—she paused, imperceptibly, at this—although not of an absolute likeness, bearing a passing resemblance to the two of them! The same high forehead, the same nose; the thin line of the lips obscured beneath an elegant moustache. He stared at her as she crossed to the side door, a look of astonishment on his face.

Once out the door, she stopped and leaned against the wall, panting for breath. "Good God," she heard the stranger say. "Her figure, her air, her features—"

"I dread the events of the future," her brother said. "Not in themselves, but in their results. I feel that I must inevitably abandon life and reason together in my struggles with some fatal demon of fear."

The nurse found her where she had fallen and helped her back to her room. As they passed the staircase, her gaze fell downward. The physician stood in the foyer addressing two men. Their thick, ugly faces were smeared with dirt, as were their tattered clothes. One wore an eyepatch; the other's teeth were rotting out of his head. "It won't be long now, boys," she heard the physician say. "When I give the word, be ready."

IV

There had been moments of comfort, of relative contentment and peace. When Roderick had finally returned from school to stay, she had felt an overpowering sense of relief. There had been many pleasant hours. He had played his guitar; she had accompanied him on her flute. There had been many books and many conversations. The absence of others seemed no absence at all.

But as they moved through their twenties, he changed. He had always talked, in moments of depression, about "the family curse," "the flaw in their house." She had paid him no heed when he was in those moods. Did they not have the house, and servants, and money? Did they not have each other? They needed nothing else, no one else. She would inevitably wean him from his sadness, and everything would be as it was.

As the years passed, though, her strategies gradually failed. He grew into himself and away from her. His nature, always sensitive, became more and more intolerant of the sensations of life. Her flute, he said, pierced his ears like nails; she abandoned it. The light hurt his eyes, so the house went dark. Their conversations became monologues, she listening patiently to his increasingly eccentric pronouncements:

"Do not question the acuteness of my senses! You call them morbid? Observe!" he would cry, holding his index finger aloft. "If I venture to displace the microscopial speck of dust which lies now upon the point of my finger, what is the character of that act upon which I have adventured? I have done a deed which shakes the Moon in her path, which causes the Sun to no longer be the sun, and which alters forever the destiny of the myriads of stars!"

The sounds of his guitar became muted and erratic; his paintings, which she had formerly enjoyed, became abstract, unfathomable. His looks grew wild; sometimes he seemed to regard her with nothing less than pure loathing. Then he would break down, grab her in his arms and sob that she was all he had, was everything; he could not lose her; they could not lose each other.

Over time, she ceased to feel. Her senses, with the lone exception of her hearing, attenuated. Avoiding Roderick's chambers, she wandered through the creaking hallways, peering into unused rooms whose dim light only worsened the darkness. Down sometimes even into the sub-basement, the vault where they had played as children, not realizing then the fierce use to which the room, as a dungeon, had been put in remote feudal times, nor its more recent incarnation as a repository for powder and other combustibles. She walked about the grounds, circling the tarn in which their house lay reflected. She would stop and gaze at the house, its vacant, eye-like windows seeming to pierce her where she stood. There was a scarcely-noticeable crack in the stonework, beginning underneath the roof and zigzagging down to the ground. She breathed deeply of the unceasing fog which seemed to rise from the stagnant water and the moldering walls. She wished she could disappear into it.

Eventually she no longer left the house. Her strength ebbed; her body grew gaunt; her sleep was increasingly prolonged. The physician could do nothing. Her brother wept. She fell silent.

V

She felt her eyes open but could see nothing. Had she finally gone blind as well? Then her vision cleared, and she found herself staring at a thick white cloth. She thought someone had pulled a blanket over her head, but the whiteness held several inches from her face. She tried to reach up and touch it, but her arms would not respond.

Then she felt a sudden shock beneath her, a bump and a scraping sound. She was inside something and was being moved. Her eyes fell shut again. She had no perception of her own breathing.

Down, and then down again; she was being carried beneath

the house—if, indeed, she were still in the house. For the first time in months, she felt the urge to speak, to cry out, but her voice was frozen along with her limbs.

She came to a halt, was set down with a thud. There was a soft creaking sound and a sudden gush of air; someone had opened the lid. She was dimly aware of two male voices from somewhere above her, fading in and out:

"—faint blush upon her bosom and face. Almost—"

"—oh my sister, my love! You cannot understand—"

Allan. Roderick.

"—sympathies of a scarcely intelligible nature have always existed between us. It is the end of the line, our line—"

She was in her coffin. They thought her dead and were preparing to bury her.

"But are you certain this is what you wish, Rod? Would it not be perhaps more fitting to give her a proper burial, with proper rites?"

"We had the priest in last night. And as I conveyed to you earlier, I have no choice. You yourself remarked on the commingling of perplexity and low cunning on the physician's face. A rare malady such as Madeline's calls to the betrayer of Hippocrates as surely as the dead and rotting animal calls to the vulture. I dare not entrust her to the remote and exposed situation of our family burial ground."

She tried with every fiber of her being to move, to speak, but remained motionless and silent. Allan muttered something in Latin; Roderick moaned, "Farewell, dear sister!" There was a gentle thump followed by the tightening of screws. Footsteps, a tortured screech of metal, a final, hopeless thud. Mercifully, the lassitude overcame her once more, and she slept.

VI

One day when they were fifteen, lounging in his bedchamber, she told him what the old servant had said of them being dressed alike as children. "I remember," he replied. "That would be passing strange now, would it not?" She had laughed at the thought and, for a joke, left the room and returned wearing one of his outfits, shirt and breeches and a slightly oversized vest. "We are truly identical now," she had declared. He looked at her with eyes shining even brighter than usual. He walked over to her, caressed her cheek with his hand. "On the outside, yes. But what about underneath?" He unbuttoned his shirt and stripped it off. She looked at his chest, as naked and smooth as his face. He reached to the top button of her shirt; she finished for him and let it fall to the floor. She had removed her corset but kept her other undergarments on. He dropped to his knees, pulled off her trousers, buried his face in her belly. She could feel his breath through the thin white linen. She stroked his hair, stared up at the ceiling. He rose and removed the rest of his clothes. She stared at the wisp of hair, the rope and sac of flesh beneath. She had seen his body before, when they were children, but not like this. She felt her own private parts clutch, moisten. She let the linen fall as she followed him to his bed. It was quickly done. Over time, they learned more. It was the easiest and most natural of things; years later, when he finally drew away from her and she fell silent, she missed it dreadfully until feelings left altogether and she no longer missed anything.

VII

She awoke again to voices, but this time unknown, muffled by the closed lid:

"Hurry up, damn you!"

"Why? She ain't goin' nowhere." Laughter and the creak of wood pried from wood.

"I don't care. God knows you made enough noise getting us in here to have the whole house down on us. I don't like this place, and I don't like this job, and I don't like you much either, so get that damned lid off and let's be done with it."

"Whining like a woman, Christ almighty. I suppose you'd rather be back on that worthless farm squeezing cow tits."

"I'd rather be in bed squeezing your wife's tits."

A harsh, mirthless laugh. "God damn you, I'll give you something to squeeze when I get this lid open." A final sharp, wrenching sound. "Ah! There we go." She heard the lid open, felt—felt!—a gush of cool, damp air, followed by heat. A light burned through her closed eyelids. "Take a look, eh? She got right peaked there at the end, but she's still a woman. Shame for the doc to want to cut all that up." A hand rested on her right breast, grasped roughly, calluses scraping against her skin. Foul breath washed over her face.

"For God's sake, Jeremy, are you mad? It's bad enough what we're doing—"

She opened her eyes and sat up. The man with the rotting teeth jumped back from her coffin screaming like a woman and dropped his torch on the floor. The one with the eyepatch, standing at the foot of the coffin, shouted "Christ save us!" and fled through the open door.

She blinked her eyes wildly; even the dim light seeping in from the open door seemed bright, and the glow of the torch cut painfully into her vision. She was in the vault beneath the house. Her coffin rested on two pillars; there was nothing else in the room. She raised her arms, clutched the side of the coffin, winced from the agony of unused muscles.

The man who had been molesting her stopped screaming. "Devil!" he cried, pulling out a knife. "Back to hell with you!" He ran to her, swinging the knife wildly. It cut her shoulder and her face. The wounds burned like fire. She tried to scream, but the only sound that emerged was more like the hiss of a snake. Her arm shot up reflexively, and her untrimmed nails scraped the man's face. He screamed again and fell unconscious to the floor.

She pulled herself out of the coffin and stumbled bleeding to the door. The entire room was lined with copper, walls and floor alike the same reddish-brown hue. A gritty substance crunched under her feet. As she staggered into the corridor, she heard the crackle and buzz of something igniting behind her. Her wounds were superficial but bleeding profusely. She wiped her face and went to find her brother.

VIII

Once she had awakened in the middle of the night to find him standing over her with a knife. The light from the doorway gleamed off the blade and illuminated his eyes. Much of madness and more of sin. He was unaware of, or ignored, her uncomprehending gaze. Then he lowered the knife, turned, and walked away.

IX

The doors to the drawing room were shut, but she heard voices within. Her hearing, so acute for so long, failed her; she recognized Roderick's voice, and thought the other belonged to Allan, but she could not make out what they said. Roderick's voice grew louder. As she reached the door, his words came clear in a scream that frightened her more than the men in the vault: "Madman! *I tell you that she now stands without the door!*"

She pushed the doors open. Allan sat in a chair in the middle of the room holding a large, leather-bound book which he let fall to the floor as she entered. The windows were thrown open; a tremendous storm raged outside, and the curtains were soaked. Lightning dazzled the room. She stood motionless, trembling with a sudden chill, weak from her paralysis and loss of blood. Roderick stared at her, all expression gone from his face. She tried to call out his name but could only manage a wordless moan. She moved to him, lost her balance, threw out her arms. They fell to the floor together, and Roderick did not move again.

She heard Allan run out of the room as she lay motionless atop Roderick. She raised her head and looked down at her brother. She tried to weep, knew she should weep, but there were no tears. She closed his eyes and mouth, smoothed his hair, kissed him gently on the forehead. With great effort, she arose and made her way out of the room, down the corridor and staircase, and out of the house through the closer-by back entrance.

She got only a few steps before she collapsed. She lay sprawled on the grass and looked up at the house. The sky churned with the final spasms of the storm. There was a rumbling sound from within and beneath the house; the windowpanes began to shatter, and one by one the rooms went dark, like eyes closing. There was a great cracking sound from the other side of the house, and the fissure that ran along the front suddenly appeared under the back eaves and ran like a fuse down to the ground. There was more rumbling, and more, and an explosion, and another, and the house crashed down before her under the light of the blood-red moon. Beyond the rubble of her home she could see the tarn churning as if it boiled, and beyond that, the figure of a man running away.

She lay on the ground for a very long time. Then she got up, brushed herself off as best she could, and began to walk toward the road that ran some distance away from the house. As she neared it, she could see the light of torches and the shadows of wagons come to investigate the catastrophe. When the wagon arrived, she regarded its startled occupants, took a deep breath, and cleared her throat. "My name is Madeline," she said. "Please help me."

THE SEXUAL COMPONENT OF ALIEN ABDUCTION (THREE-HEADED ALIEN BLUES)

> *". . . it has become painfully clear that sexuality is a major part of abduction. A vast majority of the abductees felt that the experience went well beyond reproductive curiosity and smack dab into lusty sex."*
>
> —Kevin D. Randle, Russ Estes, and William P. Cone, Ph.D., *The Abduction Enigma* (1999), p. 91.

Well the guys around here don't know how to treat a girl

Chad insists that Jolene keep her cowboy boots on and grind the heels into his hips at the moment of orgasm. He does request that she remove the spurs. She considers that cheating.

No the guys around here don't know how to treat a girl

Hank demands that she take her boots off, but wear chaps. She does her best to hide her impatience when he complains that the chaps are not real leather. The lasso placates him somewhat.

Now I got me something that's really out of this world
Initially, Jolene thinks nothing of the light that winks on the periphery of her vision. The clear night is filled with stars.

Well he's got three heads and he uses them all on me
The stirrups are familiar. The examination area is not unlike the side room at the Country Rock Café, the table on which she lies reminiscent of the pool table in Chad's rec room. At this point, she is relatively unconcerned.

Yeah he's got three heads and he uses them all on me
She awakens precisely seated behind the wheel of her Grand Am. There are scratches on the inside of her thighs and blood caked between.

Now I'm as happy as an Earthling girl can be
She tells no one but Floyd, her cat, who remains noncommittal.

Well he takes his first head and puts it on my mouth
The light turns blue, then red, then both, then white, brighter even than the spotlight beneath which she danced at her third grade recital. The clicking sounds of her examiners are not unlike the sound of her tap shoes striking the stage floor. She ascends, smiling.

Then he aims his second head a little further south
The probes fill her. They are not cold like her doctor's.

When he uses his third head it makes me scream and shout
Through squinted eyes, the middle one vaguely resembles Hank in his cowboy hat.

Oo-oo-oo-ee, first head on my mouth
Dissatisfied with Floyd's unresponsiveness, she permits herself to get drunk with Hank and Chad and informs them of her activities. Chad is dubious. Hank looks pointedly at the lasso coiled on her living room wall.

Oo-oo-oo-ee, second head going south
Chad, naked, bent double, the probe inserted with cool efficiency, does, in fact, squeal like a pig. Hank looks pointedly at the examiners coiled on the chamber wall. Jolene smiles.

Oo-oo-oo-ee, third head makes me scream and shout
[guitar solo]

Well he's got three heads and he uses them all on me
There is no charge for the abduction survivors' support group other than the occasional donation for refreshments. Still, Chad and Hank decline to attend.

Yeah he's got three heads and he uses them all on me
After several meetings, Jolene awakens suddenly one night lying fully clothed on top of her freshly made bed. Her boots are covered with mud. Outside her window, the clear night remains filled with stars.

Well, fuck these humans—I'm happy as I can be!
They came all that way for her.

Well it's hi-yo, Silver Surfer,
Hi-yo, Silver Surfer,
Hi-yo, hi-yo Silver, away!

MARIA WORKS AT OCEAN CITY NAILS

We're standing outside of Ocean City Nails, where Maria works, when Bobby walks up. Bobby was always a fat kid. When he was younger his mother Patti, my dad's cousin, used to say that it was OK if he was a fat kid, that when he was a teenager he'd get tall and slim down. When he turned thirteen he started getting tall but he didn't slim down any. He's fifteen now, at least I think he's fifteen, and when he walks up he kind of jiggles all over. None of it's muscle.

"Sup," Nick says. It's me and Nick hanging with Leo while Leo's waiting for Maria to get off work.

"My dick," Bobby says. "Got to get me some tonight."

Bobby's always going on about getting some, acting bad. Like anyone would even give this fat fuck a handjob under the bleachers Friday night if they were so bored out of their fucking minds they could convince themselves it was a joke and better than being bored. He's shameless, though, totally fucking shameless, thinks it's funny, knows it's stupid, just goes right ahead. When the Demetrios twins started filling out he waited around after school just so he could follow them down the street to their uncle's restaurant and then come tell us how he followed them down the street to their uncle's restaurant and how he had to get himself some of that. He was such a hopeless fat fuck they didn't even complain to their uncle, who would have been happy to chop Bobby's balls off and serve them in a salad.

"My Big Fat Greek Pussy," Bobby would say to us and then laugh like it was funny.

"He just got out of the clinic," Nick says. "The one where the celebrities go for sex addiction. You a sex addict, Bobby?"

"Fuck yeah," Bobby says.

"Asshole," Leo says. Leo's never had any use for Bobby. I don't mean like the rest of us who know Bobby's a stupid fat fuck and don't pay any attention. I mean getting this wrong look on his face whenever Bobby's around. My grandmother Bataglia used to say that there was a difference between dislike and hostility. It's OK to dislike someone, you can't be a human being and go through life without disliking some people, but you shouldn't feel hostile towards anyone. Then she'd quote something—she used to teach in a college—in this old form of Italian that even my dad, who spent a year back in Italy when he was about my age, didn't even understand, quote it like it meant something to anybody besides her. The point being that the rest of us kind of disliked Bobby if we thought of him at all, but Leo felt hostile towards him, and I never understood why. It's not like Bobby mouthed off about Leo's sisters, because he didn't have any, just the two older brothers and one of them died in the war. And it's not like he talked shit about Maria. Nobody, including Leo, talked shit about Maria. Even stupid fat fuck Bobby understood that.

"Whose asshole? Yours?" Bobby says to Leo. "You got a personal problem? Something stuck up there?"

"Shut the fuck up," Leo says.

Bobby laughs and doesn't notice Leo shifting his weight and clenching and unclenching his right fist, but I do, and I say, "So when is Maria getting off work?"

"Soon enough," Leo says, his fist still clenched. Bobby's grinning like the fucking moron he is, hands stuffed in his hoodie pockets, bobbing up and down on the balls of his feet so everything's jiggling.

"Let's go in," says Nick, who I can tell also sees how pissed Leo's getting.

Leo's fist finally relaxes. "Whatever," he says, and we all go into the salon, Bobby too, still grinning, not caring that nobody wants him there.

Inside Maria's working on some old lady's nails. They're the only people in the place. I don't recognize the old woman. She kind of looks like my grandmother O'Donnell but not quite. Grandma let her hair go and didn't give a shit. This old lady's hair is some kind of fucked-up orange. Like anyone would think that's real. She's sitting straight up in a padded chair that looks like my dad's recliner and got her hands stuck in something that looks like one of those rollaway TV stands. Everything else in the place looks beat to shit but this TV stand thing is bright and shiny. Maria's sitting in the chair by her.

"Hey," Leo says.

Maria cuts her eyes up at Leo and he doesn't say anything else, just nods. Then she looks back at the old lady, who looks like a ghost next to Maria. Even with her hair tied back and in her Ocean City Nails blouse and slacks that make her look like she should be working in a hospital, Maria just drowns the old woman right out, her and the beat-to-shit recliner chair she's sitting in, and the whole room, really, like Maria was some sort of special effect they spliced in over the boring real actors.

"Look at you, Madge," Maria says to the old woman. "Looking so beautiful. You're all ready to go out man hunting."

Madge snorts and I think for a second I see her drool but then I look closer and she's not. "I've had a man. One was enough. I don't need another one."

"Ow! Jesus Mary and Joseph!"

Somebody's yelling and me and Nick and Leo all look toward the back of the store where the tanning booth is and some kind of partition beside it, which is where the yelling came from. Even Bobby is distracted for a moment from staring at Maria, which I guess Leo has decided is OK as long as he keeps his distance and doesn't fucking say anything.

"Waxing," Maria says without taking her eyes off of Madge's nails.

I immediately think of some woman lying back there with her legs spread and I know the others are thinking the same fucking thing, especially Bobby, but we don't say anything because Maria is right there and so is the old lady Madge.

"Waxing," Madge says. "Shaving. My mother always said these young girls should never start shaving."

"Oh come on, Madge," Maria says. "You want us to look all hairy and gross?"

"She said that if they just let it grow for a while when they first start becoming young ladies and don't start shaving it'll just grow in like fine down and nobody will ever notice."

"Really," Maria says, like she was seriously considering this as some kind of option. "Did you do that?"

"Ah! Jesus Christ!" From the back.

"Oh, no," Madge says. "When do we ever listen to our mothers?" And she and Maria both laugh like it's the funniest goddamn thing in the world.

"Listen to you," Maria says.

"I guess it wasn't so bad," Madge says. "A little blood every now and then."

Maria laughs again, reaches over and flips a switch on the side of the thing that looks like a TV stand. "There! All dry now. You're all done." She stands up and pulls the thing away. Madge's nails are this bright candy red that practically glares. There's this blotch of bright red nails and this patch of faded orange hair and some dried-up pale old woman I don't know in between. Maria helps her out of the chair. Madge barely comes up to Maria's shoulder and looks like she's going to fall flat on her face but manages to shuffle over to the cash register behind Maria and pay for her nails. She shuffles on out the door and I realize she's even older than I thought she was. I wonder if someone is picking her up or if she's walking home, and why she's here at closing when I thought old ladies did this sort of shit during the day because they didn't have anything else to do.

When Madge finally leaves Maria says, "Give me a minute guys," and goes in the back. The yelling has stopped.

Bobby starts in like I knew he would. "God damn! That girl back there was getting her pussy waxed."

"How do you know it was her pussy," I say. "Maybe it was her legs."

"Fuck no," Bobby says. "It was her pussy. That little squeak right at the end when she was yelling? That's how they sound when you're doing something to their pussy."

"Oh, right," Nick says, "you're such a fucking expert."

"Fuck yeah," Bobby says, looking back where the yelling came from. "Might have to get me some of that."

"Right," Nick says.

I look at Leo but he's not listening. He's too busy waiting for Maria.

When she comes out, she's not in her Ocean City Nails uniform anymore. She's got a short jean skirt and a white tank top and a leather jacket that stops before the top of her skirt, and she's put on boots that make her taller than Leo. Her hair is down and sprawling all around her face and her lips are the same color as Madge's nails were, and her own nails, that I hadn't noticed one way or the other before, now look really long and black, black as her hair. I thought girls usually wanted their nails to be the same color as their lips but I guess not.

Leo's not looking pissed anymore, just that kind of stoned look he gets whenever Maria's around and dressed to go. Can't say I blame him. Standing next to Maria he fades almost like shuffling old Madge, and it's not just that Maria's half Portuguese and half Italian, at least that's what I think it is, while Leo's pale Irish ass should be on a poster for the Celtic Festival, should be wearing a fucking kilt. I wonder sometimes what it's like, being Leo with Maria.

"Let's go," she says.

Nick looks back at the partition and Maria says, "Oh, Tiffany? What a wimp."

"She coming out?" Nick says.

"She went out the back," Maria says. "She's already gone. I'm outta here," she calls to whoever's still back there. "Lock up! See you tomorrow." She takes Leo's arm and we follow them out the front door.

Leo starts walking towards his car but Maria says, "Let's take Tommy's car, there's more room. You don't mind driving, do you, Tommy?"

I automatically say, "No problem," although I'd really hoped that Leo would drive so I could get fucked up if I wanted to. Time was I wouldn't have given a fuck but after last summer when my cousin Dennis got killed and they cut his body out from behind the wheel of his car and there was an empty fifth of Jamison's under the seat I've tried to have some fucking sense about shit like that. Dennis was a good guy. Leo looks pissed but doesn't say anything. We walk the block up to the Dunkin Donuts where I'd parked. Nick starts for the rear passenger door and Maria says, "Wanna sit back with us, Bobby?"

"Fuck yeah," Bobby says, rocking up and down on the balls of his feet so everything's jiggling more than ever. Leo looks like she just asked him to go clean out the toilets at that pizza place her father used to own but he doesn't say anything, just gets in the back and slams the door. Maria gets in the middle and Bobby gets in beside her. Nick shrugs and takes shotgun. I get behind the wheel and we take off.

"Where to?" I say, trying to sound like some sort of limo driver, but I don't know how a limo driver sounds, so I guess I just sound like myself. I start to ask where they want to get some beer but then I think if I'm stuck being the designated driver then somebody else can worry about it.

Nobody says anything for a second, which makes sense. Nick's waiting to see what Leo wants, Leo's waiting to see what Maria wants, and Bobby's got to be so freaked sitting by Maria in back that he doesn't give a fuck what we do as long as we stay in the car as long as possible.

"Let's go down the shore," Maria says. "I want to see the ocean."

"It's dark, yo," Nick says. "What's there to see?" He laughs this little laugh that's more like a cough and before Leo can tell him to shut the fuck up Maria says, "I like it at night. It's beautiful at night. Let's just go down there and drive for a while." I could swear I hear Bobby breathe in sharp and then let it out like somebody punched him but I'm not sure. "OK," I say. Service with a smile.

Maria makes it sound like it's some huge fucking expedition but really it's only a couple blocks from where we are to Lynnshore Drive. Something Mr. Tomlinson said in social studies pops in my head. Urban density. He had some chart up on the screen comparing Boston with New York and Chicago and shit like that, and I don't know why I remember, because Mr. Tomlinson is a fucking bore and his fucked-up Power Points don't even have any sound or animation or anything, but I remember that phrase, "urban density," and I see as we drive how at night all the houses and stores and shit are just gray on black like that chalkboard Mr. Tomlinson never uses but never seems totally erased and how easy it is to forget with all this shit piled up on top of itself that there's a whole fucking ocean back there somewhere. We go past the coffee shop where my dad goes every Sunday morning to pick up the Globe and brings back grand lattes for him and Mom. There are two or three kids about our age hanging out in front and some older guy sitting in a chair by the entrance talking on a cell phone. We go past the Oceanside House Assisted Care Retirement Home, where some of the windows are lit but most of them aren't. I wonder if Madge lives there. I wonder if she's right now standing in front of her door having trouble finding her keys.

The street in front of Oceanside House ends on Lynnshore Drive. "Which way?" I say.

"Which way you guys want to go?" Maria says, which surprises me a bit, but there you are. Nick shrugs even though Maria probably can't see him do it. Leo says, "Take a right," and before Bobby can open his fat fuck mouth I turn right and we're driving along the shore just like Maria wanted.

All the big houses with their ocean views roll by on the right, and Lynn Beach is just a blot on the left. "Turn the music down," Maria says. We've been rocking Mastodon but I turn it down and put the window down too. It's chilly but not too cold. I take a deep breath and the air just smells like air. During the day this stretch of the shore smells like low tide even when it's high tide, but it's better sometimes at night.

With the window down things look clearer somehow and I can see the waves rolling in. It's low tide and the beachfront looks the same color as the water, which is the same color as the sky. There's a three-quarter moon. There are darker blotches on the beach, rocks, washed-ashore kelp or some shit, that look like holes where there used to be something.

Nick is chill shotgun looking straight ahead. I look in the rearview mirror. Leo has his arm around Maria but is staring out at the houses to his right. Maria is leaning into his shoulder, but she's got her ass pushing against Bobby's, and her left arm is—no. Fuck. I wait for the next streetlight and yeah, fuck me, she's got her hand on the top of Bobby's thigh. Her nails look like they're exploding every time we pass a streetlight. Bobby's moving a bit and singing along under his breath with the music but I can't see his left hand and I know, I just fucking know, he's got it in the hoodie pocket trying to position it so he can rub his dick without anyone noticing, or maybe he even sneaked it into his sweats for a clearer shot. Oh my fucking God. Maria's talking about how beautiful the ocean is, how she wishes it were summer so she could just dive in and swim swim swim, but Bobby's mouth is hanging open even more than usual, he looks fucking hypnotized. I can swear there's movement on his left side underneath the hoodie. That stupid fat fuck. If we get out and there's a damp spot on the crotch of his sweats I swear to God I'm going to beat the motherfucker with a tire iron.

"You wanna keep driving?" I say, trying to calm down. "You wanna go on to Nahant?"

"I know what," Maria says, and then stops like she's waiting for someone to say, "What?"

So I do. "What?" I say.

"Let's go up Lynn Woods."

"Huh?" Nick says. "What the fuck is at Lynn Woods? We won't be able to see two feet in front of us."

"It's great in there at night," Maria says. "It's like you're on another planet or something. Like a fairyland."

As hypnotized as Bobby is he still manages to snort when Maria says fairy.

"Can you even get in at night?" I ask.

"I know how," Maria says. "I know just what to do. Right, Leo?"

"Whatever," Leo says. He's back to staring out the window.

"C'mon, Bobby," Maria says. "Want to go to the woods?"

Bobby says, "Sure," just as we go under a streetlight and I look back and can swear I see Maria squeezing his thigh, clutch release clutch release, like she's working out with one of those hand grips trying to get strong. "Sure! Fuck yeah."

So when we get to the rotary I bear right and go downtown past the common. There's a few cars out but basically nobody's there. I don't think I've been to Lynn Woods since I was in junior high. I go down Walnut Street towards where I think the turnoff is for the main entrance but Maria says no, turn here, and we wind up on Lynnfield Street at a small dirt pulloff. There's a fence between the lot and the start of the woods with a gate like at a railroad crossing or a parking garage, and it's down, so you can't drive past it but there's nothing to keep anybody from getting out and walking. We park the car and everybody piles out. "Come on," Maria says. "I know exactly where to go."

Bobby runs ahead and makes a big show of charging up to the gate like he's going to jump it, once, twice, and the third time he just ducks under it and stands on the other side and goes, "Ta-dah!" like he's some kind of fucking miracle. Nick does jump the gate but stumbles when he lands and almost goes flat on his face. Leo and I duck under and Leo hangs back to give a hand to Maria when she ducks under even though she doesn't need any help. When she's ducked down I pretend like I'm not looking at her tits, which even in the dark you can tell are about to fall out of her top.

"This way," Maria says, and as we follow her into the woods I realize that nobody ever said anything about stopping for beer.

Somebody gave a talk at school once about the history of the woods, comparing them to Central Park or some shit, but the fact is there's nothing park-like about them at all. There's paths and a reservoir, and I guess it's nice enough to walk around during the day, but mostly it's just trees and bushes and more trees and bushes and an assload of rocks, some of them pretty fucking huge.

Maybe it is historic. The guy at school told us that some pirate had some kind of underground bunker or some shit that was filled with treasure but it got covered up in an earthquake, and then a couple hundred years later some dumb fuck spent his life savings digging a tunnel trying to get to the treasure but he never found it.

I've heard Dad and Nick's Uncle Don and some of the other adults talk about what a hangout the woods were when they were in high school, booze and dope and shit, and sex for sure. I guess some of the kids still hang out there but I don't know why. Why go out in the fucking dark and dirt and get eaten by bugs or freeze your ass off when there's always a parking lot or somebody's house? I want to ask Maria this exact question but she and Leo have gotten ahead of the rest of us. There's just enough moonlight that I can see them, barely. Bobby's trotting along, huffing and puffing and jiggling, trying to catch up to them. Nick's just a little ahead of me with his hands in his pockets and his head down like he's watching each step he takes. So I jog up beside him and ask him.

"What the fuck?" I say. "Why are we marching through the fucking woods?"

"Cause Maria wants to."

"Shit."

"What Maria wants, Maria gets, yo. Like that song in that movie."

"What movie?"

"The one with what's-her-name, you know, with all the old-time gangsters and shit, where she killed that guy?"

"Oh, yeah. I watched that on HBO. My dad thinks she's hot."

"You don't think she's hot?"

"I guess."

"You'd fuck her till your dick broke if you got the chance."

"Well, yeah."

Nick laughs, and then I remember. "Wait a minute. That's not in the movie."

"What?"

"That's not the song from the movie."

"It's not?"

"No. You're thinking about the senior musical last year. The one about the Yankees and the deal with the devil or some shit."

"Fuck the Yankees."

"I know, but that's what you're thinking about. That's where the song's from."

"Whatever. So what's the song from the movie?"

"That's the one where she kills the guy and says they all had it coming."

"Whatever," Nick says again, and then he points to where the others are up ahead of us. "Bobby's struggling, man. Can't keep up. Look at that."

"Fuck him."

"Probably the most exercise he's had all year."

"Maybe he'll have a fucking heart attack and keel over."

"Harsh, yo."

"No more 'gotta-get-me-some-of-that' shit."

"He's harmless."

"He annoys the fuck out of me."

"Well, yeah."

The wind's picked up and the leaves in the trees are making about as much noise as the ones crunching under our feet. I zip up my jacket, then I see the others have gotten into this clearing with a big flat rock in the middle. We get to the clearing and Maria and Leo are off to the left. It's still wicked dark but with the trees set back from the clearing the moonlight comes through a little more. I can see Maria leaning back against a tree and Leo leaning in kissing her. Bobby's standing beside the rock, which comes up almost to his fat gut. Maria's jacket is on the ground at her feet. Her top is pushed up practically under her chin and her skirt up around her waist. I can see the curve of her tit rubbing against Leo's jacket and the curve of her ass rubbing against the tree. Leo's moving against her and she's moaning.

"Fuck," Nick says. "I gotta take a leak," and he goes off into the woods like nothing's going on.

I look over at Bobby against the rock and he's not even trying to hide it, he's got his hand down his sweats and the front of them is moving like there's an animal down there or something. He's saying something quiet, over and over again, but I can't make out what it is. I want to go over and slam his fat pig head against the rock. I want to go over and yell at Maria and Leo. *What the fuck is wrong with you? He's right there watching! I'm right here!* But I can't move, I just stand there watching them, just like that fat fuck, watching Leo grind into Maria and Maria wrap her arms around him and dig her nails into the back of his jacket, and I could swear they're cutting grooves in the leather, and before I know it my dick is hard and I try to pull my jacket down but it doesn't matter because nobody's looking at me.

I hear a crunch in the bushes and look over and Nick's standing there looking too, but he doesn't come back over. I can't see his hands and I wonder if he's jerking off too.

Suddenly Maria gives this gasp like she's about to sneeze and shudders all over. Then she pushes Leo away and pulls down her top and her skirt and walks over to Bobby like nothing's happened, like I'm not even there, and says, "Like what you see, Bobby?"

Bobby's just finishing wiping his hand on the side of his sweats, and then for once in his life he's perfectly still. "Like it?" Maria says again.

"Yeah." Bobby's voice is flat like he's pretending to be a robot.

"Me too. I like it a lot. And I like you too, Bobby. I really do."

"Fuck," Leo says from over by the tree.

"Shut up, Leo," Maria says, and then to Bobby, "No, really, I do. You're a stupid little fuck, even stupider than the rest of them, but you know exactly what you want. But you're so afraid of it, so fucking ignorant, and in a weird way, Bobby, that's kind of endearing. It really is."

It's so dark now I can barely see them, but Maria seems somehow more visible than the others, more there.

"You know what you are, Bobby?"

Bobby doesn't say anything.

"Well, I do. Get up on the rock."

Bobby doesn't move.

"Leo, come over here and help Bobby up on the rock. You too, Tommy."

In my head I say, *What the fuck is wrong with you?* In my head I say, *Fuck you freaks, I'm outta here.* But when Leo walks over and grabs Bobby by one arm, I walk over and grab him by the other, and I don't know why, and we push him up against the rock and then pull him over on top of it. He's heavy as fuck, like I knew he would be, and the fact that he's not even trying to resist just makes him heavier. Why isn't he putting up a fight? I look back and Nick is still standing off in the bushes. Maria doesn't seem to notice him at all.

I've got Bobby by the ankles and Leo has his wrists, and Maria walks up, and I still want to scream at them and run away but at the same time I'm ready to stand there and hold Bobby down. Then Leo steps away and Maria says, "Get back, Tommy," and I do, and

Bobby just stays lying there spread out on top of the rock. He's still saying something over and over I can't understand.

"Bobby Bobby Bobby," Maria says and shakes her head.

She walks up to the rock and stretches her arms out over Bobby, who's not saying anything anymore. Leo comes over and pulls Bobby's hoodie and T-shirt up and his belly looks swollen and pale and his tits look like a woman's plopped above his belly. Leo steps back. Maria leans over Bobby and starts moving her hands up and down him, and he's not moving, not jiggling any more, not making a sound. Then she holds her hand out and Leo steps back up. He reaches in his jacket and pulls something out and places it in Maria's hand. She takes it and Leo steps back again. She flicks her wrist down and back up and all of a sudden there's a knife blade hovering over Bobby's fat gut. I yell something but it's not words, it's just a sound. I can make the sound but I can't move. If she was holding the knife over me, I couldn't move.

And then the blade goes down. She starts moving it across Bobby's chest and belly, short strokes, up down sideways. Bobby's flesh quivers and I can see lines of blood starting to form, starting to drip down his side onto the rock, but he just lies there and doesn't make a sound. She makes a couple of final strokes under Bobby's left tit and then motions toward Leo with the knife. When he comes up and takes it, Maria leans over and whispers something to him. He shrugs. "You're no fun," she says out loud. Leo shrugs again and pulls a cloth out of his jacket pocket and wipes the blade, then he does the same thing with his wrist that Maria did, only up first and then down, and the knife closes and he puts it inside his jacket. While he's doing all that Maria's gone back to work on Bobby, only now she's using her nails. She's put her fingers together like she's going to do a karate chop and it looks like she's tracing over all the marks she made with the knife. Bobby's moving around more and he's talking again but I still can't make out what he's saying. When she finishes she steps back and shakes out her hands. I can hear the click of her nails. I take a breath and realize I can't remember the last time I did.

Maria goes over to Leo and takes his arm like he's escorting her somewhere. She kisses him on the cheek and then looks over at me and smiles. "Tommy knows how to have fun. Don't you, Tommy?"

Bobby has slid off the rock and is lying in a heap on the ground, and now all of a sudden I can move again and I run over thinking he's dead. But he's not. He's breathing. He looks like he's asleep.

"He's fine," Maria says. "Help him up."

I reach down to try to get him up and I see his chest. There's a bunch of marks on it. It looks like writing in some sort of foreign language. I stand over Bobby and stare at the marks and try to make sense of them, and then I realize that the marks are letters, but they're backwards, so that if you put them up to a mirror they'd be normal. If Bobby was standing in front of a mirror he'd see the words FAT FUCK carved into his chest.

I shake him like I'm trying to wake him up, and he coughs and sits up. Leo comes over and we help Bobby stand up. "You OK?" I ask and then immediately think, *He's not OK. I'm not OK. Nothing is OK.* But Bobby stands up and brushes the leaves and dirt off himself from where he fell on the ground and pulls his T-shirt and hoodie back down. "OK," Bobby says. "OK."

"Yeah," I say. "Let's go."

I start to help Bobby to get walking, but Leo pulls me away and leans into me, holding onto my arm, and with everything that's happened I don't know what he's going to do, I'm afraid he's going to bite my ear off, I'm afraid he's going to kiss me, but all he does is say, real soft, "You're not going to tell anybody, and you're not going to forget." Then he lets go.

Maria and Leo start walking back toward the car and Bobby walks right behind them, not exactly like nothing's happened, because he's walking very carefully and his body isn't jiggling and going all over the place like it usually does, but he doesn't act like he's injured or anything either.

I look back at the bushes where Nick was standing but he's not there, and I don't see him while we're walking back to the car, and when we get to the car he's not there either. I unlock the car and Leo puts Bobby in the passenger seat and then gets in the back with Maria. I sink into the driver's seat and feel like I've just played full court all night, it's like I can barely lift the keys into the ignition. "Home, James," Maria says, and laughs.

All the way back Maria chatters to Leo about work and school and what they're going to do this weekend, like we just picked her up from Ocean City Nails. Leo says, "Yeah," and "Right," and "Sure," but mostly lets her do the talking. Bobby leans back like he's asleep. I take them back to the parking lot where everybody's cars are. Bobby gets out and doesn't say anything, just starts walking towards his house three blocks away. Part of me thinks I ought to walk with him until he gets home but the rest of me is exhausted and just doesn't care, doesn't care if I never see him again, or Leo, or Nick wherever he is.

Maria and Leo get out. Leo heads straight for their car but Maria comes up to my window and leans in, smiling. She says, "Thanks for the ride, Tommy. Let's do it again sometime." She reaches in and touches my shoulder and I think my heart's going to stop all over again but nothing happens. Her nails are still wet. She didn't wipe them off.

I look at her hand with its wet nails on my shoulder, and then I look at her and try to think of something to say that will get her to tell me everything I need to know. But I can't. I just stare at her, and her smile fades and her face sags and for just a couple of seconds she's not drowning out everything else, she's just there. For the first time I can remember, she looks like she doesn't know what she's going to do next, and like that makes her unbelievably angry. She starts to say something and stops. Then she gets her smile back and squeezes my shoulder twice, hard, before she takes her hand off and turns around and walks away.

When Bobby and Leo and Maria are all gone I drive back down to the shore, past the coffee shop where the kids are gone but the guy is still out front talking on his cell phone, and past the retirement home where all the lights are out now. I park on Lynnshore Drive and get out and walk over to the sea wall and down the stairs to the beach. There's some guy out walking his dog right by the water. You're not supposed to walk your dog on the beach, they've got signs posted. The moon is gone. I look out at the sand and the water and the sky that are all one big dark blot, and then I turn around and look up at the houses that look out over the ocean, and I think about when my grandmother Bataglia was dying. She lay in the hospital bed with the tubes going in and out of her, and she was pretty much with it right to the end, but one day I was there when my folks were out of the room, and she just lay there with her eyes closed and the monitors hissing and clicking, on and off, and she said, "Something's wrong." Over and over again. "Something's wrong. Something's wrong."

ELIMINATION OF RESTRAINT AND SECLUSION: THE ROAD TO ENGAGEMENT

Promote best practices in a compassionate environment
"Do you understand why it was wrong for you to eat Dr. Simon's brains?" Barron asked.

"I ... was ... hungry," the zombie replied.

"I know you're always hungry. But we have to behave in ways that are appropriate."

"They ... were ... good ... brains."

Barron sighed, tried to remember his training—what there had been of it. "Violence in any form hurts the community and adds to life crisis."

"Good ... brains?" The zombie chewed what was left of its right index fingernail. The entire tip of the finger came off with a wet crunching sound. The zombie chewed momentarily and then spit the fingertip on the floor.

Provide non-coercive, collaborative treatment that neutralizes power and control

After the virus had come and gone and the worst of it was over, there were still all those zombies to deal with. In some parts of the country they just wiped the slate clean—a tire iron to the head did just fine—but in Washington state there was an officially sanctioned desire to help the former living as much as possible, to see them as victims, too. But there was only so much funding available, especially given the cost of repairing Seattle. An official diagnosis was announced—Consciousness Deficit Hypoactivity Disorder—but not embraced. Crisis and counseling centers were established, but they weren't very big. Counselors were recruited, but their training was minimal. Keep the zombies from eating the living, and help them cope. But mostly, keep them from eating the living.

Create a healing environment that promotes patient involvement
"How do you feel when you kill somebody?"
"... nothing ..."
"Do you remember what it was like to feel? Try to remember."
"Good ... bad ..."
"Good or bad. Try bad. Remember what bad felt like?"
"Yes ..."
"You don't really want to make someone else feel like that, do you?"
"Bad ... now ... always ..."
Barron looked at the thing that used to be human sitting in front of him, closed his notebook, leaned forward, grateful for the ointment under his nose that fought off the smell. "Good. Let's go with that. Let's see what we can do, you and me, to make it not bad always."
"... nothing ..."

People's strengths emerge when you believe in them
They recruited Barron because someone in charge had read one of his books and thought that he might understand. Someone else had a file that contained Barron's actual history, and that sealed the deal. He hadn't really wanted to do it, but the corpses that littered the landscape from coast to coast had, funnily enough, diminished the already-tenuous market for horror fiction of the highest literary

quality. There wasn't a lot of money, but there was enough. And his reluctance did not offset the fact that he wanted to help. Of course he wanted to help. Those poor dead bastards.

Social norms are the most useful source of power
Barron sat in a circle with six zombies. "Melinda, how has the week been for you?"

"... nothing ..."

"Can you tell me something you did in the past week to make our community a safe place?"

"... did ... not ... kill ..."

"Great! Very good, Melinda. We're all proud of you. Now, Jerry, what about you? Can you tell me something you did in the past week to make—"

"... brains! ... brains! ... good ..."

Barron sighed. "OK, Jerry, we'll come back to you. Now, Kim ..."

Violence is not an acceptable behavior in this community
The day Melinda walked down a street without lunging at anyone, Barron almost wept with pride, a feeling that was only slightly diminished when she paused to gnaw on a cat. Baby steps. One foot in front of the other.

Everyone shares in the responsibility of community safety. If we follow these basic beliefs, respect one another, and treat others as we wish to be treated, then we may begin to heal.

WHAT THEY DID TO MY FATHER

I was nine years old. Daddy had come in from the field hot and tired and hadn't wanted to talk. He never did want to. That used to bother Mama. It didn't bother me. Mama dipped up some water for him but he threw it on the floor and went into the other room and slammed the door. Mama turned back to the stove and didn't say anything.

My sister Becky had gone into Kingston but Uncle Cody was there. Don't pay him no mind, Cret, he told Mama. He's fretting about the crop is all. Mama didn't say anything and kept stirring. It was about time for Mollie to be born and Mama had to stand back a ways from the pot. I know she didn't feel good, and it seems a shame since Mollie didn't last but a week anyway. Mama's face was still bruised from last night when Daddy was mad.

Uncle Cody told me once after Daddy had been even madder than usual that I shouldn't take it to heart, that Daddy worked awful hard and didn't get much out of it, and he didn't like having to give part of the crop to Mr. Monroe even though it was Mr. Monroe's land we were farming. It's hard on a man that way, Uncle Cody said. We were out by the pond south of the house. He took me there sometimes when things got bad. We were cleaning up branches from the storm the night before. He'd bend over to pick up branches and when he straightened up his head would poke into the leaves if he was under a tree. Uncle Cody was taller than anybody I knew, lots taller than Daddy. Becky used to say that Uncle Cody was so tall Jesus cut his hair. But why won't he leave Mama alone, I asked. That's not for us to mind, Uncle Cody said. What's between husband and wife is between husband and wife. But she's your sister, I said. She's your daddy's wife, he said. He took a big branch and broke it over his knee.

Becky came in from town with the flour and the cloth for Mollie's things. She started across the room to put them on the table and Mama made her go back out and knock the mud off her shoes. Lord knows I try to keep a clean house, Mama said. Becky came back in and put the things on the table and asked where Daddy was. In back, Mama said. Becky looked at the door to the other room and then looked away. She'd let her hair get real long and it hung down all around below her shoulders and where she'd started to swell out up top. Mama used to brush it for her every night before they went to bed and I used to watch her do it. The light from the fire made the shadows long and Mama and Becky looked like each other.

See anyone in town, Uncle Cody asked. Nosir, Becky said and went to help Mama with the cooking. Later she told me that had been a lie, that on the way back from town she'd seen the root man and he'd come up and started talking to her. You mean that old colored man that lives out at the edge of Camp Swamp, I asked. I reckon so, she said. Daddy'll wear you out if he hears you been hanging around colored men, I said. Especially that one. He's crazy, everybody knows that. Becky said whatever he was the root man gave her a bag of special dirt and said if she'd draw a line in the ground and sprinkle the dirt in it nobody would cross the line to bother her. I guess maybe I just will, she told me, and then Daddy can rip and roar as much as he pleases.

That night Becky took some blankets outside and made a bed for herself. Then she took a stick and drew a line in the dirt between her and the house and poured the dirt out of the root man's bag on the line. Mama had already laid down for the night and Uncle Cody had left after supper. Daddy went out in the yard and started talking hard to Becky. I couldn't hear all they said but I did hear Becky tell Daddy that he couldn't bother her no more. Daddy came back in and put on his shoes and hat and went out again. I went to the window. He was headed east toward the Strickland woman's place. Becky was turned over and looked asleep.

Later that night was when they burned the cross outside. Becky had waked up and seen it and forgot about her line and come back inside and got us up. We all went outside and looked at it. It was as tall as Mama and bright in the night and even lit up the smoke that came off it. Becky got scared and told Mama about talking with the root man. She thought that's why they were burning the cross. It was right out in the road and people were passing by, she said. I let him put his hand on my shoulder. I'm sorry. I'm sorry. Mama put an arm around her and told her to hush and that the root man didn't have nothing to do with this. She held tight to my hand and took us back inside and put me back to bed. Later I got up and went to the window and the cross was still burning. I saw someone coming up from the road. It was Daddy. He started cussing and ran over to the well and got a bucket of water and poured it on the cross. It took three buckets to get it out and the smoke hung in the air for a long time.

It was after that Mollie was born and died. Mama didn't get sick like they said she did after I was born but she was awfully sad and quiet. They used the cloth that Becky brought from town after all because they dressed Mollie in it. Daddy built a coffin out back that was the littlest I'd ever seen. He was quiet too. Uncle Cody said he'd do it but Daddy said no, it was his cross and he'd carry it on up the hill.

I went out where Daddy was working and asked if I could help. He acted like he didn't notice me at first and just kept on hammering. I asked again and he stopped and looked up at me. He had tears running down his face and that scared me more than anything to do with Mollie. You go on back inside, boy, he said. You shouldn't have to be concerned with this. I turned around to go back inside and Daddy said, Your Mama ain't going to be having no more babies. You and Becky are all we've got now. Then he went back to hammering.

When it was done Daddy brought the coffin in the house and they put Mollie in it. People came and brought food and said how sorry they were. Mr. Monroe drove up in his Model-T and gave Daddy money for the funeral. Daddy put it in his pocket and said thank you sir and looked like he wanted to spit. The women all stood over Mollie. Her eyes and mouth were shut tight and her hands were squeezed into fists. Becky cried more than the rest of them.

They buried Mollie quick. It was cloudy but it didn't rain. On the way back from the cemetery I cut away from the rest of them and went over toward the river. There was a big oak there that was good for climbing. The biggest branch hung out over the water. I wanted to be by myself and look down on things.

When I got to the river there was a colored man sitting under the tree, fishing. He was real old and looked like he was asleep with his pole almost touching the water. I wasn't going to pay him no mind but before I could get up the tree he woke up and started talking to me.

Your little one's gone, he said. Gone on to a better place. I asked him how he knew that but he wouldn't say. How's your sister, boy, he asked. Your daddy don't bother her now. No sir he don't. What you know about my sister, I said. I know enough, he said. I know all kinds of things.

You're the root man, I said. He winked at me and smiled. He didn't hardly have a tooth in his head and his eyes were cloudy. He wasn't dressed different from anyone else. He said that he had an interest in us, me and Becky, and he was glad to help if he could. I asked him why he hadn't done something for Mollie if he was so almighty interested in my family. He quit smiling and said, I got a family. We all got families. He looked tired and mad at the same time and I took a step back. Then he started smiling again and said there were some things that just couldn't be helped.

He stood up and put down his pole. He was about the tallest man I'd ever seen, maybe even taller than Uncle Cody. He stretched his arms up and they brushed the branch that hung over the water, and that was too high for me to jump safe into the shallow edge. He put his arms down and said, I know your name, boy. What is it then, I said. He just smiled and said, I know your name. Then he picked up his pole and left. I got up in the tree and leaned out over the water. It was muddy and I couldn't see any fish.

For a while after Mollie died Daddy was pretty quiet. I guess he was still sad about her. But soon enough he started in on Mama again. Becky had come back inside and sprinkled the dirt around her bed. I didn't hear Daddy up in the house at night any more but he was awfully hard on Becky during the day. It got to where he'd slap her if she looked at him wrong. He wore his belt out on me, too. Nothing any of us did was right. He got to leaving earlier in the evenings, heading east, and Becky and I were glad to see him go.

One night when Daddy went out Mama was sitting in the rocker sewing. I went over to her and said, I hope he don't come back. She put down her sewing and looked at me. I said, I hope he falls in the river and drowns. She leaned over and shook me. I won't have such talk in this house, she said. I won't. Why don't he leave us alone, I said. Why can't someone make him stop. She leaned back in her rocker and didn't say anything. Then she said, The Lord watches out for us. My place is right here, and so is yours, and so is Becky's. Ain't nobody supposed to have it easy in this life. She picked up her sewing and went back to it.

Uncle Cody didn't come around so much any more. One of the times he did I heard him talking to Daddy outside. I know what you're up to, Mace, he said. You're hard enough on Cret without going after that Strickland woman too. You mind your own goddamn business, Daddy said. Cret ain't been no good since she lost that baby. All cold and not a word out of her. Might as well be living with Coolidge. I'd like to know what you'd do. Uncle Cody said it didn't have nothing to do with that and Daddy knew it, that it had been going on since before Mollie died. I work as hard as any man in the state of South Carolina, Daddy said. I work like a dog and what do I get. Nothing. I'll do what I please with myself. They already burned that cross in your yard, Uncle Cody said. What more do you want them to do. Daddy laughed and said he wasn't afraid of that trash. Uncle Cody told him that they killed a whole colored town down in Florida last year. Thought one of them had raped a white woman. They came in and burned the town. Got every last one of them. How black do I look to you, Daddy said. Don't have to be one, Uncle Cody said. They don't like white men that don't behave themselves. Daddy laughed again. Those white sheet sons of bitches, he said. They don't scare me.

The night it happened I woke up in the middle of the night. I'd been dreaming about the river. Mama and Becky were up in the oak tree holding me out over the water. They held on tight and didn't let go. I sat up in the bed. The moon was bright through the window. The wind was blowing and I thought I heard the root man outside calling my name.

I looked out the window but there was nobody there. I heard him call my name again and got scared. Daddy had gone out again and there was only me and Mama and Becky. Daniel, he called. Come on out, boy. Got something for you to see. I started to go in to Mama but then he said some more. Ain't gonna hurt you, Daniel. Remember how I helped your sister? Come on out. You'll like this.

I got on my clothes and went outside. There wasn't anybody there. The wind was rising and I thought I saw something move down away from the house going east. I went that way and kept going. I kept hearing the root man just ahead of me. He didn't say anything but kept laughing low to himself. The wind made the trees creak and blew twigs and leaves around my feet.

After a while I started hearing other voices. It sounded like a bunch of men were arguing. Someone was yelling and I though I heard a woman crying. There was light coming through the trees. I didn't hear the root man any more. I cut over through the brush and went toward the light and the noise.

I came out in a clearing near the old way into Kingston. Nobody used it much anymore and Mr. Monroe had put up a barbed wire fence to keep his livestock in and everybody else's out. There were a whole bunch of men standing there and they all had on robes and hoods. They had two torches stuck in the ground and burning. I ducked back in the trees so they couldn't see me.

The men were all talking so loud I couldn't tell what they were saying. I still heard a woman crying but couldn't see her. Then a couple of them moved over toward the fence and I saw her tied to a tree. It was the Strickland woman. Her hair was all cut off short and jagged. Her dress was torn and she was hanging out of it. She was pulling at the ropes and crying and yelling. Let him alone, she said. God damn it don't you do nothing to him. Stop it. Shut up, whore, one of the men said. The man who told her to shut up stayed where she was tied up. He was a head taller than anyone else and the top of his hood brushed the leaves. The others were moving around by the fence. One of the men picked up a torch and moved it over toward them.

I could see as clear as day now. They had Daddy down on his knees. They were kicking at him and hitting him over and over. The one with the torch stuck it back in the ground by the fence and walked over and grabbed Daddy by the hair and jerked his head back. Daddy's face was all bloody and dead white in the light from the torch. I heard him say something but the man holding his hair slapped him with his other hand. Whoremonger, the man yelled. Can't keep your pants zipped, can you? Can't stay home and see after your family. Can't act like a decent man. Got to act like some tomcat out prowling around. You go to hell, the Strickland woman yelled. The man standing by where she was tied up slapped her and tore her dress some more. She kicked at him and missed and he laughed.

The men over by Daddy picked him up off the ground. I could hear what he was saying now. Don't whip me, he said. Don't whip me. The man who had been yelling at him laughed and so did the others. Whipping's too good for trash like you, one of them said. We're going to take care of you good.

They dragged him over to the fence near the torch. One of the men climbed up a fence post and jumped down on the other side. He took hold of Daddy's left arm and stretched it out across the fence. Another man held the arm on this side and they started pulling it back and forth across the barbed wire. Daddy started screaming up high like a woman and the Strickland woman started screaming too and the men started laughing and whooping and hollering. Take a good look, whore, one of them yelled. Monroe ain't gonna help you now, poor bucker, said another. Daddy was still screaming and they were still sawing and the blood gushed out and ran down to the ground black against the dead white skin.

After a while Daddy went limp and stopped screaming. They took his arm off the fence. They had sawed it just about off and the bone was showing through. The tall man who has been standing by the Strickland woman came over and took Daddy's arm and broke it over his knee and dropped Daddy back down to the ground. Daddy's arm stuck out and was all twisted like a snake. The man who broke it went over to where the Strickland woman was vomiting. Next time it'll be you, whore, he said.

Then the men pulled the crosses out of the ground and cut the Strickland woman loose and she ran away. They left Daddy on the ground and started to leave except for the man who broke his arm. He stood right there and didn't move. One of the other men came over and took hold of his arm. You've had your fun, the other man said. Let's go. They both moved away and joined the others and they all left.

I don't remember going back to the house or getting back in bed, but I must have because that's where I was when I woke up the next day. They brought Daddy in about mid-morning. His arm was all cut open and looked lumpy under the skin. Mama was crying just as hard as she did when Mollie died and Becky wouldn't come out and look at him. Uncle Cody held Mama and shushed her and the doctor said that Daddy wouldn't be using that arm no more but he would make it through if it didn't get infected. It'll be all right, Cret, Uncle Cody was saying. It'll be all right now.

Daddy seemed to be doing all right but after a day or two his arm got dark and started to smell bad. The pain was real bad. I heard Mama up with him. He was crying and cussing and thrashing around and Mama kept saying Hush, Mace, you lie quiet now. They called the doctor back and he looked at Daddy's arm and said it was going to have to come off. They sent me and Becky out of the house while they did it. When we came back Daddy was asleep. I'd never seen him asleep in the daytime before. Mama went outside with something in a sack soaking through like fresh kill. I went out after her but she ran me back in the house. I looked out the window and saw her walking around back carrying the sack and a shovel.

That night I couldn't sleep. I lay there and tried to think about something good when I heard somebody out back. I got up and went outside and found the root man digging up Daddy's arm. He had it out of the sack and was holding it up in the moonlight and laughing soft like he had when they got Daddy. I must have made a noise because he turned around and looked at me. His eyes were shining in the dark but they were cloudy like the river. He held out Daddy's arm and said, Got some power now for me and mine. You be getting yours by and by. Then he put his shovel and Daddy's arm in the sack and put it over his shoulder and walked away. I went back inside and went to sleep.

Daddy stayed home for a long time after that. Mr. Monroe came by and paid all the bills. After a month or so Daddy went back out to work with his shirt sleeve pinned down over where his arm used to be. He never went out again at night and he was quiet for a long time. Then one day Becky did something he didn't like and he hit her just like before. You mind, girl, he said. I've still got one good arm.

I never saw the root man again. Becky said she heard he did something to make some white people sick and then disappeared. The Klan went after him and his family but they couldn't find any of them.

When I grow up I will take Mama and Becky away from all this. Then I will find my power and I will come back.

WHAT WE DID ON OUR VACATION: SHE HEARS MUSIC UP ABOVE

At Exit 10 Olivia asks Peter how they're doing on gas. He checks the gauge and says they'd probably better stop. She asks not because she has any real sense of how long it's been since they last filled the tank but because she wants him to stop talking. He had begun to outline a theory of the fundamental differences between living on the coast, where they are both from, and living in the mountains, where they are now, and suddenly, with a certainty that startles her, Olivia realizes that, at the moment, she just does not want to hear any theories.

They take the exit and stop at the first convenience store. Peter suggests that they drive into the town whose name was at the top of the exit sign and is, according to the smaller sign by the convenience store, only a quarter-mile down the road. Olivia nods and looks out the car window, vaguely dissatisfied that he's still talking.

As they drive by the village common they see a group of people with musical instruments gathering on a small stage with a shell over it, and others arranging themselves in front of the stage on collapsible lawn chairs and blankets and on the lawn itself. Peter asks if they should stop, and Olivia says sure. He pulls over and parks. Olivia gets out of the car and immediately hears music. Not from the bandstand where the musicians are still gathering, and not from the radio in the car, and not even inside her own head. A woman's voice, a steady pulling melody as if a magnet had started singing. Not in her head but somewhere up above.

*

Life since college has been a mixed bag for Peter. He failed to parlay his undergraduate degree in computer science into one of the cyber-fortunes that at one time seemed to hang like ripe clusters of virtual fruit, ready for the picking; the fact that his was not the only such disappointment was little comfort. A return to school and a Master of Liberal Studies was intellectually fulfilling but unprofitable. A semi-random but wholly desperate application to a small university on the Massachusetts shore yielded a job in the registrar's office, where, to his surprise, he has not only remained, but advanced. His position as Registrar is relatively safe from economic fluctuations—students may enroll in greater or lesser numbers, but someone has to be there to register them—and he is good at it, keeping both faculty and administration content with his ability to arrange times and locations that flow smoothly and steadily through the academic day. A month after he started he met Olivia, two doors down in Human Resources. They have been together ever since. His parents like her; her parents are dead. Recently he has considered returning to his roots and enrolling in the college's online graduate program in Information Assurance, which he can do while continuing full-time in this safe and steady job with a retirement fund in which, three years hence, he will be fully vested. He and Olivia can afford to take weekend excursions such as their present trip into the mountains of central Vermont.

But next year he will turn forty, and while he has no reasonable grounds for complaint, while he understands completely that his best years lie ahead of him, he sometimes wonders what those years could possibly contain that would be at all different from right now. It is a perilous sequence of thoughts: things are fine now, but things could always be better, but how likely is that, and would it be a bad thing if they weren't, and are things indeed fine? Are they really? Olivia loves him, he is certain, but they don't talk like they used to.

She is unfailingly pleasant and frequently passionate, and when he asks her how she is, her answers are always positive. Yet there are times when the pleasantries seem reflexive, the passion rehearsed, the answers slow in coming and brief when they arrive. There are nights when he cannot sleep and his present and his future churn within him like small sharks circling dead and bloody meat.

He looks at Olivia as they sit on a wood-and-iron bench to the left of the bandstand, behind the bulk of the crowd but still close to the stage. Her face is ever so slightly heavier than it used to be; he is as struck by her pale, unfreckled skin and the red silk of her hair as he was when they first met. Once, early in their relationship, he called her his Celtic beauty, but she gave him a dubious look and he never called her that again.

As the band begins to tune up he resumes the conversation they had been having before they turned off the interstate. He repeats that coastal areas, by definition, offer easy access; people can drift in and out at will and with little notice. It's easy to enter and easy to exit. If you're in the mountains, though, you have to make an effort to get there, and you have to make an effort to leave. Thus the shifting demographics of their college town by the sea, as opposed to the constants of northern New England: Yankees firmly planted for centuries; ex-hippies not far removed from their ex-communes; people who came for a skiing vacation and never left. Olivia tells him that the coast is home to plenty of old things and looks intently at a row of houses on the other side of the common.

Olivia's father died when she was in high school, killed in a collision not five miles from their tidewater Virginia home. It was the other driver's fault. Her mother held up brilliantly during the funeral and throughout the five years that followed before the tumor in her left breast metastasized. Olivia's father's death taught her that terrible things can happen for absolutely no reason, and her mother's final illness taught her that knowing the reason doesn't make any difference. Her parents loved her and she loved them with no significant complaints. Each loss was like a layer being peeled away from her, leaving raw and exposed the dizzy uncertainty of being alone in the world and the guilt she felt because she didn't miss them more than she did. When she met Peter she could feel a layer being added back on, slowly and carefully. It felt wonderful to begin with, and then it felt good, and lately it has not felt any particular way at all.

The band on the common begins their first song, which she does not exactly recognize—some old American standard or other. The sound of the band is white noise to the music that continues to hover above her, like the wash of the floor fan Peter runs to help him sleep at night but which never completely obliterates the sounds of the night: the furnace groaning on, a neighbor's dog barking, a car speeding away into the surrounding darkness. It does not occur to her to ask Peter if he hears this music; she knows she is the only one who can. The woman's voice draws Olivia's attention across the grass, wilted in the breezeless July heat, past the swing set on which a boy and a girl swoop past each other like scissors clicking open and shut, toward the middle house in the row of three that stands on the other side of the common.

Olivia knows she will cross the common and enter the house, but she does not want to just yet. She is thirsty. She looks behind her and sees a small strip shopping center, one unit of which is a grocery store. She tells Peter she is going to get something to drink and leaves him sitting on the bench.

The members of the band, like the members of the audience, are mostly older people, although there are a scattering of men and women Peter's age and younger. The musicians all wear green polo shirts and khaki pants. Each shirt has a left breast pocket bearing some kind of logo patch Peter doesn't recognize. The musicians are all wearing sunglasses, cheap knockoff mirrorshades that you can buy for a dollar at a roadside flea market. Their playing is surprisingly smooth, much better than Peter had expected, with only a hint of the dissonance of a group of musicians that has a limited amount of time to rehearse. The songs they play—"In the Good Old Summertime," "The Sidewalks of New York," "A Bicycle Built for Two"—could have come from a songbook a century old, and when Peter sees a page fall from the music stand of one of the trombone players, he thinks it looks yellowed, tattered. He is suddenly aware of the very old people sitting closest to the band, and the younger families sitting farther away, and the children running freely as their parents listen to the music, and he has the same feeling he has at night when he can't sleep and the sharks are circling. He tries to push it aside, assigns the twinge of wrongness he feels to other things: his mild dread of the tiresome drive back to Massachusetts, his continued indecision about returning to graduate school. The band is now playing "The Tennessee Waltz," and he thinks first of his grandparents dancing at his parents' twentieth anniversary party, and then of the story his mother had told him of his great-grandmother who died giving birth to her ninth child, and her second husband who died of an infected blister on his heel. He taps out the beat of the music on the arm of the bench; soon he is hitting the iron with the heel of his hand on the downbeat, *one* two three *one* two three, and he has to stop before he injures his hand. He does not understand his mounting anxiety; he has no explanation for why this tranquil place and this innocuous music, this idyllic summer day, fills his thoughts with the deaths of people he never knew. The late afternoon sun dips behind the maple tree that rises from the middle of the common. He feels a sudden chill and does not understand that either. He wonders what is taking Olivia so long.

The temperature in the grocery store is at least twenty degrees cooler than the temperature outside. When Olivia first arrived in

Massachusetts from Virginia, many people asked how she could stand the southern heat, secure in their New England conviction that anything south of Maryland is the tropics. Rather than give them a geography lesson, she replied that yes, the South was hot, but everything was air conditioned—unlike New England, where air conditioning seemed largely confined to movie theaters and grocery stores.

The music above her is coming from speakers in the ceiling; the other voice she left on the common.

The glass doors of the refrigerated wall cases are fogged; she opens one, pulls out a plastic bottle of water. She doesn't recognize the brand, but there's a strawberry on the label. She is the only customer in the store. The woman at the cash register, who must weigh at least three hundred pounds, has enormous, dilated eyes; Olivia wonders if she's an addict on some kind of halfway house work release. Or do drugs make your pupils small? She used to know. There are many things she has forgotten and she would like to remember them. She pays for her bottle of water and walks out into the steady heat and diminishing afternoon light.

She crosses back to the common, where Peter sits on the bench, transfixed by the band. The music above her returns and grows stronger as she walks across the grass. Peter does not seem to notice her return. The boy on the swing is gone but his swing still moves; the girl's twig-thin legs stretch out from her thickly piled skirt as she pushes herself incrementally higher. Olivia walks past her, drinking the strawberry water. The boy's empty swing continues to rise. The music from the band recedes and the song above her grows stronger as she climbs the front steps of the middle house.

Peter is starting to panic. The other people on the common sit tranquilly listening to the band, but the dying notes of "The Tennessee Waltz" elicit images of a septic world where babies are fatal and blisters kill, and the crowd's polite applause conjures a vision of his own sterile deathbed. The afternoon light is starting to fade. The band director, who is notably younger than most of the rest of the musicians, takes off his sunglasses and wipes them on the hem of his shirt. He turns to the audience to announce the final song, and Peter is amazed at the size and darkness of his eyes, almost as if he still wore his sunglasses. The band director turns back to his musicians and raises his baton, and as the band launches into "The Stars and Stripes Forever" Peter looks across the common and sees someone on the steps of the middle house. A flash of white, a mist of red. Olivia? He looks again and this time clearly sees her open the door and enter the house. He rises from the bench and heads across the common; by the time he passes the empty, motionless swing set he is running.

The song is all around her now.

The red brick Federal style house has undoubtedly been there longer than anything on the band's program. The symmetrical windows are bordered with green shutters; the yard is overgrown but not neglected. Steps set parallel to the front of the house lead up to a screened-in porch that wraps around the left front and side of the house. Peter leaps up the steps, but when he gets to the porch door he is not sure what to do. Knock? Call out? He tries the door; it pulls easily open and he steps in. The porch is empty: no plants, no furniture, nothing. The only entrance to the house itself is a white door with a brass knocker. There is a half-empty plastic bottle of water on the floor by the door. He knocks repeatedly, calls Olivia's name. No reply. He turns the brass doorknob and has to lean in with his shoulder and push before the door opens. He leaves the door open and walks inside.

The room he enters is like the yard, cluttered but not ignored. A sofa bracketed by lace-covered side tables, a recliner, a coffee table and scattered chairs date from no particular era, but the walls are done in a frantic Victorian wallpaper. Opposite the sofa above a bricked-over fireplace hangs an elaborately-framed painting of mountains dropping to a stormy beach; small boats dot the waves while ill-defined figures wait on the shore. There is no television and no phone, no books or photographs, but there is a girl of about ten or eleven sitting on the sofa, thin legs crossed at the ankles, hands folded serenely in her lap. Her dress is too thick for July, her hair is the same color as Olivia's, and her eyes are the same as the band leader's.

Before Peter can apologize for walking in unannounced and say he is looking for his friend who came in just a minute ago, the girl gets up and walks to the far wall of the room, where there is a white door with a heavy brass knob. She opens it and beckons him to follow her.

This room is lined with shelves filled with books, old, oversize volumes. Against the far wall is an enormous old roll top desk, closed and locked, with a padded wooden desk chair on wheels. In the center of the room stands an aquarium tank in which swims an enormous fish. A boy about the same age as the girl stands beside the tank. He wears a shirt and trousers that appear to be made from the same material as the girl's dress, and his eyes are closed.

Peter walks up to the tank. The fish appears to be some kind of eel. Its head is disproportionally large, its eyes protruding and black, its mouth filled with needle-thin fangs. Its body is covered in a cloud of fine, waving antennae. It circles methodically within the tank, adding a quick burst of speed each time it reaches the corner nearest the desk. It looks like a picture Peter had seen in a grade-school reference book of sea creatures from the aphotic depths, creatures so ominously unlike anything he had ever seen before that he had dreamed of them for a week afterward.

The girl walks over to the tank and removes the eel, which immediately falls limp in her hands. The boy reaches into the left pocket of his slacks and produces a folding knife. With his eyes still closed, he opens the knife and carefully slices off the eel's antennae, which float to the floor like dust. When he is done, the girl returns the eel to the tank. The creature comes to life and thrashes in the water, coiling and uncoiling, its body helpless to locate itself and its regular path, its fanged mouth open as if to scream. Water splashes from the tank and hits Peter's hand. The smell of brine is overpowering.

The girl takes the boy by the hand and leads him to a staircase on the opposite side of the room. They stop at the foot; the girl gestures to Peter. He walks between them and climbs the stairs.

He finds himself immediately in a room with no windows and no visible source for the soft light that fills it. There is a background wash of sound like air-conditioning but the room is the same temperature as the rest of the house. The room contains no furniture other than a large four-poster bed covered in loose white sheets on which Olivia lies supine. Her head and shoulders move gently as if to music; her hands flutter by her sides. Her legs are still. Her eyes are closed. Her lips form words but she does not speak. There is nothing random about her motions; they are orderly, purposeful.

Peter walks up to the bed and looks down at Olivia. She is smiling as her lips move. He considers lying down beside her but decides that would be a mistake. Instead he leaves her to whatever she has found, the music he cannot hear, and descends the stairs. He avoids looking at the tank; he cannot bear to see if the eel continues to thrash, or has resumed its ordered circuit, or floats motionless on top of the water. The children are not in the study or the living room or on the porch. He walks carefully down the outside steps and returns to the common.

The sun has set; the band is gone. Only their car remains. Peter sits back down on the same bench where he listened to the band's old music. He will make no effort to leave. He will wait for Olivia here in the mountains, in the darkness, in the silence beneath the cold and nameless stars.

THEY GOT LOUIE

"Did you hear?" Ralph said.
"What?" Eddie said.
"They got Louie."
"No!"
"Yeah."
"Those fucks."
"I know."
"Those murderous fucks."
"I know."
"How?"
"They put out the green shit."
"The green shit?"
"Yeah."
"And he ate it?"
"Apparently."
"How the fuck could he do something that stupid?"
"I don't know."
"How many times have we been told, since practically we were born, 'Don't eat the green shit. It smells good, it tastes better, but don't fucking eat the green shit.'"
"I don't know. But you know what they say."
"What?"
"That if you eat just a little bit, just the right amount, it's the best high ever."

"What?"

"That if you eat exactly so much and no more, it's this intense rush, it opens up your mind—"

"The fuck you're saying. Your mind?"

"—and you see, I don't know, God and everything."

"See God? Well, I guess that's pretty fucking well taken care of. I guess Louie's just getting an eyeful of God right about now."

"Well, maybe he is."

"He's sitting down at God's feet, and he's saying, 'Hey, God, why does this green shit that kills you taste so good? And while we're at it, why did you make those giant fucks who try to sucker us into eating it?'"

"Come on, Eddie."

"See God. Fuck! See your own limp dick."

"I know. I'm just saying."

"See blood squirting out of your fucking mouth. See your guts pouring out of your ass."

"Come on, Eddie."

"That's what that green shit does to you."

"That's not how it was."

"How do you know?"

"Because I saw it."

"You saw it?"

"I saw it."

"And how the fuck did you see it?"

"I was hiding under that thing they keep pushed against the wall. That thing they use for a nest."

"Yeah?"

"Yeah. They found him under that smaller thing they use for a nest—"

"How many fucking nests do they need?"

"—they were wiping the floor with that big thing that makes all the noise, and they picked up the smaller nest, and there he was. All still, his tail curled around him, looked like he was sleeping."

"Sleeping?"

"Yeah. No blood, no guts."

"What did they do?"

"The guy starting making some noise, and the girl made a lot of noise. They got all excited and started running around. Then they got something and scooped him up and put him in a bag and took him outside."

"Where was the cat?"

"The cat?"

"The cat. Where was the fucking cat?"

"The cat's gone. Hasn't been around for ages."

"No shit?"

"Pay attention sometime. When's the last time you saw the cat? I think it's dead."

"Good."

"It never touched us, though."

"Goddamn right it didn't. All ferocious and shit, but all you had to do was rear up and squeal as loud as you could and it backed right the fuck off."

"True. It really took out the mice, though."

"Mice! Useless little fucks. Think they're so little and cute they can get away with shit. Fuck 'em."

"Yeah, I guess."

"Where was the dog?"

"Outside, I think."

"Louie had been lying there dead under that thing for how long and the dog didn't notice?"

"Guess not."

"Figures. At least the cat did its job, more or less. Did I tell you about the time I ran right past the dog?"

"Yes."

"I ran right past it, and nothing. The cat would have at least chased me, but the fucking dog just lay there snoring."

"Amazing."

"It was like, 'Give a fuck, I'm busy snoring over here.'"

"Well, it sure didn't do anything to Louie. Poor Louie."

"Those murderous fucks."

"I know."

"We ought to rise up and take them out!"

"We?"

"If there were enough of us, we could do it."

"Rise up and take them out."

"Didn't you tell me that story about way before, a long-ass time ago, how we killed millions of them? Not even biting, we just made them sick or something?"

"That was thousands of generations ago. Those are just stories."

"Eating the green shit and seeing God is a story. Killing the giants is fucking history."

"But there's not enough of us."

"Not now. But maybe. It would help if it wasn't just this place."

"Huh?"

"We need something bigger. Just a place like this, who wants to live here besides sad fucks like you and me?"

"I don't know. It's warm. They drop enough food to keep us going."

"If only we had a barn. Then we could build up some numbers."

"You're probably right."

"I'm totally right. You got a barn, motherfuckers'll show up."

"But we don't have a big place, do we?"

"No. We don't. But it doesn't take a lot of us to fuck with them, at least. You know what Louie told me once?"

"What?"

"He said he got into their main nest once—the thing they sleep on?"

"Get out."

"No, really, he did. He was in the nest with them and he said he got close enough to the guy's dick that he could've bitten it off."

"So why didn't he?"

"It was a *dick*, Ralph."

"You know, I always wondered about Louie."

"What?"

"I mean, there he was in their nest with both of them, so he's got this giant pussy lying right there—"

"Shut the fuck up!"

"—and all he can talk about is the guy's dick?"

"Shut the fuck up! Show some respect! He's dead, for fuck's sake!"

"What respect? What if he had gone after the guy's dick? Nothing wrong with that."

"What's the matter with you?"

"Nothing at all."

"So now what?"

"I don't know. They're just so big."

"Fucking huge."

"I mean, what can you do? What're you going to do?"

"Yeah. I know."

THE END OF ALL OUR EXPLORING

18 April 2037

Dear Paul,

I'm sorry it's taken me so long to reply to your letter, which arrived three weeks ago. I was so stunned to hear from you I didn't know if I'd be able to write back. Literally. I used to joke that I could barely write my name without a computer, but I wasn't really joking, and even though I've had—we've all had—to make do for a long time now without much of anything, I half convinced myself you'd never be able to read my handwriting. Then I wished I could really flip you off by writing in Chinese—in your face, Mr. New Internationalist, see if I care—but I remembered how pissed off you were when I wouldn't enter the Continuing Asian Studies program with you when the university reopened, and I suddenly didn't want you to have won that particular argument. Stupid, yeah, I know. And I know you gave me a number, and I know the land lines never completely failed anywhere, but I made an excellent case to myself as to why it would be impossibly painful to just pick up the phone and call. I never could talk anybody else into anything, but I've always been able to convince myself of whatever I needed to.

I've read your letter dozens of times by now, but I don't know how to respond. When you made your decision to go back home I tried to respect it. I tried my best. But I don't think you ever understood completely what your leaving did to me. How could you? You had someplace you were from, someplace to go back to. Vermont was never home to me, not the way South Carolina was to you. I know there was a lot you didn't like here. I remember how you used to say that the only thing that kept the new hippies from taking over was the fact that the old hippies just wouldn't die. I know the winters were hard. But I always felt you recognized Vermont as its own place, and you thought of it as my place, my home, something I'd always have in me, just like you'd always have the Carolina coast in you.

But it doesn't work that way for everyone. You never understood, did you? You played the expatriate well, I admit; everyone was charmed by your progressive agenda and southern accent. You used to tell me that Vermont would be warm part of the time, but your hometown was stupid year-round. I guess you thought you were paying me and my home state a compliment. But you were always so caught up in your own alienation it didn't even occur to you that I might feel the same way, that I didn't have to be a thousand miles from home to feel a million miles away. Remember I told you how I felt when I was a teenager, not just different, but like there was a big plate-glass window, and there I was on one side, and there was everyone else on the other side, and just walking through the world was like watching something going on in another room? And how that feeling had never really gone away? How the only thing that made me feel better was looking up at the sky, at the stars at night (the nights are clearer than ever, by the way, explosively clear, and I know damn well you don't get that where you are). You got that I-hurt-for-you look in your eyes, and kissed me, and I felt better—you always made me feel better. But deep down I knew you never really understood.

I'm sorry. Here you are, making this amazing effort to get back in touch with me, and here I am bitching and whining. I ought to tear this up and begin a new letter, but I'm afraid if I stop, I'll never start again.

I'm glad you're doing well. It does sound as if they're picking up the pieces down there faster than I would have thought. Your job at the Yang Liwei Center sounds as if it were just waiting for you to show up. I know how you used to say that sooner or later someone would figure out that the eastern Carolinas were good for something besides tobacco and tourists—I can't believe the program is so far along. A launch every other month. Amazing.

The improvements up here aren't quite so dramatic. There's rail service down to Boston now, and the mail seems reliable enough that I'm not too worried about your getting this. The Governor made a big deal last week about the windmills in the Northeast Kingdom being 80% online and a new wood pellet plant opening near Rutland. Things are getting better, I know.

But the pit where they buried the plague victims from Northfield is still there by the road that runs behind my parents' house. Every time I walk that road, I can still see the spot. Remember how all the doctors kept saying that the viruses wouldn't hang around a bunch of dead bodies, but people insisted on "sterilizing" the pits anyway? There are still hundreds across the state. Nothing will grow at those sites. They're like giant scars that will never, ever heal.

Speaking of scars that won't heal, can you believe that I saw one of those old "Take Back Vermont" signs the other day? It was almost falling off the side of a barn that was almost falling down itself, but it was still there. I couldn't believe that anybody would even remember all that nonsense, much less try to perpetuate it. I remembered Mom talking about how uncle Charles and his boyfriend had their civil ceremony within days after they passed the original law, they were so scared it would be repealed, and how grateful I was our wedding didn't have to be like that. And then I remembered how I felt when you said you were going home, to a place that might still hate us, and there went another three days before I could think about picking up this pen.

I guess people always need someone to blame. They blamed the doctors for preparing for the wrong flu, right? And for not being ready for what the mosquitoes were carrying when the flu ran its course. And the government for not being ready for the mosquitoes in the first place. (Yes, I know, why didn't it occur to them to blame themselves for wanting so much stuff we had to boil the planet to get it. Sometimes it's still like you're in the next room.) And the scientists for not bothering to mention that if you go a decade or so without any new satellites going up, the old ones just quit working. (Yes, I know—the scientists told them; they just weren't listening.) But sometimes I just can't help blaming China for profiting so from our catastrophe. Now, don't get huffy—you know I never bought into that conspiracy crap about them being responsible for the first flu. But "mutual prosperity," my ass. An invasion by any other name . . .

Never mind. It's just hard to think about how many wrong turns we took—not just you and me, but everybody. I remember when I was a kid how convinced my parents were that once the Democrats were back in power everything would be OK. Boy, were they wrong. (Mom sends her best, by the way. She always liked you. Did I tell you she married that guy she had just started seeing before you left? I was kind of surprised it took her so long, what with Dad being one of the first to go, but she was never in much of a hurry about anything, I guess. Zhang's a decent guy. I was afraid he'd make trouble about my staying on the farm after you went away, but not a word.)

But the hell with all that. Let's face it. If we say anything's more important than our own pain, we're lying, and the only person I can blame for my own pain is myself. Not you. There, I said it (wrote it).

Truth is, I could have left lots of times. If there was a plate-glass window between me and the world, I could have taken a hammer to it and stepped right on through if I'd had the nerve. I just didn't, is all. Of course, if I'd left when I was young enough to make something out of leaving, I'd have never met you, and despite everything, that's the scariest thought of all. But I remember something somebody told me once—your letter's making me remember all kinds of things—about this writer, I can't remember his name, who decided to run away from home, basically, just leave his wife, and he packed his bags and loaded up the car and drove off. He drove around his neighborhood for almost an hour, and then he pulled back in his driveway, took the luggage out of the car, and went back inside. That's me, Paul. I never could leave.

But then, you know that, don't you? I know how bad I was that last time we were together. I've had a lot of time to think about that, and I realize now that there were things I didn't understand, either. I know now I didn't (wouldn't?) realize what it did to you when you found out your family was gone in the second epidemic. No more jokes about your stupid hometown after that. I remember how when the net started coming back up you began checking the local news from Myrtle Beach—you didn't think I noticed, but I did. I should have understood. But no, there I was at the end, screaming and crying that I would not follow you to a place that would hate me, would hate us, and that I hoped you choked on the sand and salt water you had decided you missed so much, and that the sun over your beloved home gave you cancer, and—oh, Jesus, Paul, I am so sorry. I was amazed to have survived, and I was scared to leave the little bit of safety and comfort I had. I hated you for not understanding that. Maybe you hated me for what I didn't understand. I'm sorry.

But now you write after all this time to tell me you're going even farther away? You say you never stopped caring about me and you want to come see me before you leave? You want me to consider going with you?

The night sky gave me comfort because it was impossible. I knew I could get to Europe if I really wanted to, but not Jupiter or Betelgeuse, and that was such a relief.

And here you come saying the training program isn't as hard as I might think? That immigration to the colony is doubling every six months? That they're ready to accept non-specialists?

You expect me to be happy because our Chinese benefactors are letting you go to Mars, and that if I really wanted to, I really could go with you?

You'll probably have already left by the time you get this letter. You're probably in Boston by now. (There was a pamphlet on the commons the other day that said the new rail system was proof that the railroads helped the Chinese spread the flu in the first place. Like I said, someone to blame.) I don't know what I'll say when you get here. I know the world is starting to put itself back together, and I know you want to be—or at least you're not afraid to be—a part of that.

The fact that we never divorced—with the world falling apart in front of us, it felt kind of beside the point, didn't it?—now seems the most significant fact of my life.

Will I go with you? If I'm here when you arrive, you'll have your answer.

Here I am at the end of my handwritten letter, and every word seems legible to me.

> Your husband,
>
> Martin

WHERE WE WOULD END A WAR

When Amanda came home from the war her family was there to greet her at the platform. She knew what to expect when she rematerialized, but she'd forgotten about the mortar-like *chuff! chuff! chuff!* as the others arrived after her. It didn't scare her—she was beyond being scared by loud noises—but it added to her disorientation as she stumbled off the platform into her dad Ernie's arms. Her grandmother Rosie and kid brother Larry rushed in to grab her as well. She could hear her dad Neal crying, but the thin skype almost got lost in the other families' laughing and crying and shouting as their loved ones popped back home. Gramma Rosie smelled like her perfume and their kitchen and Amanda held on tightest to her.

All the way home Neal kept apologizing for not being able to be there in person, but the teardown in Indianapolis came up at the last minute and with the economy being what it was and all, he couldn't afford to turn it down. Everything he did was for her and her brother. He hoped she understood. Ernie tried to reassure her that the light media presence at the platform was probably because her group was one of the last to get back and they'd moved on to the next cycle, you know how the nets are. It didn't mean people didn't care, because they did. Then he quit apologizing and just stared at her like she wasn't real. From the back seat Gramma Rosie kept reaching up front to rub her shoulder. The car steered itself through the traffic even smoother than she remembered, almost as smooth as the sensed-up transports outside of Cotabato City had dodged IEDs. Probably the same tech by now. Larry was playing a game in the back seat but she knew he was glad she was home.

When they got back to the house Amanda went straight up to her room. Gramma Rosie had told her in the car that her room was just as she left it, which was technically accurate. Nothing had been moved, nothing was missing. But when she had been there it had never been that neat, and when she had come from work or school it had never felt that empty, so it wasn't just like she left it, not really.

For the first week or so she slept in late every day. Ernie and Gramma Rosie were fine with that, and so was Neal when he skyped in from his next job in Ft. Wayne. Gramma Rosie kept saying she knew Amanda needed to catch up on her rest. That was true enough, but soon her days had more darkness than light. At night, when everyone else was asleep, all there was to do was watch stuff on screen, and there was nothing that she wanted to watch on, which meant all there really was to do was think, and she didn't want to do that. So she started setting her alarm again.

Once she got back on schedule, she still mostly stayed at home but made it a point to go out during the day, not just to get out of the house but also to try to get a sense of what she had come home to. Before she left for the war she was in the same cycle as most people she knew. Get up, go to school, go to work, go out, come home, go to sleep, get up, do it again. Where she lived was just there and not anything to notice. Now she walked around the town and tried to notice things. While she was deployed she had had this recurrent dream where she was walking around the town and finding all sorts of new places that hadn't been there before. But the town she returned to was like her room. There didn't seem to be anything missing, but there was certainly nothing new, and the town didn't feel any different than it had before when she wasn't noticing it.

The closest thing to something new was the American Legion

post. At some point while she was gone the town had found the money to fix it up. Parts of it were shiny and parts were fake old-timey, but it was at least somewhere to go now that she was a veteran. There weren't too many people there her age, mostly older folks who had been in Iraq and Afghanistan, shooting pool, chugging beer, dancing on robotic limbs. There was one really old guy who supposedly had been in Vietnam. He had two robot legs but he mostly sat by the window and looked out at the town.

One evening she found herself talking to a woman named Sally who didn't look much older than Ernie but said she had done three tours in Afghanistan. She still had all her original limbs. Sally couldn't get over the jaunting.

"What's it like in between? Do you feel anything?"

"No. You just stand there and they throw the switch and then you're someplace else." That wasn't true. There was a split-second when you felt like you were leaving your body, like you were dying, and the first time that happened was still the most terrifying thing she had ever experienced, way worse than anything she had encountered in the war. After a few times you got used to it. But she didn't tell Sally that. She didn't want to frighten Sally, but she didn't want to reassure her either. Sally was just someone to talk to over a couple of beers. She didn't know Sally, who shuddered and said, "Not me, sister," and gulped down the rest of her beer.

"Never say never. You know they're starting to phase it in for civilian travel."

"Like I said, not me."

"They say it'll help the economy and the climate. Less fuel. Less time."

"The climate was already fucked when I was your age. And time? Time for what?"

Amanda couldn't answer that one.

"Besides, it was bad enough being back in the world just a couple of days after you'd been out in the shit for a year. It can't help you guys any to be out in it and then back home just like that." Sally snapped her fingers. "Turnaround in seconds, not days. How can that be any kind of advantage?"

Would having a day of travel time have made the return any less jarring? Amanda decided it wouldn't have, but she didn't tell Sally that, either. Instead she ordered another round. She looked past Sally, who was already talking about something else, at two guys her own age who were at one of the tall tables that lined the wall. One of them was wearing a T-shirt that said, BOG? AIC. TMF!

Sally noticed her staring, looked over at the guys, and smiled. "Cute. You should go over and talk to them. Maybe they were out where you were."

"Nah. Drone jockeys."

"How can you tell?"

Amanda gestured towards the T-shirt, but not enough so the guy might notice. "'Boots On Ground? Ass In Chair. Telebombing Mother Fuckers!'"

"Shit. What are they even doing here? Like they're really soldiers or something."

"They are, officially. They get medals and everything."

"Yeah, I know, but . . . shit." The next round arrived and Sally raised her glass. "Here's to real combat, girlfriend. Here's to actual fucking risk."

Amanda raised her glass, drank, and excused herself to hit the head. On the inside of the stall someone had scrawled, BJ4F. It seemed familiar but she couldn't quite place it. Blow Jobs for Free? How generous.

When she came back they finished their beers and Sally asked if she wanted to go to another place she knew about that was quieter. Amanda begged off, and when Sally left Amanda went over and started talking to the two guys at the table, who really were cute. Turned out the guy wearing the T-shirt was the boyfriend of the other guy, who was the actual drone pilot. The T-shirt guy was an accountant or something. They were nice and it wasn't too bad talking with them about nothing in particular, but when they started technobabbling about the war and the drone pilot started getting all superior about how trying to jaunt bombs to targets didn't work, how any explosive device moved with the transporter showed up at its target scrambled and useless, she lost interest and went home. The next night she came back and met a guy who had been Boots on Ground and had even been in Bravo Company just like her, although they'd been in different platoons. They went back to his place and fucked, and it was OK, but the fact that he had seen combat didn't really make any difference. Neither did the fact that he had a robot left leg. She said she'd call him but they both knew she wouldn't.

The next morning she was in the kitchen with Larry and Gramma Rosie. Ernie had already left for work and Neal hadn't skyped in yet. Gramma Rosie made morning talk as she prepared breakfast: how'd you sleep (fine), did you have a good time last night (yes, which wasn't completely a lie), did you see the news, what is Congress thinking trying to push another impeachment so soon after the last one (how should I know, and what difference does it make?). But then when they were seated she started trying to talk to Amanda about what her plans were.

"I know you haven't been back all that long, dear, but your fathers and I both believe you need to start thinking about what you want to do next."

"You mean get a job? I told you I was setting aside part of my pay to help out."

"I know, and that's wonderful, it'll really help. But that's not going to last much longer, and—oh, what am I saying, it's not anything to do with money. You don't need to worry about that. Go back to school if you want."

"I'm thinking about it," Amanda lied.

"I'm sure you are, sweetheart. But don't you need to make some plans? I'm glad you've got some friends to hang out with, and God knows you deserve some time to yourself, but—we just worry, is all.

We just want what's best for you."

"They're afraid you have PTS," Larry said without looking up from his eggs or his screen.

Gramma Rosie glared at him, caught herself, and said, "Larry, that's not true. Amanda is just fine. I'm sure she doesn't have post-traumatic stress disorder."

"It's not a disorder," Amanda said. "They haven't called it that in years."

"That's what I told them," Larry said. "I told them if you had PTS you'd be seeing things and shooting at them, right?"

The mandatory session before she left the islands: *During a traumatic event, your higher brain functions are subordinated to the amygdala, the part of your brain that controls emotional responses and memories. When you remember those events, the brain wants to recreate the same processes that controlled your response to the original event. That's what flashbacks are: your brain wanting your body to crank up the adrenaline and cortisol, to try to survive all over again. But even if you're not reaching for your weapon if you hear a balloon pop, you can still be at risk. Some of our scientists think the trauma can actually shrink the amygdala, which also shrinks your emotional responses. That's when we start looking at depression. . . .*

"Right. I'm fine. Don't worry." So far she'd managed to put off the mandatory check-in at her local veterans' center.

"Of course you are, dear," her grandmother resumed. "But you fathers and I still—"

"Why do they call it jaunting?"

Larry put down his fork and looked up from his screen. It took a few seconds for Amanda to answer, she was so struck by his eyes, how deeply brown they were, almost red. Had she forgotten that? Had she never noticed?

"What?"

"The transport. Why do they call it jaunting?"

"It's from that sci-fi movie. That's what they called transport in the book."

"Did they use it for troops?"

"They used it for all kinds of things." Amanda had seen *The Stars My Destination* like everyone else and then read the novel while she was deployed. There was more down time than people realized. She had read a lot.

"How was it?"

"It was OK."

"Maybe you should watch it, Larry, and then you and your sister could talk about it."

Larry tapped his screen three times. "Got it."

Gramma Rosie smiled. A bonding moment between her grandchildren seemed to have taken her mind off her granddaughter's future. Amanda was genuinely glad if her grandmother felt better. Gramma Rosie had always been there, and when Amanda was in second grade and her dads needed some time to work things out, Gramma Rosie had been pretty much the only one there. Amanda loved her grandmother and wanted her to be happy, wanted to please her, but what she wanted now more than anything else was for everyone to just stop talking. The three of them cleared the table and Amanda headed upstairs. Out of the corner of her eye she caught on the news crawl on the living room screen the words BLIND JAUNT FOR FREEDOM, and she remembered. That was what BJ4F scratched inside the stall had meant.

When she got up to her room she checked online and yes, there it was. She had heard rumors when she was deployed, but it looked like since she'd gotten back the whole thing was starting to get noticed. Some people were calling it a fad. Others were calling it an epidemic. Veterans who had gotten to the war and back by jaunting were breaking into the control booths after hours, setting random coordinates, and running onto the platforms just in time to jaunt wherever the coordinates sent them. Some wound up just down the street. Others wound up in another country. A few found themselves a hundred feet above a thousand miles of ocean, and some found themselves inside a wall. Some even found themselves back on the front lines. But the ones who survived and chose to talk about it described how they'd felt before in terms that Amanda immediately recognized, and they all said afterwards they felt better. Some of the contractor firms were starting to post guards at the control booths.

Amanda read some more and decided the whole thing was crazy. Things weren't that bad. Not for her. They just weren't. She switched the screen to a book and closed her eyes. The book's voice made her drowsy. She slept through lunch. Over dinner Ernie tried to have the same conversation with her that Gramma Rosie had tried to have over breakfast, but it didn't last very long, and he wound up kissing her on the forehead and saying, "Just let us know when you're ready," without telling her what it was, exactly, that she was supposed to be ready for.

And then a couple of weeks later Amanda was out walking around town when she got lost. Not lost like she couldn't locate her destination, because she didn't have one. She was walking down Pickett Street towards Main, and when she turned the corner at Carter's Drug Store, she realized she didn't know where she was. She knew she had just turned onto Main Street and was walking past Carter's. She knew Gramma Rosie kept her prescriptions there even though Wal-Mart was a lot cheaper because Carter's was where she had bought her comic books when she was a kid; she knew it was where Larry had had his first summer job. But if the leader of the New People's Army himself had at that moment put a gun to her head and asked her the name of the town she was in, or even what day of the week it was, he would have had to pull the trigger. Everything outside her was like a screen with the contrast turned way too high, and everything inside her felt almost like it did just before she jaunted. She dropped to her knees and stayed there until a girl about Larry's age came by and helped her up. She said she was OK and walked away before the girl could start asking her anything. After a couple of blocks everything came back and she made her way home.

That evening down the post she told Sally what happened. She kept running into Sally and had decided she was OK.

"I told you that jaunting wasn't right," Sally said.

"It never bothered me before."

"It's a delayed reaction."

"Don't you fucking dare say I have Post Traumatic Anything."

"I'd say dematerializing and popping up halfway around the world is pretty goddamn traumatic, wouldn't you?"

"That's not what it was."

"Then what was it? I saw a post yesterday that said jaunting actually shrinks part of your brain, flattens you out—"

"Bullshit."

"—makes anything that fucked you up in combat even worse."

The mandatory session: . . . *you may have heard that some preliminary studies have indicated that the jaunting process may affect the limbic system. At this point there is no conclusive evidence that this is the case.* . . .

"There's no evidence for that."

Sally looked triumphant. "There you go. If someone says there's no evidence for it, that means someone else thinks there is."

"I just got dizzy, OK? I shouldn't have skipped lunch."

Sally lost her triumphant look. Now she looked more like Gramma Rosie over breakfast. "OK, whatever you say. But if it happens again, let someone know, all right?"

Amanda promised that she would. They had another round and Sally again brought up going someplace quieter, and this time Amanda said OK. By the end of the evening they were back at Sally's place, but when it didn't work and Sally started crying Amanda just walked out.

A week later, Amanda went with Ernie and Gramma Rosie to see Larry's summer league baseball game. Neal skyped in from South Bend. It was the closest thing to a family outing they had had since she had gotten back. She hadn't told any of them about what had happened outside of Carter's, and she certainly hadn't told them it had happened two more times since then.

The sun beat down as hot as it ever had in Mindanao, but she liked the flat perfect grass and the flawless lines of the diamond, and she liked watching the players. They weren't scattered. Orderly. They were exactly where they were supposed to be. Larry looked perfectly at ease in center field, and when he came to bat she cheered as loudly as anyone. He struck out, walked, and was left on first when the next batter flied out, hit a single that drove in a run, struck out one last time. It all made perfect sense, even the fact that the other team won.

On the drive back she was unaware of anything anyone said. None of the streets seemed to have names, and when they got home she wasn't sure where she was.

That night she lay in her bed in her room that was still, technically, just as she had left it, and still, actually, had never felt so empty. She lay in her bed and stared at the blank ceiling and tried to understand what had happened, where it had all come from. The killing field where the bodies in the mud were so rotted away they didn't look like bodies, they didn't even smell. The housecall where the parents were silent and the little girl wouldn't stop screaming as they tore the place apart before Lt. Jeppson declared that it was the wrong fucking house. The guy sleeping beside her waking up screaming with a leech on his tongue—but that hadn't happened, that had been in one of the books she had read. It all should have meant something, but it didn't. Knowing the New People's Army had put those bodies in the field didn't make her want to be there. Watching the lieutenant drag the screaming girl's father outside and throw him on the ground and act like he was going to shoot him didn't make her want to leave. It didn't mean anything then, and it didn't mean anything now, and she didn't want it to. Not her dads, not the vets down the post. Not the guy from Bravo Company. Not Sally. Certainly not Sally. Gramma Rosie? Larry? She didn't want any of it to mean anything, but she wanted to feel something, she wanted to be somewhere. So she went downstairs and got in her dads' car and drove to the platform where she had popped back home and, feeling no surprise at all that it was completely unguarded, went in and set the controls just as the net instructions had said. "Here's to actual fucking risk," she declared to no one in particular and ran as fast as she could for the platform that was as perfect as the baseball diamond, as brown as her brother's eyes.

NOTES AND ACKNOWLEDGEMENTS

"Legacy" was inspired by a sidebar to the Bell Witch legend described in an article by William Gay in *The Oxford American*, September/October 2000. Some of the story's background details match the legend; some don't. The description of the prostitute's room derives from the photographs of E.J. Bellocq.

"Suspension," "What They Did to My Father," "When John Moore Shot Carl Bell," "Up Above the Dead Line," and "The Last Testament of Major Ludlum" are all taken from various events and circumstances in Conway and surrounding Horry County, South Carolina, in the 19th and early 20th centuries. "Moore," "Dead Line," and "Ludlum" are based on actual murder cases. The specific events in "Suspension" and "Father" are wholly fictional but based on historical situations. For information both general and specific I am indebted to the Horry County Historical Society's *Independent Republic Quarterly* and numerous conversations with my late parents.

Richard Henry Stoddard (1825-1903), George Henry Boker (1823-90), Bayard Taylor (1825-78), Edmund Clarence Stedman (1833-1908), and Thomas Bailey Aldrich (1836-1907) were all 19th century poets and men of letters identified with the "genteel tradition" of American literature. Richard's wife, Elizabeth Drew Barstow Stoddard (1823-1902), was a respected novelist and critic whose reputation, like that of her husband and his friends, vanished after her death. While the specific events of "The Light of the Ideal" are wholly fictional, many of the details of the characters' lives, and some of the details of their conversations, are adapted from a variety of sources, especially John Tomisch's *A Genteel Endeavor: American Culture and Politics in the Gilded Age* (1971) and Richard Henry Stoddard's own *Recollections, Personal and Literary* (1903). In the late 20th century, Elizabeth Stoddard's works were rediscovered, and she is now a fixture of American literature anthologies and college course syllabi. Her husband and his friends are not.

"Flannery on Stage" was directly inspired by Lewis Shiner's 300-word miracle "Oz"; much later, I discovered Karen Joy Fowler had explored similar territory in "The Elizabeth Chronicles." My story includes information regarding the lives of Flannery O'Connor and Sinead O'Connor available in *Dictionary of Literary Biography* and *Contemporary Biography*.

Background information concerning the Skull and Bones Society, the life of Geronimo, and the Apache War Dance incorporated into "Petition to Repatriate Geronimo's Skull" may be found in various online locations.

I first learned of the activities of the Reverend John Murray Spear in Joseph A. Citro and Diane E. Foulds' *Curious New England* (2004). Many of the events described in "Mary of the New Dispensation" are documented in numerous sources. I am particularly indebted to John Buescher's entry on Spear in the *Dictionary of Unitarian and Universalist Biography*, Robert Damon Schneck's "The God Machine" in the May 2002 issue of *Fortean Times*, Slater Brown's *The Heyday of Spiritualism* (1970), Andrew V. Rapoza's "Touched by the Invisibles" in *No Race of Imitators: Lynn and Her People* (1992), and Judith Walzer Leavitt's *Brought to Bed: Child-Bearing in America, 1750-1950* (1986). My wife has family in Lynn, and that had something to do with it, too. I am grateful to the members of the 2005 Sycamore Hill Writers Workshop for their invaluable feedback on this story.

All locations depicted in "My Whole World Lies Waiting" exist, as does one of the doors.

While visiting the International UFO Museum in Roswell, New Mexico, I discovered Jennie Zeidman's *The Lumberton Report: UFO Activity in S. North Carolina, April 2-5, 1975* (Evanston, IL: Center for UFO Studies, 1976). Since I was born in Lumberton, I was immediately intrigued. Some of the details of the sightings in "It Came Out of the Sky," and much of the voice on the radio, derive from that fascinating document. Both "It Came Out of the Sky" and "The Deep End" are strongly informed by memories of my childhood and adolescence, except when they're not.

"The Sexual Component of Alien Abduction (Three-Headed Alien Blues)" was inspired by a quote falsely attributed to the Reverend Jerry Falwell. The epigraph is from an actual book. "Nylon Seam" is my tribute to Bettie Page fandom. The lyrics in both stories are of songs I wrote and recorded with the band Argon Connection.

The title of, and all italicized passages in, "Elimination of Restraint and Seclusion," are taken from a flyer publicly posted in a Massachusetts hospital. The phrase "Consciousness Deficit Hypoactivity Disorder" is taken from Matt Mogk's *Everything You Ever Wanted to Know About Zombies* (Galley Books, 2011). The entire story was posted on my now-moribund Livejournal page as part of a surprise tribute to Laird Barron. For a fuller treatment of the topic, see Daryl Gregory's award-winning 2014 novella *We Are All Completely Fine.*

For "The Serpent and the Hatchet Gang," I am deeply indebted to two books by Eleanor C. Parsons, *Hannah and the Hatchet Gang: Rockport's Revolt Against Rum* (1975) and *Rockport: The Making of A Tourist Treasure* (1998), and to J.P. O'Neill's *The Great New England Sea Serpent* (1999). The town of Rockport, Massachusetts, remained dry until 2005.

"Madeline's Version" and "Where We Would End a War" are my contributions to the honorable tradition of repurposing classics: respectively, Edgar Allan Poe's "The Fall of the House of Usher" and Ernest Hemingway's "Soldier's Home." But "Madeline" would not exist without my brooding over Karen Joy Fowler's assertion that she wrote because nobody listened when she talked, and "War" would not exist without my having taught veterans at Norwich University. I am also indebted to *Writing War: A Guide to Telling Your Own Story* by Ron Capps (2013), as well as numerous online sources, for information on post-traumatic stress. The title is taken from Brian Turner's poem "A Soldier's Arabic."

The song that was in my head as I wrote "She Hears Music Up Above" was "Sister Rosetta Walks Before Us," written by Sam Phillips, as performed by Allison Krause on her 2007 collaboration with Robert Plant, *Raising Sand*. This story, "Maria Works at Ocean City Nails," "Road Dead," and "Consider the Services of the Departed" stand as my attempts to write something where I didn't have to look anything up. "The Amnesia Helmet," written after watching a Buck Rogers serial on Turner Classic Movies, almost fits into this category, although I did have to double-check a couple of things. (For a different take on the young garage genius, see Terry Bisson's 2010 short story "Teen Love Science Club.") My wife introduced me to the work of Peter Barnes long before I wrote "Consider the Services of the Departed," so that doesn't count.

I remain deeply grateful to all the members, past and present, of the ongoing Cambridge Science Fiction Writers Workshop for their invaluable feedback on many of these stories. And permanent thanks to the Norwich University Department of English and Communications, College of Liberal Arts, Office of Academic Research, and Faculty Development Program, all of which have unceasingly supported my writing.

ABOUT THE AUTHOR

In addition to the fiction in the present volume, F. Brett Cox's poetry, plays, essays, scholarly articles, and reviews have appeared in numerous magazines and anthologies. With Andy Duncan, he co-edited the fiction anthology *Crossroads: Tales of the Southern Literary Fantastic* (Tor, 2004). He is a co-founder of the Shirley Jackson Awards and currently serves on the SJA Board of Directors. He is also a member of the Cambridge Science Fiction Writers Workshop. A native of North Carolina, Brett is Charles A. Dana Professor of English at Norwich University and lives in Vermont with his wife, playwright Jeanne Beckwith.

PUBLICATION HISTORY

"Legacy" originally appeared in *Lady Churchill's Rosebud Wristlet* (2003) | "The Amnesia Helmet" originally appeared in *Eclipse Online* (2013) | "See That My Grave Is Kept Clean" originally appeared in *Tales in Firelight and Shadow*, ed. by Alexis Brooks De Vita, Double Dragon Publishing (2014) | "The Light of the Ideal" originally appeared in *Century* (2000) | "Flannery on Stage" originally appeared in *Indigenous Fiction* (2001) | "The Serpent and the Hatchet Gang" originally appeared in *Black Static* (2007) | "Petition to Repatriate Geronimo's Skull" originally appeared in *Phantom* (2006) | "Consider the Services of the Departed" originally appeared in *Geek Theater: 15 Plays by Science Fiction and Fantasy Writers*, ed. by Jen Gunnels & Erin Underwood, Underwords Press (2014) | "When John Moore Shot Carl Bell" originally appeared in *Carriage House Review* (2001) | "Mary of the New Dispensation" originally appeared in *Postscripts* (2007) | "What We Did on Our Vacation: My Whole World Lies Waiting" originally appeared in *Rabid Transit: Long Voyages, Great Lies* as "My Whole World Lies Waiting" (2006) | "The Deep End" originally appeared in *Submerged*, ed. Joshua Palmatier and S.C. Butler, Zombies Need Brains LLC (2017) | "Nylon Seam" originally appeared in *Interfictions Annex* (2009) | "Up Above the Dead Line" originally appeared in *The Dead Mule* (2000) | "It Came Out of the Sky" originally appeared in *The North Carolina Literary Review* (2001) | "Suspension" originally appeared in *The Spectator* as "The Waiting Is the Hardest Part" (1992) | "The Last Testament of Major Ludlum" originally appeared in *The Sucarnochee Review* and *Climbing Mt. Cheaha: Emerging Alabama Writers*, ed. by Don Noble, Livingston Press (2004) | "Road Dead" originally appeared in *Shadows and Tall Trees*, Undertow Books (2014) | "Madeline's Version, originally appeared in *Crossroads: Tales of the Southern Literary Fantastic*, ed. by F. Brett Cox and Andy Duncan, Tor Books (2004) | "The Sexual Component of Alien Abduction (Three-Headed Alien Blues)" originally appeared in *Say...Was That a Kiss?* (2002) | "Maria Works at Ocean City Nails" originally appeared in *New Haven Review* (2013) | "Elimination of Restraint and Seclusion: The Road to Engagement" appears here for the first time | "What They Did to My Father" originally appeared in *Black Gate* (2001) | "What We Did on Our Vacation: She Hears Music Up Above" originally appeared in *Phantom*, ed. by Paul Tremblay and Sean Wallace as "She Hears Music Up Above," Prime (2009) | "They Got Louie" originally appeared in *See the Elephant* (2016) | "The End of All Our Exploring" appears here for the first time. "Where We Would End a War" originally appeared in *War Stories: New Military Science Fiction*, ed. by Jaym Gates and Andrew Liptak, Apex (2014)

OTHER TITLES FROM FAIRWOOD PRESS

The Sacerdotal Owl and Three Other Long Tales
by Michael Bishop
trade paper $17.99
ISBN: 978-1-933846-72-9

Cat Pictures Please
by Naomi Kritzer
trade paper: $17.99
ISBN: 978-1-933846-67-5

The Experience Arcade
by James Van Pelt
trade paper: $17.99
ISBN: 978-1-933846-69-9

Other Arms Reach Out to Me
by Michael Bishop
trade paper $17.99
ISBN: 978-1-933846-65-1

Seven Wonders of a Once and Future World
by Caroline M. Yoachim
trade paper: $17.99
ISBN: 978-1-933846-55-2

Amaryllis
by Carrie Vaughn
trade paper: $17.99
ISBN: 978-1-933846-62-0

On the Eyeball Floor
by Tina Connolly
trade paper: $17.99
ISBN: 978-1-933846-56-9

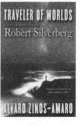

Traveler of Worlds:
Conversations with Robert Silverberg
by Alvaro Zinos-Amaro
trade paper: $16.99
ISBN: 978-1-933846-63-7

Find us at:
www.fairwoodpress.com
Bonney Lake, Washington

CPSIA information can be obtained
at www.ICGtesting.com
Printed in the USA
LVHW031812151118
597259LV00004B/632/P